"Now that you've seen the view, I'd be gr
if you'd allow me to see to it that you come
down off the roof now."

She didn't reply to this. But she did knot her
shawl snugly about her in preparation for descent,
and he plucked up the lamp.

Then she turned to him again. And because he
wasn't about to deny himself the pleasure of it,
he drank her in by lamplight and moonlight one
last time, the way she'd drunk in that view. He
was still amazed that this magical combination of
features, animated by this particular maddening
person, could cause him to lose his breath.

She knew precisely what he was thinking.

"I'm *not* naive, Mr. Cassidy," she said. Deadly
earnest. Her voice was barely above a whisper.
"Not completely," she added. It was very nearly
a plea.

Oh God. It was like a kick in the solar plexus.

It sounded less like a dare than an invitation.

But it was definitely both.

He imagined how he would begin. How her
face would feel cradled in his hand. Her delicate,
clean-lined jaw, her skin like a petal. The path his
lips would follow

By Julie Anne Long

I'M ONLY WICKED WITH YOU
ANGEL IN A DEVIL'S ARMS
LADY DERRING TAKES A LOVER

THE FIRST TIME AT FIRELIGHT FALLS
DIRTY DANCING AT DEVIL'S LEAP
WILD AT WHISKEY CREEK
HOT IN HELLCAT CANYON

THE LEGEND OF LYON REDMOND
IT STARTED WITH A SCANDAL
BETWEEN THE DEVIL AND IAN EVERSEA
IT HAPPENED ONE MIDNIGHT
A NOTORIOUS COUNTESS CONFESSES
HOW THE MARQUESS WAS WON
WHAT I DID FOR A DUKE
I KISSED AN EARL
SINCE THE SURRENDER
LIKE NO OTHER LOVER
THE PERILS OF PLEASURE

JULIE ANNE LONG

I'm Only Wicked With You

AVONBOOKS

An Imprint of HarperCollinsPublishers

I'M ONLY WICKED WITH YOU. Copyright © 2021 by Julie Anne Long. All rights reserved. Printed in the United States of America. No part of this book may be used or reproduced in any manner whatsoever without written permission except in the case of brief quotations embodied in critical articles and reviews. For information, address HarperCollins Publishers, 195 Broadway, New York, NY 10007.

First Avon Books mass market printing: September 2021

Print Edition ISBN: 978-0-06-304508-8
Digital Edition ISBN: 978-0-06-304412-8

Cover design by Guido Caroti
Cover illustration by Juliana Kolesova

Avon, Avon & logo, and Avon Books & logo are registered trademarks of HarperCollins Publishers in the United States of America and other countries.

HarperCollins is a registered trademark of HarperCollins Publishers in the United States of America and other countries.

FIRST EDITION

Printed and Bound in Barcelona Spain by CPI BlackPrint

21 22 23 24 25   CPI   10 9 8 7 6 5 4 3 2 1

For Sylvie, heart of my heart

Acknowledgments

$\mathcal{M}$Y DEEPEST gratitude to my splendid editor, May Chen; to all of the hardworking, helpful, talented people at Avon; to my stalwart agent, Steve Axelrod, and his wonderful staff, Lori Antonson and Elsie Turoci; and much love to the reader, reviewer, and blogger community. All of these people make this extraordinary job both possible and a joy.

I'm Only Wicked With You

Chapter One

❦

THE KITCHEN of The Grand Palace on the Thames was usually a soothing oasis of feminine gossip, camaraderie, and industry, and one of Mrs. Angelique Breedlove Durand's favorite places in the world. Today, however, a chilling snatch of overheard conversation froze her just as she was about to cross the threshold.

She pressed herself against the wall outside the door and surreptitiously listened.

"Two succulent hams, I should think."

Helga—their cook, of all people!—was speaking in the kind of hush Guy Fawkes likely employed when conspiring to blow up the House of Lords.

"My thoughts immediately went to two roasts of beef." Dot's reply was similarly uncharacteristically cagey.

Angelique was mystified. Hams and roasts amounted to the kind of budget massacre Helga would likely never countenance even if the king were to take a room. (And he *had* appeared, one fateful day.) For The Grand Palace on the Thames's budget was a temperamental, intricate thing, requiring tinkering and babying, prone to sudden expansions and shrinkages. Managing it was an art and a science that Angelique and Delilah, the boarding house proprietresses, and Helga, relished.

She thought, furiously. Then she bit back a smile when realization dawned, peeled herself away from the wall, and strolled in.

"Were the two of you discussing the thighs of the footman Mrs. Hardy and I interviewed yesterday?"

Thank God she and Delilah hadn't hired anyone who could lie glibly. Helga and Dot froze. Their eyes were luminous with guilt.

"Amusing. But if any of these men should become members of our staff, I trust you will refrain from comparing their anatomy to food." Last night her husband had compared a part of Angelique's anatomy to a luscious, ripe peach just before he'd nipped it. But it was the *context* that was important here. "I know you will be as respectful of them as you would hope they'd be respectful of you. Unfortunately, while the man under discussion was indeed possessed of fine thighs, he stole a teaspoon on his way out the door. Captain Hardy was compelled to chase him down the street and pry it from his clutches. Needless to say, we won't be hiring him."

Captain Hardy—Delilah's husband—had also been compelled to give the footman a good whack with it.

Neither Delilah nor Angelique had anticipated that the search for a footman would prove both harrowing and undignified. It was clear that finding a qualified man willing to work long hours for modest wages at a lovely and comfortable boarding house (granted, one in a somewhat challenging location near the docks) would be easier if they'd relaxed their standards to include scoundrels, lechers, and the just plain thick.

"A spoon? The *devil* you say!" Helga was incensed. The kitchen was her kingdom, which meant the spoons counted among her subjects. She hadn't been present for this theft, as yesterday's interview had taken place in the reception room. "And don't you fret, Mrs. Durand. We will be all that is respectful when the right bloke joins us."

Dot nodded vigorously in agreement.

Getting the "right bloke" to join them was a matter of some urgency now that they'd nearly finished refurbishing the adjacent building, which was now connected to Number 11 Lovell Street (The Grand Palace on the Thames's street number) by means of a cleverly built passage. Perhaps the most thrilling part of the Annex was the ballroom—Angelique and Delilah hoped to entice Londoners of all stripes to buy tickets to musical evenings held there, which would help recoup their renovating investment. They could begin as soon as the little stage was completed. And it would have been this week, if the workmen they'd hired to build it hadn't disappeared.

It was possible "disappeared" was a trifle prematurely dramatic. It had only been two days.

Angelique frowned when she realized that one of the kitchen maids charged with slicing apples for tarts was all but motionless, staring vaguely toward the buttery. Every few seconds or so she languidly moved the knife up and down. It missed the apple entirely.

Angelique lowered her voice and said to Helga, "What's wrong with Maggie?"

Helga spoke in a hush. "Mr. Cassidy returned from Devon this morning and do you know the first thing he did?"

Angelique shook her head.

She crooked her finger for Angelique to move closer. "He *smiled* at her."

Angelique sighed. "Oh, dear. I do wish he'd be more judicious about his smiles. They ruin the maids for half the day. They walk into walls and collide with each other while they're dusting."

"They used to take the bones right out of my knees," Dot confided. "I once spilled an entire tea tray because he smiled at me!"

Other reasons Dot had spilled an entire tea tray included carrying one when she noticed a spot on the ceiling she fancied looked like an elf; attempting to sing and walk while carrying one; and bending to pet Gordon the Cat with one hand, forgetting both were needed to hold the tray. Dot's thoughts sailed like a kite into the clouds while her feet were forever consigned to the ground, and the two struggled to work in tandem.

"Now I'm used to them, you see," she added sagely. "I smile right back."

"A testament to your fortitude," Angelique said encouragingly.

"*For*-ti-tude," Dot repeated, under her breath.

"'Fortitude' means strength and endurance," Angelique clarified, because once a governess always a governess, even if she was now blissfully and happily married to the notorious bastard son of a duke. And Dot, who had once been Delilah's lady's maid, was the best kind of student: she was all but an educational blank slate and *loved* collecting new words.

Angelique went to stand beside the maid, who was still all but miming moving the knife through the air. "Maggie," she said softly, as to one sleep-walking. "Maggie? Maggie, dear. It's Mrs. Durand."

Maggie turned to her, her eyes hazy and starlit.

"I understand it was your turn to light Mr. Cassidy's fire and bring his coffee this morning."

"Drew the long straw, so's I did," she confessed, dreamily.

Hugh Cassidy was usually up and dressed and restlessly moving about even before all the maids were yawning through the dark halls to light fires and trim wicks, a habit of a lifetime from when he'd been up to do chores and to watch the sunrise over the tops of tall pines. But one unforgettable morning a maid had come upon him still sleeping. Half of his coverlet had been tossed off, exposing a vast bare shoulder gleaming like a gold mountain by the light of a single glowing log. The maid who'd witnessed this glory had returned to the kitchen all but speaking in tongues. She'd been given smelling salts.

Ever since then the maids had drawn straws and bickered over the opportunity to wait upon him. Because while fascinating men did tend to appear at the door of The Grand Palace on the Thames—notably, the notorious bastard son of a duke and a handsome if taciturn blockade captain—the dark haired, blue-eyed young American was the one who notched most comfortably into their fantasies. He seemed to *see* them. He somehow seemed more real, and therefore more deliciously devastating.

Delilah and Angelique had always found Mr. Cassidy to be all that was charming, courtly, proper, and helpful—he'd even helped build part of the Annex—and he was infinitely patient with Mr. Delacorte. He'd been a guest for some months now, and they were quite fond of him. And yet, he wasn't precisely easy to know. He was a trifle guarded. And there was a suppressed energy to him that suggested he'd be moving on as soon as he was able. Mr. Cassidy was clearly a man with plans.

"I suspect you returned to the kitchen and brought Mr. Cassidy one more scone this morning than you ought to have, didn't you, Maggie?"

Maggie went still. Then she squeezed her eyes closed, as if awaiting the blade that would separate her head from her neck. And then gave one short, sharp nod.

Angelique sighed again.

Maggie turned a pleading expression up to her. "When he smiles . . . it's like when you look at the sun, Mrs. Durand. You can't see nothing else after that."

"Yes, well, he has a fine smile and he knows it." He in fact had a number of different kinds of fine smiles, all of which she also enjoyed, but the slow crooked one, all intimate warmth and wry, mischievous pleasure, that wrapped the viewer like a sensual net—well, that was the one that typically did the maids' heads in. "Do you know what a budget is?"

"Well, yes. You and Helga and Mrs. Hardy talk and talk about it and you seem to have great fun."

Over Helga's muttered, "Ha!" Angelique said, "Well, it *is* a bit like a game. You have to be clever, you see. It's all about strategy. We earn money by providing a service to our guests, but everything costs money. For instance, what if I told you that smuggling an additional scone to Mr. Cassidy each morning could eventually mean we won't be able to afford to hire footmen?"

She was *greatly* simplifying the concept of budgets, but the word "footmen" had inspired all manner of excitement for months now, for reasons not entirely related to shared work. Angelique now had all Maggie's attention.

"It's a bit like that. We make choices all the time about what to spend according to what we earn. We must be resourceful and thrifty *while* still providing exceptional comfort and service so that The Grand Palace on the Thames can continue to enjoy its stellar reputation . . ." "Stellar" was a bit aspirational, but it made her point. ". . . and so that we can continue to employ all of our staff members, too. Do you see?"

Maggie nodded eagerly.

"And while Mr. Cassidy is a gentleman through and through and I know he would *never* do anything untoward, men are deucedly clever about getting what they want, because most of them assume we're not as smart as they are."

"And that only proves they are fools," Helga added. "With precious few exceptions."

"Mr. Cassidy is better than most, by far. And Helga's scones can entice a saint," Angelique allowed.

"But we have to be stronger and cleverer than men are and not give them what they want simply because we find them charming. At which point, contrary creatures that they are, they will find us irresistible."

"Oh, I should *love* to be irresistible!" Maggie breathed.

"It takes many years of practice," Angelique added quickly. "Many, *many* years. So all of you, smile politely and repeat after me in a polite but grave tone: 'I shall have to speak to Helga about additional scones, Mr. Cassidy.'"

"I shall have to speak to Helga about additional scones, Mr. Cassidy," everyone present repeated sternly.

"Now please properly cut the apples, Maggie."

The maid gave a start. The knife went through an apple and she soon established a speedy rhythm.

Angelique exhaled as Delilah sailed into the kitchen. It was one of her favorite places, too. But Delilah's expression suggested she had unwelcome news to impart.

"At least Mr. Cassidy loves my food," Helga said worriedly. "Lady Lillias hardly touches it. Too plain for the likes of her, I suppose."

Delilah and Angelique exchanged a look. The Earl and Countess of Vaughn and their family were the very first occupants of one of their handsome, newly completed suites.

Difficult people had been guests at The Grand Palace on the Thames before. Delilah and Angelique had, in fact, married those difficult people. Difficult people were looked upon as an opportunity to sharpen their wits and exercise compassion. And if all else failed, a blockade captain would drag their deservedly unconscious body out the door. (Fortunately, that had so far only happened once.)

The two of them just hadn't yet decided what sort of difficult person Lady Lillias was.

As the rules compelled, she dutifully sat in the parlor four days a week and was absent for the other days. A sketchbook sat before her, as did a crayon in a holder, but no one had ever seen her so much as lift it. She did not knit (she'd been invited); she did not embroider (likewise). She spoke when spoken to and her voice was lovely and her manners were faultless. She was a beautiful conundrum, a still presence but not precisely a mild, or even benign one. She seemed to be mounting a sort of personal protest, the object of which was known only to herself. She seemed alive with thoughts.

She made Delacorte so nervous he'd accidentally uttered a curse word out loud for the first time in two weeks, breaking a record of which he was proud and necessitating a trip to the epithet jar.

Her parents and her brother and sister had gamely settled into the routine of The Grand Palace on the Thames and for the most part seemed happy. Though St. John spent his evenings in the sitting room primarily leaning against the mantel, clearly hoping to be admired.

"The rest of the Earl of Vaughn's family are clearly *more* than satisfied with your cooking. As well they should be," Delilah said stoutly.

Angelique and Delilah knew how to dispense comfort. Every gifted artist remained at heart insecure about their art, and Helga was no exception.

Delilah drew Angelique aside. "I've been to have a look at the ballroom."

"Ah. And have the workmen returned?" Angelique said this almost mordantly, because Delilah's expression told another story.

"Oh, yes. Long enough to steal the rest of the lumber, it seems."

"Something tells me they won't be returning," Angelique mused.

Neither one of them wasted a moment on indignation; or rather, they'd long been accustomed to turning adversity and indignation into fuel. It was a problem needing solving.

"Should we have apple tarts or scones for tomorrow?" Helga called over her shoulder.

That's when inspiration struck.

"Delilah . . . I think I know how to get our stage built. And it involves guilt, scones, and a certain strapping guest."

Chapter Two

෨ඞඥ

$\mathcal{H}$UGH CASSIDY had arrived two minutes before curfew the previous night, when everyone was already tucked into bed—he knew and respected, nay, *cherished* the rules at The Grand Palace on the Thames—and up well before dawn, shaved, dressed, and seated at the little writing desk thoughtfully provided to every guest, because he was no damned coward and he was determined to get what was bound to be the worst part of his day over with first and fast.

He pulled the foolscap toward him. Dipped the quill.

Paused.

Hell's teeth. What to say?

He'd never had a formal education, but he'd happily go toe to toe with any of those bloods whose intellects had been incubated at Eton or Oxford. More than they ever could, he appreciated the power and magic inherent in words—to charm, to open doors, to strategize, to seduce. History, economics, politics, natural sciences, newspapers, pamphlets—in exchange for labor, he'd been set free in Mr. Woodley's vast library and he'd methodically absorbed the precise things he needed to know. For Hugh had a plan. Hugh's father had been the best man he'd ever known, but his struggles to rise in life had essentially shown Hugh the way. It was all in the tools. Words were the tools.

But as far as he was concerned, the point of the written word was delivery and consumption of information (with the possible exception of the thrill that was *Robinson Crusoe*). He recognized the difference between his own courtly manners—instilled by his parents and rooted in respect for the dignity of all men and women—and the filigreed, rapier elegance of Lord Bolt's, for instance, or of the more typical English aristocrats, the ones marinated in privilege. They used words as playthings. Hugh knew too well the value of everything—and that included ink, paper, and quill—so he was disinclined to waste them on an attempt at eloquence.

But that wasn't the only reason he kept his missives short.

> *Dear Mr. Woodley,*
>
> *I hope this letter finds you well. I have returned from a fortnight's worth of making the discreet inquiries in Dover as I described to you in my last letter. I made the acquaintance of a Clay family, who, alas, have never visited New York. I have been directed to another family by the name of Clay in Surrey, just outside of London. I will visit and report apace.*
>
> *I thank you again for the introduction to Sir Bentley Tigmont. He was kind enough to invite me to tea and he is as genial and interesting as you described.*

*We enjoyed our conversation and I like
to think I now count him as a friend.
I will not return without your daughter.
I remain as ever,
Hugh Cassidy*

He released the breath he hadn't fully realized he'd been holding. He'd felt nearly every scratch of that sharpened quill right across his heart.

Your daughter. With each letter he sent to Mr. Woodley, he found himself more and more reluctant to write her name.

A few months ago, the comely, demure young Miss Woodley had shocked everyone by slipping away from her New York home and boarding a ship bound for London. Hugh had offered to pursue her across the Atlantic as a favor to her frantic father; he'd gone as soon as he could get passage. Still, she had six weeks' lead on him and he only had one clue: she had allegedly run off with the visiting Clay family—their daughter Kathryn had become her friend. No one knew from which part of England the Clays hailed.

He'd meant it when he'd written "discreet"; honor was the pivot around which all of his actions and decisions turned. He'd followed leads and written letters; he knew how to ease into inquiries without making them sound like inquisitions. In pubs and churches and shops, people were usually happy to talk to him. "Back in New York, I've friends by the name of Woodley, who hoped to visit Dover. They're friendly with a family called Clay. Perhaps your paths have crossed." That sort of thing.

Woodley's daughter's honor deserved protecting, regardless of what she'd done. If she was still alive, she'd need it.

Was she well? In danger? Having simply a *wonderful* time?

Sometimes he wondered if he'd get further, faster, in his inquiries if he'd said, "Her eyes are the color of a sky on a spring day. Her hair never can stay in its ribbons. The top of her head reaches about to my collarbone. And if you make her laugh, it'll likely be the best thing to happen to you that day."

Words might be magic, but he'd learned they hadn't invented the ones that could adequately breathe life into people who were gone. It almost seemed a disservice to try.

He pushed his hair back and blew out a breath and read the letter again. It was notable for what it didn't convey: his impatience to be home, so he could unleash his ambitions and build the life— the empire—he'd long envisioned. The methodical, needle-in-a-haystack nature of the search and its urgency. The infuriating mystery of it all: why the *devil* did she do it?

He allowed himself a few minutes of wild conjecture about all of that before sleep, and no more. Nobody was more dogged. He would find her.

But now he had a new problem: his conscience.

A fortnight ago, Miss Woodley was his first thought in the morning and the last at night. A fortnight ago, he'd met another woman.

Their encounter had lasted all of three minutes.

It had been sifting down around him like ash from a forest fire ever since.

He had looked into the barrel of enemy rifles, the slavering jaws of a furious bear, the lifeless faces of his father and brother. He could build a home from the stripped timbers on up, shoot to kill nearly anything, expertly hold a newborn baby. He figured he'd been tested in more ways than Hercules, and in the end he supposed he was grateful that the war had sorted the entirety of life into two categories for him: what was worth living for, what was worth dying for. And now he had land, some money, plans, and fierce ambition. If the devastation of the past eight years left one gift, it was the confidence that he didn't have a single weakness left. The world was his to conquer.

But when Lady Lillias Vaughn had emerged into view from the dusty twilight of an unfinished part of the Annex at The Grand Palace on the Thames, he'd been struck dumb. Like the child he'd been when his father had pointed up and shown him Polaris, hanging up there like a diamond pin holding the black, black sky in place.

He'd never seen anything so beautiful.

Or so clearly out of reach.

She'd been, improbably, smoking a cheroot.

She'd assessed him with a swift, expert glance. Having reached her conclusion—American, possibly a peasant, despite that, good looking—her voice was all refined velvet and bored, amused disdain when she spoke.

"Well? Aren't you going to bow to the daughter of an earl?"

Underestimating him was tantamount to handing him a weapon.

He'd disarmed her instantly with silky, ruthless directness. "Why waste a second doing that, when I can remain upright admiring you?"

He'd had the pleasure of seeing her blink. And then he'd assessed her with a glance more swift and expert than hers. The lines of her body seemed expressly designed to shorten a man's breath.

He'd become aware of a very low, simmering anger that had nothing and yet everything to do with the girl.

He'd learned over the years that anger often masqueraded as fear. After the events of the past few years, surely he wasn't afraid of a damned thing. Particularly not a woman.

And just before he'd plucked that cheroot from her fingers and crushed it beneath his boot, he'd seen the pulse beating in her throat, the fine strands of hair fluttering near her parted lips. He'd seen himself reflected in the velvety dark of her pupils. Her silvery eyes had gone nearly black.

He'd never so profoundly disliked a woman while simultaneously wanting to take her up against a wall.

He wasn't proud of it. He had all the skills but none of the inclination to be a first class rogue. He was practical. He was disinterested in being encumbered by its consequences.

With any luck, that earl's daughter had learned a valuable lesson. The thing that made her pupils go the size of dimes and her breath go short . . . it didn't give a damn who had a title and who didn't. It alone dictated who was at its mercy.

And yet.

He couldn't fight it. The need to prove to himself

that he wasn't at anyone's or anything's mercy had driven him back to London.

He sprinkled sand over the message. He'd have it posted, then spend the day making inquiries, be back in time to join everyone in the little drawing room. While he waited for the ink to dry, he stared wonderingly at the leaping fire, the little vase with a bud in it next to his well-worn precious copy of *Robinson Crusoe*, a gift from his Uncle Liam, who was even now on a ship heading for English shores from China. At the crumbs remaining of the two glorious scones the maid had brought up to him this morning. All of those things lifted his mood. He still wasn't fully accustomed to being waited upon. The sheer *luxury* of his shirts being mended (and even laundered if he paid a little more), a maid to poke up the fire and bring in his coffee and maybe even return with an additional scone. He could do all of that himself, and had for years.

He reached for his hat, jammed it on, and grinned to his reflection.

But the maids seemed to enjoy it so *very* much.

LADY LILLIAS VAUGHN looked out of the window of the dungeon to which she'd been consigned for the past week (a pretty, bright suite at The Grand Palace on the Thames Annex; her little room featured a rose-colored counterpane and a blossom in a vase). Two sketchbooks sat beside her, one full but quite ruined. One new and blank. She'd gotten her paints out.

She hadn't so much as made a twitch toward

them since she'd arrived at The Grand Palace on the Thames.

Her current view offered rooftops and distantly, like hairline cracks in the blue sky, the masts of ships with furled sails going anywhere and everywhere from the East India docks. Dover. China. America, from whence her new nemesis—that bloody American—had come. *He* was the reason she was confined to the room.

The nerve of him, looming up out of the dark like a cliff, the sort ships founder on in storms. Shoulders blocking the light, the shadows clinging to the valleys created by his cheekbones and jaw sculpting him rather starkly, and when he'd come closer—she perhaps should not have allowed him to get so close, but then, he'd felt like a dare from nearly the moment he appeared, and frankly, once she began looking at him it had been strangely difficult to stop—she discovered his eyes were not as she'd expected. Somewhere between blue and gray.

Alas, he in fact proved to be not at *all* what she'd expected.

But was she to blame for that? It had, after all, begun with him staring as if she were a genie he'd accidentally summoned from a lamp.

You might as well stare. They all do. That was the first thing she'd said to him.

If only she'd had the sense to make it the last thing she'd said to him.

Well, it was true. Because most men were exactly what she'd expected.

For instance, there was the "poem" that accompanied a great wad of hothouse flowers some handsome young fool sent to her a fortnight ago.

*I took one look at you
and my heart broke in two*

Lady Lillias Vaughn's mere presence could break a heart the way a soprano could shatter glass—or so the bloods of the *ton* loved to pretend. It had been exhilarating at first, a silly game, typical *ton* nonsense. She couldn't quite pinpoint when it had all gotten away from her. She was reminded of that gray mare Giles had begged her not to attempt to ride at Heatherfield when she was twelve years old—which of course had only ensured that she would. Now there were times she felt as though she was standing outside of herself, watching that gray mare with a twelve-year-old girl clinging to its back disappear into the distance.

"Broke in two" made heartbreak sound as simple as treading on a twig—snap! She could now speak with some authority that the sensation in the actual moment—two months and two days ago, to be precise—was less a break and more of a swift *harpooning*—she had full access to her father's library and read a good deal; she was good at choosing words. And there was nothing simple about it. It wasn't just one emotion. A whole flapping Pandora's box full of them had been released: astonishment, wounded pride, mordant amusement about the wounded pride, mordant amusement about the astonishment, confusion, scalding grief, a flailing loss. They took to tormenting her in turns, until she got used to them. Now their combined efforts only made her numb. It was a testament to how stalwart her pride truly was that not one other soul suspected her condition. Particularly—and most inexplicably and maddeningly—the person who'd unwittingly done the breaking. Her family would have fussed, and she could not have borne their suffering over her. The *ton* would have whispered and laughed, and that would have been just as bad if not worse.

Restlessly, reflexively, for the thousandth time, she fished from her reticule the little river rock she'd carried about for the last two years. Silvery, etched into little tiers on one side, smooth and speckled with olive green on the other, impulsively given to her during a picnic in Richmond on a gloriously sunny day. It used to reliably bring a jolt of joy; it had felt like a promise. Now she could almost feel it lodged in her chest, cold and angular, like the thing that had cracked her heart instead of the thing that had stolen it.

She rubbed it between her fingers and entertained an impulse to hurl it out the window. At least the rock could be free.

Upon reflection, she put it back into her reticule instead. She was practical enough to consider that she might occasionally need a reminder to never be a sentimental fool again.

If she could at least . . . oh, go for a ride in The Row. Or a long walk, somewhere new. She could do nothing to assuage her own restlessness, and it was because her new nemesis, Mr. Cassidy, had tattled on her for smoking a cheroot.

"Why?"

This was the word—really more of an exasperated sigh—her father had finally produced after he'd fixed her with the stare he usually deployed to elicit babbling admissions of guilt from his children. It was about the cheroot. It was their first night at The Grand Palace on the Thames. St. John and Claire had gone to bed and Lillias had been kept up for castigation purposes.

Her mother sat beside her father. Her expression was awfully similar.

It wasn't the first time she'd faced a matched set of incredulous parents.

"You . . . never said I couldn't?" she tried. She could usually make her father laugh with a little cheek.

His face remained stony.

"That's what you said when we caught you in the garden at midnight in your night rail last month," her mother replied evenly. "Perhaps try another excuse, if only for the sake of variety."

She'd been caught in the garden at midnight in only her night rail and a shawl. She'd been outside because she'd suddenly very much needed to know what it would feel like to be in the garden alone at midnight in a night rail and a shawl.

Which was almost the same reason she'd climbed up to the top of the tower of their country church. She'd wanted to. And she'd suddenly, desperately needed to see as far as she could see.

And while up there, she'd rung the bell, because there it was and why not?

And coincidentally it was the reason she'd suddenly torn off on her mare at such a breakneck speed that the startled groom chasing her had taken her bonnet in the face. It had broken free of its pins.

She could not adequately put into words—and normally she could adequately put nearly anything into words—the "why" of these things. Ever since that fateful day two months and two days ago, it was as though she, like paintings in her ruined sketchbook, had blurred and run off the page and continued on and on out of her own sight. She could no longer quite sense the boundaries that once constrained her. Where she began and ended.

"I suppose I was curious. I helped myself to one from your humidor before we arrived here and I found it in my reticule and . . . you said they relax you. The docks are unnerving and . . . smoking a cheroot seemed like just the sort of thing one would do near the docks," she'd improvised hurriedly and shamelessly.

This was greeted with palpably baffled silence. They both knew little unnerved Lillias.

She took a breath. "I'm sorry . . . Papa."

The word "Papa" usually made the thunderous crease between her father's brows disappear.

This time it deepened to a trench.

He allowed Lillias to look at this trench for a full thirty seconds.

"You'll ruin your looks if you smoke cheroots," her mother finally said.

"Yes, dear. *That's* why she shouldn't smoke cheroots," her father said dryly. "Her looks."

"Would it matter so very much if it did ruin them?" she said, a little desperately. Not entirely joking.

Her parents swiftly exchanged the kind of glance that contained entire paragraphs worth of that silent language married people seemed to share. She could almost hear them discussing whether she ought to be tucked into bed with a foul tisane and a hot water bottle. Perhaps the doctor ought to be called for. Perhaps some leeches or trepanning would suit.

"Go ahead then, and ruin your looks. I'm an earl. I can buy you a husband if it comes down to that," her father said finally.

He was only half jesting. But it was the beginning of a thaw.

"We're very fortunate that pleasant young American man was so very discreet. He understood immediately how horrified and concerned I would be if I'd known you were off smoking a cheroot. He has a sister, he told me, and his conscience wouldn't let him leave you out there. He had a sense of the dangers you might encounter in an unfamiliar place, a young woman, all alone."

The *dangers* she might encounter! That was almost funny. She ought to tell them she'd seen her own riveted expression in the American's pupils, because that's how close he'd been. That she could have reached out and touched her finger to the tiny crescent-shaped scar next to his bottom lip.

"And what would the proprietresses of The Grand Palace on the Thames think of us if they learned the oldest daughter of the Earl of Vaughn was wandering off alone to smoke a cheroot in a dangerous area under construction, full of nails and loose boards and whatnot? We've our family's reputation to uphold. It's been unassailable since the Conqueror."

This was a bit much.

"To be clear, you're concerned about impressing the proprietresses of an inn by the *docks*, where we've been compelled to relocate in part because

Father shot at an escaped poisonous snake that St. John won in a bet and inadvisably brought home. And is nobody concerned that the word 'rogue' is *very* faintly visible on the sign in the front, and that the pub nearest seems to be called 'The Wolf and'? The Wolf and *what*?"

Lillias said all of this slowly. The unspoken words were, ". . . and you think *I'm* the looby."

Her parents were subdued for a moment. "It could happen to anybody," her father said finally. "Shooting at a snake."

Lillias couldn't help it. She laughed.

Her father's face finally relaxed into something like its usual content lines. He loved her laughter and cleverness and loathed being upset with her as much as she usually loathed upsetting him. "Come now, Mrs. Hardy and Mrs. Durand are everything that's kind and genteel and charming, and they run a tight ship and it's clear the staff is happy and well-trained. The place is spotless, the food is *wonderful*, and I feel safe and very much at home already." The earl gave the settee he sat upon a happy thump, as though it were a beloved pet. "And frankly, the lemon seed cakes we were greeted with were like the food of angels. Angels!"

Lillias said nothing. The place—a shining white building tucked into a somewhat notorious and begrimed if essential part of London near the East India docks—was frankly a fever dream. The formerly notorious Lord Bolt—Lucien Durand, the bastard son of a duke, former denizen of the broadsheets, back from the presumed dead— roamed the halls because he was *married* to one of the proprietresses; the other proprietress had once been a countess, allegedly, and apparently the king himself had recently sat on a worn pink satin settee in one of the parlors. And God only knew what Delacorte was, apart from somewhat loud and somewhat egg-shaped.

"But . . . those *rules*. And . . . and Mr. Delacorte."

Mr. Delacorte (as he'd informed the earl) imported medicines comprised of things like the horns and testicles of exotic animals, herbs and flowers, and other interesting things crushed into teas, powders, and pills, and sold them to apothecaries and surgeons up and down the British coast. He carried them about in a case of samples. He'd said "bollocks" out loud in the parlor after Lord Bolt had made a skillful chess move.

This gave her mother a bit of pause. Then she brightened. "He's a bit like a character in a pantomime, isn't he, Mr. Delacorte? You like pantomimes! We can all play our part. It will only be for a short time. We shall endure." She said this firmly. This "endurance" was clearly an order. "And it's absurd to think *any* of this should drive one into smoking cheroots."

"And a list of rules won't do you any harm, Lillias," her father added, "given that you are either forgetting or disregarding the ones you were raised with."

Don't say it. Don't say it, Lillias.

"Disregarding," she clarified. Gently.

It was almost funny when her parents' eyebrows dove in perfect unison, like birds of prey.

Their mutual scowl held for about three seconds. Then suddenly her father's face cleared and he snapped his fingers. "You know, by God, I think she *does* need a husband," he said. "Something to settle her down, keep her occupied, on her toes. No time to *wonder* about church bells or whatnot with a husband and children."

It was acid poured on a wound.

Lillias's mouth dropped open.

After a moment, an arid sound emerged from it.

"Henry, darling, I think you've hit upon the problem *and* the solution." Her mother was pleased.

The earl slapped his hands cheerfully on his thighs, as though it was all settled. "Suitable young men abound in our circles. Pick one or I will! As long as he has a title and a long lineage and piles of money, you'll be fine. They're most of them decent lads. They've got all their limbs and teeth and the right manners and belong to the right clubs. You're a wonderful catch."

A high-pitched humming sound had started up in her ears. "You make it sound as though it's a sale at Tattersall's!"

"In the end, is it truly much different, dear?" her mother said practically.

She was teasing, of course. And two months ago, Lillias might have laughed. She'd been confident that her own match would not only be forthcoming, it would be as spectacular as the *ton* had long anticipated with delicious degrees of envy and resignation, and as blissfully content as her parents'.

Now she felt as though someone were holding her over the edge of a cliff while her feet thrashed about in midair.

"But—I—"

"You'll make some titled young man very happy. Just look how happy I made your mother. She finds nothing more satisfying than time spent with her family."

"Yes, it's *delightful*," her mother said dryly. "If you like finding new gray hairs every morning."

Her parents were happy. Lillias was learning that happy people tended to live in a land with its own happy culture and rules and language. They could be utterly baffled by the notion that someone might feel otherwise, and were often incapable of noticing it at all.

"So that's settled," her father said with great satisfaction. "You've had a few seasons of fun. It's time to be serious."

"To be clear, you're equating marriage with the end of fun?" It was a risky gambit, pitting her parents against each other, but she wasn't about to go down without a good fight.

"Aren't you clever. Of course," her father said blithely. "Now off to bed with you. And I should think a fortnight's confinement to the premises of The Grand Palace on the Thames will give you time to reflect upon the wisdom of smoking cheroots. No social calls, no riding in The Row, nothing but gazing out the window and reflecting upon your choices. But of course . . ." he added on his way out of the little sitting room, ". . . you will join everyone in the drawing room . . . as the rules compel."

She'd been confined to the premises ever since.

She eyed her paints, but she couldn't seem to bring herself to touch them.

Lillias plucked up the little printed card handed to her family when they'd arrived and, improbably, been interviewed about whether or not they'd be suitable for The Grand Palace on the Thames.

Imagine the Earl of Vaughn and his family not being considered *suitable*. Laughable.

All guests will eat dinner together at least four times
per week.

Day by day over the past near fortnight, her
father had fallen more and more in love with the
food. "I don't know what it is," he said with almost
pained, misty reverence. "It's simple . . . eel pie?
But *flawless*." Perhaps it was. Lillias put a certain
amount of food in her mouth every day, but it had
mostly lost its taste about two months ago.

All guests must gather in the drawing room after
dinner for at least an hour at least four times per week.
We feel it fosters a sense of friendship and the warm,
familial, congenial atmosphere we strive to create here
at The Grand Palace on the Thames.

Her parents had been enchanted by this outlandish requirement. "You'll all be grown and
out of the home soon enough and I'd like us to be
together every night. Perhaps it's a blessing that
St. John won a snake." And if her father said it,
then it was law. Claire was enjoying it. Lillias was
enduring it.

But her brother St. John was suffering. He reliably left a trail of blushes and a veritable breeze
of fluttered eyelashes and fans behind him when
he strolled through *ton* ballrooms, but he'd failed
to engender much more than bemused, kindly tol-
erance among the ladies of The Grand Palace on
the Thames. Not even when he'd tried striking
his most insouciantly masculine pose against the
mantel during the evenings in the parlor. Not even
when he strode from one end of the room to the
other "like a panther—it's my panther walk" he'd

told Lillias and Claire, which was a grave mistake as they never, never let him forget it, and often slinked about after him growling softly, then falling apart in giggles.

And almost no one adored being handsome as much as St. John did. He wasn't wholly insufferable. He was just male. They did tend to abuse such gifts.

All guests should be quietly respectful and courteous of other guests at all times, though spirited discourse is welcome.

She wondered if Mr. Delacorte muttering, "Oh, bollocks," fell under the definition of spirited discourse. So far, the most spirited discourse had been regarding a book called *The Ghost in the Attic*, about which the maid Dot and guest Mrs. Pariseau seemed to hold very strong opinions.

Perhaps, "Go back inside, little girl, you wouldn't know daring if it bit you," was an example of spirited discourse. She clamped down on her back teeth. She could think of a dozen retorts now . . . now that he wasn't hovering over her, all blue-eyed self-righteousness.

Guests may entertain other guests in the drawing room.

The phantom words ". . . but not in their bedrooms" practically throbbed from the end of that sentence. If a girl had eyes, half a brain, a father with a decent library, and maybe a loquacious older brother, she was hardly going to remain ignorant of such matters. She'd even been kissed—chastely and swiftly—a time or two. It had not changed her world.

She supposed such a rule was necessary if one

was going to rent rooms to men hailing from the wilds of America, for instance. One never knew what they would get up to. How *had* Mr. Cassidy passed the interview? He must have impressed them with his *moral superiority*.

Curfew is at 11:00. The door will be securely locked then. You will need to wait until morning to be admitted if you miss curfew.

This one had sent her brother St. John into a panic. "What could you possibly want to do after 11:00?" their father demanded, clearly experiencing amnesia over being young once.

So far he'd managed to be in by curfew. Lillias and her sister had a private wager—two pence— over how long this would last.

If the proprietresses collectively decide that a transgression or series of transgressions warrants your eviction from The Grand Palace on the Thames, you will find your belongings neatly packed and placed near the front door. You will not be refunded the balance of your rent.

She wondered if anyone had ever sufficiently transgressed. Would producing a cheroot in the parlor get *her* evicted, or her entire family?

Was it worth attempting?

Claire flounced into the room, a happy vision in striped muslin, her face alight with a mischievous secret.

"What are you doing, Lillias? Are you drawing?" She peered at the sketchbook.

"I suppose I was thinking about it." This wasn't untrue.

"I wish you would. I love your drawings."

"That's very sweet, Clairy."

"Did you know the king visited here?" Claire announced. "I sat on the very spot on the very same settee. Mrs. Hardy told me all about it."

"The king has visited a lot of questionable places."

"He has? Where?"

"Good try, Claire, but if I told you, Father would disown me, because you wouldn't be able to keep it to yourself."

"Fair enough. It's cleaner than our townhouse, this boarding house."

"Well, isn't everything at the moment, since father shot a hole in the wall?"

Claire laughed.

Lillias smiled. Making her sister laugh was always a reliable way to make herself feel a little better about everything for a second or two.

"But don't say that to Mother or you'll get all the maids replaced, and they're only now getting used to us," she added quickly.

"Of course not. Guess what was sent over from the house today, Lillias. I sneaked it out of the stack of mail sent over when Mother wasn't looking."

From behind her back, Claire slowly and theatrically produced what was clearly an engraved invitation. She held it out as if her palms were a tray.

Reflexively, absently, Lillias took hold of it.

When she saw what it was she dropped it.

Her hands went cold.

It wasn't as though it was unexpected. The Landover Ball came about every year, after all. She'd been to three of them, and thoroughly enjoyed herself. All the bloods and the people who wrote gossip for the newspapers had made cakes of themselves over her.

This year it was not so much approaching as hurtling toward her like a cricket ball she couldn't possibly duck in time.

A fresh wash of dread lapped up over her heart.

Fourteen more days. A fortnight until the last of her dream would be murdered, and she would have no choice but to be there and witness it.

She was half tempted to grind her heel on the invitation as Mr. Cassidy had done away with her cheroot.

She felt invigorated by the little flame of fury that reared up at the very thought of him.

Go inside, little girl.

She rubbed her hand against her cheek as though the words were a glove with which she'd been struck.

She knew she could ascribe her beauty to the roulette wheel of fate and a couple of pleasant-looking parents. It wasn't something she'd *achieved*. She wasn't daft about it. But women were afforded so little power as it was, and if someone had handed an unarmed man a sword and sent him into battle, wouldn't he learn how to use it? Since her debut she'd deftly parried everything from worship to bitter envy and she couldn't honestly say she'd been above wielding—and enjoying—a certain queenly, if benevolent, social supremacy. It still hadn't gotten her what she wanted.

And now here she was, confined to her room like a child for her transgression, as though she'd never had any power at all and never would. But now she understood the most infuriating thing of all about him: two minutes with Hugh Cassidy had given her a taste of the *true*, thrilling, unnerving power she possessed.

And then he'd stripped her of that power with a few words.

She intended to take it back from him.

Chapter Three

✥⟨⟨⟨⟩⟩⟩✥

*H*UGH HESITATED on the threshold of the sitting room at The Grand Palace on the Thames, feet planted firmly on the marble of the foyer, postponing his entrance the way he would any rare pleasure, taking in the view. Mrs. Pariseau was emoting from a book fanned open in her hands. He counted four other shining heads bent over knitting and embroidery—Delilah, Angelique, the Countess of Vaughn, and a girl of about fifteen with red-gold hair who must be Lady Claire, all leaning into the story like it was a quenching rain. Mr. Delacorte, who'd been teaching Dot how to play chess, was sitting across from her at a little table, chin in his hands, looking ever so slightly martyred, which was inevitable when facing off against Dot in anything, really.

Against the mantel leaned a tall young man in exquisitely tailored clothes, dark hair swept artfully back from a fine, high forehead. His sole occupation appeared to be insouciance.

And then Hugh saw her.

She was sitting alone at one of the little tables placed about the room. One hand propped up her chin as she gazed toward the curtained window as though she could see right through it. She was still, but not inert. He imagined a queen of yore might adopt the same posture—patient, absorbed, at peace with her blue-blooded birthright—while her ladies in waiting settled ermine capes about her shoulders and a crown on her head. She was wearing a dress the approximate shade of new leaves, and the firelight in fact had given her something of a flaming coronet. Her hair was precisely as he recalled: a half-dozen shades of mahogany, the color of good, old, gleaming wood.

She turned slowly, her brow furrowed slightly, as if she'd caught a snatch of elusive music.

She saw him, of course.

Sparks ought to have arced from the collision of their gazes.

Slowly he stepped over the threshold into the room.

And . . . well, he recalled hearing that Sir Galahad had been speechless when he'd first clapped eyes on the grail. It was a bit like that. Words seemed both pointless and impossible.

But Galahad had allegedly been pure of heart, and that's where the comparison ended.

Hugh's thoughts were anything but.

Taking refuge in manners, he bowed. A little sardonically.

"Good evening, Mr. Cassidy," she said, when he was upright again. "I see you've returned. I was *just* thinking that the only thing missing from this cozy evening was a moral arbiter. The epithet jar's presence notwithstanding."

Her voice was just as he remembered—all velvet superiority.

"Good evening, Lady Lillias. I'm surprised you

could bring yourself to say my name, as it doesn't begin with 'Lord.'"

Having each thrown an initial blow and established how they meant to go on, they assessed each other for weakness or injuries. Neither of them blinked.

"It's the very Americanness of 'Cassidy,' perhaps," she said thoughtfully. "You look as though your best friend might be a bear."

"Lillias," her mother said reprovingly from over in the corner, and somewhat doubtfully, as if perhaps there was nothing at all wrong with having a bear for a best friend. As if one never knew with Americans.

Hugh didn't reply. Instead he found himself slowly peeling his gloves from his hands, as though he were preparing for a bare-knuckle fight, or demonstrating how he would undress a woman whose body he intended to thoroughly savor.

Lillias's gaze flickered.

And then dropped.

And she watched, transfixed, until Hugh's hands were entirely bare.

A shade of deep rose moved into her cheeks. He knew triumph when her shoulders rose just a little as she pulled in a subtle steadying breath.

She returned her eyes to his with evident effort.

He didn't smile.

"He did once *spring* upon a bear!" Delacorte said hopefully.

"It was the other way around," Hugh said evenly.

This sentence naturally caused a startled silence in the room. Knitting needles went still.

Delacorte sucked in a breath to speak. "Tell the sto—"

"Another time, perhaps."

Never had a silent conversation been louder than the one he was conducting with Lady Lillias Vaughn.

No one seemed to notice anything amiss. The ladies took up their knitting again, and Mrs. Pariseau gave her throat a clearing before she continued.

"Speaking of moral arbiters, surely a lady of your refined nature appreciates the care taken to maintain a civilized environment, Lady Lillias." Hugh gestured at the epithet jar. "Not to mention protect your virgin ears from the stinging trauma of epithets." He imbued every one of these deliberately chosen words with tender condescension.

She pressed her lips together and tilted her head, sympathetically. "Have you need of civilizing then, Mr. Cassidy? I suppose recognizing one's deficiencies is the first step toward correcting them." Her eyebrows met in concern.

He gave a little nod. "All Americans are feral. I thought you would know that, given your obvious knowledge of our habits, friends, and accents."

"Cassidy is always a perfect gentleman," Delacorte, who was listening, maintained loyally. "He is always very polite to the ladies in pubs who try to sit in his lap."

Midway through this sentence Delilah had gracefully risen to pretend to adjust the ribbon in Lady Claire's hair, and in so doing happened to casually slide her hands down to cover her ears.

It clearly wasn't the first time she'd needed to do that since the Vaughns had arrived.

She resumed her seat just as gracefully and took up her needles again, and Mrs. Pariseau cleared her throat and read on.

He was sorely tempted to laugh, but he didn't want to miss a single twitch of Lady Lillias's reaction. He kept her pinned in the beam of his gaze.

"How devastating it must be to be mistaken for furniture, Mr. Cassidy," she said finally, on a grave hush, her eyebrows still canted sympathetically.

"On the contrary," he said with silken matching gravity. "What's a man's body for if not to ensure a lady's comfort and ease and safety? It's in fact my honor and privilege to do so."

A screen of caution moved over Lillias's features.

He was aware of playing fast and loose with the line between impropriety and innuendo. That the ruthlessness he felt was perhaps out of proportion to the circumstance. He wanted to win, whatever that meant. Though it was clear that he might as well attempt to prove to a riptide that it had no pull at all.

"Well, the epithet jar is clearly having the intended civilizing effect upon you, Mr. Cassidy, if you've progressed so far as to put the comfort of . . . ladies . . . first," she said ironically.

Was this a rebuke? He didn't care. "How astute of you to notice. And you'll be gratified to know that should anyone inadvertently utter an epithet in your presence, I'm certain Mrs. Hardy and Mrs. Durand could provide smelling salts. Or should something stronger seem necessary, I understand tobacco can be vivifying."

This occasion marked the first time in his life he'd said the word "vivifying" out loud. He'd said it primarily in the hopes that she would stare at him fixedly and with animosity, as he suspected she would.

And she did.

Every angle of her was alarmingly interesting and good. Her eyes were pale silvery blue and her lashes were black. Losing his breath had never been so delicious.

"I've something in my case what will wake the dead, if it's a good strong smell you're after," Delacorte volunteered brightly over his shoulder.

Lillias looked at him curiously. Then gave him a polite little smile.

Delacorte's smile faded and he pivoted away again.

"Mama, may I smell what's in Mr. Delacorte's case?" Claire asked.

"Certainly not, Claire," the countess said absently and rather shortly. She was absorbed in Mrs. Pariseau's story.

Claire shrugged with one shoulder, clearly accustomed to hearing, "Certainly not," a good deal. She shot a quick little smile at her sister, who flashed the tiniest smile back.

The unexpected, fleeting sweetness of this exchange stopped his breath with a jolt of homesickness: for his sister, Maeve, for New York, for people he'd lost, for things that would never be the same, for the simple pleasure of sharing sly mischievous smiles with people who knew and loved him.

It left him briefly winded.

He wondered if she'd noticed.

"Interestingly, the epithet jar didn't prevent Mr. Delacorte from sharing a new word with all of us," Lillias said suddenly.

"Oh? What did you say, Delacorte?" Hugh turned to him.

"Oh, I said boll . . . ha. I'm not falling for that again, Cassidy."

Hugh laughed. "I'll take responsibility for the first syllable." He flipped a half pence into the jar with such accurate vigor that Lillias gave a little jump. It clinked loudly, because it landed on a little metallic bed of already present pence.

The heads of the knitting ladies came up abruptly at the sound.

"You might be curious to learn, Mr. Cassidy, that a half pence is the exact cost of a scone," Mrs. Hardy said very sweetly, yet significantly.

Hugh looked toward her sharply. She *could* be making that up on the spot, though one never knew—but then, Angelique and Delilah knew their budgets down to the last pence. She was clearly making a point, and he suspected what it was.

"Well, that is interesting information, indeed. The scones are worth their weight in gold, of course," he said carefully. "Suppose a man had innocently eaten more than his fair share of scones and wished to compensate for . . . ah . . . succumbing to their divine qualities?"

There was a little pause while she studied him.

"Innocently?" She wrinkled her nose skeptically.

Hugh grinned.

"The man in question could assist with completing the construction of the stage in the Annex as the crew, and be paid with scones and gratitude," she said briskly.

"He'd be willing to do that." He'd actually love to do the work; he loathed having nothing constructive to do while he waited for letters that might never arrive. "I wonder what became of the men doing the work?"

"So do we," Angelique said darkly.

"It's so difficult to get good help," the countess said brightly, as though delivering a line in a play.

Dot had gotten hold of her knight and was making little clopping sounds against the roof of her mouth as she pretended to gallop it across the board. She claimed this helped her concentrate.

Delacorte lifted pleading, deeply regretful eyes to Delilah and Angelique. He was as sturdy as a Welsh pony and his hair tended to tuft out above his ears when it got a little long, which made him look a bit like a squirrel. And his eyes were lovely. Large and misty blue, the eyes of a dreamer.

They shrugged and smiled back at him with limpid, impish gratitude. The truth was, thanks to him, Dot already played a creditable, if unorthodox, game of chess. One day Dot was going to win a game. With somebody. Most likely with herself.

"I should say it's so lovely to have you back, Mr. Cassidy, as we're reading stories about gods and goddesses," Mrs. Pariseau, a dashing, worldly widow whose dark hair was streaked in striking white and whose sense of humor was bawdy, said. "Would you like to take a turn with the voices? You've such a fine baritone you ought to be on stage. I should think you'd make a *wonderful* Hades."

Mrs. Pariseau thought everyone who possessed a gift she appreciated ought to share it with the world via the stage.

She patted an empty chair near her. Hugh, contentedly, pulled it out and settled. He rather savored knowing Lady Lillias couldn't help but note that he, and his fine baritone and carpentry skills, was so welcome and appreciated.

"Tell me, Mrs. Pariseau . . ." All the ladies turned abruptly, eyes wide, when Lillias spoke, as it was the first time she'd voluntarily addressed them in the little sitting room since she'd arrived. "Isn't the myth of Hades and Persephone about a woman compelled to be, or shall we say, *trapped*, where she doesn't want to be? Thanks to the perfidy of a man?"

Her innocence was entirely feigned.

Hugh leaned back in his chair. "If you'll allow me, Mrs. Pariseau, to address the question?" he asked politely. Mrs. Pariseau gave a magnanimous nod. "Your interpretation is interesting, Lady Lillias. I confess *I've* always thought of it as a story of a woman who was searching for an excuse to succumb to temptation. Because confronting her true desires would have scandalized not only her parents, but the entire world. Imagine wanting to be with a man who is *literally* beneath her. So she ate a pomegranate seed and blamed her desires upon it."

The pretty flush in her cheeks seemed to begin at Lillias's collarbone.

A startled, rather impressed silence fell upon the room.

"Demeter and Zeus," Mrs. Pariseau contributed helpfully. "Those were her parents." She sounded fascinated. "Do go on."

"Thank you, Mrs. Pariseau," Lillias said pleasantly. "I do think it's rather distressing to imagine that there Persephone was, minding her business, innocently picking flowers, when Hades just decided it would be wonderful to . . . take her."

She fixed him with an unblinking gaze.

Well, that was surprisingly well done.

Take her take her take her. The words echoed through his mind, accompanied by swift, flickering scenes and carnal little prepositions and possibilities: backwards, forwards, sideways, behind. He dug a fingernail into his palm to stop them.

He eyed her warily.

Did she understand the full implications of what she'd just said? Or was he just inclined to sift everything she said through an innuendo filter? Doubtless she'd learned that men were just that easily distracted.

"But *was* it . . . innocent?" He furrowed his brow. "Persephone's actions? Or was she doing something she oughtn't be doing out of sheer boredom, courting an outcome she was entirely unprepared for, as she had no real notion of the dangers or consequences? It strikes me as a situation in which she would never . . . possibly . . . win."

Their eyes locked in deadly, silent combat.

Mrs. Hardy and Mrs. Durand each sported slightly puzzled furrows in their brows. Mrs. Pariseau was now frantically scanning the pages of the book for anything that might support his hypothesis.

Lillias's head tilted sympathetically. "Poor Hades," said softly. "How *weak* he must have been to do such a thing. How very savage and desperate it must have felt to be at the mercy of a need he couldn't ever ... dream ... of satisfying."

His jaw tightened.

"Oh my goodness," Mrs. Pariseau breathed. She touched her fingertips to her collarbone. "What a powerful and *unique* interpretation, Lady Lillias."

Everyone else looked rather puzzled.

She lifted slightly and let fall one shoulder with a little self-satisfied smile.

Hugh took pains to make his own faint smile pitying. An intimation that, while her goad was amusing, she hadn't a clue who she was up against.

Her satisfied expression flickered a bit.

Hugh rubbed his chin pensively. "Well, it certainly relieved her of the need to make that decision for herself, didn't it? Perhaps being swiftly taken by someone so uncivilized was a dream she'd never, ever admit to ... given that she was so above him."

He had the pleasure of actually seeing her breath hitch.

"Then again, at least he's the *lord* of the underworld," he added. "I'm sure that eventually brought her a good deal of comfort."

Mrs. Pariseau was now madly flipping through the book. "*What* a stimulating discussion," she enthused. "I didn't know you were a scholar of mythology, Mr. Cassidy. I must say I'm impressed with your conjectures. I'm eager to hear your thoughts on Odysseus. The poor fellow lashed himself to a mast in order to avoid being lured to his death by sirens."

"Odysseus was weak," Hugh said idly. "Resistance is child's play."

Lady Lillias seemed a trifle subdued. She turned her head and resumed gazing toward the curtains.

It was in all likelihood merely a tactical retreat.

He studied the back of her head. He suddenly imagined putting his lips against the pale inch of skin just above the lace of her collar. Blood rushed to his head.

"So what you're all saying is that Hades *snatched* her and took her to live in, er . . . *Hades*?" Lady Claire said suddenly. She'd been listening to all of this raptly, and evidently was both thrilled and scandalized. "*The* Hades? Where the devil lives?"

The countess looked up uncertainly, belatedly realizing that the classics were essentially full of moral pitfalls. "Er, doubtless she was quite comfortable there for the duration, Claire, dear," her mother soothed. "It was a palace and she was the queen, after all. And she would have been waited on hand and foot. We would have *all* been quite comfortable there, I'm certain, if we went."

Lillias turned toward Claire, her eyes lit with suppressed laughter, and Hugh was briefly dazzled.

"Are you advocating for all of us to go to the devil, Mother?" Lillias said innocently.

Claire bit her lip on a laugh.

Delacorte's head shot up at this. It pivoted be-

seechingly this way and that to note reactions.
Surely this warranted a trip to the epithet jar for
the young lady.

"Did you hear . . . what she . . . what she said . . ."
he prompted weakly. Chagrined at his lack of chiv-
alry, itching for a little justice. And perhaps a little
revenge.

It could not be denied that Lillias had said "go
to the devil." One simply did not say that in proper
company any more than one ought to say "bollocks." It could not be construed as anything other
than naughty.

A slightly uneasy silence settled over the room.

It was a conundrum.

Angelique, the former governess, finally spoke.
"Well, you pose an interesting question, Mr. Delacorte. I think perhaps it's a bit of a technicality, as
her reference in this instance was to Hades, the
place. Perhaps it would warrant a trip to the jar if
she had requested that one of *us* go to . . ." she lowered her voice delicately ". . . go to where she said
we ought to go."

"May I choose which person should go?" Lillias
said gravely.

"Lillias," her mother said exasperatedly.

"If Hades has comfortable knitted pillows and
Helga's scones *I'd* willingly go," Hugh said, as if
Lillias hadn't been talking about him all along,
"but something tells me Persephone isn't the type
to condescend to see to a man's comforts." He
paused, pretending to mull. "Might I suggest that
in instances where the intent was not so clear—
where indeed the speaker might be attempting to,
oh, *get away with something he or she ought not*—we

ought to take a vote? It would be a useful prece-
dent going forward."

Lillias made a small indignant sound in her
throat.

"I do like voting!" Dot enthused.

"Well, what sort of ambiguous circumstances
do you anticipate, Mr. Cassidy?" Mrs. Hardy wondered.

He gave it some thought. "For instance, what if
I told Mr. Delacorte that I was looking for a place
to store my cricket balls, and I had a fine wooden
box to put them in. But wanted to prevent thieves
from opening the box. What would I need?"

"Why ball locks, of course," Delacorte said at
once, with a satisfied smile.

Which flipped upside down with horror when
he realized what he'd said.

"In this circumstance," Hugh said, "I would say
that Delacorte ought to be exempt from the penalty."

"I should say so!" Delacorte agreed, indignantly.
"Entrapment!"

"Well, that sounds like a fair solution." Delilah
could sense some sort of mischief was afoot but
couldn't really see a good reason to stop it.

"Ha," Mr. Delacorte said under his breath.

Lillias shot him a glare that had him ducking
his head into his shoulders again. Her glares were
powerful indeed.

All of this was for Delacorte's sake, really, Hugh
told himself. She was enjoying herself just a little
too much at his expense.

"The rules are the rules, Lady Lillias," Hugh
said, sorrowfully.

Even her withering gazes were worth withstanding. Although . . . there was something lurking at the corner of her mouth that might—*might*—have been reluctant amusement.

He shrugged one shoulder, pityingly.

"We shall recuse ourselves from the vote, as we are your hostesses, and we will abide by your decision," Angelique said. Delilah and Angelique lowered their knitting to their laps.

Mr. Cassidy spoke. "All those in favor of Lady Lillias putting a pence in the jar, raise your hand."

And up went Hugh's hand immediately. "I think it's for the best," he said sadly. "When one wants civilizing, the epithet jar is there to help."

Up went Delacorte's hand boldly. He didn't offer an explanation apart from righteously raised brows.

Predictably, up went St. John's and Lady Claire's hands, as did the corners of their mouths. Siblings being siblings.

And then, in an interesting twist of plot, up went the countess's hand.

Lillias's stared at her balefully. "*Et tu*, Mama?"

"I voted in favor because you ought to stand and move about the room, dear. For heaven's sake. You're not doing a thing but sitting."

Lillias sighed heavily.

Hugh noticed that Mrs. Pariseau had not raised her hand.

"Mrs. Pariseau?"

"I feel a lady ought to utter an epithet now and again, if only to experience the feeling," Mrs. Pariseau said, quite modernly.

Lady Vaughn's eyes widened.

"Is it a good feeling, Mrs. Pariseau?" Claire asked somberly. She darted another glance at Lillias.

"Don't worry, Mother, Mrs. Pariseau is just discoursing spiritedly, as per the rules," Lillias said tautly. "Very well, then. If I put a pound in the jar, may I buy one hundred epithets?"

"Lillias," her mother warned again.

"I'm bound to learn one hundred new ones by the time we leave here," she said, quite pointedly. "It seems a wise investment."

Delacorte aimed a somewhat pleading look at Hugh.

"One pence is the penalty," Hugh said firmly as a magistrate. "The people have spoken. The penalty is now due."

Chapter Four

❦

THE LOOK Lillias fixed him with was fueled by the fires of a thousand silent epithets.

And then she had her revenge on him.

Lillias did not so much rise as *bloom* from her chair in a way that compelled him to watch every moment of that motion, which seemed to last forever and yet not long enough.

And regally as a queen about to go to the gallows, she squared her shoulders, lifted her chin, and moved.

And time seemed to slow in a both merciful and punishing way as Hugh watched the silk of her dress fall into soft folds and contours which would have prevented Galahad from ever setting eyes on the grail, so impure would have been his thoughts.

She moved across the room, and every one of his muscles tensed as though they were getting ready to pin her to a mattress.

And he knew with almost a sense of doom how Hades must have felt when he'd seen that girl in a meadow picking flowers. *I must have her or die.* It was that simple.

She put a pence in the jar, neatly.

Then returned the way she'd come.

Watching her return offered the same baffling, exquisite torment.

"Satisfied, Mr. Cassidy?"

"It was well done, indeed," he said softly. Subdued and baldly earnest.

Color moved into her cheeks again. She turned away abruptly, offering him a three-quarter view of her profile.

"*I'm* satisfied," muttered Mr. Delacorte.

"Well!" said Mrs. Pariseau. "Now that we've settled that, shall we read the story, or save it for another evening?"

"To be truthful, Mrs. Pariseau," Lillias said suddenly, sounding a trifle peevish, "I don't know why a myth about a young woman being *held prisoner* against her will is entertaining reading."

Her mother snorted.

"Yet aren't most novels about people compelled to be where they don't want to be?" Hugh said. "No doubt because we've all had that experience at one time or another. If they weren't, we'd hardly have any stories at all. For instance, *Robinson Crusoe* made the best of things. He even had a pet parrot."

"Oh, certainly every story would be improved by the addition of a pet parrot," Lillias said at once, rather reflexively.

Their gazes clashed in shock, then ricocheted away from each other.

They were shaken and none too pleased by this awkward moment of accord.

A little silence fell.

"How clever of you, Mr. Cassidy. And then

there's *The Ghost in the Attic*," Mrs. Pariseau chimed in. "Certainly our heroine had reservations about going into the attic."

"It gave me shivers, that book," Dot declared. "She should not have gone up into the attic! She was ever so brave."

"Ever so stupid, that is," Mrs. Pariseau muttered. "It's right *there* in the title."

Dot cast her eyes up from the chess game and met Mrs. Pariseau's in a mutual brief, stubborn glare.

"Oh, I should like to hear a story about the ghost in the attic. Have you any ghosts here at The Grand Palace on the Thames, Mrs. Durand and Mrs. Breedlove?" Claire was diverted.

"We've none at all," Delilah assured her as Angelique said sweetly, "Eleven or twelve."

The truth was probably somewhere in between, given the building's history before it was resurrected as a charming inn. But none had made themselves a nuisance, or even known, yet. Perhaps Gordon the Cat had seen them.

"Perhaps The Grand Palace on the Thames has an attic or a secret stairway?" Claire asked hopefully. "I saw a very tall ladder propped against the wall in the ballroom when I walked by."

"Well, the ladder is there because I'm helping to finish repairs to the Annex roof, Lady Claire," Hugh explained. "At the moment, if you climb that ladder, you can see right through to the stars and across the tops of roofs and ships."

He smiled at her.

Claire's face went utterly blank.

And then before everyone's eyes, a sheet of scarlet furled up her face like a venetian blind and her eyes turned to hazy stars.

"Oh for God's . . ." Lillias muttered.

"We'll read *The Ghost in the Attic* again," Mrs. Pariseau assured Claire. "We're all quite fond of it."

As she was still recovering from the cudgeling beauty of Mr. Cassidy's smile, Claire could not reply.

"I saw the ghost of the word 'rogue' on the sign hanging outside," Lillias said. "Did you perhaps change your mind about the nature of your business, Mrs. Durand, Mrs. Hardy, or did you think it would be helpful to label the contents of the building?"

She aimed this right at Hugh.

Delacorte pivoted eagerly, delighted to be able to enlighten her. "It's such an interesting story. Once upon a time this place was called The Palace of Rogues because *OW!*"

Delacorte glowered at Dot. She'd kicked him. She'd been present for the naming of The Palace of Rogues and it was a sacred moment for her.

"Not a single rogue has ever set foot through the door of The Grand Palace on the Thames," Delilah assured everyone in the room, which was more or less true, give or take an interloper, and depending upon how one defined the word, and given that it had been christened that only when she'd inherited the building. But she crossed her fingers in her lap beneath her knitting all the same. "Our interview process is very thorough for that precise reason."

"They even interviewed *us*, Lillias," her mother reminded her.

Hugh coughed unsubtly at that.

Everyone's heads turned at the sound of foot-steps in the foyer. They heralded the arrival of the Earl of Vaughn, back from a meeting with his Man of Affairs, and he swept into the room cheerfully.

"Good evening, all! And well, well, if it isn't Mr. Cassidy! Welcome back from . . . Dover, did you say when we last met?"

They'd only met briefly a fortnight ago, long enough for Hugh to tattle on Lillias for smoking a cheroot.

Hugh was on his feet at once. "Yes, sir. Thank you. It's a pleasure to see you again. I hope you're enjoying your stay at The Grand Palace on the Thames."

"We are, thank you. It's been an adventure!"

Delilah and Angelique exchanged a look. This wasn't precisely how they preferred to character-ize The Grand Palace on the Thames. Though ad-mittedly the description fit more often than not.

"As it so happens," Hugh said, "I recently had the pleasure of meeting with your cousin, Sir Bent-ley Tigmont. I found him altogether amiable and knowledgeable. He mentioned your name when we discussed horses."

"Ah, *Tiggy*!" The earl was thrilled. "Good man, good man, indeed. Bought a gelding from him just last year. We were at Eton together. Dear Tiggy. Are you also in imports and exports, like Captain Hardy, Lord Bolt, and Mr. Delacorte, Mr. Cassidy?"

"No, sir. I was flattered—and tempted indeed—when they invited me to join the Triton Group. And while my business interests are similar, I've long intended to run for mayor of my hometown of Wolfdale when I return to New York. And then, one day, for the United States Congress."

The little silence that followed this sentence was total and impressed. Some of them were already aware of Mr. Cassidy's ambition. It was the utter cool confidence and conviction of his delivery that made Mrs. Pariseau surreptitiously fan herself.

Lillias's eyes were fixed on him suddenly in speculation.

"How very enterprising of you, Mr. Cassidy," Lady Vaughn said. "Tell me, do they have gentlemen in America, or does every man work for a living?"

Hugh went still. Then he slowly, gingerly turned to her, his expression carefully neutral. In an instant, he could see at once that her question held no malice. It was entirely born of curiosity.

Lillias had one sardonic eyebrow up as if she wanted an answer to this question, too.

"Everyone is considered a gentleman until he demonstrates otherwise, Lady Vaughn," he said gently. "And that goes for the ladies, too."

"It must get lonely there in New York, with just trees and those little fellows with masks for company—raccoons," she delivered brightly, but almost . . . tentatively. As though it was the first time she'd said "racoons" and she'd been looking for an excuse to say it out loud.

He narrowed his eyes. As surprises went, it was a good one. How on earth would she know about *raccoons*, of all things? They weren't native to this part of the world. What other secrets was she harboring? She'd likely meant to startle him with quite a specifically American reference.

She looked a little triumphant.

"My best friend the bear and I sit on the porch and play the fiddle. And occasionally play chess. He lets me win. Unlike my friend Mr. Delacorte."

"Well, that's rather sweet of your friend," the countess ventured, after an uncertain silence.

Lillias smiled slowly in sheer delight.

"It's an actual city," Hugh said gently to the countess. "We've shops. A pub. A church. Taxes. I've human friends."

"Oh, shops!" The countess was relieved on his behalf, which was rather touching. "I don't suppose it's anything like London, though."

"Is anything truly like London?" Hugh decided to say, with a smile that made the countess visibly melt.

Lillias snorted quietly.

But her father heard the snort. "Daughter, perhaps you'd like to knit or draw or something rather than snort at things."

In truth, he sounded a little concerned. It was as much question as admonishment.

"The devil makes work for idle hands, Lady Lillias," Hugh said gravely.

He was rewarded with a dagger stare from beneath her straight, dark brows.

"How very on theme, Mr. Cassidy," Mrs. Pariseau approved.

"Lillias is a talented artist," her mother said proudly. "Her watercolors are exquisite and her teacher says she has a gift! All the ones she did of Heatherfield over the years are—"

"Ruined," Lillias said so flatly and abruptly it echoed in the room a bit like a door slamming.

There ensued an awkward silence.

"Heatherfield is the Bankham estate in Richmond," the countess explained benevolently, and though none of those words meant anything to him, their inflection made it clear that they were synonymous with "money" and "power" and he was meant to be impressed. "We've spent many happy days there as a family with the Earl and Countess of Bankham and their son, Giles, and her drawings were rather a chronicle of that. It's disappointing to lose them."

Lillias did not concur. She in fact had gone curiously motionless, like an animal who hopes a predator won't notice it. Quite as though she hoped all questions along those lines would stop.

Intriguing.

"Ah," Hugh said sagely. "Have you any new drawings in your sketchbook, Lady Lillias?"

Lillias looked up. "Oh, yes. It's a chronicle of all the fascinating things I've experienced during my stay here," she said earnestly. "Would you like to see it, Mr. Cassidy?"

She raised her brows and extended the sketchbook to him.

He hesitated. And when he took it, his bare knuckles just scarcely—but quite deliberately—brushed her bare fingertips.

Skin against skin. Just that much was as potent as a shot across a bow.

Their eyes met, held. It was an absurd moment before either recovered.

And then he slowly took temporary custody of the sketchbook.

Carefully, and with a sort of held-breath anticipation and, truthfully, respect—drawing was a talent he would have in fact loved to possess—he opened the cover of the sketchbook to the first page.

It was blank.

So he delicately turned to next page.

It was also blank.

He did that, carefully and deliberately, for every page of the book. About twenty of them.

Every last one was a clean, white blank.

He handed it back to her.

"You are *very* talented," he said softly. "I look forward to seeing my face on every page."

He flashed Lillias a wicked, crooked little smile, turned his back, and made for the smoking room without another word.

THE GENTLEMEN'S SMOKING Room looked and felt like an animal den in its scale and color—snug and primarily brown. The carpet was scrolled in cream and brown, the furniture was brown, the curtains were velvet and brown. A man could heave his boots up on the table, smoke, curse, or, as was often the case of Delacorte, silently break wind with impunity, in such a room. Hugh was touched by his proprietresses' thoughtfulness every time he set foot in it. It was quite lovingly masculine.

Delacorte had followed him in. The Earl had not. At least not yet.

Hugh leaned against the wall and inhaled his lit cheroot into smoking life.

No one looking at him would have known that

his entire being was vibrating as though all of his cells were little gongs that had been individually assailed with little mallets.

Lady Lillias Vaughn was a problem. He'd confirmed that much.

A unique-in-his-lifetime problem.

There seemed to be only one solution to this problem.

Which meant the problem was unsolvable, because he could not avail himself of this solution. Which involved the two of them, a bed and no clothes.

Cheroot tucked between two fingers, he pondered. She was a worthier competitor than perhaps he had anticipated, but he liked to think he'd won this round. He'd at least gotten the last word. But in truth there would be no winners, and he understood there would never be peace, not even in this cozy smoking room, until she was gone or he was. And he wanted to be gone, and to do that he needed to find Woodley's daughter, and none of this did anything to sand the jagged edges of his mood.

There was some minute comfort in the absolute certainty that he was also Lady Lillias Vaughn's problem.

Neither he nor Delacorte spoke straightaway, but that was usual. For the male guests of The Grand Palace on the Thames, the first moments in the smoking room were rather like unbuttoning one's trousers after a big meal. A spiritual exhale.

"When she's in the parlor I feel as though . . ." Delacorte tipped his head back, exhaled, consulting the wreath of cigar smoke about his head like an oracle. "I feel as though the back of my neck isn't quite clean enough."

He didn't have to explain who "she" was.

Nor was Hugh going to describe how she made him feel, which was, at this very moment, as though her nude body was pressed against his skin but his hands and legs were tied.

It would have shocked even the well-nigh unshockable Delacorte.

He said instead, "What a strangely specific thing to feel."

"I don't know quite how else to describe it."

Hugh stared at him.

Delacorte gazed back.

"*Is* it clean enough?" Hugh asked.

"Have a look." Delacorte twisted about.

Hugh heaved a resigned sigh and peered. "Like new-fallen snow back there."

"I don't quite cut the same dashing figure as you or Bolt or Hardy. Clean is all I've got."

"Oh, you've likely one or two other as yet undiscovered charms, Delacorte."

"Ha!" Delacorte loved being teased and quite liked himself. "And it's not so much what she says. It's about her whole . . ." and he gestured again with the cigar and the smoke.

And Hugh could almost see the shape of her in that smoke, like a succubus conjured. He had a feeling he would see the shape of her stamped on his eyelids when he closed his eyes.

And all that made him want to do was close his eyes.

"She's just a woman, Delacorte," Hugh said shortly. "And bored, spoiled women are a danger to themselves and everyone around them."

Delacorte's furry brows launched upward. It would never occur to him to use the words "just" and "woman" in the same sentence.

"I expect you're right," he said cheerfully enough. "She's like one of them goddesses. Not one of them seems the type to want to sew a button on a bloke's waistcoat."

This was remarkably astute.

Since Delacorte had moved into The Grand Palace on the Thames, his waistcoat buttons were always securely sewn on, and they were taxed, indeed. From the side, he rather resembled the letter "D" on legs.

"What do you think of the others?" Hugh asked. As if anyone else mattered at the moment.

"Well . . . I'd say the Earl and Countess are decent enough for being an earl and countess, but it's a near thing. The younger daughter, Lady Claire, asks a good many questions and laughs quite a bit and gets on with the others. The boy seems to like himself a good deal. Doesn't know how to play chess."

Those last sentences were about as close to a character indictment as Delacorte had ever uttered. Rather like a spaniel, Delacorte tended to like everyone and ultimately gave people no choice but to like him back, despite themselves. Hugh was intrigued.

A polite rap on the door heralded the entrance of, one after another, Lucien—Lord Bolt, Mrs.

Durand's husband—and Captain Hardy—Mrs. Hardy's husband—both of whom had been out at the ship on business with the Triton Group.

Followed by the Earl of Vaughn.

Hugh tried not to look as though he'd freshly imagined taking the earl's daughter from behind.

"Cassidy. Good to have you back." Captain Hardy and Bolt shook his hand and brandies were poured. The new entrants lit cigars and all at once they all leaped into satisfying talk of the business of the day—hiring new crew for the ship, discussion of adding another cutter to their fleet down the road, silk prices.

"Have enough money to run for mayor, Cassidy?" This was a question from the earl.

"Is there truly such a thing as enough money, sir?"

The earl laughed. "I knew I liked you, Cassidy."

"As it so happens, I believe my endeavor will be quite adequately financed. I've been fortunate in my investments. The Triton Group here being one of them." He gestured expansively to the other men in the room.

Hugh always looked for opportunities to champion his friends.

"Lord Vaughn, I may know a fellow who can help you capture that snake," Delacorte said suddenly, to no one's surprise except Vaughn's. Delacorte always knew somebody who could do something unusual.

"You don't say?" The earl was intrigued.

"Chap hails from India. He says he can do it without hurting the snake at all—seems you need to entice it with dead snakes or other tasty tidbits and whatnot and a brazier for warmth. I'll take you to go and have a chat with him, if you'd like."

The earl hesitated. "Well, that's big of you, Mr. Delacorte. Thank you. I'd like that. How did you meet this fellow?"

"Works for an apothecary friend of mine. Met him the other day. They took a dozen of the new impotence cure I've just got in from the orient. I don't suppose you could use some of those, too?"

And then he winked at the Earl.

The earl appeared immobilized by astonishment.

A faint spasm in the area of one of his eyebrows signaled they were undecided about diving in out-rage.

All the men in the room held their breath in hushed, anticipatory glee.

"Thank . . . you?" the Earl said finally, very, very carefully. "It's kind of you to ask, but at the moment I don't anticipate a need."

All of which made everyone in the room rather like him.

There was a little relieved silence.

"But . . . you wouldn't happen to have anything to . . ." the earl cleared his throat ". . . er, calm . . . the female nerves, would you?"

"Mmmm . . . not as such," Delacorte said, exhaling smoke. He was often the deliverer of shocking questions, but a question hadn't been invented that could shock *him*. "Females all being different people, you see. Perhaps if I knew more about the complaint."

Not one other man in the room wanted to know more about the female complaint and they prayed the earl wouldn't expound.

The earl hesitated. Then sighed. "My oldest daughter. She's grown into such a fine young lady over the past several years, you know . . . perhaps you've read an item or two in the gossip columns?" He looked up, half proud, half abashed. Everyone just smiled politely. "They do like to write about her. She has been everything that is proper and elegant, and we are so proud. But lately she's been a bit . . . unpredictable."

He glanced at Hugh, who was the only one in the room who knew about the cheroot.

Hugh suspected the earl had no idea of the true scope of Lillias's capacity to surprise.

"The only predictable thing about women is their unpredictability," Lucien said knowledgeably.

"Well, out of the blue a few weeks ago Lillias suddenly climbed the church tower. Bolted right up it after church."

Of all the things Hugh had expected to hear in the brown smoking room, this was perhaps last on the list.

"Did she say why?" He shouldn't have asked. It occurred to him that it was better that she remain a problem akin to an irritating noise on the periphery of his awareness, and not evolve into a person who would take deeper root in his imagination.

"Said she suddenly wanted to see as far as she could see. And while she was up there . . . she rang the bell."

There was a nonplussed little silence as they all pictured this. It was difficult to reconcile with the lovely, imperious young woman who sat so quietly in the drawing room with someone enthusiastically yanking on a bell rope.

"I should think the temptation to ring the bell would be irresistible once you're up there," Delacorte said, quite reasonably and charitably, given that she was, after a fashion, his enemy.

Imagining Lillias succumbing to temptation made Hugh want to ask Delacorte about remedies for male nerves.

"Has she ever done anything like that before?" Hugh asked before he could stop himself.

"Not as such. She was a bit of an adventurous child. Never a tomboy, mind. She loved her dresses and ribbons and whatnot. Just not a shrinking violet. Not afraid of much of anything, not fussy. Loved to read and still does. I encouraged it, and I . . . well, I sometimes wonder if that was wise, because you get notions when you read, don't you?"

He looked about the room for approbation.

Hugh was recalling how touchingly pleased she'd looked to say the word "raccoons." This must be how she'd learned it.

He was irritated to realize that it frankly . . . charmed him.

On the heels of this, unbidden, that sweet little smile she'd exchanged with her sister winked in him like a light in the dark. It came with an odd jab in his solar plexus.

"But a few weeks before the church bell nonsense, she was out for a ride and tore off on her horse without warning. Nearly scared the life out of her groom."

Hugh was silent.

He thought about her stillness in the sitting room. As he viewed her through another lens, it occurred to him that there was something stoic about it. As if she were waiting for something. Or waiting *out* something.

He found himself frowning faintly, then willed the frown away.

Everyone was regarding the earl with gentle sympathy. He was clearly concerned about his daughter.

"No doubt it's just an excess of high spirits," the earl said absently. "It's probably just time for her to get married."

"That'll fix 'er," Bolt said absently.

Captain Hardy stifled a smile. They both counted themselves lucky to have married complex, utterly singular, perfectly imperfect women.

No one man in that room truly suffered from the delusion that a remedy imported from any continent could solve women.

Chapter Five

❧❧❧

"You LIKE towers, if you'll recall. You can pretend you're Mary in the Tower, to make it more interesting," Lillias's father said mordantly the following morning. "Only infinitely luckier than Mary, of course . . . as long as you stay on the premises."

And then he'd gone off with Mr. Delacorte to speak to a man who "knew how to coax snakes out of hiding"—how one acquired that skill she could not begin to guess, as it didn't seem like something one could or should practice, like shooting at Mantons. St. John had gone for a ride in The Row in order to be admired by young ladies in carriages as not enough of that was taking place at The Grand Palace on the Thames. And her mother and Claire had gone to Leicester Square to view an exhibit of Miss Mary Linwood's exquisite needlework.

Lillias had smoked a cheroot, and this, like original sin, threatened to haunt her for the rest of her days.

She could lay this, and the fact that she would not see Miss Mary Linwood's needlework, at Hugh Cassidy's door. His transgressions were piling up like wood about Joan of Arc's ankles.

She could now add to them the fact that she hadn't slept much at all the previous night. Not that she'd slept much in recent weeks. She'd become accustomed to using the time between sliding under her blankets at night and the time the maids came in to poke up the fires for calculating the hours, minutes, and seconds remaining until the Landover Ball. Much more effective than counting sheep and practical, too: Why not use her encroaching doom to improve her math?

She'd begun to dread going to bed.

Last night she lay awake, all but winded, exhilarated as though she'd survived a climb up a crumbling, narrow mountain road, around whose corners stunning vistas or fanged predators were just as likely to appear. She felt she could not take her eyes from Hugh Cassidy when he was near. It was some combination of wariness—as though he were indeed feral—fascination, and irritated wonderment that such an arrogant, self-satisfied man should possess such a riveting collection of features. Skirmishing with him had demanded the kind of wily strength of wit she'd all but forgotten she'd possessed. She so rarely encountered a will as strong as her own.

He was entirely too pleased with himself, and this could not stand.

"Ball locks." Her mouth slowly curved into a reluctant smile. Very well, *that* was funny. And if she was being honest with herself, so was the way he'd orchestrated her trip to the epithet jar. She might have done something similar to one of her siblings.

The way he'd watched her walk to the jar wasn't at all funny. It was perhaps the most soberingly adult thing to happen to her in her twenty years of life.

She wasn't unfamiliar with lust. Nor was she naive about where it led. But she could not deny there was no relationship between the occasional thrill that traced her spine when she waltzed with a handsome blood and the inexplicable all-out siege Hugh Cassidy's mere presence had waged on her senses. Even now, in this empty, quiet suite, her skin hummed like a crystal glass tapped with a fingernail. The caress of her silk dress along her shoulder blades as she pulled it over her head, the cool glide of sheets against her bare legs, the warmth of the fire on the back of her neck—she was suddenly acutely reminded of her capacity to experience pleasure.

Doubtless the death of her dreams had left a vacancy in her soul and lust, like an opportunistic demon, had seen an opportunity to move in when she was at her weakest. What other reason could there be?

Inexplicably, it was the most alive she'd felt in weeks. There was a good deal of unworthy satisfaction in knowing that Hugh Cassidy would not be getting what he wanted, either.

And what he wanted was her.

She sighed, drank another cup of growing-cold coffee, and contemplated what to do with the empty, quiet hours ahead of her.

She would never dare tell anyone in her family that she'd come to rather enjoy having them underfoot. She liked all the bickering, laughing, and rustling about in the mornings and evenings. There was so much echoing space, so much coming and going in their London home and their country home, and so many servants to tidy them and manage them as they moved through their days so that no evidence of actual living—crumbs, a stray stocking, an open book—was left to linger for long.

Although it was admittedly convenient to come in the door from a walk and hold out her pelisse and have an arm take it away at once to be hung in her wardrobe. That sort of thing.

From the window she could see, down below in the courtyard of The Grand Palace on the Thames, an improbably lush little garden about the size of four picnic blankets sewn together, complete with little trees and blooming flowers, enclosed in a wrought iron fence. She hadn't yet visited it.

"Even the poor flowers are in jail," she muttered.

Surely it wasn't violating the spirit of her sentence if she were to have a look? Of a certainty, it *was* on the premises. She hesitated.

Then she snatched up her sketchbook and a packet of pastel crayons and a holder, and made her way down the stairs and burst into the cool, clear morning.

She lifted the latch on the gate and ventured in. The shortest little flagstone path led to a pair of wood and wrought iron benches arranged across from each other. A dense little thicket of tall, healthy trees stood at one end. Some of them were the fruiting sort, and were now breaking out in blooms; flowers on stalks were crowded chummily between them, and arranged in a circle at the center.

She settled on one bench sporting a little engraved plaque and stared down at her sketchbook.

Perhaps she would draw a flower.

The impulse to move her hand across the page,

a sensation once so delicious, seemed to have deserted her. She wondered if it was because it had once been born of joy.

She stared at the blank page until she saw black spots before her eyes. Then she shaded her eyes with her hand very briefly, a fleeting, despairing gesture of the sort she seldom allowed herself to indulge in. And certainly never when anyone else was about.

She let her hand heavily fall to the blank page again, sighed, and raised her eyes absently toward the cluster of trees.

Her heart leaped into her throat.

Standing as still as a tree—in fact, looking like a cousin to a tree—was Hugh Cassidy.

He was wearing buckskins, boots, a black coat, and a gradually growing, rather wicked smile.

In his hand was what appeared to be a letter.

"Well, *good* morning, Persephone. Something about your expression suggests you wouldn't mind if Hades would burst through the earth right now to pull you under."

It was a moment before she could pull enough air to speak.

"Forgive me for disturbing you, Mr. Cassidy. It's just that I might have easily mistaken you for a tree if you hadn't been staring so intently at me."

He offered a gently solicitous smile. "My apologies. Would you prefer that I do something else to you, instead?"

Her heart thunked as though toppled from a turret. Blood rushed into her cheeks. The backs of her arms went hot.

She couldn't speak.

His sympathetic smile was the sort a master fencer would aim at a novice.

Mr. Cassidy, she realized, *always* came out fighting. Which she supposed was flattering: it was a measure of the sort of adversary he saw in her.

He moved toward her slowly. Then lowered his large self slowly, gracefully, down on the bench across from her, as if he didn't want to spook her.

They regarded each other.

A flake of gold sat next to the pupil of one of his eyes. Something made her want to hoard this discovery as if it were actual gold.

"You want very badly to tell me to go to the devil right now, don't you, Lady Lillias?" He was all hushed sympathy. "There's no epithet jar or witnesses. Go right ahead, if it will make you feel better. I shall withstand it manfully."

"I'm not as prone to histrionics as all of that, Mr. Cassidy. Or as easy to shock."

"I'll certainly have to try harder, then, won't I?" More seriously he added, "I am sorry if I frightened you. I didn't mean to. Would you like me to leave so that you can be alone with your sketchbook?"

What she would like was for his eyes to stop being so interestingly blue so she wouldn't be compelled to look at them. He was unfortunately no uglier by daylight than he was by lamplight or by the dim light of the under-construction Annex.

She knew how to handle the bloods of the *ton*. After all, they'd been raised with the same manners and mores and institutions as she had, and they essentially adhered to the same rules. The lines of propriety were distinct and kept her safe.

She didn't know what the rules were here.

All Americans are feral.

"You didn't frighten me. And it seems I was intruding upon your private time, Mr. Cassidy. I should be the one to leave."

"It's no intrusion at all," he said smoothly. "I am awaiting the arrival of a cart full of lumber and decided to take the opportunity to read a letter from my Uncle Liam, sent to me by my sister." He lifted the letter. "As it so happens he's sailing into Portsmouth on the *Tropica* from India. I'll be off to meet him there."

She was so arrested by the warmth of the words, that for a moment, she couldn't speak for wondering what it would be like to actually be at peace in Mr. Cassidy's presence, as Uncle Liam presumably was.

"'You won't believe what I'm about to tell you,' Uncle Liam always says," Hugh continued, when she said nothing. "Which, coincidentally, is how I always begin when I tell the story of finding the daughter of an earl smoking a cheroot."

She gave a soft snort. "You seem to believe I'd be appalled to hear that."

He grinned fleetingly at that. "You'll be relieved to learn that I only told your father," he said, with mock conciliation.

"And that was well done of you, too, Mr. Cassidy. That's one woman saved from perdition. Now to do something about the ones who want to sit on your lap in pubs."

"Oh, I'm not certain those ladies want saving," he said with wicked sincerity.

She stared at him.

"'Ladies,'" she muttered to herself, ironically. She cast her eyes upward in a near roll.

That quick grin flashed again, and it was a thing of beauty. He seemed much more at ease this morning.

Perhaps *he'd* had a decent night's sleep. Perhaps last night's encounter was as routine in his life as swinging an axe, or whatever it was Americans routinely did.

The notion made her feel a little peevish.

"What brings you to Helene Durand Park, Lady Lillias?"

She paused, wondering whether entering into a civilized dialogue with Mr. Cassidy was signaling détente and whether she ought to encourage it.

"I thought I might draw," she said stiffly.

Although she half suspected she might never draw again.

He looked at her sketchbook. Then up at her.

After a moment, he arched a skeptical brow.

He was probably beginning to think she was a looby who merely carried about an empty sketchbook for effect, but so be it.

With an extraordinary effort, she turned her head away and pretended to scrutinize an apple blossom as though she intended to render it. As if anything could be more fascinating than what was sitting on the bench opposite her.

While she studied the blossom, he studied her. She could all but feel the rays of his attention illuminating her.

"Perhaps . . . you're mourning your ruined sketchbook?"

The question sounded serious. Almost tentative. And was so startlingly astute that she could only turn to him in speechless, somewhat hunted surprise.

He didn't pursue it.

"Did you just use the word 'histrionics' because you thought I wouldn't understand what it meant?" he said at once, instead.

She was still a little rattled. The truth was: she had. Unworthy of her, perhaps. It was interesting to know how swiftly she was willing to play dirty in order to retrieve the upper hand from him.

"I said it because it was the right word for that particular sentence," she hedged.

"Mmm. Well, I approve of exactitude." He wasn't blinking.

"And your approval means *everything* to me, Mr. Cassidy."

His smile was slow, and contained such a combination of genuine amusement, self-deprecation, and appreciation for her that for an instant every part of her felt illuminated, warmed, and too exposed.

She remembered poor Claire and the scarlet furling up her face.

She looked quickly away, at the apple blossom, in order to avoid that fate.

It was a point for Mr. Cassidy, and he knew it.

He leaned back against the bench. She watched, out of the corner of her eye, the grace of the lines of his body as he settled in and stretched an arm across it.

It seemed entirely rational to want to sit in his lap.

"Why raccoons?" he asked suddenly.

She was unaccountably flattered. It meant he'd listened carefully—and remembered—every word she'd said last night. Men were often such terrible listeners.

"They seem like charming animals."

"They *are* charming. Clever and clownish. Did you know their name comes from a Powhatan word? They also make fine warm hats, should the need arise."

She had no idea what to say to this. She suspected he was being very American in an attempt to unnerve her.

"I ask," he continued, "because I didn't go to Eton with 'Tiggy,' Lady Lillias. I learned 'histrionics' the same way you learned about raccoons, no doubt."

"Because my father has a large library and books on many subjects and I . . . read them."

"As does my friend, Mr. Augustus Woodley. He allowed me the use of it while I worked for him, building out his library shelves and stables."

A reminder that Mr. Cassidy was a *laborer*.

Or had been. Albeit an ambitious one.

There was an awkward little silence, during which she realized that nearly all of her interactions with men to date had been governed by the kinds of rules and assumptions that kept her, like a train, on a track, rolling toward one destination and quite blinkered, to boot.

Doubtless there were very good reasons for this. She probably ought not be isolated in a little garden by the docks with a laborer from America, even if he harbored political ambitions.

"Are you a great reader then, Mr. Cassidy?" She

gave this a doubtful lilt, lest he be lulled into thinking she was enjoying this conversation.

"Apart from *Robinson Crusoe*, of course, which my uncle"—he raised the letter—"gave to me, I read in order to learn everything I'll need."

"Need for what, pray tell?"

"To build an empire." He said it easily, matter-of-factly.

But the words had the ring of prophesy. She almost felt them in her chest, as one might feel the vibrations of a church bell.

She stared at him.

Unaccountably stirred, she swiftly looked down at her sketchbook again. It was inconvenient to have no drawing to pretend to inspect.

She simultaneously and equally wanted nothing more than to ask questions and to not ask any questions at all.

Curiosity killed not only cats.

"What manner of 'empire'?" She gave this last word an ironic lilt, too, for the same reasons.

He took a breath, as though he were about to embark on a story. "Well, it began with my friend, Mr. Woodley. He's in shipbuilding, and American ships are the finest in the world. I've learned a good deal about trade and imports and exports from him and I've been tempted to join Delacorte, Hardy, and Bolt in the Triton Group. But I think railroads are the future. I'd like to build a consortium in New York to bring the railroads to the United States. Canals we have, and they're a start, but moving goods and people across a growing country will be a perpetual and increasing need. I want to be part of building it—and shaping laws and policies—which is why I want to run for mayor, and then Congress. *Everything* is new in America. The possibilities are infinite."

She'd heard both awe and relish, flavored with the faintest hint of censure—even condescension—in those words: "New." "Infinite."

The implication was that everything in England was old and had been done, of course.

No man had ever really spoken like this to her before—about trade and business and plans. She was at once full of more questions; ideas of her own began to form. And perhaps that was the reason no one had spoken to her like this—in her experience, few men liked to answer to much, particularly to women. But she could see how each of Mr. Cassidy's ambitions connected to and supported the next. His plan was like a well-drawn map or a network of roads that fanned outward. She was impressed despite herself. She suddenly wanted very much to hold such a map in her hands.

She'd been sheltered from his world of work and trade and men and striving and ambition. But it existed parallel to her own; it in fact made her world of elegant ease—well-sprung carriages, servants, marble floors, new dresses every season—possible.

But she had a point to make.

"I've always found a sense of strength in being surrounded by centuries of history and tradition, Mr. Cassidy. England feels eternal. As if it has always been and always will be. I find all of this quite safe and . . . peaceful."

"Mmm," he said again. He paused at length. "Do you?" he asked quietly. It seemed a genuine question. Flustered, she dropped her eyes again, briefly to her blank page.

He noticed. "Speaking of tradition, what does Heatherfield look like?"

Interesting that he'd remembered that, too. Speaking of Heatherfield would be like grinding her thumb into a bruise. But it would help her to illustrate her point, and for this opportunity she would suffer.

"The house is . . . well, as stately in its way as St. Paul's Cathedral, or Westminster Abbey. Its history stretches back more than a century. And when you step inside . . . you can feel the age of it, and sense the centuries of Bankhams who've lived there. Carrera marble and Savonnerie and Axminster carpets are everywhere, and vast windows hung in yards of brocade and velvet . . . and the grounds are comprised of miles of soft grass, and fine, lush gardens. There's an oak forest surrounding it . . . and it's quite old. A long drive lined in cypresses leads up to it, and they always reminded me of soldiers. I am not doing it justice, I'm afraid."

"Sounds very nice," he damned with faint praise.

She looked at him askance. A little silence followed, which would have been a fine time for either of them to depart.

"Do you know, Lady Lillias . . . the first thing I did with the money I earned was buy land."

"I suppose one would have to do that if one doesn't inherit land with a title," she said offhandedly.

"Yes. One would," he said, ironically amused, after a pause during which he clearly decided against saying something he was tempted to say. "And . . . well, we haven't churches like St. Paul's . . . and cypresses don't line my drive, as I haven't a drive and cypresses don't just spring up out of nowhere in New York. But the trees on my land, Lady Lillias . . . they're like cathedrals." He lifted his hands up, like a God summoning rains. Illustrating. "Ancient. Their spires reaching high, up into an endless sky. I've oaks, too. My land is surrounded by these magnificent trees . . . and it overlooks the Hudson River Valley."

She was riveted.

He closed his eyes briefly, as if he was in fact dreaming of it. There was a tension in his face, very like yearning, and it started in her a surprising ache she could not name. "The mountains begin their days in deep blues and purples—the colors of the sky around midnight—and the sun paints gold light right up them as it rises. And then when it's high in the sky all you see is dense green velvet mountains, fields and forests as far as the eye can see, and the colors change with the season. The scale of everything is . . ." He gave a short, awed laugh, and spread his arms wide. ". . . majestic. As if everything is aware of how much room it has to grow and breathe. It's beautiful and unforgiving and mysterious. Makes a man want to . . . tame it and worship it all at once."

The words sifted down around her like a shimmering net. She was transfixed. She half suspected if she closed her eyes now, at once, she would see it, too. But she would need to do it quickly, before it drifted away.

She didn't. But she knew he was going to be

a *gifted* politician. He was even more formidable than she'd thought. Mainly because she was certain he not only sincerely felt every word he'd just said, but also knew precisely the effect they would have. Which is why he'd said them.

Particularly that last sentence. *Tame it and worship it all at once.*

She ought to look away just to prove that she could.

She could not. Nor did he.

She wondered how he'd gotten the little crescent-moon-shaped scar next to his lip. She imagined tracing it.

She realized she was already absently running her fingertip in a slow caress over the little plaque on the bench. And he was watching this rather fixedly.

"I wonder who Helene Durand was?" she said idly.

She stopped tracing the plaque.

He lifted his head with apparent effort.

His eyes looked somnolent. Rather stunned. He'd clearly been imagining something, too.

He took a breath. "She was the mother of Lucien Durand, Lord Bolt. Mrs. Durand's husband. You've met him, no doubt. His father, as you likely know, is the Duke of Brexford. And the duke was . . . ah . . . not married to Bolt's mother. He was unkind to both of them."

"While your attempt at discretion is both touching and wholly inadequate, I *have* heard the word 'bastard' before, Mr. Cassidy."

He smiled slowly. "But you probably never truly felt like using it until you met me."

She quirked the corner of her mouth wryly. "I think it's very sad, though. I don't understand how he could be so callous to his son and his . . . er . . . Helene Durand. Family is family. My own father knew his father, and his father knew his father, on back for centuries. It's extraordinarily comforting. After all, the strongest trees have the deepest roots."

"My father didn't know his father at all," Mr. Cassidy said offhandedly.

She was silent.

"Now you're shocked," he noted accurately.

She was. An entire branch of Mr. Cassidy's family tree was all but invisible to him. For an instant, she could almost feel the wind of the abyss under her feet. This seemed nearly inconceivable to her. And yet there were likely many people just like him.

It was another thing that felt like a challenge, like raccoon hats and manual labor.

And perhaps *this* was why he liked the newness. He would need to create *something* of lasting value, and he could do it where everything was new. A person needed a foundation.

"In other words"—he stretched his arms casually above his head, reaching for the sun, and Lillias watched that movement because she was helpless not to—"my father was a *literal* bastard, Lady Lillias." His implication being, that he, Mr. Cassidy, was of course being the figurative sort. "It seems reprehensible treatment of women isn't confined to the upper classes."

"I suppose it isn't," she said politely, after a moment. She was freshly, acutely certain she should not be participating in this conversation.

There was a lull.

"Do you perhaps need a cheroot for your shaken nerves?" he said with gently ironic solicitousness. "Perhaps a half of the light ale at The Wolf and . . . ?"

She supposed no one knew what that fourth word on the sign used to be.

She craned her head toward the little pub. She half wished she could, just to see the inside of it.

Still, she didn't speak. She'd already been given a good deal to think about.

He seemed to sense this. Mr. Cassidy pressed his lips together, and looked off toward the end of Lovell Street. Then he returned his gaze to her. "Well, all's well that ends well, Lady Lillias, because my father met my mother and they are responsible for my presence here before you, for which I know you are grateful."

She had the sense that he was inspecting her as closely as she'd been inspecting him, and similarly wishing he did not want to ask more questions.

"I suppose it's a fortunate thing there was only ever one of you, Mr. Cassidy."

He offered a quick, crooked smile. "I have some devastating news for you. I had a brother, and he was even better looking than I am."

Just then a cart pulled by a stocky gray horse clattered into the courtyard. It appeared to be filled with lumber.

They both shot to their feet.

And just like that, they found themselves standing mere inches apart, just about a single exhale away from touching. In seconds, those inches evolved into a trap. Dense as velvet. Subject to its own natural laws.

Because surely this was the only reason that neither of them seemed able to move even as the elapsing time . . . five seconds . . . ten seconds . . . twenty . . . became officially unseemly.

And then undeniably a contest.

It was long enough for the heat radiating from his body to join the heat radiating from hers until her eyelids felt weighted and she yearned to close them. Long enough for her breathing to go shallow, and rather spiky.

She was close enough to see herself reflected in his coat buttons.

And to see that reflection rise . . . and fall. Rise . . . and fall.

One inch. A slight forward tilt of her head. And then her cheek would be against his chest. She could feel the beat of his heart. This seemed an eminently reasonable thing to do.

And she knew, too, that his view from where he stood was the pale swell of the tops of her breasts, and the little shadowy divide between them.

And so she continued standing absolutely motionless. It might have been the most wanton thing she'd ever deliberately done.

He would not win this.

Suddenly there was his voice. Low, slow, far too intimately close. "I imagine it's maddening when something comes along to disturb those centuries of peace you described, Lady Lillias. Something that causes you to lose sleep. To toss and turn . . .

toss and turn. Something over which you've no . . . control . . . at all."

He no doubt noticed how the breath she took shuddered.

She needed it in order to get the last word. She knew she would.

"I wouldn't know, Mr. Cassidy. But Odysseus lashed himself to the mast, if you're looking for a solution to your current dilemma." She addressed this to his waistcoat buttons.

"Adorable suggestion. You'll be disappointed to learn that I have greater trust in my powers of resistance than that poor bastard did."

And then she mustered all of her courage—which was in truth considerable—to tip her head back. The sudden sight of the sensual curve of his mouth so close caused a jolt right between her legs. She found his eyes were heavy-lidded. Inscrutable. And as hot as the lit ends of two cheroots.

"Perhaps that's only because they haven't yet been sufficiently tested, Mr. Cassidy."

She stepped back just as his expression changed to something more fierce.

And the only thing that kept her from turning around as she walked away was the certainty that he would watch her, helpless not to, until she was no longer in view.

Chapter Six

❦

"*D*O YOU remember Mrs. Locksley?" Delacorte said wistfully a few hours later, over two pints of the dark at a pub they'd escaped into after a misguided foray into a music hall. "She was pretty."

Delacorte had indoctrinated Hugh into the types of entertainment thrifty men who were not debauchers could enjoy in London, including donkey races, festivals oriented around people chasing pigs that had been greased, lectures, boxing matches, darts in pubs, singing flash ballads in various pubs, meals in pubs, and walking about the city.

The pub was smoky and crowded and lively. A fire was leaping. No drunks were starting knife fights. The waitresses were pretty and flirtatious and none of them had yet attempted to sit in his lap. The dark ale wasn't terrible. He'd had worse.

Which was a blessing, as Hugh felt he needed to drink more than the usual restrained taste of brandy he usually indulged in after dinners at The Grand Palace on the Thames.

He was here to smugly prove he did indeed have greater powers of resistance than that poor bastard Odysseus.

The Grand Palace on the Thames's rules required that guests be present in the little sitting room for at least four days of the week, and he'd rather be there right now.

Only he knew he wasn't actually proving anything at all. He wasn't so much lashed to a mast as he was lashed to the woman by an invisible cord that tugged and sawed at him even when she was well out of sight.

While he'd measured and sawed boards for the stage this afternoon, he'd thought about the tops of her breasts. He suspected they rivaled the apple blossoms in the little garden for their silkiness.

A minute part of him thought he might die, as if from starvation, if he didn't lick one soon. She'd certainly played that moment with deuced skill, he thought grimly. She was clever and fierce and did not back down from a challenge and these were qualities he admired in anyone . . . to an extent.

But she was playing a reckless game.

A different kind of man would have her on her back with alacrity.

He found at once that he gravely disliked the notion of her playing a similar game with any other man. This realization blackened Hugh's already capricious mood around the edges.

Delacorte offered him a roasted chestnut from a paper cone of them he'd bought out on the street.

He'd actually been holding it out to Hugh for close to half a minute, but Hugh hadn't noticed.

Hugh took one. "Mrs. Locksley was pretty, indeed," he said absently.

Mrs. Locksley been a guest at The Grand Palace on the Thames not too long ago. Blue eyes? Why couldn't he quite recall at the moment? They'd all been mildly smitten.

She smelled like a damned garden. Lillias, not Mrs. Locksley.

"How is your sister?" Delacorte tried, when Hugh failed to pick up the conversational torch.

"Oh, she's well." Hugh smiled faintly, because Maeve lived in Baltimore with their aunt and he missed her like the devil.

"I take it you've had no luck finding the Clay family, otherwise we'd be . . . celebrating?"

Hugh had told Delacorte, in general terms, that his search for Woodley's daughter was how he came to be in London, his only lead.

"No. There are an unconscionable number of families named Clay in the general London area, and I learned the Clay family in Dover was not the one I'm seeking. I've been directed to a possible likely Clay family in Surrey."

He fell silent again.

Delacorte chewed noisily and drained the last of his tankard.

"I should say we've been lucky at The Grand Palace on the Thames, surrounded by so many pretty women, the likes of Brownie and Goldie and our handsome Mrs. Pariseau," Delacorte said.

Brownie and Goldie were the pet names Delacorte had given the brunette Delilah and blonde Angelique, quite unbeknownst to them.

"Indeed."

"All that said," Delacorte told him, "it looks like you could use a woman. Or be well used by one," Delacorte added cheerily.

Hugh stared at him. "The *devil* are you running on about?"

"You've been a moody cuss all night."

"A 'moody cuss'?" He didn't know whether to laugh or bang his tankard down with a scowl. Which he supposed would have proved Delacorte's point.

"And you're usually an even-tempered fellow."

"Which, believe me, is no mean feat around you."

"Ha," Delacorte said, and popped a chestnut into his mouth and chewed.

"Or . . ." Delacorte mused. He finished chewing before he went on. "Perhaps you're moody because you're *already* being well used by a woman."

"Or perhaps we don't need to talk about women," Hugh said very evenly.

Delacorte's brows went up. "I see. Fair enough." Delacorte glanced down, then shook out the bit of paper in which the roasted chestnuts he'd purchased were wrapped. He read silently for a moment.

"Well, would you look at this."

He read aloud:

The yearly Landover Ball is well-nigh upon us and all the ladies of the ton are atwitter with speculation about what the lovely Lady Lillias Vaughn will wear. If history is any indication, we can anticipate an enchantress set loose in a ballroom specifically to bewitch all the bloods. The ones not in love with her are bound to be by the time the night is over, and hothouses all over England will be denuded of flowers as heirs spend their inheritance to fill her foyer with flowers. Oh, whom, whom will she choose in the end?

Young Giles, Lord Bankham, lately in town

*from Heatherfield, was out riding in The Row
today looking like a modern Adonis on his
new gray hack. Rumor has it that a certain
young and fetching Lady Harriette will be
making her debut at the Landover Ball, and
perhaps soon after a debut as a wife of an heir.
Care to speculate which one?*

"Good God," Hugh croaked. Appalled.

"Do you hear that, Cassidy? 'Denuded.' 'Enchantress.' 'Heirs.'" He said this grimly, as though it were instead a list of criminals scheduled to be hung. "Told you she was like one of them goddesses."

A dozen disparate thoughts and impressions beset Hugh: those paragraphs were *hilariously* florid, and deserved to be roundly mocked at once, and yet all of his words seems to be lodged in a lumpen mass in his throat; the ridiculous cost of hothouse roses; the utter absurdity that she occupied a world in which a paragraph featuring the words "enchantress" and "bewitched" would be written and published about her; the probable bald truth of the "enchantress" bit; the fact that every bit of it, from the hyperbole to the ball, was foreign and possibly antithetical to his experience and everything he believed in; her blush as she'd watched him remove her gloves. The word "raccoon."

The quick little despairing hand over her eyes today as she stared at her blank sketchbook, as though he'd pressed a wound with his question.

Her eyes fixed on him as if she was drinking in his description of his land in the Hudson River Valley.

The fact that he'd tried to avoid her and she had somehow found him here in this dark pub, anyway.

He was motionless.

"I can tell from your expression that she's gotten under your skin, too, Cassidy." Delacorte held up his hand for another round, and the pretty waitress beamed at them and raced over in the hopes that the big blue-eyed man would finally look her full in the face.

Hugh's jaw set. She was a bored debutante confined in a boarding house near the docks, and naturally she'd found a diversion in him, and he was here because Woodley had entrusted him to bring his daughter home.

He would leave for Surrey the minute he'd finished building the stage.

"I hope The Grand Palace on the Thames doesn't become one of those duke and earl places," Delacorte added.

"Clearly those are the worst places," Hugh said casually. He startled Delacorte by scraping his chair roughly back, standing abruptly, and striding over to hurl that gossipy scrap of newspaper on the fire.

"I'll have another of the dark, darling," he told the waitress when he returned. And with a smile he looked her full in the face.

"THAT'S THE WAY it was done at the Stevens Hotel. I would do errands for the guests, like."

The maids were still going about the business of lovingly waking up The Grand Palace on the

Thames with fires and scones and coffee when Mr.
James Barton, the latest candidate for footman, arrived, and now Delilah and Angelique sat in the
kitchen across from him at the kitchen table, while
behind them Helga pummeled bread dough and
eavesdropped.

It was unlikely that odes would be written to
Mr. Barton's thighs, but he was tall and appeared
sturdy and clean. He'd demonstrated manners
and a decent command of the English language,
and claimed to possess experience and letters of
reference from the Stevens Hotel. If they were not
bowled over by his charm they could not find fault
with his manners.

"Why are you seeking a new position, Mr. Barton?" Delilah asked.

"I thought a smaller establishment might be a
bit cozier, you see, and the guests more exclusive."

This was meant to flatter them and it did,
though they weren't credulous. The word "exclusive" whistled a bit through the little gap between
his front teeth. The fact that he was able to produce a word with three syllables nearly had Delilah and Angelique reaching for each other's hands
to squeeze in hopeful disbelief.

"And Mr. Barton, are you able to read?" Delilah
thought it best to make sure. Their footman would
need to carry and deliver messages on occasion
and find the directions of vendors.

"I can, indeed. If you would like to see my
references . . ."

He reached into his coat and pushed across two
letters. Delilah and Angelique each took custody
of one and read them quickly. Written on statio-

nery from the Stevens Hotel, they did not immediately appear to be forgeries. Though one never
knew. They would of course investigate.

"Well, thank you for coming this morning, Mr.
Barton. We'll write to you at your direction once
we've reviewed your references."

They stood up to allow him to move around the
table. And as he passed them he dragged his hand
across Angelique's hindquarters so deliberately
one would think he'd gotten up so early to do precisely that.

Helga growled and hoisted her rolling pin like
a cricket bat, and James Barton felt the wind of her
swing in his flying coat tails as he fled at a run,
Helga on his heels.

Angelique and Delilah were so surprised they
couldn't say a word.

They heard the front door slam, and the thunder
of Helga's footsteps heading back up the stairs. She
was shaking her head.

"They do not think with their *brains*," is all she
said.

Not one them was a fragile flower or prone to
hysterics. It was hardly the worst thing to happen
to any of them.

But *honestly*.

"What a pity. At least he seems fit," Angelique
said finally.

They all laughed, darkly.

"We're lucky Lucien wasn't here, or there would
be bloodshed," she added, more morosely.

Lucien—Lord Bolt—and Captain Hardy were
out at the ship. And they both knew that The
Grand Palace on the Thames was the province of

their wives. They did not involve themselves with the running of it unless specifically requested. But there had indeed been a few disconcerting occasions when a man on premises would have been useful for something other than heavy lifting or reaching the higher sconces. Ironically, this was one of the problems a footman was supposed to solve.

Captain Hardy had made certain everyone in the house knew how to shoot. Even Dot. But only Delilah and Angelique knew about the loaded pistol in the buttery. The "just in case" pistol.

"At least they're weeding themselves out," Delilah said. "Imagine if we'd hired him and he did that to any of the girls on staff."

They shuddered.

Helga sighed heartily and returned to pummeling the bread while Delilah and Angelique settled back in at the table, chins in hands.

"Are you beginning to despair, Delilah?"

"Of course not," Delilah said firmly. Although she'd hesitated just a little before she'd said that. "Perhaps we ought to advertise in the newspaper."

"Perhaps," she said, with less conviction. They hadn't yet, as it was costly to advertise. "Speaking of the newspaper, where is Dot? She's normally in with it by now."

Dot liked to read the gossip aloud to everyone in the kitchen before breakfast. Newspapers being dear, it was then usually passed about and read by everyone who lived under the roof of The Grand Palace on the Thames until it was in tatters.

As if summoned, Dot drifted into the kitchen

just then. Her eyes, normally wide and round, seemed haunted.

They glanced down. Her hands were empty.

"Dot, is aught amiss?" Angelique said.

Dot turned her alarmed expression toward her.

"Didn't you . . . go to fetch the newspaper, Dot?" Delilah asked gently.

"I did . . ." she began. Then she sighed and folded her hands like a penitent. "Well, I suppose I will just tell you. Today I read the gossip straight off! I couldn't wait. You know I like to. I'm so sorry. I know I normally read it to everyone in the kitchen."

She said this as though gossip was something that, once consumed, was then digested like a lemon seed cake, and could not be re-shared.

"Yes. Of course, understandable. No harm done."

Dot took a breath. "There was a bit about Big Bartholomew Bellamy's last words before he went to the gallows. 'I will see this through!' My heavens, so thrilling. So I read that. But then I read a lovely bit about Lady Lillias and how she was an . . . enchant . . . enchanter? Enchantress. And about Lord Bankham, of Heatherfield, who was an Adonis, and isn't he a friend of their family's? I thought she might like to read it, as she seems to be a bit out of sorts and I thought the pretty words might cheer her a little."

Dot was kind. And she noticed a good deal more than most people suspected.

"So I brought it up to her and showed her and she was ever so kind. I stood by while she read it and . . ." She gulped. "She went white as a ghost!

Oh my, she went so still! I thought it might be apoplexy. Cor, it gave me quite a fright." She clapped her hand over her heart.

Delilah and Angelique exchanged baffled glances.

"And then Lady Lillias said"—and Dot adopted, amusingly, Lillias's gilt-edged, dulcet aristocratic tones—"'oh, dear, my hand slipped'—and she dropped the whole newspaper right into her fire. It was ashes in seconds."

Angelique and Delilah absorbed this in amazement.

Something was indeed troubling the girl. What on earth could it be?

"I'm so sorry." Dot raised her hands to her cheeks. "I didn't know how she felt about Big Bartholomew."

Angelique and Delilah had no idea what to think. "You were trying to do a kind thing, Dot, and you're to be commended. Thank you," Delilah said. "We'll just have to fetch another newspaper. You might be able to find six pence in the epithet jar."

"Thank you!" Dot was relieved.

She dutifully went off to have a look.

"Six pence up in flames, just like that," Delilah mused. "What is *troubling* the girl?" She meant Lady Lillias.

"I suspect we'll learn eventually. Things have a way of coming to light here at The Grand Palace on the Thames. For now, we'll just add it to their bill," Angelique said serenely.

Chapter Seven

❧

WHEN SHE was eight years old, Lillias, Gilly—Lord Bankham—and her brother St. John decided to try to ride down part of the stairs at Heatherfield on a little carpet.

Once they got going it was rapidly clear the ride wasn't going to be as amusing as they thought it would be, but there was no way to stop once they'd gotten it going. Bump . . . ka bump . . . bump . . . her head banging on her collarbone, her teeth clacking . . . no choice but to endure it until they got to the floor. Intact but wiser.

That's a bit how it felt now that her cherished assumptions about life had crumbled into dust. *Everything* was a jolt now.

There was nothing she could do about the uncomfortable forward jolt of time toward the Landover Ball apart from distract herself from it, or pretend it wasn't happening at all.

This wasn't easy to do when the well-meaning maid brought up a newspaper filled with gossip.

And Mr. Cassidy had not appeared in the drawing room last night. That was yet another jolt.

Of course, *she* might have left the boarding house if she'd been able. To make the point that she could. Just like her brother, just like all men, who could up and go where they pleased as whim took them.

It was just . . . she'd been so certain he would be in the drawing room. After this afternoon in the little park outside, it seemed as inevitable and inexorable as that carpet trip down the stairs. He'd been enthralled. She'd wanted the balm of the distraction. The tribute of his attention.

She'd felt thwarted. Which was to be expected.

She hadn't expected to feel . . . bleak.

Or strangely . . . ever-so-slightly panicked.

Finally, she was coolly resolved. He was merely an American laborer, his way with words notwithstanding. If they were not confined together here at The Grand Palace on the Thames, she likely would not have taken any notice of him at all. As of course their worlds would never have intersected.

She had time to come to this resolve as everyone in her family was out again today. Her mother had taken Claire for a fitting for new shoes. Her father had gone off to do something related to being an earl, and St. John was off enjoying being an heir.

"Enjoy your day in the tower, darling. Your sentence is almost up!" was how her mother bade her a cheery farewell.

And now it was quiet. She was left alone with her shattered assumptions, encroaching dread, restless, nascent, inappropriate lust, and worst of all, a badly shaken sense of herself. The fact that all of this was occurring away from her usual environment, in a suite of rooms by the docks, lent to the air of unreality.

Only seventeen thousand two hundred and eight

minutes until the Landover Ball. There was nothing unreal about that. It was going to happen.

Partly from reflex, partly to comfort herself by doing something familiar, she stood and poured water from her basin pitcher into two little battered tin cups she carried about with her for that purpose.

She brought them to the table nearest the window, the one looking out toward the ocean and the garden.

She hesitated again.

And then she fetched her paintbox.

She gently, almost tenderly, settled it before her, and slowly unlatched it. As though whatever lived inside was sleeping, and might bite if awakened.

She hadn't opened it in a few months.

"Good day," she whispered to it. "Sorry I've been away."

She peered inside and her pulse quickened a little with joy.

All those colors represented infinite possibilities.

"Infinite" . . . where had she last heard that word?

Oh, of course: Mr. Hugh Cassidy.

She set her teeth at the thought of him, as though that alone could push it away.

But suddenly she understood in a way that she hadn't before that all of these colors represented a sort of freedom. She could do with them what she would. Make them into anything she'd like.

She lined up her brushes.

Gingerly, almost reluctantly, Lillias opened her sketchbook. She stared at the first thrilling white page.

She pensively tapped her brush. An inspiration gnawed at her; it had begun yesterday. She resisted it. It remained persistent. And as she didn't have a spyglass, there was no other way to bring this vision into focus other than to try to coax it out of the paint.

She dipped her brush and added red to blue on her palette, eyed it critically, added a bit more blue.

Once delicious contact was made between brush and paper—how she loved that first moment—the brush seemed to know what to do.

Almost unnervingly, little by little, she began to reveal to herself something she'd never before seen.

In merciful absorption, in a world luxuriously free of expectation, disaster, or barbed anticipation, she worked in a deep black-purple.

Then with slate blue and deeper grays.

Then with greens.

At some point she became aware of a rhythmic thumping. How long had *that* been going on?

She paused and frowned, and listened, hand frozen over the paper.

Could it be footsteps on the stairs?

Just in case, she threw her torso over her painting, just shy of touching it. Her heart slammed as if she were about to be caught in the act of smoking another cheroot.

Seconds later she realized she knew the sounds of her family's footsteps as well as she knew their faces. That sound wasn't caused by any of them.

She opened the door of their suite and peered

out. The hall was empty of maids; the light through the windows at the far end of the hall was pale; candles burned in sconces. She appeared to be alone.

The sound stopped.

Then started up again.

She left the door of the suite open a crack, and followed the stop-and-start pounding down the stairs to the main floor, as it grew louder and louder.

All the way to the ballroom.

She peered in at the glossy expanse of golden floor.

A very long ladder was pushed against the far end of it, and from the hole in the roof a shaft of sunlight poured through.

Suddenly, a pair of booted, buckskinned legs appeared on the ladder. Her breath stopped when a bare, vast-shouldered, wedge-shaped, gleaming, pale golden torso came into view. So dumbstruck and riveted was she by the little gap between the waistband of his trousers and his narrow waist and the elegant play of muscles beneath his skin during his descent that realization lagged. It only arrived with a resounding jolt when he reached the bottom rung. She was beholding Hugh Cassidy.

Shirtless.

He was holding a hammer in one hand.

The banging sound was now officially her own heart.

He jumped down gracefully, pushed a hand through sweaty hair, and his shoulders lifted and fell in a sigh. And then he turned around.

Because he must have heard her heart beating from where he stood.

He froze. She was caught.

He didn't reach for his shirt.

She was fairly certain he didn't even pull in a breath. Those magnificent shoulders, that broad chest, didn't appear to be moving.

He just stood in that shaft of sunlight pouring through the little gap in the roof, like a wild animal caught in a clearing, fully, gloriously illuminated. Or like some pagan god. Half-naked and gleaming with sweat.

She turned her head swiftly away, heat roaring through her like a flame up a fuse. Her hair would surely ignite. She squeezed her eyes closed.

Centuries of propriety ran in her veins. It did put up a bit of a fight. All of her female ancestors had been taught to be chaste and modest. She understood at once the very good reasons for that.

Because in seconds she flung modesty out the window like slops, and her head was turning of its own accord.

Her muscles tightened as if the shape of him were being stamped upon her, as if she were wax, or a coin. Marked by him. He was made of distinct lines cutting his torso into sections of muscle and gleaming slopes and curves; a slim trail of ferny dark hair divided his ribs and vanished into the waist of his buckskins. And scars—a white slash across his torso, a darker round mark where a bullet must have struck. Battered and beautiful and all too alarmingly real.

Her skin burned and hummed as though each

cell was keening softly in recognition. As if she were born already knowing how his skin would feel pressed against hers and craved it.

She could hear her own breath in her ears.

Even from this distance his eyes were as blue as a distant sea. Perhaps as blue as that lake viewed from his land in the Hudson River Valley.

What did Mr. Cassidy see when he looked at her? Parted lips, scarlet cheeks, virginal shock?

His expression was inscrutable. He still didn't pull his shirt on, and a gentleman most decidedly would have.

He was making a point.

But she thought there was a hint of a question in the angle of his head. Something fierce—a yearning, suppressed—in the tension of his features.

He knew precisely what she was feeling.

And for that reason, he'd already won.

She didn't quite understand why she felt a thwarted sense of fury. Which, in fact, inched toward despair.

He reached for his shirt.

She watched the slide of muscles beneath his skin as he swiftly stretched upward; furry armpits were exposed, and then all of that disappeared beneath his shirt.

She backed away. Leaned against the wall.

She closed her eyes and drew in a shivering breath.

Less than twenty seconds. Twenty seconds that altered her notions of perfection forever and drew a line beneath precisely how dangerous this game was.

She whipped around and ran back up the stairs.

SHE SAID SHE was not prone to hysterics. He was inclined to believe her.

He wasn't particularly worried that he'd be evicted from The Grand Palace on the Thames for emerging, half naked, from a hole in the roof, for the riveted audience of the daughter of an earl.

But both he and Lillias were subdued that evening in the little sitting room.

She carefully did not meet his eyes. It called to mind the way one might, out of an excess of caution, avoid looking directly at an eclipse. She seemed contemplative. Perhaps even a little sullen. As though she'd gone confident and well-armed into a sword fight only to discover her opponent had a secret weapon, like the ability to shoot quills.

She was wearing a blue wool dress and a loosely draped shawl.

He could have told her that the pearly expanse of skin between her bodice and chin was enough to drive him to his knees. That he could well extrapolate about the rest of her from there. That he could close his eyes, and had, and followed in his mind's eye the curve of her lips, the angle of her jaw, the arc of her throat as it sloped to her collarbone to the swell of her breasts, then down, down along that sensual violin curve of her waist to her hips. All the places he would follow with his tongue and fingers if he could.

That he could have himself hard in seconds if he imagined it.

Her evolving expression during those twenty seconds in the ballroom haunted him. Stunned, blushing innocence to carnal yearning to a sort of . . . fury. How dare he make her want him?

He understood every one of those things all too well.

It was so cripplingly, distractingly erotic that he lost quickly and badly in chess to Delacorte, who fixed him with a disbelieving, rather baleful, almost wounded stare.

Hugh did the only honorable thing and removed himself to another chair and pretended to be fascinated by the coverlet unfurling from Mrs. Hardy's needles. Dot took his place in front of a beleaguered Delacorte.

Mrs. Durand was also knitting. Mrs. Pariseau was trying to get up a game of Faro. Lord Bolt was in the corner, contentedly reading from a little book. Captain Hardy had gone to dinner with his friend and former subordinate, Sergeant Massey, who was in London with his wife, and St. John was holding up the fireplace, counting the minutes until he could bolt to his club.

"So when do you plan to run for office, Mr. Cassidy?" the Earl of Vaughn asked, blissfully unaware that Hugh and his daughter were locked in morose sensual torment. The earl liked to merely sit for a bit, digesting and reminiscing about the wonder of his dinner, before he decided what delightful parlor pastime to partake in for the evening. In the smoking room for the past several nights he'd thrown himself with gusto into conversations about business with the other men, more after the fashion of enjoying a novelty, or the way one would enjoy an exciting novel, like *Robinson Crusoe*—he had no wish to be shipwrecked on an island, really, just as he'd no real need or desire to work. But he did like to hear about it.

"When I return to New York, sir, hopefully within the next few months. The current mayor's term is up at the end of the year."

"Think you'll win?"

This Hugh could answer readily. "Yes. I know personally nearly every member of my prospective constituency—mainly because I've done work for most of them from the time I was a child. They've experienced firsthand my work ethic and commitment to the well-being and prosperity of the town. I know their needs, their families, their hopes for the future. And they know me as an adult who unfailingly keeps his word and knows how to turn these dreams into realities."

"Well, my heavens! Listen to you! Spoken like a politician," the earl said, sounding pleased. "You have my vote." He raised his voice a little. "Tell Mr. Cassidy what *you* did last year, St. John."

"I bought a horse," St. John said easily.

"With my money, to boot," his father expounded mockingly, as if praising a child for a well-done lesson.

"Indeed," St. John replied. "I ruminated about it for a good day or two, too." His lazy little smile was entirely self-mocking, but not self-loathing.

Hugh had been prepared to thoroughly dislike St. John, but he couldn't, quite. The difficult people were those who made others uncomfortable by trying to be something they fundamentally were not.

"You'll need a wife if you go into politics in America, Mr. Cassidy." The countess smiled at him cheekily.

"Oh, of a certainty," Hugh said gravely.

In his peripheral vision, he saw Lillias lift her head slowly.

In fact, all the women were on alert now, such was the interest in Mr. Cassidy's romantic life, as he'd been an object of speculation and hope since he'd arrived.

"And she'll have to be able to shoot anything from the porch," Hugh continued thoughtfully. "Because of all the rabid pumas and grumpy Indians, of course. As well as look elegant in silk and velvet. Also, she'll need to know how to skin rabbits. And charm foreign dignitaries during balls and dinners. Fell a tree with an ax. That sort of thing."

It was probably unfair to set out to deliberately disconcert the aristocrats. But once he started he couldn't seem to stop. His mood revealed itself to him as bristly and a little untenable, and he was a bit too tired to attempt to rein it in completely. His usual control was swaying like a rope bridge in a stiff breeze.

They eyed him uncertainly.

Except Bolt and Delacorte, who were thoroughly amused.

"Well, Mr. Cassidy. I hope for your sake that those kinds of women abound in America," said the countess. Which was actually a very kind thing to say.

"I was jesting," he said gently. "Forgive me. My wife will be treated like a queen. Or rather, since we don't have those in the United States, a goddess. We'll have a full complement of servants and a beautiful house on beautiful land. But if she should like to shoot dinner, I won't stop her."

Lillias still didn't turn to look at him. Her own mood, it appeared, was quite determinedly bristly.

"Oh! Just a week or so ago Lord Bolt read aloud a sonnet that mentioned something about goddesses," Mrs. Pariseau said suddenly. "Perhaps he'd like to share it again? It's lovely, and he reads so well."

"Oh, I believe you're thinking of Sonnet 130, Mrs. Pariseau." Lord Bolt—who knew it by heart—began:

My mistress' eyes are nothing like the sun;
Coral is far more red than her lips' red;
If snow be white, why then her breasts are dun;
If hairs be wires, black wires grow on her head.

This was followed by an appreciative stillness, because there was no denying he was a skillful orator.

"That's . . . oh my . . . that's not very kind." Dot was aghast. "Wires! Her hair! I ask you! In a poem!"

"It has a happy ending, Dot," Lucien assured her. "It turns out he's rather fond of his mistress, after all. It goes like this:

I love to hear her speak, yet well I know
That music hath a far more pleasing sound;
I grant I never saw a goddess go;
My mistress when she walks treads on the
*   ground.*
And yet, by heaven, I think my love as rare
As any she belied with false compare.

"A goddess who treads on the ground," Hugh repeated quietly.

"That's the sort of wife you need, Mr. Cassidy," the countess said.

He looked at her, surprised.

Mrs. Pariseau sighed happily. "Ah, the Bard. Wouldn't it be lovely if recitations were held on the stage in the new ballroom?"

"It's nearing completion," Hugh said shortly. Absently. He'd be almost sorry when it was. It had been cathartic to have something to beat with a hammer.

"And we're so grateful to you, Mr. Cassidy," Angelique said. "Before we hold any events, we'll need a fine curtain to complete it. We'd love to have velvet . . . but we'll need so *much* of it," she added wistfully.

"It'll come very dear, curtains like that," Mrs. Pariseau mused.

"Velvet is *indeed* dear," the earl said. "We've velvet *everywhere* in the country house."

He wasn't bragging. But he perhaps hadn't quite heard how this sounded to a pair of proprietresses who had furnished The Grand Palace on the Thames more by bartering, repairing, reusing, begging, and sheer acrobatic ingenuity than by throwing about pound notes. They were earning fairly well now, but almost all of the profit was immediately reinvested in their business.

"The stage will be beautiful when it's done," Hugh promised them.

They smiled at him.

He felt a little better. It was undeniably soothing to be smiled at by kind women.

"What a fine thing it will be, too. I do believe Lord Bolt and Mr. Cassidy could enthrall an audience with recitations of poetry," said Mrs. Pariseau. "The public might even pay to see it."

Hugh was far from sure of this.

Lucien was amused. "Cassidy has *no* patience at all for poetry."

Hugh smiled ruefully. "I'm afraid he speaks truth."

"Why, that is a shame, Mr. Cassidy," the countess said. "We've spent many a pleasant evening reading poetry aloud to each other by the fire, haven't we, Vaughn?" She beamed upon her husband.

Hugh sought the right words. "It's just that . . ." He pushed his hair back. And then he sighed. "I feel that if one is *properly* living life . . . an excess of rumination and metaphor can put you at a remove from all that's beautiful about it. If one takes advantage of all the senses—breathing, feeling, seeing . . . touching . . . tasting . . ." he tried not to look at Lillias ". . . then merely being alive is poetry."

There was a little lull as everyone reexamined their beliefs.

Lillias turned to him, then, and said her first words of the evening.

"So what you're saying is that you're a bit like an animal, Mr. Cassidy."

The quiet in the room was instant, total and shocked.

And not just because these were the first words she'd said all night. Something about her tone, even as elegant as it was, seemed so nearly accusatory that even the fire seemed to stop crackling in order to hear how Hugh would respond.

"No," he said finally, gently, with great patience. "Exactly like an animal."

He met her eyes. It was warning, an apology . . . and, after a fashion . . . a promise.

She turned away again abruptly.

He watched her profile avidly. Which is how he saw her throat move in a swallow.

He looked down at his hands while a bolt of lust sliced right through him.

He drew in a steadying breath. He ought to be ashamed to be beset by such carnality while her parents sat right next to them.

"Interesting point of view, indeed, Mr. Cassidy." The earl was tapping his chin thoughtfully. "But wouldn't you agree that the ability to create art, music, and magnificent architecture elevates the human above the animal? The sense of tradition and ritual? The ability to reason? Governments? The, er, ruling classes?"

Nervousness about insurrection doubtless ran through every aristocrat's blood.

Hugh leaned back. "Well, isn't it about perception? How do we know whether, for instance, the ruby-throated hummingbird doesn't consider her nest a towering architectural achievement? Gyrfalcons return to the same nests again and again, year after year. One might consider that tradition. Generations of falcon may in fact use the same nest for thousands of years."

"A thousand years!" Delacorte marveled. "Imagine how much bird shite is in those nests by then!"

The clicking of knitting needles ceased. Delacorte was fixed in the beam of reproachful feminine eyes.

He sighed, resignedly pushed back his chair, and fished a pence from his pocket. He made approximately the fiftieth trip to the epithet jar since he'd arrived at The Grand Palace on the Thames.

"You should have heard me before I lived here," Delacorte volunteered weakly, when he returned to his chair.

Dot had yet to make her move.

Lillias gave him a small, taut smile.

"Of course, the aristocracy never makes messes of their own nests," Hugh said, slyly.

"Papa shot holes in our nest," Claire pointed out. "There is plaster *everywhere*."

"Thank you, Claire, that's very helpful," her mother said acidly.

"Perhaps the snake has already had snake kittens in our furniture," Claire added.

"I don't think that's what baby snakes are called, Claire," St. John said.

"What are they called?"

"Horrifying," her mother said firmly. "Horrifying is what they're called."

"Perhaps it's in the variation, Mr. Cassidy," Lillias said suddenly. "The evolution of architecture over the centuries is a reflection of the sophistication of the mind of man. Heatherfield, for instance, is an achievement on that scale. And cathedrals. Whereas birds build the same types of nests over and over."

He turned to her, grateful to have a reason to meet her eyes. "Perhaps the nests are exquisitely unique from the point of view of the bird. Ruby-throated hummingbirds use spider silk to knit their nests together, which helps them cling to branches and to stretch and move as their children grow. And they use bits of moss, lichen, even silk or yarn. Every nest is different and subtly beautiful. My mother used to put out scraps for them to see which ones they'd choose."

Lillias was clearly listening to all of this avidly. One would have sworn it was nectar. He could almost *see* the pictures her mind was forming: his mother with the nests, the birds.

"Which scraps did they choose?"

Her question surprised him. It was somewhat quiet, and sounded as though nothing, nothing but unbearable curiosity could have compelled her to ask it of someone who had the temerity to possess a very fine torso.

"Not always the silk, believe it or not. They seemed to like green." He offered a tentative smile.

She held his gaze a moment. She seemed to want to say, or ask, something else.

Then gave a short nod and turned away again.

"Are the Indians truly grumpy, Mr. Cassidy?" Claire wanted to know, shyly.

"Ah. Well. I'm sorry, but I was jesting. And I'm uncertain how much you know about this, Lady Claire, but 'Indians' is a word applied by European settlers to the original occupants of the continent. There are, in fact, many tribes with many different names. It's considered impolite to shoot at them if they don't shoot at you." He gave her a little smile; enough to intoxicate but not devastate her. "It was, in fact, an Algonquin friend who taught me about gyrfalcons. I met him through my infamous Uncle Liam, who has been everywhere in the world, and will soon be coming to visit England."

"I can't wait!" Delacorte interjected cheerfully. "He sounds a right card."

"An Algonquin friend!" the countess repeated slowly, in quiet wonderment. "Imagine!"

"But didn't Indians shoot at Americans during the war?" St. John was stirred to ask.

"Some tribes fought with the British and Canadians. Some fought with the Americans. I was born an American, and I proudly fought for my country." The issues surrounding the war were complicated and could be viewed from many angles, but the time to explain it wasn't now.

"Mr. Cassidy's brother and father lost their lives in the war." Bolt said this quietly, but in a way that made it clear that more talk of war was discouraged.

Hugh knew why he'd done it, and was grateful.

And that's when he felt Lillias's eyes on him.

This time it was he who carefully did not meet her gaze. Another yearning for home swept through him with a sudden visceral violence. For the smells and sounds and sights. Usually he could muster patience and diplomacy. But he was weary. Bridging the gulf between his way of life and that of the blue blood he wanted to ravish was abrading.

"The most useful thing I learned in war is that there's not much difference between men when they're naked and dead," he said shortly. "Indian, American, British, titled, untitled."

There was a stunned little silence.

"Oh . . . my . . ." The countess swiveled her head. "Ought we . . . that is . . . that word . . . Mr. Durand? Mrs. Hardy? Do you really think that . . .

that word . . . is appropriate immediately after dinner?"

"Which one, 'dead' or 'naked'?" Hugh said calmly. His mood had officially shifted to mutinous.

"Good night!" St. John all but bolted from the room.

Lillias was staring at Hugh now. A flush had traveled from her collarbone up to her forehead. He sensed that she was experiencing the sweet hell of picturing him entirely naked.

He fixed her relentlessly in his gaze.

"The . . . latter word," the countess said.

"I've never quite thought of 'naked' in that light," Delacorte mused, happy to have a problem to mull.

"It does rather conjure a vivid picture," Lillias reflected, slowly. "The word 'naked.'"

Her delivery of that last word—slowly, savoringly, her eyes level with his—was a masterpiece of torture.

Hugh almost closed his eyes. He cast about desperately in his mind for an erection queller and hit upon Delacorte breaking wind in the smoking room. It worked.

The countess stood up and sat down then stood up again, turning this way and that in a little panic, as though each "naked" was a spot of fire she might need to stomp out.

"Lillias, stop conjuring," she said finally. Sitting down.

"Do as your mother said," the earl echoed.

"It's difficult to stop once you start," Lillias said softly.

"Entirely my point," Hugh ground out evenly. Tautly.

She turned away from him and tucked a tendril of hair behind her ear.

Hugh began to wonder what sound she would make if he traced her ear with his tongue.

"Naked!" Lady Claire muttered, just to say it before it was forbidden.

The countess's brow furrowed. "Perhaps Mrs. Hardy and Mrs. Durand ought to introduce another jar for words like that that are just a hair too . . ."

"Foolhardy? Potent? Dangerous?" Hugh suggested, relentlessly.

"Thank you, Mr. Cassidy. I see you *do* have a grasp of the situation," the countess said.

"I'm afraid 'grasp' might be another of those words requiring review, Lady Vaughn. One can grasp so many things . . . in so many ways."

Lillias's gaze flared hot and stunned. Flickered. Dropped.

He'd conclusively won that round.

"Oh, dear," the countess said sadly. "You may be right."

"Lady Vaughn . . ." Delilah ventured. "The presence of more than one jar might make our guests feel a trifle inhibited from spirited conversation, though spirited conversation may encompass disagreements about words. Perhaps monitoring ourselves is the best solution for now?"

"Perhaps we ought to compile a list of words that may prove to be controversial?" the countess countered weakly, desperately but valiantly sensing she was losing this battle that she possibly should never have undertaken, and feeling about for a way to be gracious.

"Words besides 'naked,' you mean?" Hugh said gravely.

The countess closed her eyes.

And when no one said anything else, a little relieved, awkward silence ensued. Cautiously, knitting needles were taken up and began to move again.

"I nominate 'moist,'" Delacorte said brightly. He'd clearly been giving it some quality thought. "Because when you think about it—"

Delilah and Angelique had already risen as one, and in a swift, graceful, coordinated blur of garnet and gold silk, traversed the room, and settled in at the piano. The rest of Delacorte's sentence was lost in a jaunty little duet.

"Well, that's rather lovely, isn't it?" The countess exhaled. "Music."

"Music has charms that soothe a savage breast," Mrs. Pariseau agreed happily.

The countess sighed.

Hugh found himself on his feet. He was, he realized, about to bolt, though there wasn't a place he could go to evade his mood.

His room would be as fine a place as any. But he'd need to walk past Lillias on his way out. And suddenly he understood Odysseus's mast-lashing precautions.

But he'd meant it when he'd said his powers were greater, and just to prove it, he slowed his pace when he was abreast of her table.

"How *do* you suppose beasts become savage, Mr. Cassidy?" she said softly, her brows furrowed in mock innocence.

Her struggle to hold his gaze was apparent in the bright pink spots on her cheeks, but she managed.

"By wanting what they shouldn't," he said grimly.

Chapter Eight

❦

$\mathcal{H}$EAT COLLECTED and hovered over him like an extra blanket in his room that night.

He was awake. He resented it.

And *why* was he awake? She was the reason he was awake.

Damn her, anyway.

Because when he was awake and not occupied, memories rushed in to fill the space. And then he was held hostage by another kind of unassuageable ache.

He'd seen how swiftly a forest recovered from a fire. How the new, tender green growth moved in with gentle but nearly unseemly speed, until one would never see the burn scar, or the dead trees. But that wasn't until the rains came. And they wouldn't come until he was home, and building his new life.

He ought to go to Surrey in search of the Clay family. Apart from his promise to build the stage, there was no reason he ought not go immediately. But that was another reason to resent Lillias: the image of Woodley's daughter was as elusive now as one of those rainbows thrown about by the crystals dangling from the chandelier in the foyer. He'd been driven by a promise and his own need for answers. His own hope. And it was slipping from his grasp. He felt guilty.

Hugh gave up, sat upright, and began by casting off his nightshirt and hurling it across the room as though it were the cause of every frustration he'd ever known.

He followed this by kicking off the lovingly sewn coverlet.

And finally he lay naked and sweating, but that was hardly better.

Christ.

He rolled out of bed, strode nude across the room, and heaved up the sash window. In came a great gust of fetid air and the unearthly screeches of two cats fucking.

Or perhaps fighting.

Perhaps both.

Was there a difference, really?

"Lucky cat," he muttered.

He *felt* feral, standing naked—clearly the word of the day—and perspiring at an open window, irritable and restless, acutely aware of every inch of his skin, or, more accurately, the full contours of his being. As though it had been coiled into a cramped place and newly freed, and now was needling him as the blood flowed again.

Skin was useful for more than being the thing between his viscera and bullets, for instance. It was capable of knowing glories.

And he remembered diving into a swimming hole naked with his brother when he was about ten. The delicious icy shock of the plunge that took the breath out of him, sinking from the gold-green dappled surface into the olive dark depths, sinking, sinking until his toes found the sandy bottom and pushed off to launch back into daylight. That triumph of moving with grace in both worlds, on water, on land. Darting like little silver fish to the rock they called the Whale, their limbs pulling them through the water, pouring over their backs. His brother was faster but when it came to longer races Hugh always got there first. His will was stronger than possibly anyone's.

And the feel of his skin covering a woman's rippling body. Her nipples chafing against his chest, her fingers digging into his shoulders as they bucked together, her hot breath in his ear huffing *more, faster*, the two of them running down the merciful, obliterating blackness of that ultimate, near unholy pleasure. He had a few friendly widows to thank for his sexual education. He gloried in the textures of women and there was almost nothing more gratifying than discovering the kinds of touch that made a particular woman wild, so he could build her desire up like he would a fire started with a flint.

But Christ.

This.

Was this *fair*?

He didn't usually think of things in terms of fair or not fair. You played the cards you were dealt as they were flipped your way. But apparently, unlike an angry bear, he couldn't shake this thing. Nothing ameliorated this restless, clawing want. Nothing ever could.

Because he of course would not be seducing the virgin daughter of an earl.

He pressed his palms against his eyes and took

in a long breath, blew it out at length. He imagined her lying naked on his bed, and all of his muscles tensed as if he were about to cover her with his body. He wrapped a hand around his tightening cock and gave it a speculative heft. Then decided, no, it wasn't a good use of his time to spend the night exercising his elbow and nurturing an obsession.

But he needed to burn some of this off or he'd never sleep.

He'd go have a look at the work remaining to do on the stage. Perhaps sweep up a little.

He poured water from his pitcher into the basin and splashed his face with it. Took a long breath.

Suddenly a slight breeze, tender as an exhale, slipped in the window and curled around his neck. A breeze was never far behind when the ocean was just outside. He said "thank you" to whatever deity might be listening, aloud because he would never not say thank you for the gentle, small graces. Because life was comprised of pretty much nothing but that, between battles.

Beyond that, far beyond the ocean, was home. As soon as he finished building the stage he would go to Surrey.

He seized his shirt and pulled it on over his head, got into his trousers and boots. He hooked his fingers into an unlit lantern, then closed and locked the room behind him.

Even in his sturdiest boots he could walk nearly soundlessly, a habit learned from hunting in the woods. He made his way in the dark, at first. He'd learned which stairs creaked and which patches of floor tended to groan when weight was applied.

He passed Gordon the Cat on the prowl for mice and rats and probably just for the sheer pleasure of sniffing about his kingdom, and nodded to him.

Gordon raised his tail in salute and gave a soft chirp.

Another floor down and he grinned when he heard Delacorte snoring like a tree being ravaged' by a rusty saw. Delacorte could vibrate paintings from the walls.

And then went down through the quiet kitchen and into the breezeway connecting the inn to the Annex. In there all the Vaughns slept.

He imagined Lillias's head on a pillow, her coppery brown hair a sweaty tangle thanks to lovemaking.

"Christ," he whispered.

Only then did he pause to light the lantern as he made his way toward the ballroom.

He'd taken the ladder down from the wall, but someone had pushed it upright again.

He froze, heart in his throat.

And a pale blur had just vanished up it, headed for the roof.

He wasn't certain if he was afraid of ghosts or even believed in them. He guessed he was about to find out.

Up the ladder he went.

And there, in a night rail, a shawl pinned closely about her and a braid down her back, about to settle on the edge of the roof, was Lillias. She didn't look as though she was about to jump. She looked, in fact, like a colt who'd just been released from a winter stall to find it was suddenly spring.

She whirled.

"Don't scream, for God's sake!" he said. He kept his voice just above a hoarse whisper. "And don't move or I might scream. Perhaps you should step back from the edge."

"Good evening, Mr. Cassidy."

"Good *morning*, more accurately. The watch just cried half past one."

It *was* possible he was dreaming. He looked down swiftly to verify that he was clothed.

"Are screams even noticed much around here?" she wondered dryly. "I've heard a couple tonight. I think only a few of them were animals."

"The heat brings out the best and worst in everyone. And everything. I can only assume the latter is why you're on the bloody roof."

She smiled at that. "Oh, now we hear your true colors, Mr. Cassidy, when the epithet jar isn't standing watch."

"I think this is an exceptional circumstance. A vote would vindicate me."

She snorted. "Are those dark creatures moving about rats?" She was peering avidly below.

He perversely liked that *she* wasn't screaming. She sounded more curious than anything.

"Gordon takes care of the rats in the boarding house." He answered her question before she could ask it. "What are you doing on the roof?"

"I've noticed he's rather fat. Gordon."

"Draw your own conclusions."

She gave a soft laugh at that.

And like everything about her, that laugh charmed and infuriated and inflamed him.

"I wish I could have a cat. They make Claire sneeze."

"That is regretful. Lady Lillias, I've an honest question. Are you quite mad?"

"No," she said, after some thought.

"Why. The bloody hell. Are you on the roof?"

There was another silence. They had a half of a moon to light things. Below, not everyone was sleeping. Sounds echoed. Coughs. A laugh. A snatch of an argument, complete with oath.

"It's your fault." She said it shortly. Resigned.

"That you couldn't sleep?"

Because why should he mince words?

She turned to look at him. Whenever their eyes met, neither seemed able to look away. It was some combination of dare and the sort of fascination one experiences stumbling upon an exotic landscape that offered endless vistas. They'd seen each other in all lights now.

Except perhaps firelight, in bed.

He could reach over, draw a finger lightly over her lower lip. He knew he would feel her breath sigh out. The sweet beginnings of surrender.

His head felt tight in solidarity with his groin.

Her gaze dropped, flicked across his torso. A frown flickered. And then she gave a restive head toss and turned away from him. Perhaps she was alarmed by her own directness. She didn't answer.

Seconds later, he watched her throat move in a swallow.

"I notice you're *also* awake rather late," she said somewhat stiffly.

"Yes. Would you like to guess why?" He said this dryly.

Apparently she hadn't the nerve to pursue the same line of questioning.

Perhaps she suspected he would tell her the truth about why she kept him awake at night, and guessed rightly that it would be more potent than she was prepared to hear.

"Well, I'll get to the reason I'm up here. You can't stay here. It's self-indulgent and reckless to climb out on the roof in the middle of the night just because you took a notion."

She ignored this and settled on the edge. "Fancy you having an opinion about what I'm doing. Who would have thought? I take it you've never been self-indulgent or reckless in your life."

"It requires the opportunity to be bored and I can't say as I've often had the pleasure."

"No? What sorts of pleasures have you had, Mr. Cassidy?"

He drew in a long breath. "Let me put it this way. I've never before been alone in the dark with a woman who wasn't beneath me, begging me to take her faster and harder. That, Lady Lillias, is a singular pleasure. You shouldn't be alone on a roof in the dark, let alone in a night rail, let alone with me."

The breath audibly went out of her in a gust. She jerked her head away again.

It was ruthless. He didn't apologize. He was certain she could take it. And if he could shock her sufficiently, perhaps they'd both be spared wherever this thing between them was headed.

She said nothing for a time.

The sweet breeze that had earlier circled his neck returned, and this time it was cooler. It filled his shirt, and he knew if he closed his eyes he could imagine he was on the porch of his cabin in New York.

"I have an honest question for *you*, Mr. Cassidy. Is it that you think *I'm* a weak, naive fool requiring constant shepherding, or do you think all women are?"

He drew in a long breath and blew it out. Resigned, he settled at a safe distance from her on the roof edge, where they perched like the world's most attractive gargoyles.

It was yet another world, like swimming or sex, the immersion in the night with the stars above them woven into the mist like diamonds in a woman's hair. He was suddenly glad to be a part of it.

He carefully settled the lamp down between them.

"Lady Lillias . . . my mother could shoot a deer from the front porch of our cabin. She could load a musket as fast as my father could. She could skin any animal, though my father was better at it, and I'm better than both of them—and turn it into a delicious dinner. There wasn't one thing she was afraid of, unless it was harm befalling any of us."

He said words like "cabin" and "skin" and "shoot" deliberately. He laid them down like fortifications between her station in life and his.

She remained wordless and watchful.

"The ladies of The Grand Palace on the Thames created all of this"—he gestured to both buildings—"from what was essentially a ruin. That takes guts and wits and resourcefulness to spare, especially when you start out with nothing to begin with. In other words, some of the smartest, bravest people I know are women. But even my mother with a musket would be no match for a man truly intent on harming her. That is just the way of the world. You could shout 'I'm the daughter of an earl' all you want in the dark down below but that isn't going to save you. The dark has a way of equalizing everyone, same as death."

She shifted and brought her knees up, wrapped her arms around them. And still she didn't speak.

"So it's a man's duty and privilege to keep women safe in every way until or if a day comes when that is no longer necessary. Even when a woman happens to make a special effort to put herself, and therefore maybe others, in harm's way. I just . . . it just isn't in me to let it be."

Her expression was oddly intent now. The breeze caught hold of her shawl and attempted to tug it from her, and she maintained her grip. It was the strangest thing, but she looked *right* up here. Right and happy. She was clearly reviewing everything he'd just said, and he appreciated it. She was difficult, but she was no fool.

"Lillias," he said softly.

It was difficult to align the complicated things he felt with the proper words. So he said the truest thing he could, slowly and softly.

"I should hate for any harm to ever come to you."

She studied him in silence. By lamplight, by moonlight, by any light, she was enthralled.

"All right," she said gently, finally. "I'm sorry to worry you."

It surprised him. He released the breath he didn't know he was holding as though it was a burden.

"Do you mind if we stay a few moments longer?" she asked evenly.

"No."

She turned her head toward where the spires of ships rose darker than the night, and he got the sense that she was drinking it in, the strangeness, the newness. As if it were nourishment of which she'd been deprived.

The wind found nooks to howl and whistle through, turning the city into its own eerily beautiful orchestra. It rose and fell again, yanking at her shawl, inflating his shirt a little, boring of them, moving on. The half-moon was an opalescent arch above them, like the doorway to another world.

"Mr. Cassidy . . ."

"Mmm?"

"Can your mother still do that? Shoot from the porch?"

"My mother is dead."

She went still. "I'm so very sorry."

"Thank you," he said shortly. "So am I."

She was thoughtful for a moment. "You tend to use words like bludgeons, Mr. Cassidy. 'Dead.' 'Naked.' Don't you think it would be kinder, sometimes, to use a euphemism, to ease people into the blow of the revelation? Because words *do* conjure."

"I'd like to point out the irony of someone perched on a roof wishing to be eased into a blow. A stiff wind would make a kite of you."

To his surprise she laughed. It was the loveliest

sound, like bloody spring bursting out all at once. "I'd *love* to see the city that way, from way up above." She sounded wistful.

He couldn't argue with that. "So would I. I imagine it would be extraordinary."

"What does a gyrfalcon look like?"

"A bit like the daughter of an earl in flight in a night rail."

She turned to him and smiled, radiantly, unguardedly delighted.

And for just that instant, he knew precisely what it felt like to be soaring high above the city, made of light, utterly free.

"It's a magnificent creature, the gyrfalcon," he said, softly. "Rare, beautiful, and more than a little dangerous."

"Oh, I'm certain he is." Lightly said, and only a little ironically.

The wind caught the end of her shawl and she reached up. The moonlight shone through her night rail, and briefly, distinctly, the full arc of her breast was delineated in shadow.

His lungs ceased moving.

She captured her shawl again.

It seemed an unnecessarily brutal thing to know precisely how her breast would fit in his hand.

"I think you do it," she mused, "the blunt words, that is . . . so people won't ask you more questions about it. It's a bit like a shield."

She turned to face him directly.

His mind blanked an instant. Bloody hell.

He eyed her warily. For a moment, he felt like he'd been flushed like prey from the underbrush. Exposed. And yet . . . he could not explain it . . . he also felt safer, somehow, than he'd been just a few moments before. As though one more veil twisted about his spirit had been unwound. He could breathe a little more freely.

He thought she deserved an answer. "You're not wrong."

She didn't gloat. "You're safe up here with me, Mr. Cassidy," she teased.

As *this* was patently untrue and a bit of a goad, he answered that only with an ironic little smile.

The bark of a dog carried to them on the wind. And he thought about his old hound, Tuesday. Damn, he missed that dog.

He could feel weariness setting in, even as his body was but buzzing from the nearness of her.

What on earth was he doing here in London, on a roof with a woman who was discovering the power of her own sensuality and treated it like a plaything? He could not rebuild his life in earnest until he was home again. He was chasing a phantom in the form of Woodley's daughter. And he could not and would not touch the woman in front of him.

Lillias cleared her throat. "Mr. Cassidy . . . I hope you don't mind . . . I could not help but notice . . . you've a few scars."

"I've scars," he confirmed.

"You were shot?" she asked carefully.

"I've been shot," he said gently. So as not to bludgeon. But there was really no way to pillow that word.

She was quiet. The hair that escaped from her braid danced all about her face and in the lamplight. She cleared her throat again.

"I find . . ." She turned to face him, her expression unguarded but composed. "I find that I don't like the idea of harm coming to you."

All of those words lined up in the order she'd delivered them suddenly seemed more dangerous than the words "naked" or "dead."

He gave a curt nod.

It suddenly seemed imperative that this interlude end.

"Perhaps you should consider coming down. Your mother and father are decent sorts, and I believe they would mind very much that you were up here."

"Ah, but I've you to protect me," she said, lightly. Somewhat ironically.

He sighed.

"I want you to know . . . it's not boredom," she said suddenly. "The reason I'm up here. And it's not recklessness. Not really."

She turned to him, searching his face.

"What is it?"

She seemed to be struggling for words. "I find . . ." She shoved her hair self-consciously away from her face, as though she, too, were dropping a veil. She cleared her throat. "I find that something in me feels lighter if I can see across a vista. I feel more like myself if I can see far as the eye can see."

Almost nothing else she'd said could have surprised him more in the moment. He had the sense that she had never admitted that to anyone before.

She was watching him cautiously. Afraid, perhaps, of being mocked. "That makes sense," he assured her.

She was visibly relieved. "I can ride like the wind. I'm a competent climber. I'm afraid of very little, actually. After a fashion nearly everything I do is reasoned, Mr. Cassidy. Even now."

But what weight did the daughter of an earl carry about? Or was it just that she craved the exhilaration that arises from realizing one is smaller than everything and that the world is vaster than can be imagined?

Or was there a wildness in her that simply had no place to go within the confines of her life?

He didn't ask. But he thought he knew. The bands of muscle across his stomach tensed, as if the restraints she lived under were suddenly binding him, too.

"Has this . . . predilection for views come upon you recently?"

"Ah," she said shortly, a little bitterly. "You've been talking to my father. You probably laughed when he told you about the church tower."

"No," he said. "Nothing about you, or this moment, is a joke."

She studied him as if to ascertain the truth of this, then turned away, for one last look at the view. "If I may presume . . . but I should like to say that I'm very sorry for your losses, Mr. Cassidy."

"Thank you."

"I don't know how I would do without my family. Even St. John."

He'd thought he'd dreaded those spaces unfilled with work or activity because memories inevitably crowded, and loneliness would corner him. And blunt words usually quite effectively forestalled

the need for soul baring. They had indeed been a
sort of blind he could take refuge in while his soul
stopped ringing from the losses.

It was easier for him, somehow, to talk about
it in the dark. He wanted to give her an answer,
because it was clear she was thinking about loss.
And he didn't want her to spend a moment suffering over his own suffering.

"For what it's worth . . . I don't think anyone you
love is ever truly gone. I do very much feel their
absence . . . but I also feel their presence all the
time, in a new way. In some ways they're with me
now more than ever. I don't know if that makes
sense."

"It does," she said shortly.

That was enough unexpected soul mining for
the night.

"All right," he said briskly. "Now that you've
seen the view, I'd be grateful if you'd allow me to
see to it that you come safely down off the roof
now."

She didn't reply to this. But she did knot her
shawl snugly about her in preparation for descent,
and he plucked up the lamp.

Then she turned to him again. And because he
wasn't about to deny himself the pleasure of it, he
drank her in by lamplight and moonlight one last
time, the way she'd drunk in that view. He was still
amazed that this magical combination of features,
animated by this particular maddening person,
could cause him to lose his breath.

She knew precisely what he was thinking.

"I'm *not* naive, Mr. Cassidy," she said. Deadly
earnest. Her voice was barely above a whisper.

"Not completely," she added. It was very nearly a plea.

Oh God. It was like a kick in the solar plexus.

It sounded less like a dare than an invitation.

But it was definitely both.

He imagined how he would begin. How her face would feel cradled in his hand. Her delicate, clean-lined jaw, her skin like a petal. The path his lips would follow.

One kiss. What harm could there be?

His breathing went shallow.

Fate was such a *bastard*. A rush of fury at feeling like its plaything. It had fitted him with an iron-clad sense of honor and presented him with the cruelest of temptations. Even now, a rationalization was forming: she wanted him. It was a torment. He could ease it.

And she might have a good sense of the mechanics of sex—that was easy enough for anyone to learn, even the sheltered daughter of an earl. But he'd wager his life that she didn't fully understand the rest of it: the complications. The way it could make you lose your reason. He would be damned if he would be her experiment.

He took a subtle breath. "While I don't doubt that," he managed evenly, with just enough regret to protect her pride, "I will not be relieving you of the balance of your naivete."

The effort cost him. And she likely knew. She studied him, her mouth quirked. She did turn sharply away again, taking one last look at the spires from this height.

Then she briskly tucked some of the loose strands of hair behind her ears and stood. He almost smiled. She was made of sterner stuff than anyone would have suspected.

"I'll go down first to make sure you don't fall," he said.

"All right."

There was really no hope for her modesty or his sanity at this point, but there wasn't another choice, either. He was going to get a look up her night rail. But as it turned out—and this amused him—she'd put pantaloons on beneath it. And while they were in essence an undergarment, there was nothing particularly erotic about frilly muslin trousers. He hadn't heard that women were wearing them with any stylistic conviction yet under their dresses.

Oddly, the fact that she'd thought to don them made him think she might actually possess more than a grain or two of sense to go along with the intelligence. He imagined at the planning process: lacing on the sturdy boots, seizing up the sturdy shawl, then tippy-toeing through the dark to the ladder.

He caught that glimpse but he didn't keep looking. He wouldn't look when a woman was vulnerable, or when her safety was in his care. His eyes were on her feet.

Rung by rung, they went back the way they came. He watched carefully, breath held, making sure her feet found the rungs, every now and then pausing, hand raised in midair, as it seemed she might need a little assistance to find the next rung. But she never did, and he didn't know why he should feel proud of that fact, but it somehow was a relief to consider that if she ever took it into her head to do such a thing some other time, when he was back home in

America and she was God knows where, perhaps in the library of the duke she was bound to marry, climbing up to the tallest shelves, well, maybe she wouldn't break her neck.

And together they descended more or less with alacrity. From the world of the roof and sky back into the Annex.

As his foot settled on the last rung it groaned.

And then made an ominous cracking sound.

He yanked his foot back and looked down.

Confronted with a final rung comprised of two jagged, splintered, dangling pieces of wood.

"Lillias, stop," he said.

She froze midstep and peered back down at him, her face a pale blur, half shadowed.

The jump was about three feet. Easy enough for him.

Potentially perilous to the ankles of a smaller person in a night rail and a shawl.

There was no hope for it.

"I'm going to lift you down."

He knew at once that touching her would be like Persephone and the pomegranate seeds. There would be no going back.

She paused to study him, gauging the distance over her shoulder.

Then she turned, carefully, and contemplated him, perhaps entertaining an objection and recognizing its absurdity. They both understood she was at his mercy.

He knew a surge of possibly unworthy, purely primal pleasure at this realization.

He reached up for her and she leaned into him, his hands fitting the notch of her waist, her ribs, and he lifted. She was so light in his arms, and so at once trusting he was shocked by a ferocious wave of tenderness.

She sailed lightly, her hair braid brushing against his cheek.

Seconds in duration, a hundred impressions held him fast.

His hands lingered there, lightly. Long enough that he could feel the lift of her rib cage when she drew in a long, shaky breath. Long enough to feel the soft, warm give of her waist.

She slowly raised her eyes to his.

He lifted his hands.

"Go inside, Lillias," he whispered. He said it almost roughly. "You don't know what you're doing."

"I'll warrant you'll spend the rest of the night thinking about me, Mr. Cassidy," she replied softly. "And that alone proves I know exactly what I'm doing."

And then, like one of the eleven or twelve ghosts Angelique had teased about, she turned and vanished swiftly through the door the way she'd come.

Chapter Nine

❧❧❧

"LILLIAS, CLAIRE. Something terrible has happened!"

Lillias was in the midst of splashing water on her face—the way she began every morning—and flew, dripping, out of her bedroom, nearly colliding with Claire dashing out of her own room.

For the next few seconds, a veritable abyss of horrible possibilities opened and howled at her feet.

"Your father tried to hire away the cook. And now the ladies of The Grand Palace on the Thames want to throw us out."

Lillias stumbled to the settee and sat down hard, then dropped her face in her hands. "Thank God!"

The worst thing she could imagine was losing anyone she loved.

Claire sank down next to her.

Relief made Lillias weak. Which was how epiphany swept in with a violence: Hugh Cassidy had lost so many people he loved. How on earth was he still able to face each day?

Let alone climb a ladder to the roof, lecture her, and refuse to kiss her when she'd all but stood there in the misty, starlit moonlight and, like a wanton, implied he ought to go ahead and do it?

"It's rather embarrassing," her mother added, more mildly. "And your father and I don't want to leave."

"More embarrassing than Papa shooting a hole in our walls?" Claire said somberly.

Lillias peered through her hands at Claire and flashed a smile.

But her mother seemed genuinely distressed.

"But Mrs. Hardy and Mrs. Durand wouldn't make us leave . . . would they? But . . . they're so very amiable," she pointed out gently.

"And strict," her mother reminded her, with a certain regretful relish.

"There are other places we could go . . ." Claire ventured, reluctantly. There likely were, but there was no guarantee that rooms would be either available or comfortable for all of them.

"Your father and I like it here," her mother said firmly. "We like having everyone together in one suite. And it's so inconvenient to move everyone all at once."

Her mother poured tea for the daughters she'd startled awake and a lull settled in and heartbeats slowed and nerves quieted.

And it was strange . . . but as of late, when Lillias awoke in the morning, she enjoyed three blissful seconds of consciousness before Landover-Ball-dread rolled in like a cloud bank.

This morning, her first thought had been of sitting with Hugh Cassidy out on the roof.

It had also been her last before she'd finally, just before dawn, slept.

From his first appearance on the roof holding a lamp, like Diogenes looking for an honest man until he swung her down from the ladder—she'd spent the balance of the night poring over every moment as though they were tea leaves. But *now*, in the hard light of day, the dread set in.

Ten more days.

Lillias suddenly realized she didn't quite want to leave The Grand Palace on the Thames yet, either. The whole place seemed suspended in time, though being confined to the place for smoking a cheroot had something to do with that. But it had begun to feel a bit like the withdrawing room at a party, during which one retreated to repair a trodden hem or hair that was coming out of its pins, life and music and merriment going on faintly outside the door. The time between her life had unraveled and . . . whatever her life would be after the Landover Ball.

A time that contained a big American who had quietly sat beside her while she drank in the view of London from the rooftop, lectured her, and refused to kiss her.

Her cheeks went hot all over again.

She held her tea up to her face so her mother would only suspect steam if she noticed the rosiness.

But oh, he'd wanted to.

And that wasn't all he wanted to do.

I've never before been alone in the dark with a woman who wasn't beneath me, begging me to take her faster and harder. That, Lady Lillias, is a singular pleasure.

It was yet another infuriating version of, "Go inside, little girl." He'd said that in order to both unnerve and enthrall her. It had worked on both counts.

But it had enthralled more than unnerved. Burning with curiosity and jealousy, her very sheets against her skin were a sensual torment as she imagined his beautifully battered body covering her own.

I should hate for any harm to ever come to you.

He'd also said that.

Of course he worried. How on earth was he still able to face each day, knowing how ephemeral life was? Let alone climb a ladder to the roof, lecture her, make her laugh, and refuse to kiss her.

What was the *matter* with him?

What was the matter with *her*?

Maybe she *was* quite mad. His will was stronger than hers. Largely precisely because life had buffeted him quite a bit. Absurdly, this infuriated her. How was she ever going to get the better of him?

And yet in some ways she already had. It had nearly *killed* him to take his hands from her waist after he'd lifted her down. She'd felt the war he waged with himself humming in his body.

Why did this make her want to . . . protect . . . him?

He was from an entirely different world. He was practically a brute, albeit one possessed of a nimble vocabulary and a startling swift wit. And yet, in the dreamlike world of the roof, in the dark, outside of time, Hugh Cassidy sitting beside her, she had briefly made sense to herself.

Why should any of this make her feel close to tears? It was all a bit too much, and she had only herself to blame.

"So where is Father now?"

"Mrs. Hardy and Mrs. Durand have him down in the receiving room and it looks serious, indeed.

Oh, and St. John was locked out last night, as he missed curfew. He hasn't yet come home."

Claire and Lillias exchanged an uncertain glance. Lillias's stomach tightened again.

"Oh, St. John is a grown man. He can look at his watch now and again, for heaven's sake. He's been out all night before. Docks or no docks. He's not an *utter* fool. I'm certain he's just fine," her mother said firmly.

Lillias knew her parents loved all of them. What degrees of fortitude must one possess to allow their children to do what they did—ride horses, shoot rifles, stay out all night? How did *anyone* manage the fortitude to love anyone? It was fraught with peril and pocked with hazards one could not foresee. She'd never before asked these questions of herself, but suddenly she understood it was why Hugh Cassidy had such an expansive plan for his life. She suspected this was how he'd imposed order on chaos, and gave content to emptiness, and form to dreams. Because lately, this was what her sketchbook had become to her. It was the only place in which she could shape anything at all to her satisfaction. The one thing she could control.

"I suppose we'll just have to await the verdict," the countess said. "I think some more tea to settle our nerves would be in order."

She refilled her daughters' cups.

Lillias could have told her that she'd become an old hand at anticipation, that more genteel word for dread.

"The maid brought up the newspaper with the tea." Her mother rattled the pages open. "Oh, would you listen to this. 'The whole of the *ton*

wonders what that heavenly heartbreaker Lady
Lillias Vaughn will wear to the ball.'"

Claire rolled her eyes.

"And there's a bit about Gilly, too!" her mother
exclaimed. "The rumors about Lord Bankham's
impending nup—"

Lillias yawned so loudly, widely, and deliberately
her mother was startled into silence. And then fixed
her with a puzzled little frown.

"Won't it be lovely to see Gilly and his parents
at the Landover Ball, Lillias—it's been at least two
months since we last, hasn't it? And it's only ten
days away," her mother said with some satisfaction.

*Actually, Mama, it's about ten days and about sev-
enteen hours. Or about fifteen thousand four hundred
twenty minutes.*

"Oh, who's counting?" Lillias gave another
cavernous and entirely feigned yawn. "The tea is
excellent, but I think I need to splash a bit more
water on my face in order to adequately face the
world."

Startling her mother and sister, she stood
abruptly. If only a face full of water was all it
would take to face the Landover Ball.

"It's DIFFICULT TO convey the depth of the betrayal
we feel, Lord Vaughn. We've grown quite fond of
you and your family."

Delilah and Angelique occupied one settee in
the reception room. The earl had been bidden to sit
on the other. Dot had not been requested to bring
in tea. This was not a social call, and tea was not
the traditional accompaniment for perfidy.

The earl was subdued. "She told you everything. Helga did."

"Of course she told us, Lord Vaughn," Delilah said reproachfully. "We're like family here."

He fidgeted, as though he'd very much wanted a cup of tea, and then settled his hands in his lap. "Well, it's what one does with servants, isn't it?" He raised an expression that begged for understanding. "It's difficult to get good ones, and the marvelous ones come dear. Servants move about from place to place. It's business, isn't it, ladies? You ought to know."

Delilah and Angelique could indeed testify to how difficult it was to find good ones, the ones who wouldn't steal spoons or pinch bottoms, let alone keep good ones, but they weren't about to commiserate.

They presented a united, softly reproachful front.

"Helga was very adamant that she would not leave you," he said. Impressed and rather surprised.

"We know."

"I promised her an enormous increase in salary."

"Money isn't everything, Lord Vaughn," Angelique said.

"And a pension."

Well. Helga didn't have that, but she soon would, was Delilah and Angelique's silent communication. Hell's teeth, the expenses here at The Grand Palace on the Thames did tend to grow apace with the profits.

"We know you did," Delilah said obliquely.

"And you thought you could hire her away because . . . how did you put it . . ." Angelique touched her fingers to her chin. "'The status of working for an earl is surely infinitely preferable to working at a little inn by the docks.'"

The earl actually blushed.

"It was by way of persuasion. I think your boarding house is very fine, indeed, and we have enjoyed our stay here."

They were quiet for a time.

They let him reflect upon his shame.

Finally, he sighed deeply. "Do either of you ladies yet have children?" he said finally. A bit hesitantly.

"Neither of us has yet been so blessed," Angelique said gently.

"Mine are getting older. They are always running about, hither and yon, with their friends and so forth, which is as it should be. St. John spent so much of his time away at school. They will soon have families of their own, and I look forward to grandchildren. But this part of our lives . . . will be over soon. It flies by in a heartbeat, your time with your children. Only yesterday Lillias was sliding down a banister, and look at her now . . . a beautiful, elegant grown young lady. And although the circumstances which compelled our residence here are rather absurd, and even though my son can be a blight indeed, I have relished this opportunity to have them all so snug and close, in the comfort and welcome of The Grand Palace on the Thames. In this charming place you've created. Please don't make us leave. Please."

It was admittedly a very pretty speech.

They turned when they heard the front door open.

Slow footsteps echoed in the foyer. Then stopped.

A handsome young man paused in the doorway and looked in on them.

A coat was draped across one arm, and a crushed-looking beaver was gripped in his other hand. His cravat was askew. Whiskers darkened his jaw and chin, completing the air of rakish dissolution.

His person was liberally sprinkled with little bits of straw.

"Well, good afternoon, St. John," his father said pleasantly and ironically.

"Good afternoon, Father. Mrs. Durand. Mrs. Hardy."

The ladies nodded to him, coolly.

There was a silence as they inspected him with varying degrees of pity, humor, and sympathy, but absolutely no remorse.

He was too tired, apparently, to do anything but stand there and submit to inspection.

"You've bits of straw all over your person, St. John," the earl mused.

"I spent the night in the livery stable," he said.

"Ah."

"It was not too uncomfortable," he added, after another long pause, with a certain admirable attempt at defiance. The shadowy crescents beneath his eyes and the fine red lines across their whites suggested that "comfortable" wasn't a word he'd use, either.

He didn't apologize for missing curfew. Nobody expected him to. Nobody apologized for locking him out, either. It wasn't personal. Those were the rules.

To his credit, he wasn't wasting any of his obviously currently scant emotional resources on raising a complaint.

"Well. I think I shall go up now," he said.

"It's good to have you back," Delilah said kindly. "Would you like some tea? And would you perhaps like a warm bath prepared?"

"Yes, please, thank you," he said meekly, and turned to go share the good news of his return with his mother and sisters.

"You do recall that baths cost a little more, of course," Angelique said to the earl, quietly. "They require significant staff time to prepare. We'll add it to your account."

"Of course."

Briskly, they returned to the business at hand.

"Well. What do you say, ladies?" He offered them a charming smile. "Will you allow us to stay, and accept my abject apologies?"

Angelique and Delilah exchanged a long look.

"I'm afraid we'll have to take a minute or two to discuss it privately between us, Lord Vaughn," Delilah said. "For you see, it's not just that we consider Helga family. It's that she's part of the very lifeblood of our business, and we can attribute a good deal of our success to her talents." Every word of this was just a *little* bit of an exaggeration, but at its core was truth. "When people become our guests they find comfort in every way, and that includes the food. She also manages our kitchen and the maids, and this is no small skill. As a man of business, you likely understand that the loss of her would strike a blow at the very foundation of our livelihood."

He blanched a little and looked deflated. "I see."

It was rather sweet to see that he was truly suffering, the traitor.

And it wasn't as though the Earl of Vaughn and his family didn't have other equally or more attractive options. Perhaps another hotel in London could find a way to accommodate them; at the time of their arrival, nothing had been available for them at the precise moment they'd been compelled to hastily vacate their home. But both Delilah and Angelique believed in the quality of their service and they also knew the profound value of perceived exclusivity.

"If you would be so kind to wait here while we discuss it?" Angelique said to him, on a nearly funereal hush. Together she and Delilah gracefully rose and crossed the foyer underneath their beloved crystal chandelier, to the opposite parlor, lately the scene of such merriment. It was empty now.

"'Strike a blow at the foundation of our livelihood.' That was very good, Delilah," Angelique whispered.

"Thank you. It just came to me."

"How long do you think we ought to let him marinate in guilt and remorse?"

"Well . . . he's a good man, I think. And he's an earl. Even now he's considering offering some sort of financial solution, because most things have a financial solution when you're an earl." Both Delilah and Angelique knew this from personal experience.

"*I* have a suggestion if he doesn't come up with it on his own," Angelique said.

"I suspect it's the same as mine."

"We'll nudge him in that direction if he doesn't come up with that solution on his own. But we need to stand here another minute or so in apparent fevered discussion. What shall we talk about?"

"How to persuade Mr. Cassidy to build the rod for hanging the curtain? Pay for pensions? *And* footmen?"

"That will do quite well," Angelique said.

They returned to the reception room a few minutes later. The earl searched their faces in vain for anything revelatory of his fate.

"I believe we've reached a decision, Lord Vaughn," Angelique said very, very gently. Her tone implied regretful resolve.

He took a breath. "Before you speak . . . I've been having a little think while you were discussing matters. What if, by way of restitution . . . I agreed to buy a fine new curtain for your stage? And perhaps I can persuade a friend or two—I have in mind the Earl and Countess of Landover—to visit your new ballroom with an eye toward perhaps attending a soiree there?"

Delilah and Angelique exchanged a look.

This was exactly what they'd been about to suggest.

Delilah spoke for the two of them. "How very kind and intuitive of you, Lord Vaughn, to notice how much our new ballroom means to us, and to recognize how an elegant curtain will elevate it to something truly splendid. It's a gesture that speaks to our hearts. We'll accept your offer . . . as long as you promise not to cause Helga any anxiety by attempting to lure her away again."

"I swear upon the honor of my family that I will

only humbly *appreciate* your staff, and not attempt to abscond with them."

They smiled at him.

There was a little pause.

"We'll need the curtain straight away, of course," Angelique added gently.

"Of course," the earl replied with a little smile.

Chapter Ten

❧❧❧

*P*EACE WAS restored, after a fashion. Relief made the sitting room somewhat celebratory after a brilliant dinner of lamb in mint, artichoke soup, cheese and salad, peas and onions in butter sauce, and blancmange—all of which taxed the boarding house budget a little but which served the dual purposes of rubbing in the earl's transgression ever so slightly and making nearly everyone exquisitely happy and full.

Except Lillias.

Hugh had observed this from the moment he'd returned from Dover. Everyone else in her family ate with great enthusiasm. She ate begrudgingly, as though it was a duty. Just enough to ensure survival. It puzzled him. She struck him as someone disinclined to reject a sensual pleasure if one was available, and if ever a sensual pleasure existed, it was Helga's cooking.

Tonight she wore blue silk and sported a matching pair of pale blue shadows beneath her eyes.

She'd likely been awake all night.

This was both irritating and satisfying.

Because he had indeed thought about her all damned night. It had been disorienting, as though he'd done the night backwards: a dream first—

because that's how those minutes on the roof seemed to him—then sleep. Before he slept he was surprised to find himself gripping the counterpane on either side of him, as though he was lifting her down from the ladder again.

All of his senses had echoed with an outraged disbelief that he'd actually released her instead of sliding his hands up her night rail.

He'd spent a few minutes torturing himself into a full body sweat by imagining what would have happened next if he'd done just that. But that rooftop encounter left him echoing with a peculiar resonant ache he didn't know how to name. He only knew it had something to do with how it felt to watch her look out across the dark, gritty London view and the vast sky with hungry joy, as if she wanted to swallow it whole.

He supposed he was glad he'd been there to witness it.

And to see her safely down.

And surely there was relief in knowing that he'd as much as told her there would be no seduction. The fact that he could get those words out through the clamoring lust reassured him that he was the one in control after all, regardless of how she played havoc with his senses.

His profound instinct for self-preservation had gotten him through a war. He was satisfied it would get him through Lady Lillias Vaughn, too.

Happily fed, the guests convened in the drawing room and claimed chairs and settees. St. John leaned against the mantel. A lively discussion was immediately underway about whether a game of Faro—so daring!—or spillikins ought to be got up

or whether they ought to launch into reading about
Odysseus or some other story. Delacorte suddenly
said, "I've an idea—Cassidy should tell the story
of his hound and the bear."

"Oh, are these more friends of yours, Mr. Cassidy?" the countess wanted to know. "I'm jesting,"
she added at once.

She was catching on.

He smiled at her.

"Oh, go on, do it, Cassidy," Delacorte insisted.
"We need a little violence and heroism now and
then to offset all the embroidery and knitting and
whatnot."

The women scoffed good-naturedly at him, but
this was undoubtedly true. And Hugh knew it.
Too *much* civilization wasn't good for a man.

"Very well." Hugh leaned back in his chair. "I'll
do my masculine duty. Gather round, ladies and
gentlemen."

Chairs, and bright, expectant expressions, were
turned toward Hugh.

He gave a dramatic throat clear. "I once had a
fine bloodhound named Tuesday, for the day of the
week she was born. My Uncle Liam gave her to me
for my sixteenth birthday—he traded furs to get
her for me, because a hound was what I wanted
more than anything else in the world. That dog
was the best gift and the best friend I ever had. She
was smarter than most humans and more loyal
to boot, and was she *ever* a character, just like my
Uncle Liam."

"Dogs make me sneeze," Lady Claire said sadly.

"That is a tragedy, indeed," Hugh said somberly.
"Well, Tuesday and I were out walking through

the woods on a beautiful day, tracking deer. And for dogs, you know, smells are a whole other world and language. Through smell, they learn and understand and communicate things that we just can't. Walking in the woods for them is like walking into a whole library of books. I loved watching her just . . . savor the world . . . when were out together."

He realized that he'd inadvertently said this almost directly to Lillias. He'd sought her out, as if she was the light he was reading by.

Who was listening, as raptly as she'd gazed across London last night.

"I lost sight of Tuesday briefly that day, but usually she always ran back to me every minute or so. Then . . . then I heard her barking. A different bark. She sounded . . . terrified and furious. And, well, I went running." He paused. His voice went somber. "And that bear was going for her."

He didn't actually like to recount the story, but then again he did: it was an instant where everything could have gone terribly wrong. And yet it was proof that he could navigate chaos and violence and emerge triumphant.

The room was very quiet.

"I screamed and roared at that bear like I was the devil himself. But I couldn't get off a shot because it was happening so fast, and they were tussling. There was an equal chance I'd shoot Tuesday. So I just went in there and with every ounce of strength I had, I kicked that bear. It was like kicking a wall."

He paused.

"And then the bear came for me."

Not a person in the room was breathing.

"Before I knew it I was on my back and I could see her jaws and feel her breath and see the shine on her teeth and the rage in her eyes. She was going in for the kill."

Dot made a whimpering sound and bit her knuckles.

"I don't know where I got the strength. Or the knowledge. I wasn't going to die that day and neither was Tuesday. I remember hurling my fist like a madman into that bear's eyes and twisting so that I could fling her off and somehow . . . I did. I saw sky again and in two seconds I was able to stand and grab my gun."

He paused again. Mr. Cassidy did indeed have a flair for storytelling.

"I hope that bear is a rug on your floor now, Mr. Cassidy," the earl said. Sounding subdued, almost tentative. And very impressed.

"Well, the thing is . . . bears don't attack unless they're threatened. She had cubs and she was protecting her own. Baby bears. You all can understand that, yes? I wasn't after bear meat that day and there was no reason for her cubs to die.

"I was able to fire a shot in the air to get that bear off running. And that gave me enough time to get out of there with Tuesday in my arms. We were both bleeding and battered. I didn't feel a thing until we were back at the house. We took a few weeks to recuperate. Tuesday had some gashes. And I sport a couple of scars from that encounter. I think her tooth might have grazed me. I don't remember. But this is a memento."

He pointed to the crescent-shaped scar below his lip.

Everyone gave him the tribute of a moment of dumbstruck, starry-eyed, reflective silence.

"We always *knew* you were a hero, Mr. Cassidy," said Mrs. Hardy, sounding satisfied, which was a compliment indeed, as she was married to a hero.

"'A tooth might have grazed me,'" Delacorte quoted slowly, admiringly. "Didn't I tell you it was a great story!"

Everyone nodded.

"All that for a dog . . ." the earl repeated musingly. "Bravo, sir."

"Tuesday was my responsibility, sir, and all I knew was that if I had to, I was going to go down trying to save her. No matter what, I . . . I take care of my own."

He realized he'd directed this to Lillias. Primarily, or so he told himself, because he could feel her eyes upon him. He was suddenly certain he'd be able to sense the quality of her gaze even if they were separated by a crowd of hundreds, the way he was able to detect a shift in the wind. He deliberately, with an effort at nonchalance, turned his head and pretended to study the wallpaper.

Everyone sat in happy, quiet contentment for a time, as one does to let a good story settle in. Presently, knitting and embroidery was taken up and Mrs. Pariseau reached for the Faro box.

"All right," she said happily. "Who would like to—"

"I CAN'T TAKE IT ANYMORE!" St. John howled.

Mrs. Pariseau gave a little shriek and she and the countess clapped their hands over their hearts. Dot nearly fell out of her chair.

All the men stiffened, poised to leap in case he needed pouncing upon.

St. John took a gulping breath.

He took another.

"Mr. Delacorte," he said firmly, his voice creaking from strain.

Confused eyebrows joined the startled expressions. If they'd been accepting wagers on what St. John was about to say, everyone would have lost.

Delacorte looked up at him, expectantly.

"Will you *please* . . ."

Everyone pitched forward a little in suspense.

". . . teach me how to play chess."

It was safe to say it ranked among the most surprising things said yet at The Grand Palace on the Thames.

Delacorte studied St. John thoughtfully, sternly.

Then slowly, his face split into an expansive grin and he swept an arm toward the chair across from him.

St. John staggered over and settled in.

"I've been so bored," he half croaked.

"There, there," Delacorte said briskly as he set up the board.

It took a moment for everyone's heart to settle to its usual rhythms. Between the bear story and St. John's outburst, everyone's emotions had taken a vigorous buffeting on a full stomach, and it grew quiet.

"If he thinks standing there is humbling, just wait until Delacorte makes hay of him," Hugh murmured to Bolt, who grinned.

Mrs. Pariseau cleared her throat. "Well, perhaps we ought to finish reading—"

A vigorous rapping echoed through the foyer.

"Oh, the door!" Dot leaped up.

Until they hired a footman or two, Dot was charged with answering the door, and it was her very favorite responsibility—and she hoped it would remain her responsibility, even when (or perhaps if) they hired a suitable fellow or two. Discovering who had knocked held all the anticipatory thrill of opening a gift. A new guest? A drama? The King of England? All three of those things had appeared on the other side of the door at The Grand Palace on the Thames at one time or another.

And she was an absolute savant at describing to Angelique and Delilah the people on the other side, in her own singular way. She had not yet been wrong.

They heard some murmured words.

Angelique and Delilah exchanged an anticipatory glance.

They heard the door close with a satisfying clunk (it was a nice heavy door).

But then they heard only one set of footsteps returning. It was, in fact, not so much a step as a shuffle.

Presently, a bouquet of roses entered the room on a pair of legs. Or that's what it looked like to the already startled people seated.

It was in fact Dot, holding a great urn, from which brilliant plump roses on long stems burst forth.

Dot peered from behind them. "They're for Lady Lillias. A footman had them sent over from your townhouse."

Hugh stopped pulling air. He in fact went motionless.

All heads whipped toward Lillias. Everyone was simply vibrating with curiosity.

Lillias was staring at them as if someone had instead brought her heads on pikes. "Oh God. Not more of them. How did they know to send them here?" She sounded aghast.

But also—astoundingly—a little bored.

As though roses that cost a fortune were simply her queenly due.

The colors and shapes of the room were suddenly too bright and distinct. A lot of emotions were waiting to have a go at Hugh; all of his muscles tensed as though he could forestall the need to feel them by refusing to take a deep breath.

"Ohhh, Lillias, who sent them?" Claire asked eagerly.

"Yes, tell us who!" Mrs. Pariseau leaned forward. "Oh my, they're so lovely!"

"There's a little message with them," Dot said. She attempted to shift the roses into the crook of her arm so she could hand over to Lillias the little crumpled sheet of foolscap clutched in her fist.

It proved too complex of a maneuver. The foolscap made a break for it, and when she attempted to snatch it up, she accidentally created the perfect updraft and sent it flying through the air instead. It fluttered like a drunken bird in flight, glanced off of Delacorte's reaching fingertips, and drifted down, down, down.

Right onto the little table in front of Hugh, as if it was a falcon he'd called from the sky.

He stared down at it for a moment. His ears were ringing.

"Read it, Mr. Cassidy," Claire begged him.

He levered his head up and looked square at Lillias. Her chin was up a little too high; the cant of it was officially arrogant. But her eyes were wary and ever-so-slightly beseeching and her jaw was tense.

Everything about her expression begged him not to read it.

And that decided it.

Hugh picked it up casually.

He did. Out loud, slowly, his inflection ironic, with the oddest sensation that he was reading it over his own shoulder:

> *A humble gift for a maiden fair*
> *Perhaps you'll tuck one in your hair*
> *Or press one to your rosy lips*
> *Or caress one with your fingertips*
> *I shall see myself forever bless'd*
> *If you'd hold a petal to your breast*
> *And if you should choose to love me best*
> > Peter, Lord Eshling

Hugh found he could not look up from the fools-cap. All of his limbs felt odd and stiff, as if he was suddenly coated in frost. A sort of cold, caustic hilarity had taken up simmering in his gut. He could very nearly taste it in his throat. Finally he levered his head slowly and stared, with coldly amused irony, at Lillias.

Two hot pink circles of color sat high on her cheeks. She returned his gaze stonily.

"What rot," she said, irritably.

The funny part—well, there were two funny parts—was that he resented that the poem was competent. He didn't think he'd be able to come up with lines that rhymed like that in a million years.

The other funny part was that he felt like a fool.

But why on earth should he? He had no real stake in this.

Or in her. He was a man who'd survived things which by rights ought to have killed him, including war, a bear attack, and Delacorte's gastric emissions. And yet he'd been lying awake in what he'd believed to be unique sensual torment, while it was now becoming clear that, in all likelihood, a whole *ton* full of bloods were lashed to proverbial masts when it came to Lady Lillias Vaughn.

And who but a fool does that?

He at once vividly recalled that little snippet of gossip Delacorte had read to him from a greasy newspaper. A dispatch from another world entirely. He ought to have taken it as a warning.

I'm not completely naive, she'd said last night.

He still couldn't feel his limbs.

Or get a proper breath.

"Well, I thought it wasn't half bad. One could almost set that to music," Delacorte said. "It has a bit of a nice ring to it."

"Oh, everyone wants to marry Lillias," St. John said on a yawn. "Don't you get about one proposal a week?" He aimed this question at his sister.

"They're not real proposals. It's meant to be

amusing. For the men, that is." Lillias had gone white. She looked for some reason nearly furious.

"There's a club at White's. With its own betting book. You can't join it unless you've sent roses to Lillias," St. John expounded.

"That's *ridiculous*." Lillias was aghast, for whom this was clearly news.

"That's precisely what I told them," St. John said, with the sincerity of a sibling.

"It's like a forest in the foyer most days with all the bouquets for Lillias," her mother added happily. "It smells heavenly, most days."

"It's not," Lillias retorted tautly. "And it doesn't."

"Don't be modest, dear. You've been the belle of the *ton* and it's a memory that will last a lifetime. You'll tell your grandchildren about it," her father said comfortably.

"I won't." Lillias's voice had gained an octave. She sounded increasingly panicked.

"Lillias is going to marry a duke or some such," Claire said proudly. "I thought she would marry Gilly, he's so nice and he's going to be an earl and all, but he's probably going to marry—"

"CLAIRE," Lillias said sharply. With something so akin to anguish Hugh's heart jolted.

Claire clapped her mouth closed, good and startled.

"Well, it will be someone like Giles," the earl said jocularly. "It's what one does, isn't it, when one is a fine clever girl with a pedigree stretching back to the Conqueror? You'll marry an heir of some sort. She can have her pick of them. After all, a dog doesn't marry a cat."

It wasn't the most accurate comparison, but his point was made: there was the aristocracy. And then there was everybody else. He wasn't even being ironic or pompous.

Lillias didn't quite close her eyes. But she'd gone still again. There was a rather internal look to her as though she wished to be invisible. Hugh couldn't bear to look at her in that moment. He looked down instead, as if an explanation for all the things he felt in this moment could be found between the lines of that odious poem.

The "everybody else" in the room struggled not to exchange looks. But it was, typically, simply how things were, mostly without question.

"Perhaps cats don't marry dogs," Mr. Delacorte said reasonably, "but I know a fellow who once saw a lion and a tiger making lo—"

If Delacorte were a dartboard and eyes were darts he'd be bristling, such were the warning glares sent his way. He was stared into silence.

The silence lasted a tick or two.

"Well, how do you suppose mules are made?" Delacorte stubbornly, and a little more quietly, pressed.

"How *are* they made?" Claire wondered.

The dart glares aimed at Delacorte strengthened. All apart from Lady Vaughn, who closed her eyes, perhaps at last giving up.

Claire looked at him expectantly.

"A horse proposes to a donkey, and they get married and have a family and that's a mule," Delacorte said kindly.

"I'm fifteen, not eleven," Claire muttered.

"I should *love* to go to a donkey wedding," Dot breathed.

"Thank you for bringing them in, Dot. It was very kind of you. But would you please take them away?" Lillias had recovered her composure, and her voice was cool and polite. Hugh had to admire that self-possession. She was a lot of things, but she wasn't fragile. "Perhaps you can spread them about the rooms here at The Grand Palace on the Thames."

Hugh stood then, slowly and casually, as if to stretch his legs.

Lillias watched him rise, her gaze every bit as tethered to him as his was to her, apparently.

He delivered the poem to her table. He laid it gently down before her. "Doubtless you'll want a souvenir, Lady Lillias," he said evenly.

She stared at it. She began to look up at him, but he'd already turned his back, and his back was all she was to see for the rest of the evening.

"I think Faro would be grand," he said to Mrs. Pariseau as he resumed his seat. As though nothing at all of note had just happened. As though Lady Lillias Vaughn had never arrived at The Grand Palace on the Thames. As though he'd never speak to her again.

Chapter Eleven

❧

LILLIAS AWOKE to the smell of roses.

She growled and sat bolt upright in bed. A quick sweeping inspection of the room located the culprit: a fluffy portion of the dismembered bouquet had been stuffed into the little vase on her writing desk. Some well-meaning maid must have installed it there as she'd built up the fires. She wondered what Lord Eshling—had she even ever met him? She could not recall—would say if she told him that she'd shared his bouquet with everyone in a boarding house near the docks.

And then she wondered if one of those roses made it into Mr. Cassidy's room.

She lowered her face into her hands at the thought.

She left her face there for quite some time.

The scent of roses had lingered in the parlor long after Hugh had departed for the smoking room. He had not looked at her from the moment he'd delivered the poem to her. And she could *feel* the severing of his attention, like a physical thing. It left a sudden, shocking void, as if he'd kicked down one of the walls of her house the way he'd kicked that bear away from his dog.

His icy, thorough, casual shunning made the

jealous antics of the bloods of the *ton* seem like child's play. He did not do things by halves.

If it had only been jealousy, that would be one thing. But she knew he'd formed a judgment, and it was a patently unfair one. His self-righteous implacability made her furious. As did the brutal effectiveness of it. It very nearly made her want to *grovel*, and she had never groveled for a thing in her life.

She would not like him for an enemy.

She also—and this seemed very nearly absurd—thought perhaps his feelings might be hurt. She could not quite say why she suspected this, only that she'd learned that emotions did tend to swing between poles out of defense. If not feelings, then at least his pride.

The very idea of even inadvertently visiting suffering on him when he'd already suffered bravely in so many other ways made her so restless with misery she could scarcely draw breath.

Still! He hadn't the right to be hurt, had he? *Or* jealous.

She'd lingered in the drawing room for another twenty minutes or so after Hugh read that terrible poem aloud. The she'd pleaded a *mal de tête* and had gone upstairs, taking the poem with her.

It actually *wasn't* a terrible poem, which made it somehow worse. How was she supposed to respond? Thank you kindly, the flowers are lovely but then that's the job of roses, to look lovely, and oh, what about those appallingly familiar lines about my lips and hands? What about the *contents* of my heart? My brain? Who I am?

Once this nonsense hadn't mattered. Then it had evolved into an irritant.

Now it flayed her. Back in her room, she'd gotten the little rock out of her reticule and held it, for no reason, except that it had been given to her by someone who knew her well. Someone she'd thought had *seen* her and also cared about her. It of course yielded no comfort.

She'd spent the rest of her evening with her lamp lit, her door closed, and her sketchbook open. And she had filled it with lines and color. It was the only thing she could control.

It was still remarkably early. The stillness of her little suite suggested her family were warmly bundled and sleeping in their own comfortable beds.

She slid out of bed and dressed quickly in the nearest wool walking dress to hand, a rich brown that colluded nicely with her hair. Then she laced on walking shoes and eyed the little vase of flowers speculatively. She wanted them gone, but she couldn't countenance wasting them.

Inspiration struck. She lifted the two little cut blooms, dripping, from the vase. She could take them down to Helene Durand Park and cover them in the soil there. At least they could become mulch and help something beautiful to grow in this strange place by the docks.

She startled a yawning maid in the hall as she locked the door, then made her way quickly down the stairs.

She'd just passed the first little door to the ballroom—it was one she suspected led right up to the stage—and was just about to pass the second one when who should appear but Hugh Cassidy, striding in buckskins and rolled shirtsleeves, lumber tucked under his arm.

His eyes flicked over her. Apart from that, not one of his features so much as twitched.

But as he strode past her into the ballroom, he sardonically mimed tugging on his forelock.

FOOSH!

Just like that, her temper ignited and leaped.

She followed him into the ballroom, quietly, and pulled the door closed, none too gently.

He dropped his burden of lumber, brushed off his hands, pivoted.

And froze.

And then he planted his hands on his hips. His face, and stare, were as hard as if he was staring down an enemy soldier.

It was daunting.

He was about to learn how fierce *she* could be.

"*Good* morning, Mr. Cassidy," she said pleasantly. "I wonder if you'd share with me what I've done to earn your contempt?"

An eyebrow leaped in cold amusement. "Was I not deferential enough, my lady?"

He said it softly. Mockingly.

She clamped down on her back teeth. "What if I said 'yes'?"

He wordlessly, coolly contemplated her as though he were a bear deciding where to deliver the killing bite.

"Very well. Let's just say that 'contempt' is an interesting choice of word for someone who said 'take it away' when presented with a bouquet of hothouse flowers." He flicked his eyes down to the roses she still clutched in her fist. "I can imagine you saying 'off with his head' in the same bored tone."

He turned his back on her again, picked up a plank from a stack of boards, then hurled it aside when he saw a hint of rot.

The echoing clatter made her start.

"And how, pray tell, was that contemptuous?" she demanded.

He paused and turned again. And then very slowly and carefully, as if he'd been up all night itemizing her sins and memorizing them for recitation, he said, "Well, let's see. There's contempt for the man who made the effort to choose and send the flowers. Contempt for all the other men who've sent flowers. Contempt for the fool who took the time to write a deeply stupid poem. Contempt, no doubt, for anyone who isn't the heir to a duke. As if it's simply your queenly due."

The last words were almost but not quite a sneer.

She felt as though she were being piled with bricks. If she'd had something to throw, she might have, and she wasn't the throwing-things-in-a-pique type.

"You don't understand." Her voice was frayed.

"I think I do." He sorted through the boards and found the one he wanted, apparently. "You might want to step back. You might inadvertently get some manual labor on you, Lady Lillias."

Her head was light now with fury. In slow amazement she said, "Why you arrogant . . ."

He whirled.

"Go right ahead," he said silkily. "Tell me what you really think, Lady Lillias."

His anger was daunting, but her own gave her strength. Still, she could hear her own breathing.

The air she pulled in was hot. "Very well then, Mr. Cassidy." She was so angry that her voice shook. "Given that you're a simple American from the country, I'll forgive you for not knowing it's a *sport* to them. To all those men. The flowers and that nonsense. *I'm* a sport to them. They don't *see me*. They don't care about me. They don't know *me*. It's a ritual. I'm the *object*. It's what everyone does and I haven't really had a say in it. And every time I get a bouquet I'm reminded of that."

She realized her voice had escalated in pitch and now her eyes were burning and she was perilously close to furious tears. She went to brush her hand across her eyes. She realized she'd crushed the two roses in her clenched fist.

Oh, to be a man, able to stand there with an eyebrow up and not fall apart when ferocious emotion assailed you.

She uncurled her fingers. They both watched as the roses fell to the floor with a soft thump and a spray of red petals, like drops of blood.

And he *had* gone motionless. All traces of irony were wiped from his face. Something like epiphany lit it. Then, to her amazement, his head went back a little, and came down with a nod, as if he finally understood something. His expression gentled, and then went inscrutable, as he at once took what appeared to be an involuntary step toward her. His hand rose slightly, as if he meant to touch her arm.

He stopped himself.

He let her breathe.

She took a shaky breath, and another. "And that

fool who wrote the poem has absolutely nothing else to do with his time, any more than my darling brother does."

She said this more calmly.

They stood in this relative détente for another silent moment.

"But you'll have to pick one eventually, right, Lillias?" He was only mildly ironic. Still gentle. "As long as he's got a title."

"Yes," she said after a moment, quietly. A little desperately. "Of course. That's what's expected. That's how it's done."

She swiped at her eyes.

But in silence, in the dim, dusty light of the ball-room, they regarded each other, and it was an absurd relief to have his attention again. To be heard by him.

And yet he'd still judged her. And her anger wasn't spent.

"I want you to know . . . or rather, I should say I did like them, at first. The flowers. Who wouldn't? It's flattering, isn't it? Flowers are lovely. It's meant to be a compliment. And I know that I'm considered pretty, and I don't dislike being told. And yet do you have any idea how often men are unkind about it? Do you know how ridiculous they can behave about it? It's all *wanting* and competition and it colors their perception of me and I cannot free myself of it. All the *men* decided who I was. And you're just the same." She was ashamed that her voice was shaking. "*You* don't even really like me. It's the only reason you noticed me at all."

He took this in, his expression inscrutable.

"Actually, I think it was the wreath of smoke around your head," he said.

This surprised a short laugh from her.

It was the first time she'd said these things aloud to anyone. She felt shaky and a little exposed, but the liberation was dizzying.

"Well, let's look at it another way," he said, sounding deceptively reasonable. "Why did you notice *me*, Lillias? Wouldn't I normally be beneath your notice? I'm practically a pagan from the wilds of America, after all. No title. No pedigree. My family tree has big bald patches. And yet you noticed me. And continue to notice me, as they say. Because that's as good a word as any. 'Notice.'"

The word, the way he said it, sounded like another world altogether, one that ought to have been worth one hundred pounds inserted into the epithet jar should it ever have been uttered aloud in the sitting room of The Grand Palace on the Thames.

She felt the heat on the back of her arms. "You're impossible not to notice," she said stiffly. "You take up a good deal of space in the little sitting room at night."

"And in your mind when you're in bed, I imagine." He said this casually, almost sympathetically.

He was ruthless. But she stopped breathing. He was like someone cornering a magician into revealing her secrets.

He looked away for a moment. He pressed his lips together in thought. She took that opportunity to gulp him in like she'd gulped in the London view. Saw that dimple embedded like a crescent moon at the corner of his mouth, and the finest of lines about his eyes, and that little arcing scar he'd gotten from a bear because he always took care of his own.

Her own heart turned over hard.

He turned to her again.

"Lillias . . ." She'd never heard her name said in such a way. It had facets; it fairly shimmered with shades of emotion. Wit and exasperation and tenderness and frustration. The long pause that followed it betrayed just how much was going on in Mr. Cassidy's head.

"I don't dislike you." His voice was solemn.

He moved slowly across the room, to close that distance between them.

"Yes," she said wearily, dryly. "You might bestir yourself to do something if I were on fire, as it's your duty to look out for the safety of women, and so forth."

"Well, let me think. If you were on fire," he said thoughtfully, "I would likely spring upon you, and perhaps roll you in a carpet. Give the carpet a good patting to make sure you were completely doused, lest you ignite the rest of The Grand Palace on the Thames, a place of which I've grown quite fond."

She gave a short laugh. "Would you indeed spring upon me? Isn't springing on a bear how you got that little—" And as if of its own accord, her hand reached toward him to touch his scar.

She went still. Stunned.

His hand was clamped around her wrist.

She hadn't even seen him move. He'd captured her wrist mid-reach. It must have literally happened while she'd blinked.

She gave an experimental, minute tug.

His strength was reminiscent of an anchor thrown overboard.

He let her simmer in astonishment and a pure primal thrill of being held like that for a moment.

Then he spoke.

"In America," he said, his voice low and calm, "we learn at a young age not to touch things when we can't foresee the consequences. A lesson learned by a friend of mine who inserted his hand into a log and lost it to a badger."

"That is a very colorful story." Her voice emerged after a delay, because it had needed to traverse through a thicket of sensations. "You moved very quickly."

There was a pause, during which the realization that his skin was touching her skin was slowly seeping in and mesmerizing both of them.

"I once snatched an arrow out of the air, shot at me by an irritated Indian." He said this softly.

She managed a tense smile. "You are lying."

He half smiled, too. "Am I hurting you?"

"No."

He wasn't. He was scarcely even touching her.

His fingers had loosened, and now circled her wrist in something perilously close to a caress.

And then that's what it became. Gently. As if he were uncertain of his right to touch her. Inexorably. As if he simply couldn't help himself.

Surely he could feel her pulse thumping away against his fingers. Because she certainly could. The blood was rushing in her ears like waves beating on a beach.

She gazed up into his face, and he gazed down

into hers as if she were a landscape he was inspecting for hidden enemies. Or perhaps hidden wonders. Lost.

His voice lowered conspiratorially. "Would you like your hand back?"

The right words to say were bobbing around somewhere in the syrup her brain had become; she couldn't quite fish them out. The truth was, at the moment, her hand seemed to rightly belong to him. As though it were a trophy he'd won for snatching arrows out of the air.

"You seem to have found a use for it, Mr. Cassidy. You've used it as a sort of . . . as a sort of . . . lever."

Somehow, without either of them noticing, he had pulled her all but into his body.

Somehow, she had easily, willingly gone, as if she were on wheels.

He wasn't smiling anymore.

His expression was taut. And enthralled, in the truest sense of the word.

"Lillias . . ." His voice bathed her senses like a too-potent liqueur. She heard more than a little pain in it. "I am not a toy. I feel it only fair to tell you that I do not normally enter into a contest— and we both know this has been a contest, so let's not pretend any longer—of any sort unless I've a certainty of getting what I want. You cannot win this."

Delicious quicksilver shivers of sensation traced her limbs, sent by his thumb.

Back and forth. Back and forth. Over her pulse, which was kicking like a trapped rabbit. Demonstrating to her his power.

"Do you want me to let you go?" he whispered.

Yes, she should have said.

But she couldn't help herself.

"Tell me what you want," she whispered.

She was going to make him say it out loud.

He closed his eyes briefly. "Which words would you like me to bludgeon you with this time? In the spirit of truth, I must warn you, 'naked' is likely to be one of them. Also words like 'moaning' and 'cock.'"

She went rigid and sucked in a sharp breath.

He released her hand at once, almost roughly.

She took a step back.

And then another.

They regarded each other from this safe distance in silence.

And then he raised an eyebrow. Not unsympathetically. But once again, the "go inside, little girl" was implicit.

It was maddening.

"You aren't really winning either, are you, Mr. Cassidy, if you're helpless to stop playing the game?"

He instantly went as rigid as one of those boards he'd been hammering into place.

He wasn't the only one who could raise a single eyebrow. She could, too, and so she did. And then she turned for the door.

She never got there. And she didn't even have time to gasp.

In a single fluid motion he'd seized her, spun her about, and now she was enclosed by the bands of his arms, held flush up against his body.

One of his hands rested at the small of her back.

The other hand rested alarmingly much lower, a scant inch or so before the curve of her derriere.

Her breasts were crushed against his chest.

His groin was pressed hard, implacably, against hers.

He held her like that, for seconds or an eternity, his breath swift and angry, his eyes searching hers, his mouth a stern line. She stared furiously up at him.

And in seconds the length of his hard, hot body went to her head like laudanum. Until the breaths she drew were unsteady and hot, and ever swifter. She went pliant with surrender. Her body had transferred its allegiance to him with alarming speed.

In that moment, she wanted, very badly, for him to do with her what he would.

He'd probably always known how it would be. He'd tried to warn her.

His hand slid up her spine to cradle her head, to urge it gently back, and when his lips touched hers she moaned low in her throat, a sound she hadn't known she could make. All want. All relief.

Shocking in its subtlety, at first, the kiss. A delicate slide of his lips against hers. But this was how he showed her that heretofore unimagined sensations could be coaxed from her lips alone. And that those sensations could ignite her entire body until she was trembling with a need she could not quite name.

She felt his own need humming in his body.

Her lips fell open beneath his. And that's when the plunder began.

The hot satin of his mouth was a primal revelation. When she dared to meet the search and glide of his tongue with her own, his low groan vibrated through her body and he nearly crushed her against him. Together they turned that kiss into something furious and desperate, a clash fueled by futility and the forbidden. Every second of it uncovered in her new, fresh levels of erotic hunger.

Every second eroded the boundaries of her body and time. Until she was clinging to him to keep from spinning away.

His other hand slid down, down, and pressed her up against his hard cock.

Pleasure speared her; her head fell back on a gasp. He moved against her again. And then again. "Oh my God . . ." she moaned. "Hugh . . . ?"

She understood too late that if he didn't stop this, she wouldn't, either.

She heard her own breath sawing against his throat as he turned his head to kiss the pulse beneath her ear. He dragged his lips down, down, down to the soft swell of her breasts, to the valley between them, where her heart beat.

His lips lingered. And very gently, he kissed her there.

And that's when he lifted his head. Slowly.

He brought his hand up to cup the back of her neck. His fingers played along the fine hairs there. Her body was still pressed hard up against his cock. And like this, he held her fast.

Their breathing mingled in a little storm, their lips still inches apart. She was as dazed as if she'd been trapped in an opium den.

"Do you see the trouble now?" He said this quietly, ironically, almost kindly next to her ear. His voice was still hoarse; the words staccato. "Now you will lie awake and think of nothing but this. You will desperately want what can *never* be. You will wonder about what awaits at the end of a kiss like this and yet I assure you, your imagination will never be able to do it justice. It is *glorious*. That is the curse of playing a game like this."

She couldn't speak.

Her eyes were closed.

Her breathing swayed against his.

"This can lead nowhere good, Lillias. Because we will not be able to stop. One day you will beg me for more. And then more. By then you will want it more than you've ever wanted anything. And there may come a time when I cannot help myself, and that way lies our doom." He delivered the next words like the softest of whispered curses, right into her ear. "And rest assured . . . there is so . . . much . . . more."

Her thoughts spiraled, chaotic as leaves caught in an updraft.

"Do you believe me?" His voice was low and almost stern, a little urgent. He sounded as though he were trying to shake her from sleep while the building around her burned.

She drew a struggling breath up from her lungs, hot and shaky. She took another.

"So this stops now," he said abruptly. "Do you hear me?"

She managed to nod once.

His arms dropped and he stepped back from her abruptly, releasing her into a world that would never be the same again. She nearly staggered, but her formidable pride righted her.

There was silence.

She opened her eyes. But she refused to look at him. She looked steadfastly away, at the wall.

And a moment later, she turned and walked quietly out the door, closing it gently behind her.

Chapter Twelve

"**V**ISCOUNT BESSETTE is redecorating his Sussex estate," Lucien said in the smoking room that evening. "His wife no longer wants red in her sitting rooms. Green apparently is in favor. Everything red must go."

Everyone in the room—Delacorte and Hugh, that was—turned their heads slowly and stared at him in rank astonishment.

He was amused. "We don't just talk about horses and boxing at White's, you know."

Hugh caught on before Bolt said, with amused exasperation, "He's selling curtains. Twelve feet long, red velvet, wonderful condition, with valances. Three sets. Vaughn has agreed to pay for them. Delilah and Angelique can arrange for them to be sent or—"

"I'll go," Hugh said immediately.

Bolt, Hardy, and Delacorte swiveled toward him in surprise. Hugh realized then it was the first thing he'd said in fifteen minutes, which was as long as they'd all been in the room together. He'd been addressed. He hadn't responded, because he hadn't heard them. The desultory, contented conversation around him might as well have been smoke for how much he'd noticed it. They didn't trouble him; they all knew a man needed a good brood now and again and they left him to it.

Hugh supposed he'd been listening for a life-line. Apparently it was made of curtains.

He wasn't in the habit of being melodramatic in his thoughts. But he understood very clearly that his only chance at salvation meant never occupying the same room as Lillias, ever again. He'd been out building the stage all day and hadn't come in for dinner. He'd only come in for a cheroot. He hadn't seen her again, and that was by design.

He could hire a hack from the livery stables and easily make the trip, stop in Surrey to inquire about the Clay family, and be back in time to meet his uncle in Portsmouth.

Life had demanded a lot from him. He'd found, every time, reservoirs of strength, insight, cussed-ness, and endurance, some of it requiring acrobatic spiritual contortions. But ending that kiss had been one of the hardest things he'd ever done.

Was there satisfaction in knowing she would be just as haunted by it as he was, no matter which aristocrat eventually had the privilege of bedding her? Her voice rising in something near anguish when she talked about being pelted with roses by aristocrats, about being so visible and yet invisible: that's what haunted him.

And anytime he wanted he could relive it and experience a certain conqueror's triumph: the sound of her low moan when their lips met. And the blossom-tender give of them beneath his. Or the feel of his tongue twined with hers. Their hips moving together.

But he knew the reason he'd pressed his lips

against her breast was that he'd wanted to feel the beat of her heart.

Her heart.

It was this last realization that had him up and out the door just past dawn and all but fleeing The Grand Palace on the Thames.

She would in all likelihood be gone by the time he returned.

"I SHOULD THINK you'd be out of here like a hare out of a trap, Lillias. Off to the Galleria or The Row or some such."

Ironically, her punishment for smoking a cheroot had concluded nearly in time for all of them to move out of The Grand Palace on the Thames. The snake, still malingering on their townhouse premises, had been successfully lured into a basket thanks to Mr. Delacorte's friend. Workmen were even now beginning to patch the walls. They could be home again soon. "I would prefer you not to behave like one, if you would," her father added hurriedly. "A hare out of a trap."

"Thank you, Papa, but I've seen the error of my ways and I think I'd like to spend a little more time in quiet contemplation."

He scowled at her, unconvinced.

She gazed back at him innocently.

The funny part was that it was true.

Well, apart from the "error of her ways" bit.

And so her family scattered out on errands and entertainments, and Lillias took her sketchbook and the books she'd had sent from her father's library to Helene Durand Memorial Park and sat on the bench.

And this time she drew.

But first she contemplated.

She'd been altered in a fundamental way. She could now call forth a memory that made her weak and hot and desperate, that made some parts of her throb and other parts of her go erect, and she was certain Mr. Delacorte would make a fortune if he should ever import a pill or a tea that possessed similar powers. She'd liked it too much and had regretted its end. She was irrationally furious with Hugh Cassidy—for knowing more, for making his point, for *winning*—and grateful to him, which she wasn't quite prepared to admit, and likely never would.

Mainly because it was probable she would never see him again.

He'd gone to Sussex (Mr. Delacorte had mentioned this in the sitting room last night) and then to Surrey, and she and her family ought to be back in their own home any day.

He was walking away with a few of her secrets, and she was certain he both understood them and would keep them—after all, their worlds did not and would not intersect from this day forward. But she felt as though she knew some of his, too.

How he felt (hard as a wall, safe as a house, dangerous as a wild animal), how he smelled (sweat, sawdust, smoke, musk, sex), how he tasted (like sin, if sin was a liqueur)—taken together they should have all comprised an adventure. And a lesson. And then be rapidly consigned to history.

But now she felt strangely, ever so slightly diminished. Or depleted. As if something vital had been lost. Or as if something nearly gained had slipped from her grasp. Not dissimilar to when she'd ruined her Heatherfield sketchbook.

She had been telling the truth when she said she'd wanted to be alone. Her thoughts and body were not quite done with Hugh Cassidy and she wanted to sit and reverberate a bit, the way she would after listening to a favorite piece of music.

So she read her book—about Native American tribes, as it so happened. One her father had never opened in his own library. One she might never have chosen to read before.

And she drew.

THE RULES OF The Grand Palace on the Thames allowed guests to entertain other guests in the parlor, a contingency meant to forestall orgies or other untoward nonsense one might attempt in rooms upstairs. Their rigorous but kind interview process had thus far ensured that no rogues or roguesses were admitted . . . for long, anyway.

It was this rule that compelled the Earl and Countess of Vaughn to entertain the Marquess and Marchioness of Landover that evening in the little sitting room of The Grand Palace on the Thames. For the Earl of Vaughn was a man of his word, and he had not only purchased a grand set of curtains—which Mr. Cassidy had returned with just hours ago, and was even now hastening to hang in the ballroom—it transpired that he had extolled the delights of The Grand Palace on the Thames to the marquess in White's and mentioned that they would soon be hosting first-class entertainments in their ballroom.

"Well. What a pleasant establishment."

Mr. Delacorte, Captain Hardy and Delilah, Lord Bolt and Angelique, and Dot were arranged in chairs about the room. It was a typical evening, apart from the somewhat uneasy volume of aristocrats in the room.

"Year after year our ball is quite the crush, you see, as we've so many dear friends and they seem to grow in number year after year," the Marquess of Landover explained.

None of the people in the room were invited to the ball apart from the earl and countess. None of them minded.

"As do mine," Mr. Delacorte enthused. "Friends are wonderful. Why, just look about the room—everyone here is a friend now! And thanks to my friend McBride, an apothecary in St. Giles, we found a gentleman who was able to coax a poisonous snake from Lord Vaughn's townhouse using only a few dead snakes for bait and a brazier. They like warmth, you see. Snakes. It's on its way to a new home even now."

Lady Landover's eyes got wider and wider as this revelation wound toward its conclusion. She stared at Mr. Delacorte as if not one word of what he'd just said had been in English.

"They named the snake after me, as it so happens. Stanton," Delacorte added.

She carefully lowered her teacup.

"Are you in . . . trade, Mr. Delacorte?" the marchioness tried delicately. She was making a valiant attempt to decipher him.

"We are all in trade," Lucien said, smoothly. "The Triton Group. Imports and exports. Tea, silk, spices, and other fine things."

"Oh, yes yes yes yes yes," the marquess said politely. "Real goers, all of you. I've heard talk of you at the clubs."

"I do like silk. And spices," Lady Landover said kindly. "And tea."

"Fortunately for us, nearly all of England shares your tastes." Captain Hardy and Lord Bolt smiled at her, which meant she received a potent dose of smiling, indeed. All at once.

She dimpled.

Who knew such pleasant men could be found by the docks?

She turned to Dot, who'd been staring, rather awestruck. "And young lady, you are . . ."

"I'm Dot, Lady Landover," Dot said. Shyly. She'd read about Lady Landover in the broadsheets.

"And what do you do?"

"I answer the door. And bring the tea." She did a lot of other things, too, but those were her favorites, and awe kept her from expounding.

Or blinking.

This fixed stare gave the Marchioness pause. "Ah," she said brightly. "We've fifty or sixty people on our staffs who do that for us."

Dot merely continued staring.

Delilah and Angelique struggled not to exchange a glance. If they were being perfectly honest, they'd been a little desperate when Delacorte had shown up at the door right after they'd first opened for business. They'd liked him then. But now they knew they'd choose him over a marquess for a guest at any time. When they were fortunate to have any sort of choice, that was.

"Where are your darling offspring, this evening, Vaughn?" the marquess wanted to know. "Lillias, St. John, Claire?"

"Oh, St. John is out doing what young men do. I think he went to his club. He'll be in by eleven o'clock. Claire is reading. Lillias had a *mal de tête* and was tucked up in our comfortable rooms. Quite cozy. But I expect she'll be down to join us any minute. She's *so* looking forward to the ball."

Lillias had in fact not emerged from her room for much at all over the past four days, even though she was free to roam, if she chose. She'd declined invitations to ride in The Row or to the museum with her mother and sister. But she'd taken a renewed and rather passionate interest in her watercolors and drawing, and they attributed her sudden re-hibernation to that. This seemed like something to condone. Such an elegant, ladylike endeavor.

"So many engagements have been announced this season and others are anticipated! I wonder when Lillias will make some man the happiest man in the world?" This was the way Lady Landover decided to disguise prying as a compliment.

"Well, she receives about one proposal a week, of course," Lady Vaughn said.

"But she's a woman of singular and particular tastes, like her mother, ha ha," the earl added.

The countess smiled politely. One got the sense

she'd heard that particular joke from her husband a number of times before.

"Well, it's *quite* the fashionable thing to claim to be smitten with her. Of course, our dear Henry is just sixteen, or she might have been able to nab him. And there will be a good deal of competition for *him*, of course, when he's of age. As he'll be a marquess."

This last bit didn't need to be explained to anyone in the room.

"We hope to announce an engagement soon," the earl said. Which wasn't entirely untrue. There was at least a hope.

Delilah and Angelique exchanged surprised glances. This hadn't so much as been intimated during their previous evenings in the sitting room.

"Oh, *my*! Is that so?" Lady Landover touched a hand to her collarbone. "Well, that would be happy news, indeed. I know the *ton* waits with barely suppressed excitement to know who will finally win her. And everyone looks forward to hearing what she will wear to the ball."

Only two people in the room were invited to the ball, but no one cared. They were interested in the commerce aspect of the evening.

"I wonder if you'd like to have a look at the ballroom while you're here?" Lord Vaughn, doing his promised duty, suggested.

"Oh, yes," Delilah said. "We're very proud of it. We'll be hosting musical guests and other entertainments there and we'd so love to hear what you think of the room."

"Oh, what a charming idea!" Lady Landover enthused. "We should love to see it."

HUGH STEPPED DOWN from the ladder and walked the length of the curtains, seizing soft handfuls of it, shaking them out until they lay in fat, lustrous, smooth pleats. The hems trailed the ground ever so slightly, looking like ladies in ball gowns, and he'd haggled with the butler charged with facilitating the transaction to get him to turn over the heavy tasseled cords that came with them for no additional cost. They would now glide smoothly open from either behind the stage or in front of it via a cord.

He couldn't wait to see the expressions on Delilah's and Angelique's faces when they saw them. He smiled at the thought. Then the smile dimmed. He wondered if he'd be present for any of the entertainments held in this ballroom. Or whether he'd be on his way home soon.

His instincts told him the latter was likely. It ought to have been a more thrilling prospect to contemplate.

He'd been five days away from London; he'd gone from fetching the curtains in Sussex to Surrey to visit the Clay family. When he'd called at their genteel farm, he'd been told by a servant that none of the family was home at present. They were in Bath, apparently. They were expected home within a fortnight. He'd inquired directly about a Miss Woodley, giving her description. He'd only been recently hired, the footman who'd answered the door told him. He regretted that he was unable to answer questions about a Miss Woodley.

Hugh thought that was an interesting way to phrase it. *Unable* to answer questions.

They'd stared each other down, he and the footman.

After some hesitation over whether he even ought to do it—in case Miss Woodley intended to bolt if she knew she was being searched for—Hugh finally left his name and direction in London with the footman. Along with the message, "Your father misses you."

He'd no choice but to return to London. But he'd go back to Surrey at his first opportunity. He'd go to Bath, if he had to. He sensed he was close to the truth.

He wondered that the only notion he could currently muster about this was relief. Perhaps because he was too weary and too preoccupied.

He'd be leaving for Portsmouth to meet Uncle Liam in just a few days.

Once he'd returned to The Grand Palace on the Thames, he'd purposely gone straightaway to the ballroom to commence the hanging of the curtains.

Between this and traveling, if he was careful, he might never see the Vaughns again.

With that thought, he went motionless. As if to avoid jarring any inconvenient emotions loose.

He hesitated. Then he drew a bit of the soft weight of the curtains between his fingers and lived again the feel of the soft swell of Lillias's breast beneath his lips.

Lust nearly gave him vertigo. He closed his eyes against it.

The life of an aristocrat—her life—meant velvet anywhere, anytime. Velvet was cast away for other velvet when the whim for another color took you. Was this careless abundance better than fleeting moments of savoring rare pleasures? Did life—did a kiss—owe its sweetness to its brevity? To the fact that it would necessarily end?

He heard footsteps in the hallway outside the ballroom. Light and swift.

His heart lurched.

He went still.

The footsteps stopped.

He didn't dare turn around.

His heart had taken up a slow, hard drumming. He wasn't certain whether he wanted them to keep going, past the door.

He slowly turned.

Lillias was standing at the doorway. As surely as if the mere thought of rare pleasure had conjured her.

She was wearing a shade of marigold silk trimmed in copper ribbon and it colluded with the mahogany of her hair.

Damned if it wasn't exactly like the first time he'd seen her.

It was like a blow to the head. It was a collision with some cosmic force he could never hope to understand. He was no hero, bear or no bear. He was Achilles. She was his velvet-clad heel.

"I hope I'm not intruding," she said very formally.

"Not at all." His voice sounded husky and formal in his own ears.

"I wasn't certain whether I should . . . whether you'd want . . ." She stopped.

He couldn't say a word.

"The curtains look beautiful." She stepped into the room and mounted the little stairs to the stage, and he tracked her every move. "I saw the door open and I . . . I thought . . . I understand you're leaving for Portsmouth to meet your Uncle Liam soon."

"Yes. In two days' time. It's kind of you to remember. I'm very much looking forward to seeing him."

They were speaking as though they'd just been handed a script.

She smiled uncertainly. "We will be gone from The Grand Palace on the Thames and back in our home for good before you return."

He went still. "Is that so?"

"Apparently a friend of Mr. Delacorte's experienced some luck capturing the snake. Alive, as it so happens. And the repairs in the walls are already underway."

"Delacorte told me this was a possibility. That is altogether good news, particularly for the snake. Unless it had snake kittens."

She didn't smile.

He didn't move any closer.

Neither did she.

It seemed preposterous that this fierce, untenable, intimate association should come to an end so quietly. It had been such a consuming force. It had turned him raw side out. He ought to be relieved, the way one appreciated the drama but was pleased when a storm had spent itself.

"Well. I was on my way to the sitting room to visit with my parents and their friends. I would like to say goodbye and good luck," she said.

"Well. Goodbye and good luck, Lady Lillias."

She nodded once.

She looked away from him and he studied her

profile as if it were the notches on a mysterious key. That line of her nose, the rose swell of her lips, the luscious dips and curves of her body.

He knew what was worth living for and dying for.

He had never before entertained what might be worth risking eternal damnation for.

And suddenly he was convinced there was only one thing.

"Lillias," he said softly. He stepped forward.

He gently touched her arm. She turned to him as though he were the sun and she a sunflower. And then she was against his body and in his arms.

He kissed her with absolutely no quarter. As though they were longtime lovers. With greed and desperation. They both knew this needed to be fast. With their arms locked around each other, she met him with a hunger that fanned his own too quickly, too hot. He moved his hand to cup her breast and then his thumb grazed the bead of her nipple pressed against her bodice. He took her gasp of stunned pleasure into his mouth with a kiss. He thought he might face a firing squad if only he could hear that sound over and over for the first time. He did it again, harder. And this time his reward was his name, *Hugh*, turned into a breathy sob of pleasure in his ear.

He thought he heard voices, faintly, distantly; it was as though they were a memory, the rag-ends of a dream. Perhaps it was just the echoes of the tattered, battered regiment that was all that remained of his conscience attempting to get his attention. And he thought perhaps he'd heard footsteps. Though that sound could have been the thud of his heart or hers. And as she moved her hips against his, he groaned an oath and took that kiss deeper and harder, the plunge and stroke of his tongue mimicking what his cock would never get a chance to do, and shifted his hands to grip her buttocks and pull her hard up against his body.

And this is what the Earl and Countess of Vaughn, the Marquess and Marchioness of Landover, Captain Hardy, Lord Bolt, Delilah, Angelique, and Delacorte saw when the curtain was whipped merrily aside.

Chapter Thirteen

❧

THE ENSUING gasps probably siphoned any lingering dust, and possibly a lingering spider or two, from the rafters.

There followed a silence like the end of time. And as if the building itself had detonated and blotted the sun, and now all the smoke had finally shifted and cleared to reveal all of those people standing there.

Hugh's awareness seemed to fracture into crystalline fragments, each of them distinct, each of them possessed of its own sense of time, and it wasn't unlike perusing a battlefield or aiming at a target. And that was how he saw and felt a hundred little things simultaneously: Mrs. Hardy and Mrs. Durand nearly colliding midair as they gracefully leaped to block the views of the Marquess and Marchioness Landover while Captain Hardy and Bolt and Delacorte performed a sort of reel in their efforts to surround the Earl and Countess of Vaughn.

All the mouths opened in little dark circles.

All the eyes above them white with shock.

He'd immediately shoved Lillias behind him, on the off chance it was not too late to disguise her identity. He could feel her breathing against him. It made him fierce with the need to protect.

No one said a word for what seemed like an eternity.

And then:

"Lillias?" Lady Landover said on a stunned hush that seemed to echo and echo. "Lady Lillias Vaughn?"

Speaking of eternal damnation.

Son of a bitch, as his Uncle Liam might have said.

But suddenly he was coldly clear. He'd destroyed Lillias's reputation before the kinds of witnesses who fed gossip to the broadsheets the way rivers fed the ocean. He'd destroyed his own, for that matter.

And he may have destroyed that of The Grand Palace on the Thames.

There was only one thing he could do.

He silently aimed a request for help up to whatever deity or celestial entity would have mercy on him. He must have been heard, because he found the words. His mouth moved, and haltingly, but with remarkable coherence, the words emerged.

"We must beg for your forgiveness, as we never dreamed there was a possibility we might startle or offend. We sought privacy to celebrate the joy and solemnity with which we move forward into the next years of our lives. For you are looking upon the happiest man alive. Lady Lillias has agreed to be my wife. Our union awaits only the blessing of her parents."

Her parents were utterly motionless.

They were riveted in what appeared to be

amazement and horror, as if snake kittens had popped from the wall.

Lady Landover clapped a hand over her heart and her mouth dropped again.

"That is the prettiest speech I've ever heard." She quickly fumbled for a handkerchief and dabbed the corner of her eye.

"I always *thought* Mr. Cassidy should be on stage," said Mrs. Pariseau, proudly.

"Oh, is that his name? Mr. Cassidy! My heavens, how original of you, Lillias, to choose a *Mr.* Cassidy. And an American, at that!"

"Does this make him a rogue?" Delacorte said quietly and received a quick sharp elbow in the ribs from Lucien.

"Oh, my, Lady and Lord Vaughn, you sly things! Is this what you meant when you said you suspected her engagement was imminent?" This was Lord Landover.

Wide and perilous as the ocean was the silence that followed this question.

Hugh could hear Lillias's breathing behind him.

"We knew of their attachment," the earl said very, very slowly, sounding as though he'd just been handed a stone tablet engraved in Turkish and was translating it aloud into English. But his tone was interestingly thoughtful. Like a judge handing down a sentence. "And they . . . have our blessing."

Hugh could feel Lillias go rigid behind him. She'd stopped breathing.

"Well, isn't that exciting news!" Lady Landover said gleefully. "Congratulations, you darling, rascally young ones. You must bring Mr. Cassidy to our ball. It's typically quite a crush, but we can of course make an exception for Lillias's fiancé."

That was the first time anyone had used that word.

Both Hugh and Lillias flinched.

DELILAH AND ANGELIQUE ferried the marquis and marchioness swiftly away, followed by Dot and Mrs. Pariseau.

"My heavens, how very exciting and romantic," the marchioness ventured. "Do romantic things often happen at The Grand Palace on the Thames?"

"*Very* often," Angelique said, sensing a publicity opportunity.

"I'll have a word with you in a moment, Mr. Cassidy," the Earl of Vaughn said icily as he and his wife flanked their daughter.

Lord Bolt, Lucien, and Delacorte had surrounded Mr. Cassidy, managing to look both like jailers and medics.

Lillias was similarly escorted away by her terrifyingly silent parents.

In their suite, Claire was lounging on a settee, legs hooked over the arm of it, reading *The Ghost in the Attic* by holding it straight over her eyes. It was a peculiar way to read and her mother despaired of it.

She gaped in astonishment when the three appeared, each parent holding Lillias by one arm.

"Go to your room, Claire," the earl ordered.

Such was his tone that she scrambled upright, seized the book, and disappeared. Lillias's last view of her was the whites of her eyes before she closed the door.

Lillias was compelled down into the place she'd vacated on the settee.

And for a moment her parents hovered over her.

She was at a grave disadvantage. She felt her full complement of wits hadn't yet returned, after they'd been kissed into oblivion by Hugh Cassidy, and her body was humming with the remnants of a boiling, unsatisfied need. And the shock of it all prevented the true horror of what had just happened from sinking in, but she knew she was engaged. There was really no getting out of that.

They didn't speak for quite some time.

"Darling, your hair. I just . . ." Her mother put her hand to her mouth.

It wasn't really about her hair, which had been used by Mr. Cassidy to tug her head back for a soul-branding kiss and likely showed the effects. It was also, probably, a little sweaty.

It was just the metaphor for how disordered everything had become in a shocking second. And this on the heels of a recaptured snake. Just when the holes had been repaired, Lillias had gone and essentially, metaphorically, shot a few more holes into their house.

"It was the frank talk with the word 'naked,' wasn't it?" her mother said.

"Oh, honestly, Mother, do you think I haven't heard that word before? I know what it means. We've been to the museum. Literally everything in there is naked." It was an exaggeration, but it made her point.

"It's the peculiar alchemy of a handsome, charismatic man and the word 'naked,' perhaps."

It was very, very odd to hear her mother describe Hugh that way, because it sounded like approbation, and this was unnerving. Because she'd already begun to hope that her parents would help to extricate her from this.

"There is no one thing or one person to blame," Lillias said flatly.

She was not going to sacrifice Hugh, who had fallen on his sword with the most astonishing speech she'd ever heard, thereby saving and ruining both of their lives.

But this wasn't what her parents wanted to hear, because that left open the probability of their daughter dallying away over the past fortnight.

Her father's silence was beginning to be more terrifying than the dawning acceptance of her fate.

"Well, I suppose there are worse ways to begin a marriage than with a bit of passion," her mother mused. "Why, your father and I still—"

Lillias threw her arms up over her head. "NO. OH GOD. I can't. Please."

Her mother stopped.

"I'll admit I imagined you as a duchess or a countess," her mother said somewhat querulously. If she began to cry, Lillias would cry and perhaps not stop.

Literally everyone had. Lillias couldn't sort one single complete distinct emotion from the murky soup of shame, shock, horror.

"Darling, you talk to her. I need to lie down for a moment."

Her mother disappeared into her bedroom.

This is what she'd done to her mother. She'd literally shocked her into needing to lie down, which had never happened for as long as Lillias had known her.

The quality of her father's continued silence was like the aftermath of a dropped anvil.

Lillias waited.

Anything he said was bound to shock her. The very air on her skin right now seemed to hurt.

"You could do much worse than young Mr. Cassidy. I rather wish he was my own son."

Nothing, nothing he'd said could have shocked her more.

His tone was almost reasonable. She began to panic.

"Then he'd be my brother, and if you think the broadsheets are going to outdo themselves with *this* story . . ." she said bitterly.

She trailed off at his incredulous—almost wounded—stare.

Lillias felt tears of frustration begin to press against her eyes.

"I don't feel as though I know you anymore, Lillias. Have I failed you in some way?"

"No, Papa. Not at all. It wasn't you or Mama."

"Then . . ."

How could she possibly explain?

"Papa . . . what if Mr. Cassidy was just . . . falling on his sword, so to speak?"

"Well, I'd of course have him killed at once for having the temerity to trifle with the daughter of an earl, of course."

Lillias's limbs iced.

"Oh, for heaven's sake. Of course I wouldn't have him killed. I'd have you killed."

At least he was joking again.

Mostly.

"Lillias, it's a nonsense use of time to entertain the question because surely neither you nor Mr. Cassidy would do anything so stunningly foolish for the lark of it. You'd only do it because true, true love gave you absolutely no choice in the matter."

This was all said quite tersely and ironically. He carefully did not ask whether she was in love with Mr. Cassidy, which was somehow better and somehow worse. Her father wasn't one to entertain illusions.

She was quiet. Shame, and regret. Those emotions were nice and distinct now.

"So. Congratulations on your engagement, Lillias. It seems you have gone and chosen yourself a husband. It's not quite how we envisioned it happening, but I wish you every happiness and we will support you in this matter."

Lillias pressed her hands against the settee. It suddenly seemed as though the earth had cracked open and she was slowly, little by little, sinking into it.

"We will be attending the Landover Ball, and since Mr. Cassidy is now invited, you will introduce him as your fiancé. Because you can be certain Lady Landover will dump this little bit of news into the stream of *ton* gossip like whiskey in a bowl of ratafia. We will make it very clear that he is everything we dreamed of in a member of the family. *Everyone* will want to get an American fiancé from the wilds of New York after this, because it is such a wondrous thing. Am I making myself clear? You will speak of him glowingly, as will I and your mother, and we will make a silk purse of this. And as I said, it isn't quite how we envisioned your life *or* ours, but in the end we'd like you to be happy, and that means St. John will have to make a spectacular match. Or Claire."

She couldn't speak. Her limbs were icy and a knot in her throat prevented words from escaping. Her status in society, the life she'd envisioned . . . she'd thrown them away for a chance to kiss . . . a stranger. For that's how he seemed now, when his arms and lips weren't on her. When she'd known all those other boys in the *ton* nearly her entire life.

She almost didn't dare ask the question.

But not asking it would be the height of foolishness.

"Papa . . ." Her voice was shamefully small. "What if I don't want to marry him?"

Her father went still.

And then he sighed.

He sat down on the settee across from her, leaned forward with his hands folded, and regarded her with a complicated expression. Sympathetic, just a little. Affectionate, just a little. But utterly implacable.

"I assume you're asking a hypothetical question because surely it can be nothing else, as, clever as you are, you would have considered the following things. To wit: since your . . ." her father closed his eyes, then issued the word the way one might squeeze a shirt through a laundry press ". . . embrace . . . was witnessed by the people in a position to report in exaggerated detail the events of the evening, it would indeed become part of the *ton*'s flow of gossip. Rowlandson might make salacious drawings of it. Remember the caricature of Olivia Eversea we saw in *Ackerman's Repository*? Cobwebs hanging from her. Merciless and very funny, or so we thought at the time. Yours, of course, would be so *much* worse because of all the people who actually witnessed it. And *how* they would laugh and laugh at all of us. But most especially at you. Because you . . . would . . . be ruined."

Those last words he delivered as one might hammer in a few final nails.

"Of course." Her voice was frayed. Black dots scudded before her eyes. "Well, certainly. Noted."

"And then, of course, you'd have to take into consideration the matter of what it would mean for Claire's or St. John's prospects in marriage and society, and how this reflects on your mother and me. Once besmirched, a family's reputation can remain that way for generations, if not forever. And our history has been pristine, if uneventful. This is not an accident of fate. Generations of Vaughns have understood the value of a family name and have taken pains to protect it. We are not a family of saints. But we are, thus far, a family of people who exercise *discretion*."

Those last two words were delivered with a certain punishing exactitude.

She couldn't remember her father ever using the word "besmirched" before, and for some reason it was that that burned away a little of her shock and revealed to her the true horror of her circumstances.

Not the least of which was this: Mr. Cassidy's little speech had pulled her back from the razor's edge of ruin.

A stubborn little voice inside her insisted: *But it wasn't my fault that we were caught. I was exercising discretion.*

What other possible end could there be to their dalliance? It was explosive all along, and it had concluded, like any good show of fireworks, like a Roman candle going up.

"And so, given your nimble mind, Lillias, I do wonder what your solution would be if, as you say, you did not want to marry him. It certainly poses a fascinating intellectual conundrum."

There was quite a long pause.

"I suppose I'll have to sleep on it," she said carefully.

"You do that." He stood up with a great sigh and headed for the door. "If you can. Now, I'm off for a word with Mr. Cassidy."

"He wants to live in America," she called after him, rather desperately.

"Well, *that's* not going to happen," her father said, almost mildly.

He shut the door behind him.

HUGH WAS IN the smoking room.

He couldn't quite remember how he'd gotten here. He couldn't, in fact, quite feel his own limbs.

He felt a bit like a ghost at his own funeral.

After his burst of eloquence everything was a bit of a blur, as if every bit of his emotional and physical resources had been spent.

The hush, despite the presence of the three other men staring at him, was dense as the carpet.

Six eyes—Bolt's, Hardy's, and Delacorte's—were fixed upon him. It occurred to him that this was likely how he'd gotten there. They'd somehow escorted him away from the stage and back into The Grand Palace on the Thames's main building.

Those eyes were variously amused, pitying, sympathetic, and wondering, the expression shifting across them the way light glanced from mirrors.

Still, nobody spoke.

He *ought* to smoke. It would clear his head. The act of selecting a cigar, lighting it. The soothing familiar ritual.

He reached for the humidor. He was shocked to see his hand shaking badly.

He pulled it back as though it had betrayed him and thrust it into his coat pocket. The hand that had so recently touched a trembling, sighing Lillias.

His breath stopped for an instant.

Lucien was the first one to speak.

"Perhaps we ought to have discussed this during one of our evenings in this room . . . but getting caught is optional, Cassidy."

And at this Hugh moaned, sank down into the brown wing chair, bent forward at the torso, and crossed his arms over the top of his head, as though a boulder were hurtling out of the sky toward him.

Although of course, metaphorically, the boulder had already struck.

He breathed in.

He breathed out.

He heard his own breath as though he were

inside his little cabin in New York and the wind outside was battering at it.

Then he became aware of a faint shuffling sound, which he suspected was his friends gathering around him, and the reassuring sound of a bung being plucked from a decanter.

Delacorte cleared his throat. "I was surprised you were able to get an entire handful of her derriere," he said gravely. "I always imagined she was made of marble."

Hugh slowly levered up his head and stared at him in rank amazement.

"*Tink tink.*" Delacorte tapped the air with his forefinger. Illustrating, presumably, the sound a marble derriere would make. Interpreting the incredulous stares as need for clarification.

"Some circumstances are better served by quiet commiseration, Delacorte," said Captain Hardy, who thought every circumstance could be improved if only everyone just stopped talking.

"Oh, yes, of course, I take your point." Delacorte lowered his voice to just a notch above hushed, bent until his limpid blue eyes were level with Hugh's, and tenderly placed a hand on his shoulder. "She is terrifying and I am truly sorry for you, my friend. But I sincerely wish you every happiness."

Then he stood back and clasped his hands, eyebrows locked in a worried position.

Hugh continued to stare at him. But Delacorte said every word of what he meant. There were few enough men in the world like that.

"Thank you," Hugh managed finally, with great irony. His voice was a dry croak. He supposed it was a good thing that somewhere in the smoke and wreckage of his life, his sense of humor was still alive.

"Drink this." Hardy thrust a glass at him.

Hugh bolted it. Then coughed.

It was whiskey.

It burned a path down his gullet and he gasped, and suddenly he felt clearer but he didn't know if that was better.

"I don't suppose you're in love?" Bolt mused. As though this predicament he was in—not so much a predicament as a cataclysmic event reshaping the landscape of his life, like an earthquake— was a problem that could be solved once Bolt had enough information.

"I'm not entirely certain we even *like* each other. But she's . . ."

They waited.

"She's . . ."

They leaned forward.

"We've naught in common except . . ."

Whiskey was truth serum, damn it.

"Ah, yes," Bolt said. "That 'except' will get you every time. But here's a hint: don't say that to her father."

Hugh glared balefully at Lucien.

"I've never been so grateful to not be handsome," Delacorte mused. "Resisting all that temptation to become a rogue must be exhausting."

"I'M NOT A ROGUE."

Was he?

"Of course not," Delacorte humored him sooth- ingly, shooting an "if you say so" sidelong glance at Lucien and Captain Hardy.

Hugh gulped a few breaths.

"Bolt here was the one with a Moroccan mistress. And wasn't there a soprano who threw a vase at your head? I think those are in the *How to Be a Rogue* handbook."

"Are you implying I might be a rogue? I'm an upright, somber married man now and will be for the rest of my life." Bolt paused theatrically. "As you soon will be, too. For the rest . . . of . . . your . . . life."

"You're lucky I don't have a vase to hand right now, Bolt."

Bolt grinned, lit a cigar, sucked it into life. And then he leaned down and gently tucked it into Hugh's hand.

Hugh gripped it as though he'd been thrown a lifeline.

"She's a beautiful girl, Cassidy, and if you'll forgive the Delacortian bluntness, she looked as though she knew what she was about. Once the children come along you'll be kept so busy you probably won't have time to be miserable." This was Bolt.

Oh, God.

"Children," he repeated hoarsely. In incredulous horror.

"Stop torturing him, Bolt," Captain Hardy interjected. There was a pause. "It's my turn."

He took the empty glass from Hugh and poured another from the flask in his coat. So that's where the whiskey had come from. The ladies were wise enough not to stock anything much stronger than brandy in the smoking room.

He planted himself in front of Hugh and said

slowly, "Cassidy, did you consider how this dalliance of yours could reflect on the reputation of The Grand Palace on the Thames should it become discovered? Because it was *very* clear this wasn't the first time you and Lillias had done that."

For the first time he realized that Captain Hardy's silence, all this time, was really a sort of simmering anger.

"All I can say, Hardy, is . . . I saw the lay of things at once, as if I was floating up over my body. The people standing in front of me. The woman with me. The circumstances. The consequences for everyone, for me, for Lillias, for her family, for The Grand Palace on the Thames. I knew I needed to act immediately and decisively in order to shape a story and so I did."

Hardy studied him. "I think that was some of the quickest and bravest thinking I've ever seen a man do. And all without firing a shot."

Hugh thought, but didn't add, ". . . and with an erection, to boot."

He smiled faintly, humorlessly. "You should have seen me in the war."

"I wish I had a man like you when we're running smugglers to ground."

Hugh nodded once at the high compliment this was, which was probably much more than he deserved in the moment.

All the men were somberly quiet a moment.

He'd so hoped that life from now on would be free of battles.

"Every moment of my life has been considered. But with her . . . when I'm near her . . ."

Her. Even now the word caused an anticipatory

ripple along his traitorous nerve endings; even now his muscles were tightening in anticipation, bracing for the glut of pleasure.

She was no safer than opium. Opium only led to disaster.

And what was this if not a disaster?

All three pairs of eyes aiming at him were now sympathetic and thoughtful. Both Bolt and Hardy understood that any man, no matter how formidable, could become Achilles when the right woman—or the wrong one—came along. Delacorte only wanted a cozy domestic life and a woman who adored him for who he was.

But no one was offering suggestions for a way out of this. And that was because, given the facts at hand, there *was* no other way out of this.

He unconsciously gripped the edge of his chair, as though if he held on strongly enough he could keep the life he'd imagined for himself from snapping its tether, sailing away from him, lost forever. Cornflower-blue eyes and corn silk hair and a gentle laugh seemed like an echo now.

"Cassidy . . ."

Hugh looked up at the sound of Hardy's voice. "There's no shame in wanting to lose yourself for a little while." He said it quietly. "We could all use a little forgetting now and again."

Hugh locked eyes with Captain Hardy. He was surprised but he didn't let it show. He didn't much like being seen so clearly. He wasn't certain he liked knowing that he'd destroyed his entire future for something so human, so universally banal, as lust and . . . forgetting.

"I probably have a thing or two in my case that'll

keep you from thinking, if you'd like." Delacorte said. "I'll have a look!"

"Thank you, but no. I don't run away from consequences. I will see this through."

"Weren't those the last words of Big Bartholomew Bellamy before he went to the gallows?" Lucien mused.

Delacorte snapped his fingers. "I thought I'd heard them somewhere before."

And then they all turned at the sharp rap on the door.

THE OTHER THREE men filed out.

Hugh was left alone in the room with the Earl of Vaughn.

Despite the fact that the Earl had said, "I'd like a word with Mr. Cassidy," he said nothing for a good long while. He studied him thoughtfully, almost quizzically, from the opposite side of the room. He didn't reach for the cigars or the brandy.

Hugh met the scrutiny head on, without blinking, without flinching.

There wasn't an expression in the world that could break him, even as he died a thousand deaths internally. He could only guess at some of the things the earl was thinking.

Finally Hugh spoke. "Lord Vaughn, I deeply regret the manner in which you learned of our attachment."

The earl barked a laugh. "*You* regret it," he said dryly. "Like a bloody show at Piccadilly, the curtain going up, there you were."

Hugh didn't say, "You'd have to pay dearly for

that sort of show." He was in an agony of shame and disbelief.

And then another moody silence ensued.

"I was young once, Cassidy. I did a few inadvisable things. Not on stage, mind you."

Oh God.

"Yes, sir."

"Here is the thing," the earl said. "While I'm tempted to issue a more vociferous objection and castigation based on the circumstances—in other words, I'm tempted to have you hog-tied and flogged—the truth is I think you will be good for Lillias. She is strong-willed and too clever for her own good and I think you are just the man to keep her in line and protect her from herself. Her settlements are generous and will enable you to dabble in business here while you keep her in the manner to which she is accustomed. A house in Devon will be at your disposal. She is my oldest daughter. I'd dreamed of a grander match, of course, but her happiness is paramount to me."

It was a guillotine coming down.

Hugh stared at him. "Dabble."

What he wanted didn't matter, that much was clear, given the circumstances. And though it was more or less what he'd expected, the brief rote recitation of what his domestic life would be like—the cozy life in Devon, finances controlled by her father—settled like a cannonball on his chest. As did, oddly, the notion that Lillias ought to be "kept in line," something he might have concurred with some weeks ago. As though she was a pet requiring tethering, not a person with agency and original thoughts and restless desires.

"But I will not have you take her out of England to live," the earl said. "If you do, there will be no settlement at all. And while I do have some sympathy for your disappointed dreams, if you abandon her to return to America, I will see to your ruin. Do you understand me?"

Hugh breathed in and breathed out.

"Yes, sir. Upon my life, I will never abandon her," he said quietly.

"I know you won't. That's not the sort of man you are." The earl sounded almost sympathetic. "Congratulations. Welcome to the family."

Chapter Fourteen

❧❧❧

WORD CERTAINLY spread quickly.

Hugh realized this when he awoke much later than usual to a dark, cold room and the kind of pounding in his skull that made him immediately wish he could twist it off his neck and hurl it out the window. Memory sifted in—the glorious woman and the kind of kiss he'd told himself he'd risk damnation for followed by—surprise!—damnation. Two lives ruined and salvaged in one fell swoop, followed by sympathy whiskey and an Armageddon-like discussion with the Earl of Vaughn.

Surely he'd had a choice in all of it? It was only when he was away from Lillias that he felt he'd had a choice. He was honest enough about that.

How was *she* faring? He doubted anyone had fed her liquor.

He groaned and steadied his head between his hands.

The fire was all but dead. No steaming coffee or freshly baked scone awaited on a tray next to him.

The maids were punishing him.

Everybody's dreams had died last night, apparently.

This was when another chilling possibility occurred to him: Would he be evicted from Eden, aka The Grand Palace on the Thames? Certainly his transgression was dramatic enough. The rules allowed for it.

No worries: he was to have a cozy house in Devon, apparently.

The thought wrapped itself around him like leather straps.

He supposed, given the circumstances, he ought not be hungry.

But he was.

And so after a wash and valiant attempt at shaving steadily, he got into his clothes and went down to the dining room. It was empty, given that it was later than the usual breakfast hour. Helga had taken pity. Eggs and kippers and toasted bread, a little cold but he wasn't fussy, were waiting for him. An entire pot of coffee had been left for him, sympathetically and reproachfully.

It might have been his imagination, but the building seemed hushed. Anticipatory.

It was possible everyone was avoiding him.

Or holding a meeting about him.

And then, sauntering through the foyer, came St. John, holding his coat over one arm and his hat in the other.

They paused to stare at each other.

There was something of his sister in the bones of his face. He had his father's dark hair and his mother's blue eyes and likely his sister's knack for getting heads to pivot in his direction.

"Well, I suppose it's a fortunate thing for you

that you're bound to be a member of the family, Cassidy. Otherwise I should be obliged to challenge you to a duel."

"Whereupon I would be obliged to kill you, St. John, and it would be a shame to lay waste to all those female hearts and all your . . . potential," Hugh said politely.

St. John nodded politely in return. He shoved his hands into his pockets and looked up at the ceiling. Then back at Hugh. "I am quite fond of my sister. I don't know why."

It was perhaps about the last thing he expected St. John to say, and it was funny. Hugh might have said it about his own sister.

Hugh smiled faintly. "Good. She is . . . remarkable." Which was only the truth he was comfortable with saying out loud to her brother.

And it was this thought that brought home the enormity of what he had done. What the two of them had done.

"If you make her unhappy, I will find a way to free her from you."

A startling, rather ominous bit of gallantry. He issued a sort of half smile and damned if it wasn't almost convincingly threatening.

But it made Hugh like him better. "I would expect nothing less."

"I'm glad we're understood. I think I might like having a brother, even if he's an American." St. John leaned forward confidingly and said on a sort of hushed, only partly feigned anguish, "Two sisters is *hell*."

He moved on, Hugh staring after him. Then he

turned and walked backward a few steps. "See you at the ball. And, oh—you're going to need better clothes."

And as he turned to watch St. John going out the door, a dulcet voice came to him from the little reception room. "Good morning, Mr. Cassidy. May we have a word?"

He closed his eyes briefly. Said a silent prayer for strength.

He was a brave man, and as he'd told his friends the night before, he was unafraid to face consequences.

But Mrs. Hardy and Mrs. Durand were standing in the little reception room, their faces grave. A beautiful blonde and brunette tribunal.

He entered.

To his surprise, between them they were holding up a coat.

His heart lurched when he thought it might be his own black coat, and then his still-recovering brain realized he was already wearing it.

"If we'd known that's what you intended to do on that stage, Mr. Cassidy, we might not have been in such a hurry for you to finish building it," Angelique said.

Delilah appeared to be suppressing mirth.

Hugh smiled weakly.

"We put out word early this morning among tailors known to Lucien and Captain Hardy and were miraculously able to locate an evening coat that might well fit you, with a few alterations. Why don't you try it on?"

She held it out to him.

He stared at it, dumbstruck. He studied them warily.

"It's a coat, not a shroud, Mr. Cassidy. And it's a ball you're going to with the beautiful daughter of an earl, not a funeral. Though I daresay you'll look so well in it you could be buried in it."

He sensed a jest along the lines of, "And isn't that what's essentially happening?" would not go over well at the moment. The ice he trod upon was thin.

"I don't know how to thank you," he said humbly. "I do not deserve such kindness."

"If you're lucky, life is long, Mr. Cassidy," said Delilah. "And includes many, many acts."

He wondered if this was a sly pun about his on-stage clinch.

"And I am . . . so very, very sorry for how it transpired."

"Anybody would be," Angelique said gently.

He almost laughed.

He hesitated. Then he asked, "Are you disappointed in me?"

He genuinely liked these women. He held them in the highest esteem. He knew their good opinion was a valuable thing and not easily earned; the notion that they might be thinking he'd abused their kindness and hospitality made his throat feel tight.

"I think we have a sense of you, Mr. Cassidy. And in truth, we are the last people to judge. We will be disappointed if you are unhappy. We'll be disappointed if Lady Lillias is unhappy. For now, let's just make sure you have proper evening clothes."

And so Mrs. Hardy, Mrs. Durand, and Dot pinned

him into a new evening coat, and every now and then a pin missed and he was thoroughly jabbed.

He hadn't felt so loved and utterly chastised all at once since his mother was alive.

"You're going to marry *Mr. Cassidy*? You're so *lucky*."

"Claire. For heaven's sake." Her mother was startled by her younger daughter's effusion.

The three of them were at Madame Marceau's establishment in Bond Street, surrounded by three seamstresses wielding tape, pins, and needles.

"He's very handsome and kind. And interesting, too."

"He smiled at you once and these are your conclusions?" Lillias was terse.

"I have eyes and ears. For heaven's sake," Claire said, irritably. "I can draw my own conclusions."

"There are other qualities men ought to have, too, Claire. Good God, have I failed you both?" Her mother muttered this last sentence to the ceiling.

She was not entirely joking.

"I'm not daft, Mama," Claire said reasonably. "I know he hasn't a title or anything of the sort. But you'll have to look at him for the rest of your life and surely handsome counts for a very good deal if that's the case."

Her mother closed her eyes and muttered what could either have been a prayer or an oath.

"Don't worry, Mama, *I'm* bound to marry a duke." Claire winked at her sister.

Lillias was not in a mood to reciprocate winks. She had a headache. She had not slept much, if at all, she'd been so rigid and numb with disbelief all night.

And the ball was . . . tomorrow. She was so tired she'd forgotten to calculate the minutes. Shock was a lovely, lovely invention. It kept one from feeling all manner of unpleasant and nuanced things. She couldn't imagine alcohol doing a better job.

And yet. And yet. Her traitorous body could not but continue to relive what she had become very close to discovering in Hugh's arms behind the curtain. She'd been *so close* to something extraordinary.

"And isn't Gilly getting married soon, too?" Claire continued. "All the gossip in the newspapers seems to be hinting at it. And you'll see—"

"CLAIRE."

She wished everyone would stop talking, because all the words about her engagement were like threads thrown over a loom, and the more people talked about it the more tangible it seemed. The more it began to resemble a noose.

Claire was made of sturdy stuff. She never took offense.

"I didn't know you were in love with Mr. Cassidy," Claire said shyly, after a long silence.

"I'm not," she said reflexively. Her throat knotted.

Her mother's eyes hurled daggers' worth of warning at Lillias.

"But you were kissing him." Her sister was puzzled.

"*How* on earth did you . . ." Her mother was aghast.

"You learn absolutely nothing if you don't have wonderful hearing. And I have," Claire said. "I heard all of you talking about it."

"Well, that is certainly useful to know," their mother said acidly.

"I kissed him . . . because he is a very fine man," Lillias said carefully. "And in the moment it seemed like the thing to do."

Claire looked up at her, a little puzzled, as anyone would be.

And maybe it was because she was tired, and still rather underfed, but tears welled, filled her eyes, and spilled.

Because it was true. All of it. He was handsome (dear God, and how), she had kissed him, she did not love him, he was a fine man. And all of his dreams had come crashing down because they could not keep from kissing each other, and when she stood with her mother and her sister in a dress shop, not kissing him seemed like the easiest thing in the world to do. She had shocked and upset her family, confused Claire. And she would need to face the *ton* tomorrow with him by her side and see all manner of uncomfortable reactions reflected in the faces of people she had known her entire life, and her pride felt as though a whole layer had been scraped away. Everything hurt.

She stood in the rubble of shattered dreams while dressmakers spoke in hushed tones and tweaked and pinned the gossamer fabric of the little puffed net sleeves.

"Lillias, sweetheart." Her mother fumbled for a handkerchief. "She's to be married," she whispered to the dressmaker.

"*Mon dieu*, of course. So beautiful. The new brides, they are so emotional. If you could refrain from weeping on your dress, mademoiselle. The velvet about the bodice will stain."

SOMEWHAT PORTENTOUSLY, MRS. Hardy and Mrs. Durand were waiting for them in the now empty reception room when they returned with Lillias's ball gown. "I wondered if Lady Lillias would join us here for a moment? We won't be more than a minute or two," Mrs. Durand said.

"A gift for you," Mrs. Hardy hastily added, correctly intuiting from Lillias's expression that she anticipated some of the same iron-fist-in-velvet-glove censure they'd administered to her father (which she admittedly deserved, but didn't think she could bear).

Her mother and sister slipped discreetly away and left Lillias alone with the proprietresses, who invited her to sit down opposite them on the settee that had once supported, briefly, the bum of King George IV.

"We wanted to give this to you . . . by way of an engagement present."

Mrs. Durand held out to her a tiny package wrapped in tissue and tied with a blue ribbon.

Lillias hesitated. Then she took it into her hands and gave the little ribbon a tug, and parted the tissue. To discover a lovely little pair of satin garters, trimmed in lace.

She lifted her head. Her throat felt thick. "You are too kind to me after all I've . . . after what I've . . ."

Angelique was ready with a handkerchief and Lillias accepted it.

At the rate she was weeping today, the broadsheets would need to find a way to describe how well her red, puffy eyes suited her complexion and her ballgown. She dabbed. "Thank you so much." Her voice was thick. "I don't deserve it. I'm so sorry about . . . I apologize for . . ." She closed her eyes and took a long, long breath.

Then opened them and said, "I don't *know* myself anymore." She confided this almost wildly, on a cracked, amazed whisper. Half to herself, half to Delilah and Angelique.

The ladies exchanged a glance.

"We've come to suspect that knowing oneself is the work of a lifetime," Delilah said gently. "And this might not be reassuring at the moment, but you might in fact become a stranger to yourself a few more times over the years."

"Men are often useful when it comes to helping women discover themselves," Angelique added wryly. She didn't add, "sometimes by showing you what you *don't* want." "We think we have a sense of you, Lady Lillias . . . and we think you'll be equal to anything life sends your way."

What had Hugh said about these two ladies? That they had guts and wits and resourcefulness to spare. He admired them immensely. She understood fully why now.

"Mr. Cassidy is a good man," Delilah said cheerfully, so as not to make Lillias weep more. "And we wish you joy."

Simple words. They often sounded so rote: "We wish you joy."

She could sense that these two ladies had learned about joy the hard way, and so knew precisely what they were wishing her. Which made it feel like a benediction.

And God only knew she could use one.

SHE'D REMAINED IN her suite the entire next day. She'd ordered a bath and languished in it until she was thoroughly pink and scented and her mother fussed at her to hurry. She'd nibbled on a little bread and cheese at some point near noon, and bolted a few cups of tea, but she'd taken no actual dinner.

As a result, by the time they were to depart for the ball, Lillias didn't feel quite sober. But not in a pleasant way. Her head in fact felt light as a blown dandelion perched upon her shoulders, apt to float away if she were jarred slightly. She half wished it would. No one would expect a headless woman to go to the Landover Ball with her brand new American fiancé.

She hadn't seen Hugh since the proposal on stage.

And suddenly there he was in the foyer of The Grand Palace on the Thames, gleaming from a fresh shave and wearing evening clothes, a black coat that fit him like a pelt, a soft cravat pillowing the hard angles of his jaw, a waistcoat striped in gray and blue. He looked almost criminally fine. Otherworldly. Like a god who had suddenly materialized beneath the chandelier to drag her underground.

Unreasonably, she found she was a little relieved that he was near, as though life itself revealed itself to have a broken rung and he stood ready to swing her safely down.

His face was somber as he looked at her. He said
nothing.

But then there appeared on his lips the beginning of a smile, which spread slowly and became
crooked and rueful and almost reluctant. He gave
his head a slight, slow, disbelieving shake.

It might have been the most explicit compliment
she'd ever received.

The backs of her arms went hot.

She deserved it. She'd seen herself in the mirror before she'd come down the stairs. Worthy of
head turns, perhaps a gasp or two. She'd fastened
a small, simple diamond hung on a fine gold chain
at her throat; Claire had helped her put her hair up,
and with curling tongs they'd coaxed two loosely
spiraling curls to trace her cheekbones. Those were
her only adornments, unless one included her little
reticule. Everyone in the *ton* had looked forward
to seeing what she intended to wear. They were
unprepared, she thought, for what she intended to
bring.

But neither of them spoke.

What would she say? "How have you been since
I was pressed up against your erection?" "How
does it feel to act as though your life hasn't been
utterly ruined?" "Are you furious?" "Do you hate
me?" "Do you want me?"

He was clearly as tense as she was, and as full of
unspoken things. She warranted the inside of his
head buzzed with the same questions.

Although *he* hadn't had two entire months to
dread this particular night.

Her mother and father looked handsome indeed
together, as they always did. Her mother was in

long-sleeved dark green and pewter silk, and her father in a waistcoat striped in dark green. They'd adopted a brisk, rather serious "let's get on with it, then" air. Neither one of them was prepared to jolly Hugh or Lillias just yet.

They bundled into the waiting carriage. St. John would make his own way, as there was only room for four inside, and Claire was left to listen to Mrs. Pariseau read *The Ghost in the Attic* in the sitting room.

Horses and carriages stretched for what seemed nearly a mile before the Landover house. Atop them, coachmen and footmen passed flasks and shouted merrily to each other, and the horses nickered, shifted their feet, and lifted their tails and made liquid and solid deposits liberally and often. It was the typical dangerous little maze that led to any ball, and it could and did ruin dresses.

But just as he'd lifted her from the ladder the other night, Hugh reached up, fitted his hands about her waist and settled her and her hem down well out of harm's way.

"Thank you," she said almost shyly. The first words she'd said directly to him all evening.

"Always at your service," he said, touching his hat.

Which made her smile slightly.

But as they all drew closer to the lights and noise and music and the phalanx of footmen charged with ushering guests inside, her strength nearly failed her.

Chapter Fifteen

✺✺✺✺✺

LILLIAS HADN'T fully understood until she'd set foot into this house on this night that her expectations for her future had been as much a part of her as her own skeleton. Her entire being had grown around it. It had determined how she viewed and moved through the world, how she expected to be seen, addressed, read about, talked about.

And now that it had been quite shattered and replaced with something entirely new, everything seemed to require an odd new effort. Walking, seeing, speaking.

Her heart was jabbing away at her breastbone.

"Hold your head high," Hugh murmured. "Assume they already know. We'll enter as though we're the King and Queen of England."

Well, she could do that.

And soon it was clear that he could, too.

Lillias had made enough entrances into enough thronged ballrooms to understand how the glittering congregation could behave like a tide. How one exceptional person could start up a ripple of murmurs and rustles just by gliding through, like a hand over pianoforte keys. She had more than once been that person.

Tonight, that person was Hugh.

It was almost like a dance.

Postures everywhere straightened and male faces grew stern and alert, fans and eyelashes fluttered, kid-clad hands rose to touch a lip, move a curl behind an ear, touch a jaw, a necklace at a throat. Unconsciously or deliberately meant to point out their loveliest features to the man strolling through. If they were birds, Lillias thought, they'd all be singing their hearts out at the glory of the morning, as if he were the sun.

And then she saw the heads actually turn to watch him. Watch *them*, rather. For they were together, and this would be how they entered ballrooms and other rooms together for the rest of their lives.

The tension in her stomach coiled tighter.

And up the fans went, so gossip could be exchanged behind them.

She nodded and smiled, and her parents nodded and smiled, and Hugh, who knew nobody but the people he'd arrived with, smiled and every now and then, nodded.

It was apparent in the dream-like context of The Grand Palace on the Thames that he was different from other men. In a ballroom crammed with the cream of England's aristocracy, many of whom had known her since she was born, the contrasts became both heightened and distinct. It was instantly clear he was not *of* them. He'd been shaped by different forces.

He had the build of someone who'd labored hard and fought hard, who rode and strode over terrain more rugged than England's soft hills. He had the sensual grace and confidence born of knowing precisely who he was and what he was capable of. His confidence all but preceded him like a tide. One or two men took an unconscious step back.

"You look well together, at least," her mother said encouragingly. In a tone one might use to praise the quality paste copy of the family jewel.

She wondered if that "at least" would follow her marriage for the rest of her days.

"So do father's matched bays."

"And don't they get us to where we need to go?" her mother enthused ironically. And rather tersely. Her mother was losing patience with her.

Her mother had liked Mr. Cassidy well enough for someone who wasn't a gentleman, but she was juggling at least a dozen conflicting emotions as she made adjustments to her own dreams, too.

As through a dream, Lillias moved through the elegant crowd, the tension that had been coiling and coiling in her for two months now pulling ever tighter, until she was nauseous with it, and the voices of the room blended into a high whine in her ears. The final seconds of two months of dread seemed to throb in her ears like the boots of a firing squad advancing.

Ten . . . nine . . . eight . . . seven . . . six . . . five . . . four . . . three . . . two . . .

. . . One.

She saw Giles.

A BALLROOM. A battlefield. Was there a difference, really? The uniforms were different, but that's precisely what they were, whether they were silk and velvet or wool and stained with blood and gunpowder. They were there to indicate rank and status, to impress and intimidate. There wasn't a context Hugh couldn't navigate without some degree of competence. But he was never going to love a ballroom like this. An evening of pianoforte and dancing in a parlor suited him better, not this little jungle of gossip and competition, interrupted now and again by very good music and dancing, both of which he liked.

Hugh was no stranger to preening, and he appreciated the efforts on his behalf, and he smiled. So many lovely women. The young men all had a clean sameness to them. He imagined a hothouse full of them, rising out of rarified earth, their gloves and boots glossy as new leaves.

Suddenly some odd, inner jolt—as distinct as a finger-flick to the back of his neck, a feeling as though a song had come to an abrupt halt in the middle of a waltz—made him turn his head sharply.

Lillias was motionless. Not just motionless; it was as if her entire essence had retreated to the very center of her, as though she yearned to be invisible. He remembered her sitting like that in the drawing room at The Grand Palace on the Thames once or twice. As though she was enduring some private misery.

It would have to be a remarkable circumstance indeed that would make her yearn to be invisible.

Her eyes were fixed on one of the taller blokes.

Hugh narrowed his eyes and assessed him.

Like the others, he was otter-sleek in a lintless black coat, his neat square chin hugged by a cravat tied with what struck Hugh as unnecessary flair. His features were symmetrical. His hair was an artful toss of dark waves. If he had to, Hugh could probably pin him to the ground in less than a minute. Which was frankly the way Hugh assessed every man, even the ones he liked very much. (Delacorte: ten or so seconds, as he would be ticklish. Captain Hardy: a fight to the death. Lucien: would probably have a knife hidden in a convenient place on his person, but he could get the job done in an hour or so. Hugh was younger.)

The gleaming handsome bloke seemed to notice the quality of the attention fixed upon him, because he turned his head like a colt sniffing something dangerous on the wind.

He went still when he saw Lillias.

Anchored by a dimple, his smile began at one corner and spread into a slow curve. His eyes lit like twin sunrises. His teeth, square and blinding as pianoforte keys, appeared. Hugh had never seen such radiant delight.

The color drained from Lillias's cheeks as swiftly as if someone had pulled a bung.

Seconds later, a smile wobbled fitfully across her lips, as though a drunk puppeteer had gotten hold of their corners.

What the bloody hell was going on?

Hugh reflexively cupped Lillias's elbow and steadied her, because it seemed only seconds before her knees gave out.

The smiling man's eyes dropped to that little juncture of Hugh's hand and Lillias's elbow, and his face froze.

And then gracefully, leisurely, he separated from

his herd of brethren and strode over, aiming like an arrow for Lillias.

He had clearly decided to pretend that Hugh was invisible.

Hugh wished him luck with that. Hugh, who had never been invisible in his life, and who hadn't been raised on scrupulous English etiquette, still knew a snub when he experienced one. He was darkly amused. He could bide his time.

The man bowed.

Lillias managed to curtsy.

"Lilly. I was so looking forward to seeing you. Mother said a bit of renovation is taking place on your townhouse and you've been compelled to repair to a boarding house. It sounds rather colorful." His voice was so aristocratic.

Lillias seemed mute. That wobbly smile had shrunk, but still qualified as a smile.

"You are well? Your family is well?" the man prompted.

"All well, Giles. Is your family well?"

Ah, *Giles*, was it?

Where had he heard that name before?

"Mother, Father, Claire, and St. John are all well. Giles, I should like to introduce you to Mr. Hugh Cassidy."

Giles's head turned with what appeared to be a great, unnatural effort, as if his entire being was invested in pretending Hugh didn't exist.

He was forced to confront Hugh and his unblinking gaze.

"Your . . . dancing instructor?" Giles offered what was meant to be a puzzled little smile.

Hugh's smile was the metaphorical equivalent

of a finger drawn over a knife blade to test its sharpness.

He had the satisfaction of seeing Giles blink before he performed an elegant bow. "A pleasure, Lord Bankham. I've heard a good deal about you."

He'd heard absolutely nothing except his name. And now he recalled: Heatherfield.

"An American," Giles said predictably, because for heaven's sake, they all did.

"What a fine ear you have for accents, Bankham." The two stared at each other.

"Gilly . . ." Lillias cleared her throat. "That is, Giles, Lord Bankham, as we mentioned to you before, has been a family friend since we both were . . . very small."

"Since you fell into the pond . . ." Giles said, like a prompt to an old and beloved joke.

". . . and you tried to fish me out . . ." Lillias said weakly, smiling. "But then you . . ."

". . . fell in, too. And then you . . ."

". . . accidentally on purpose kicked you. Giles, Mr. Cassidy and I are engaged to be married."

Hugh saw the moment Giles stopped breathing.

And then Giles blinked as if something had been dashed into his face.

A long, strange moment passed during which Hugh merely observed, and the three of them seemed to be enclosed in a dome of silence while the ballroom full of revelers chattered, flirted, and gossiped behind them.

None of them spoke.

Lillias turned away to look at a cavorting statue, then down at her reticule. Then away again.

As if fantasizing about her escape path if she managed to muster the nerve to run.

"I see," Lord Bankham finally said.

Which was an odd thing to say for someone who so patently did not see.

But *Hugh* was beginning to see.

See, but not understand. Suspicion was sprouting like a noxious little weed.

Lillias looked up at Giles, Lord Bankham, and her expression was faintly pleading.

"I'm afraid I don't . . . that is . . ." Bankham had been badly shaken. "But you never . . ."

Lillias looked down at her shoes again. And this time that's where her gaze remained.

Whatever the hell was happening here, for his sake and for hers, Hugh was going to need to salvage it in order to forestall gossip.

"We were much thrown together of late during various entertainments. And when you meet the person you hope to spend the rest of your life with, you don't want to waste another moment."

Her head came up. As if he'd given her the start of a script she could convincingly follow.

And then she produced a fond smile and aimed it up at Hugh.

Bankham didn't speak.

He stared at her.

Then back at Hugh.

Then back at Lillias.

"And your . . . father . . . the earl . . . he can't possibly think . . . that is, Mr. Cassidy is . . ." Giles's voice wasn't quite a croak. But there was really no way to finish the sentence that wasn't astonishingly rude, and Hugh got the sense that nothing but a terrible shock would have caused Giles to stumble down that particular conversational road.

"Father *adores* Hugh." Lillias managed to make those three words sound like gospel. Hugh had no illusions about it being for his sake—more on the order of loyalty to her family and her father's orders—but he was impressed.

Bankham finally was very subdued. He squared his shoulders. "Well," he said. "I suppose congratulations are in order, Lilly."

These words were utterly inflectionless. They might be in order, but he didn't precisely offer them, and Hugh was not included.

"Thank you," Hugh said pointedly, anyway. "We are very happy indeed, and it's kind of you to share in our happiness."

Lillias appeared to be mute. She smiled again, and it was almost convincing. Then looked into the middle distance, where someone was still waving a handkerchief, attempting to get her attention, and then glanced into a nearby mirror, obviously worried that *she* was invisible. Lillias was staring right through her.

"I've yet to enter a similarly happy state," Giles said carefully. Like a spy delivering a code.

He'd transferred that unblinking gaze to Lillias.

Lillias's head went up sharply.

She locked eyes with Giles for a moment that was eloquent with . . . *something* . . . before looking away again.

And Hugh clamped his teeth down on a corrosive suspicion that mingled with quite a few other things he'd rather not examine closely.

"I look forward to coming to know you, Mr. Cassidy," Giles said suddenly. "In fact, I would be so honored if the two of you—and Lord and Lady Vaughn—should join my parents and me for a picnic tomorrow at Heatherfield in Richmond. Your new mutual happiness would certainly brighten the day, which promises already to be sunny."

"I am away to Portsmouth the day after tomorrow to meet the *Tropica*, as my uncle is expected to arrive within a day or so. I would be able to spend a lovely day in Richmond with my fiancée and her dear friends if I set out no later than sunrise the following day." He smiled pleasantly.

He could not recall the last time Giles had blinked.

Lillias notably did not make haste to accept the picnic invitation.

"Heatherfield is our estate, Mr. Cassidy. You may have heard of it," Giles said thoughtfully.

"Oh, I have indeed."

"It will one day be mine, of course." Giles smiled modestly.

"Fortunate you are, indeed. Land is the ideal asset, Lord Bankham. Unless, of course, the lands are entailed to a title in such a way that an endless amount of money is needed to support them. Then they've been known to quite drain the coffers. Best to have a good business head and a reliable source of income. "

Giles was silent. His face hardened speculatively.

"I don't recognize your tailor, Mr. Cassidy," he said. "Which strikes me as unusual, as Lillias is usually dressed in the first stare of fashion as such things matter to her."

Hugh almost laughed. He supposed it was an English aristocrat's version of drawing a sword.

"Mr. Cassidy's clothes were lost at sea," Lillias said suddenly.

Hugh slowly turned to look at Lillias.

"Yes," he said, after a moment. "In a tragic maritime accident, my clothing was lost at sea. Yet my enthusiasm for this evening and the opportunity to meet you was such that I found the courage to wear this coat."

Lillias refused to look at him. Her expression had altered somewhat. She knew he was angry. But, if he'd had to guess, she was almost tempted to laugh.

Although, given the mood, it would have been slightly hysterical, if she had.

The three of them stood not speaking at all, but they *were* being looked at.

And then Lillias said, "Gilly . . . I so looked forward to meeting Lady Harriette this evening. Did she arrive with your family?" It was an attempt at sounding casual.

An epiphany struck Hugh: he knew Lillias. In just a few scant weeks he'd come to know her inflections and the angles of her head and the way her face colored, the way she held herself. He knew when she was proud or angry or curious or vulnerable or bored or full of herself.

So he knew she was lying.

She was not in the *least* looking forward to meeting this Harriette.

More and more curious.

And less and less pleasant.

And that's when he noticed that her fingers, tightly clutching her little reticule and fan, were trembling.

"Lady Harriette has unfortunately been detained on her journey here. I'm given to understand a carriage horse threw a shoe and a blacksmith cannot be found for a day or so. She looked forward to the ball and to meeting you, as well. Her absence means I have a waltz going begging on my dance card."

Lillias was white and wordless. And then a breath shuddered out, as though what she'd just asked had taken all of her courage.

Enough was enough.

"I think Lillias could use some air," Hugh said firmly. "If you will be so kind as to excuse us? Delighted to meet you, Lord Bankham. I'm certain we'll become great friends."

Hugh favored Lord Bankham with a smile of such startling, irresistible warmth and bonhomie that the man's face split into a smile as of its own accord, while his eyes looked astonished over the behavior of his mouth.

He took Lillias by the elbow and walked her, gently but implacably, toward a set of doors, wide, inset with small panes—leading to the garden, and pushed the door open, onto a veranda. He said not a word.

Chapter Sixteen

❧

She PULLED away and strode swiftly ahead of him along a path of flagstones, lit up by the high, bright moon.

And then she stopped, suddenly. Whatever emotion had driven her had been spent.

Hugh saw deeper into the garden the paler outlines of stone benches, and what appeared to be a little spire of a gazebo.

"This way," he said quietly. "Go left."

His voice was taut. He didn't touch her. She followed him, resignedly.

The gazebo was tucked in amid shrubbery that needed a good trimming. It was lined with stone benches, and moonlight poured down through its latticed roof.

He stopped. He gestured at one of the benches.

"Sit down, Lillias."

"Masterful," she said, faintly, sardonically. But she sank down onto the bench as though whoever held her strings had cut them.

He lowered himself down next to her, a genteel distance apart.

They sat in silence, staring straight ahead. He wondered how to begin.

"I've eyes, you know," he said finally, carefully.

"I've seen them," she said shortly. "There they are, right above your nose."

He contemplated whether he ought to be delicate, but he was no coward. Life was short. To know what sort of life he could expect from this day on, he needed to be blunt.

"How long have you been in love with Bankham?"

Her head whipped toward him.

Her head pivoted back again and she stared stonily into the dark.

"What . . . what utter rot," she muttered.

He sat quietly. He studied her profile, turned stubbornly away from him.

What did he feel? A thousand things, pelting him lightly like leaves in a storm. He had not expected this at all, and the knot in his stomach told him he hadn't any idea what to do about it.

"Let me guess," he mused. "Since you fell into the pond, and then he tried to fish you out, and then he fell in, and you kicked—"

"Forever," she said bluntly. "Or, more specifically, two years."

He took this in.

Blew out a breath.

"Something's unclear to me. Why the *devil* are we in the mess we're in?"

She hiked her chin a little. Took a breath, and then another, and released it in a sigh. "Well you see, the trouble is . . . and I'm certain this will come as a *great* shock to you . . . it seems he is not in love with me."

He frowned, faintly recalling the man's white face, the way his smile had frozen into something

like a rictus at the word "fiancé," his luminous
pleasure at the very sight of Lillias, though this
seemed a reasonable reaction to how she looked
in that rose-colored dress tonight. She was a gift to
the sense of sight.

"How did you come to that conclusion? Did he
outright tell you that?"

This seemed stunningly unlikely based on what
he'd just witnessed. But men were often stupider
than they appeared.

She sighed. The squared shoulders slumped
again.

"A few months ago, at another picnic at Heatherfield . . . he said his parents felt it was time to
get married now that Lady Harriette was of age.
Apparently it's a long, happy family tradition for
the Bankhams and Dervalls to marry, when possible. And apparently it was decided practically
from birth. It was absolutely the first I'd heard of
it, and our families have been friends for nearly a
lifetime."

"And he said this with no apparent sign of . . .
er . . . inner torment?" Hugh felt ridiculous saying
it aloud. He was struggling altogether with the
scenario now unfolding.

"He said it . . ." She cleared her throat. "It was as
though he were commenting on the weather. Perhaps he saw it as part of the natural sequence of
life events, like coming into his majority. In that
case, why would he mention it? He might as well
mention that he was breathing. He said I would
meet Harriette at the Landover Ball."

How she must have *suffered* in anticipation of
this ball. Hugh thought again of her stillness in

the parlor, the absorption, her restless distraction. Her grief over the destruction of all her drawings of Heatherfield.

She'd been wretched. He'd half sensed it. And yet.

And despite himself, his gut went cold. He was sardonically amused at himself that the notion of the woman he was engaged to marry suffering over the man she loved should arouse any kind of sympathy or a sense of protectiveness. But there it was.

He looked at her, currently refusing to look at him, at her long throat and the elegant straight nose and the stubborn chin aloft and those soft, soft lips and thought it inconceivable that a man could look at her and not be assailed by something powerful, whether it was emotional or physical.

"I will *never* understand the aristocracy," he said, almost to himself. "What did you say to him at the time?"

"There wasn't an opportunity to say anything at all. What do you imagine I would have said or done? Thrown myself upon his feet? If he's known me his entire life and a proposal hadn't entered his head, what's to be done?"

He was struggling to absorb this. "It must have been a terrible shock for you," he said almost gently. He was absorbing something of a terrible shock of his own.

She didn't reply. He could hear her breathing. Hard breaths, as if through pain.

"Does anyone else know? Your family?"

"You're the first I've told. I don't think it crossed their minds, either. I just . . . and this might sound ridiculous . . . I should hate for them to suffer on my behalf. And then there's the pesky thing called pride."

"It doesn't sound ridiculous at all," he said carefully, after a moment. "And I, believe it or not, understand what you mean."

She turned her head then to look at him as if she'd detected an echo of something in his words. A hint of something she could not decipher.

"You're careful of your own," she said. "Of *all* of your feelings."

He made a little sound. She did rather see him clearly, and had from the very first. He didn't know why this observation should surprise him. Nor did he know why he didn't mind it.

"But Lillias . . . Bankham is *not* yet engaged. He in fact made a point of saying it once he heard about your . . . our . . . engagement."

"I suppose he did," she said, absently.

Hugh was still baffled. "So he's marrying this Harriette to please his parents? Out of duty? The vaunted aristocratic appreciation for tradition?"

"So it would seem."

He gave a short laugh. "I suppose there's something to be said for that. If either of us were more dutiful we wouldn't be in this predicament."

She just made a soft snorting sound. Not quite a laugh.

"Or it's a singular lack of imagination," he suggested.

She lifted one hand a little, let it drop, as if it hardly mattered anymore.

"He seems to esteem you, Lillias."

"Ah, yes. What every girl yearns for. Esteem. Didn't Byron write a poem about esteem?"

"I haven't a clue. But I'm certain Gilly would."

"Oh, he would, all right," she said darkly.

"Maybe poetry is what aristocrats do instead of passion. The words do it all for them."

"Ha," she said. Although the "ha" sounded a little uncertain. It wasn't the most implausible theory.

"So you've been wretched," he said slowly. "And you've been dreading this ball."

"Ever since then, it has felt as though my heart is being carved out with one of those little spoons we use to put sugar in our tea. A bit at a time. Scrape. Scrape. Scrape."

He made a soft sound, half amazed laugh, half rueful empathy.

"The pain is ghastly and quite surprising," she said with a certain dull, ironic wonderment. "I'm quite amazed and ashamed. And not a soul has noticed. They would all be astonished to learn I'm sentimental at all. So there's something to be said about being raised English, Mr. Cassidy."

The silence was such that the very stars above seemed to ring.

There was a certain relief between them. The relief was new, and this newness, both awkward and peaceful. He looked at his beautiful tormentor, this haunter of his nights. The sheer *scale* of feelings she'd stirred—the size of an American tree—somehow restored dimension to his life. It wasn't at all comfortable. But then neither had been waking up from a fever in a hospital, shot but alive.

And all of the things she felt when she was near him . . . did she feel them for Giles? His masculine pride told him definitively "no." This thing between them was its own singular natural force, like a hurricane. He knew that much.

But maybe that was Giles's appeal. He was patently not a hurricane. He was patently of her world.

"Lillias?"

"Yes?"

He hesitated. But the curiosity compelled him. He needed to know.

He tried to keep the words inflectionless. "Why do you love him?"

She gave a short, stunned laugh.

And for a time it seemed she intended to ignore the question. Or perhaps berate him for daring to ask it.

And then she sighed, and from her reticule withdrew something. "Hold out your hand, palm up."

He obeyed. Into it she deposited a little stone.

Puzzled, he held it up and angled it so that the silvery, pale moonlight would illuminate it. The elements—water, storms, who knew what else— had etched little tiers and facets on one side, smooth on the other, a sort of creamy bronze shade, with speckles. A typical, humble little river rock.

He wasn't quite certain what to do with it.

"Nice little stone," he approved. "I could probably skip this three, maybe four times across the pond back home. In winter, you can make the ice sing notes by just skipping a stone."

"What on . . . that's not . . . that can't be true." She was watching him intently.

"I wouldn't lie to you about singing ice," he said somberly.

She smiled a little. "Gilly gave it to me two years

ago. It was then that . . . well, I've always been fond of him. I knew he was fond of me. It was all very lovely, easy, and I thought our fondness for each other was apparent to everyone. Our families spent a good deal of time together; we've been friends for simply always. Anyhow, two years ago we were with our families on a bit of a jaunt down at Heatherfield and he found and gave it to me and he said, 'Lillias, this reminds me of you.'"

She stopped, as though this was explanation enough.

"You remind him of a rock," Hugh said slowly.

She sighed. "He said, 'One side shines brightly and it would catch anyone's eye. Anyone would look at it; it's why I noticed it. But they wouldn't turn it over to see the subtle shading and little freckles on the other side.'"

Damn that aristocrat. It was a rather lovely thing to say.

And he thought he understood why she'd *craved* hearing something like that. *They decided who I am,* she'd said in anguish.

His stomach contracted again.

"And just like that, you fell in love."

"He's also a nice person."

"Nice! Well, that tears it. I'm half in love with him now, too."

She gave a short, pained laugh. "He remembers things. Servants' names. Birthdays. If you've a favorite color, that I like jam with my scones but not cream. He thinks I'm clever and it doesn't upset him and as we've discussed before, some men struggle with the notion that a woman might be clever. He listens when I speak and doesn't yammer on the way so many young men do because they think they're fascinating and they are usually quite wrong."

"You'll get no argument from me there."

"He can be witty. He thinks I'm witty. We've had the same kinds of upbringings and we have the same values and memories and know all of the same people and places and we've the same friends. We love the country and going riding and picnics and such. And we love our families. He's a gentleman."

That was her list?

"You left out 'and he's obedient,'" he said rather ironically.

She was silent.

He was dumbstruck by the surprisingly gentle, mundane things that this prickly, intelligent, beautiful, sensual female who possessed a rather unorthodox sense of risk claimed to cherish in a person.

Things that had resulted in her quiet devastation. A devastation that made him restless. He wanted to undo it, even as he felt a little frayed. And perhaps betrayed.

She turned to look at him. He couldn't quite read her expression in the shadows. It wasn't the loneliest he'd ever felt, sitting here in the dark of a far too tame garden with a woman who, even as she confessed her love for another man, he would gladly lay back on the grass and ravish.

A woman, he half suspected, who would, despite her professed love for another man, welcome it.

But it was lonely.

And then one of her shoulders went up and then down.

"Why does anyone love anyone?" she said.

He shifted on the bench and blew out a breath.

"I don't know. I know it's the only thing that makes life bearable. And it's the only thing that makes life unbearable."

She turned then to him. Their eyes met. He felt that gaze everywhere in his body. The way she listened, the way she absorbed things. It was such a rare pleasure, he realized, with some surprise, to speak to her.

"Are you astonished to learn that I even have a heart?" she asked. Somewhat ironically.

But her voice cracked a little on that last word.

"I've always known you have a heart, Lillias," he said gently. "But I'll tell you something. Beyond doing what they're supposed to do, which is bump along and send blood through our veins, hearts are an encumbrance."

He looked away then, back toward the sky where the moon hung like a portal to another, shining world.

"What is her name?"

"I don't know what you mean," he said smoothly.

She waited.

His sense of fair play, and honor, told him that he would have to give her an answer. And yet it was another moment before he could speak.

"Amelia." He said it quietly.

He hadn't said her name aloud in so long that it felt like a new word he'd just learned.

"Amelia Woodley."

The name hung there in the dark for an instant.

"Is she in America, this Amelia?"

He breathed in deeply and sighed it out. "She was, in fact, last seen boarding a ship from New York bound for Liverpool. Her father, an employer and now friend, has entrusted me with finding her and bringing her home."

If she wanted more information, she was going to have to pull it from him.

"I gather her departure for English shores was unexpected and not sanctioned by her family?"

"You gathered correctly."

"Well. Another disobedient woman, Mr. Cassidy. You seem to have a predilection for them."

He didn't take this little challenge up, primarily because he was beginning to worry that it was true.

"She can't have gone alone."

"According to the letter she left behind for her father, she departed with a family by the name of Clay who was visiting New York, and with whom the Woodleys had become friendly."

"Was there a man involved?"

"I don't think so. But I don't know for certain."

The spoon Lillias described: scrape, scrape, scrape. That's what the thought of Amelia had done to him ever since.

Funny that at the moment he still could not quite recall her features distinctly. It was like peering through a scratched lens.

The first reel had begun. The ghostly strains of it reached them in the garden.

It seemed quite some time before either of them spoke again. The silence was oddly not uncomfortable. Both had laid down burdens. There was relief in that.

He realized she was studying him. He couldn't quite interpret her expression.

"And . . . you love her?" She said it tentatively. Almost reluctantly.

They both, after all, apparently belonged to the Order of the Brokenhearted.

Did he love Amelia? *Had* he loved her? What did he feel now?

There was a moment last spring, outside the Woodleys' home. They'd been walking in opposite directions along the path and had stopped to bid each other good day. He saw distinctly Amelia's soft blue eyes looking up into his, one hand pushing her pale hair from her face. The breeze had tugged it loose from its ribbon, and she had laughed in delight. Her face was like the sun.

And he'd thought later: that is what love felt like. Simplicity. Peace. Beauty. Joy. The gift of just being, crystallized in a moment.

"I had reason to believe our regard was mutual," was all he said, finally. Hesitantly.

He anticipated the next question. Still, it was a while in coming.

Lillias had the right to it. But he had no idea what to answer.

"Why?" She whispered this intently. "Why did you love her?"

He didn't have a vocabulary for this sort of thing. He hadn't been raised on poetry read in cozy parlors for entertainment. He would rather simply *be*. What he felt and thought he hoped he embodied in actions. But how could he know for sure?

He didn't know what to say. But his sense of fair play made him want to try.

"All I know . . . when I was near death in the hospital at Williamsville from a bullet wound . . . hers was the face I pictured. And I wanted to live."

He felt her eyes on him, searching his face the way he'd searched hers.

She turned away again. Her hands went up to her face and she sighed at length. And then she brought them down again.

"I've gone and ruined your life, haven't I, Mr. Cassidy?"

"Yes. I am the poor, innocent victim in this affair."

She gave a wry, bleak little laugh.

He pictured the face of that man in the ballroom lighting up at the very sight of her and almost closed his eyes. If he did, he knew he could clearly see the days she described—the warmth, the river stones beneath bare feet, the friends, the family, the picnics, the laughter. Because he'd had those memories, too. He could have happily and forever lived out his days like that; he understood their pull.

But most of the people who'd populated those memories were gone now.

Sitting in the moonlit dark next to Lillias, he could not quite bring the things he felt into focus; they were like bright fish beneath the surface of dark water, moving too quickly to catch or inspect. They flickered through him, jealousy and possession, lust and awe, betrayal, mordant amusement. But the water, the thing that held all of these and sustained them, was deeper and less easy to name.

All he knew now was that he wanted to give Lillias what she wanted. And he thought he knew how.

"Well. I believe I can impart some wisdom."

She gave a short laugh. "Perhaps Amelia fled because of your tendency for imparting wisdom."

It was a risky joke, but he liked it. "It's this. I don't believe in giving up. And I don't believe that life—even when it appears to lie in a smoking heap—is ever ruined. It's all in what you do with the wreckage. I built an entire stage from scrap wood, the wreckage of something else. And do you know how long an American forest stays dead from a fire? It's emerald and growing again nearly within weeks. New and sprouting green everywhere. It needs fire to renew itself."

"And how does this wisdom relate to the subject at hand?"

"What if we could persuade Bankham—Gilly— to be . . . disobedient?"

She frowned. Then her face cleared as she caught on. "You mean *not* marry Lady Harriette? But . . . how?"

"Exactly. Because . . . well, here's what I noticed. When you introduced me as your fiancé, he blinked rapidly." He demonstrated. "As though the news had been something dashed into his eyes. And only a man who's been startled and badly knocked off his game blinks like that, or lets another man see him blink like that. We don't show weakness to each other, especially in front of beautiful women."

"How burdensome to be a man."

"It's not a picnic at Heatherfield, that's for sure, being a man. In other words, it was clear to me he'd suffered a shock. He straightened up to his full height, which, I might add, is something a bear would do in order to frighten a man off. Or many animals would, to frighten off a predator. And then he stared at me for nearly the duration of our conversation and didn't blink once. I daresay the thoughts he was thinking were not very . . . nice. At all. In fact he likely, for a *not* nice moment or two, wished me dead. Because most men, apart from perhaps Delacorte, are *not* generally nice, regardless of what you might think. The epithet jar and the brown smoking room are the thin veneer between us and savagery."

Lillias was quiet.

And then she said: "It's brown? The smoking room?"

He grinned fleetingly. "It's brown. So in a word, Lord Bankham was jealous. And if he was a woman, even now a concerned friend would be urging him to sit down before he faints. I suspect this friend, assuming he has friends, got a look at his face and is pressing a whiskey on him. Perhaps his life is passing before his eyes. All because of the sudden, shocking appearance of your fiancé, an eventuality he probably had not considered, given that his life has heretofore been so very predictable and you were always about."

Her lips parted as if to say something. She closed them again. Sat a moment.

And then finally she swiftly pivoted her entire body toward him.

"How did you notice all of that?"

It wasn't the question he expected. "Habit of a lifetime. It often means the difference between life or death, the difference between hearing a yes or no, the difference between winning a hand or losing one. If you are not born with a title and a heap of money and a map to your future, you learn to pay attention to everything, because everything— *everything*—can be useful if you know what to do with it. It's instinct. Exactly like an animal, Lady Vaughn."

Something in her intent expression made his heart contract. And then her face was faceted by shadows; a wispy shawl of a cloud had wrapped itself around the moon.

Hoots of inebriated laughter floated to them from the balcony. They'd need to return to the ballroom soon to avoid additional layers of scandal.

"So . . ." She cleared her throat, and said almost lightly, "Do you think he . . . he cares for me?"

He was quiet a moment. Then gave a soft laugh.

"Yes," he said, quietly. "I think he does."

And if this answered more than one question, one spoken and one not, neither of them acknowledged it.

"How do you envision this 'persuasion' taking place, as you call it?"

He drew in a breath. Sighed it out. "Oh . . . I believe the trick would be to arouse his spirit of competition. If together we can persuade Giles that life without you is unthinkable, if I can honorably release you from your obligation to me and he can . . ." he was awfully tempted to say, "be a man," because it struck him as simply the truth ". . . make the decision to be happy rather than merely content."

"He'd have to be a simpleton for that to work."

He laughed. "Well, he's a man. It seems we're all simpletons when it comes to women."

"Surely not you, with all that wisdom you have to impart."

"Probably more simple than simpleton. But I have my moments. Look at me here, in my not quite right evening coat, and consigned to English shores forever, because you, Lillias, are . . ." He shook his head slowly.

She smiled.

This moment of ease and accord with Lillias Vaughn was yet another of the strangest moments in his life.

She cleared her throat. "It occurs to me that I haven't thanked you for . . . rising to the occasion on the stage, Hugh."

"No need to thank me. What else would I do?"

"Run in the opposite direction at a great clip."

He gave a soft laugh. "Firstly, I would never leave any woman to face that alone. It never occurred to me to do anything else. Not that I've ever been in that position before. And secondly . . . Lillias, I cannot imagine ever running in the opposite direction from you."

She looked up at him, eyes widening. Then she smiled wistfully, and sighed.

"It's just . . . I so very much wanted to feel something that wasn't . . . what I was already feeling.

Which was a bit empty, and lost, and miserable. And all I do when I'm with you . . . Hugh . . . all I do is feel things with my body that are so loud that everything else is muted."

The words were like a blow to the head, as if lust was delivered the way whiskey was. He half laughed, half groaned.

"Lillias, you've described seduction right there." He picked up her hand, lightly, in jest. "Sometimes I think that's the entire point of it. It's why it works at all. It mutes everything else."

He'd meant to release her hand at once.

He couldn't seem to.

Instead, he drew his thumb across her palm, musingly, gently. A caress. Tentative. As if seeing how she felt to him now that he knew what he knew, and now that she knew what she knew.

It was the strangest, most confounding thing. He might as well have lit a fuse. That little touch burned through his body and now he was alight with a restless need and he could feel hers thrumming in her, too.

"Like this," he said softly.

"Like this," she agreed, her voice lulled. "It isn't gentle. It isn't easy. It isn't safe."

"No."

"It isn't love."

"No," he said. "It isn't love. But it is . . . it has been . . . forgetting."

"Is it wrong?" she whispered. Her voice was lulled, as his fingers trailed up the satin road of her forearm. He wanted to thank her for the rare pleasure of touching her. For the triumph and thrill of hearing her breath shorten, feeling her body soften, and knowing his touch had brought her that pleasure.

"I can't imagine . . ." his voice sounded drugged, too ". . . why we were given these senses if we aren't to use them. It seems a sin to squander that gift."

"That's precisely what I would say if I intended to seduce someone," she said wryly.

He laughed, very softly. "And who are we hurting right now in this moment?"

It was as good a criterion as any.

"I wonder," she said, her words lulled, "what it would feel like to lie with my bare back against the grass, and stare up at the stars."

He closed his eyes. The image was glorious.

She wondered so many things. How many of them would she ever experience?

"There are more stars in America than there are here. I daresay naked, on a meadow of dark grass, beneath the stars, you would glow like the moon."

She gave a stunned laugh.

His fingers traced the crease of her elbow, gently. Followed the road of the pale vein in her arm. Dragged, so lightly, just above the velvet ribbon trimming her bodice, scarcely softer than the skin above it. They snagged in the little valley between her breasts, hovered there, where her heart beat. She sighed softly, accepting the pleasure.

"I've always wondered how night air would feel on the parts of my skin that . . . never feel the night air."

His fingers were on her laces, and light-fingered as a pickpocket, he had them undone.

"Lillias," he said softly, and it was all he needed

to say. The longing in it, the promise, was like a call she had no choice but to heed.

She turned her head. He dragged his lips across her forehead. He kissed her brows. He claimed her lips. The kiss was gentle, almost tentative. Because this was new, too.

And it was at once intoxicating.

Her trust and surrender did him in. He'd been careful of it for so long, for the sake of her honor and his. Mindful of the danger.

Now, for some reason, it seemed unnervingly precious.

And as he kissed her, he spread the laces of her dress gently and slowly, slowly dragged the delicate little fairy-wing sleeves of her dress down, down, until more of her back was bare to the night, so that she could feel the air, the breeze on her skin. His fingers played at the little short hairs at the nape of her neck, traced the little bumps of her spine as though they were prayer beads, and felt beneath them the quickening tempo of her breath, the shuddering rise and fall of it. And into the gap of her loosened dress he stealthily slipped his hands and grazed, with just his fingertips, the silky curve of her breasts.

She sighed and stirred and arched. Her body instinctively asking for more.

His cock was already hard. And growing harder.

And then, with the same featherlight touch, he grazed the hard beads of her nipples. Just so she would know.

Her head fell back on a gasp.

The sound cleaved him; he felt savage in a way that tightened every muscle in his body.

And the game and the test were this: up to the edge and no further.

And if all went according to hopes and plans, there would never be any further.

But he still could not resist whispering perhaps the wickedest, wickedest thing of all to her. It felt at the moment the hardest thing he'd ever done, but he slid his hands away from her soft breasts. "And yet there's so much more, Lillias."

And while she closed her eyes, and breathed in an attempt to congregate her scattered senses, as deftly as he'd undone her laces, he did them back up again.

In silence, collecting themselves once more, they sat.

"And now . . . we're going inside to dance," he said. "Our campaign begins tonight."

Chapter Seventeen

❧

IT FELT odd to do something as ordinary—in her life, that was—as waltzing with Mr. Cassidy, given that she'd only been on the roof, on the stage, and in a sitting room at the boarding house by the docks with him.

One of his hands gently held hers; the other rested at her waist.

And on that first rotation around the ballroom they didn't speak. He danced well. He smiled down at her. More of a speculative tilt of the corner of his mouth, really.

Something about that smile made her feel precisely the way she had when he'd touched her nipples.

She, who never stumbled, nearly stumbled.

The smile grew, and he righted her with a mere flex of his hand.

It seemed an unfair amount of power for one man to possess. To raise blushes—and nipples—with just a smile.

"I ought to have mentioned earlier . . ." he said offhandedly, "but you look like a Hudson River Valley sunrise in that dress."

"Thank you. I might need a little more context."

"Once you see one, you'll never forget it," he said. "They steal your breath."

Which is exactly what that sentence did.

"Oh," she said finally, on an exhale.

Even his compliments disarmed with their potency.

He noticed. He was smiling, now—for her sake and for the sake of anyone watching in abject fascination, no doubt—but his gaze was rather fixed and was it . . . puzzled?

Perhaps not precisely. But the faintest of frowns had settled between his eyes. He was looking at her somberly.

Probably similar to the way she was looking at him.

An assessment. A reassessment. They were new to each other. Revealed.

She felt unaccountably shy. A little raw.

But she also understood something: when the shock of engagement was new, when it was settling over her, she'd thought of him as a stranger. The notion seemed outlandish now.

Out of the corners of her eyes, gowns and jewels flashed by like exotic birds.

"Has he kissed you?"

She blinked. She wasn't coy and didn't ask, "Who?"

"Not as such."

"Not as such," he repeated thoughtfully, slowly. His eyes glinted, amused. "I think that's aristocrat for 'no.'"

"My hand and my cheek, he has," she said, irritably. "He's certainly capable of it."

He smiled at that again.

Her blush renewed itself.

For heaven's sake, she'd never been a blusher before.

"Are there any *other* kisses you want to mention?" he tried.

"Not unless you want to mention all of yours."

He grinned at this, crookedly.

And this, for some perverse reason, this made her smile.

She frankly didn't want to spend any time wondering how he'd gotten so good at kissing. Talent, experience, and the fact that he liked it a good deal, she supposed. All the reasons she was good at watercolors.

Although it always helped to have a muse to really surpass oneself.

"Since there will be two waltzes tonight, and he hasn't given it away, I wonder if perhaps you ought to dance with Giles to get a sense of how he's feeling in the wake of your momentous news. And while you do that, I'd like to spend a little time in the library with your father and his friends."

"Very well. A sound plan. Why the library?"

"Because I like your father and he ought to be able to face his friends over his daughter's sudden engagement to a previously unknown American. And by that, I mean I'd like him to be proud to be associated with me. And also . . . because many of his friends are wealthy and influential and could conceivably become my friends, which is splendid, because it's wonderful to have friends, and could potentially be useful one day."

He smiled at her widened eyes.

"I meant it when I'd said I'd have an empire, Lillias. Not just for my sake. But for the sake of the family I raise. For generations of Cassidys to come. My family will never want for anything, and we will never take anything that isn't our due."

There was an unaccountable quiet thrill in hearing him speak this way. He sounded deadly serious.

Who would be "the Cassidys" if their plan to arouse Giles's spirit of competition succeeded?

She felt a strange sense of restlessness, almost panic, at the notion that she would never know.

She didn't doubt he'd charm all the viscounts, barons, earls, and heirs who managed to crowd into the library. "Everything is valuable," he'd said. How rich and different and interesting, somehow, the whole world seemed when viewed through that lens. She wanted to sort through everything she knew and assess it in that light.

"And if I do make a good impression, it will inspire the spirit of competition in Giles should he hear of it, which he no doubt will, gossip being what it is."

"Well, I commend you for your strategic thinking, Mr. Cassidy."

"That means everything to me."

She gave a little laugh. Oddly, she wasn't entirely certain he was joking.

After another little silence, during which Hugh continued studying her with that intent little frown between his eyes, she said, "Did you plan to marry Amelia when you return with her to America?"

For nearly an entire rotation of a ballroom he didn't answer the question. "She was what I envisioned when I imagined the kind of wife I'd have."

"I think that's 'Hugh Cassidy' for 'yes.'"

He laughed shortly. Not entirely amused.

She was reluctant to press him. She certainly had the right to do it. But strangely, she wanted to protect him. She sensed he'd been gravely hurt, and that his vulnerability was even more guarded than her own, and possibly equivalent to his strength. And as she'd told him that night on the roof, the notion of him hurting for any reason was distasteful.

"No matter what she's done or where she's been?"

"I promised I would ensure that she is returned safely home to her father, who is a good man, a good friend, and ill with worry."

It wasn't an answer to her question.

Perhaps he didn't know.

"What does she look like?"

"Exactly like Queen Elizabeth the First."

She laughed.

He grinned down at her. "You wound me with your laughter, Lady Lillias. Perhaps it's her stellar character I'm drawn to."

Her smile vanished.

"Is it?" And suddenly there was a little knot in her stomach.

Hugh didn't answer for a time. He watched her face, as if it were a spyglass aimed directly at her heart.

"Lillias . . . have you ever stepped outside just before a thunderstorm?"

"Yes."

"So you know how the air is fresh and wild and charged. You can't wait for the show. And

you know the storm will clear the air and nur-
ture things and be dazzlingly beautiful, even as it
might destroy them, too. But even the destruction
could be all to the good. You're prepared, and eager,
for what will happen."

She stared at him.

"That's *your* character, Lillias."

She was stunned.

For an instant, the air in the ballroom felt exactly as he'd just described. The next sharp breath
she took felt just as charged.

So did the next.

It was neither gentle nor particularly flattering,
but truthful because he was truthful. A storm was
beautiful both in how it was experienced and as a
consequence of its character.

For an entire rotation of the dance floor, they
neither looked directly at nor spoke to each other.
She studied his cravat and the buttons of his waistcoat instead. If she reached over and slowly unbuttoned them, one at a time, she'd reveal golden skin
and scars.

"Have you kissed her?" she asked quietly. She'd
been dying to ask it and finally succumbed.

"No."

"Because she's a saint?" She'd meant it to emerge
lightly. It didn't, quite. Of a certainty, it could not be
said that his ability to resist temptation was weak.
But in truth, she was seeking an answer to a question she wasn't certain she knew how to formulate.

"If the perfect moment had arisen, I might have
had a go, men being what they are." He said this
matter-of-factly. He paused. "We went for walks,"
he said gruffly.

With an odd pang, she wondered what it would be like to merely go for a walk with Hugh. He'd probably cherished those walks.

And then suddenly her heart took up a strange, hard, swift beat when she asked the other question she'd been afraid to ask, because she realized any answer to it would unnerve her. "But it wasn't like . . ."

"Nothing is like us, Lillias," he said shortly.

Particularly that one.

The music ended.

They bowed and curtsied, deeply and prettily, in part to please the audience of watchers, some of them overt and others pretending they were doing something other than watching them.

GILES HADN'T YET given his waltz away.

In fact, when he saw Hugh repairing to the library alongside the Earl of Vaughn, he made what could only be described as a beeline for Lillias.

Her heart skipped like . . . a tiny stone across singing ice . . . when he approached.

It was familiar and pleasant. Not as dramatic as the violent lurching it underwent in the presence of Hugh. He splashed about in there like a bear in a birdbath.

"The next waltz . . . would you dance it with me?" Giles said at once, long friendship excusing the lack of formalities.

"Of course, Giles."

Giles seemed sober, which rather put paid to Hugh's theory about one of his friends forcing whiskey upon him. He had not, however, recov-

ered all of his color and his eyes remained a trifle
haunted. He looked a bit the way the heroine of
The Ghost in the Attic allegedly looked after she'd
returned from the attic. At least according to the
description.

It was yet another moment in a series of moments
of adjustments, a few minutes suspended between
the past and the future. Bittersweet, serrated with
hope and fear.

She'd waltzed with Giles before. They were well-
matched, both tall and long-legged, and they'd
danced together countless times, from the time
they'd learned their first reels when they were
very small.

"I have seldom seen you looking so lovely," he
began. This was a little effusive for Giles, but it
was practically a customary way to begin conversations during waltzes, so she didn't think it could
immediately be interpreted as some sort of impas-
sioned declaration. Especially since it was delivered
so politely.

"Thank you, Giles. That is indeed a compliment,
as you've seen me hundreds of times before. Or
perhaps it's a gentle hint I ought to have improved
my fashion sense before now?" she teased him.

"No," he said. "It was the first. You are always in
the first stare of fashion."

She wasn't certain what to say. This was true.
Although she didn't know why that should be the
reason she always looked lovely.

"Lillias, I had no idea you were . . . that is . . .
good heavens . . . an engagement."

As this was neither a question nor a statement, it

was difficult to know how to respond. He stopped, clearly realizing the sentence had been butchered and there was really no way to repair it.

"Neither did I," she said, truthfully. "It just . . . happened," she said even more truthfully.

She managed to produce a gentle beatific smile, which made him frown.

Even though she knew it so well, she found herself searching Giles's face for landmarks. Some equivalent to a bite from a bear, for instance. She supposed he wore his comfortable history in the flawless clean lines of his face, a face echoed in variations across the ancestors framed and hung on walls all over Heatherfield. Giles, like her brother, took for granted a degree of female adulation simply because he looked the way he looked, but he'd never used it as a reason to be a cad. He was far too well-bred and decent for that.

"Perhaps when you mentioned you were ready to be wed to Lady Dervall, my mind went to the notion of engagements. After all, we are of age and it's inevitable."

His eyes flared in something like alarm.

"Oh. Yes. Quite. Well, the notion is bound to arise when one comes of age. One can't play in creeks or gallivant across ballrooms forever, I suppose."

"Alas," she agreed.

"Your Mr. Cassidy seems an unusual sort."

"Oh, he is," she said earnestly. "That is, he is in some ways. And in other ways he isn't."

"I didn't know you would be drawn to an unusual sort." He paused. "Although . . ."

"Well, one must meet them first before one is drawn to them, I suppose, and that has happened only recently. Although what?"

"You've always been a little . . . well, *more* . . . than most girls." He said this with something like rueful affection.

"More? More what? More how?"

"More willing to wade in the water, for instance, and risk falling in . . ."

"Like in the creek."

"Or to get a little dirty . . ."

"Like the time I fell in the ditch we were trying to leap at our house in Dover?"

"Exactly. Or to try something new to eat. Remember the frog's legs? Or to ride a difficult horse. More clever. More full of thoughts. More willing to kick me." He smiled here. "More surprising, I suppose." He sounded rueful again. "More . . . er, beautiful."

He had never quite said this last aloud to her, and he sounded as though he were trying it on. His cheeks went a little rosy.

She took this in, her own cheeks warming.

She had never thought of herself this way. And it was in fact a revelation that Giles thought of her this way.

"Even your watercolors are a little *more* than everyone else's. More accomplished, more vivid, more singular. I'm so sorry your drawings of Heatherfield were ruined."

"I was heartbroken."

"I can imagine. And isn't it a little unusual that Mr. Cassidy would allow you to waltz with another man?"

"Don't be silly. Firstly, Mr. Cassidy is not 'allowing' me to do anything. He knows that you and I have been dear friends since childhood and he thought I might enjoy the time with you, which was thoughtful of him. I told him that you never indicated an interest in me otherwise. He laughed."

"He . . . *laughed*?" Giles's hand stiffened in hers.

Clearly not one bit of this sat well with Giles. He'd just been neutered in one sentence by a man he'd just met who—inconceivably—didn't view him at all as a rival.

"Well, to be fair, he thought it was madness. But then, he is very biased, and doubtless you look upon me as a comfortable old shoe."

"No," Giles said hoarsely. With genuine astonishment. "How could . . . no. There isn't a man in the world who would view you as a shoe!"

Her heartbeat accelerated as she maneuvered toward her next question.

"As . . . perhaps you see me as a little rock instead, then?" she said, almost shyly.

He smiled, amused. "I beg your pardon?"

She didn't stumble.

But for an instant, her mind blanked in shock and her heart contracted as if it had taken yet another blow.

Was it possible that something she'd cherished, a memento of a moment limned in meaning and promise, had simply been another of the many, many pleasant moments in his life? There had been as many of those pleasant moments in Giles's life as there were pebbles sprinkled over the banks of the Ouse.

For a moment she couldn't speak. And perhaps

it was just that Giles had said what she'd yearned to hear in that moment. Perhaps he saw every moment with her as special, which is why remembering a specific one was elusive.

Still, she found she hadn't the nerve to explain.

"There are no other men like Mr. Cassidy in the *ton*," she finally said quietly.

"Well, there are certainly no other coats like Mr. Cassidy's in the *ton*."

"His coat is a coat, Giles, and he looks very fine in it." An unfamiliar irritation arose. Because once coats had indeed mattered to her. In this peculiar instant, she could not remember why.

"It's just . . . you never seemed particularly partial to any of the young men of our acquaintance. You seemed to like all of them more or less the same amount."

Was he *mad*? Hadn't he eyes or ears?

"Well, perhaps that's because they've all treated me more or less the same, and I've decent manners," she said almost curtly.

But it stung to know he believed she'd had no preference at all. How on earth could someone who knew her so well not notice this?

She took a breath. "I sometimes think it's Mr. Cassidy's uniquely American attributes, perhaps, that make him so appealing," she said thoughtfully.

"What are those unique qualities?"

"He is very ambitious, for one."

"Ambition is for people who are not gentlemen, Lillias," Giles explained kindly. As if guiding her to the realization that this was not an exciting attribute but a flaw in the design. "Ambition is what you have if you've no money. Where *is* the virtue in striving if you don't have to?"

It was a difficult argument to refute. Perhaps it *was* the ceaseless internal churn of his plans and the things he knew how to do that made Hugh seem more vivid than the other men around him. A bit like a whirlpool in a calm, privileged sea.

Or it could be just that he *wanted* things more. Valued things more.

Perhaps loved things harder.

And *that* was the value in striving, she suddenly realized. Everything is useful, he'd said. But then everything won becomes also more precious.

She could not imagine saying this aloud to Giles.

"But it's thrilling to hear how someone hopes to shape the future of their country, isn't it? And to want to create things using his own unique tastes and talents? It's a bit God-like, that sort of creation. I am full of admiration for it."

"Did you see the silly item in the broadsheets where I was compared to a god?" Giles said idly. "Adonis, I think it was. Ha. If you can imagine."

"Oh. Indeed. I read that." She hadn't read it, actually. It had been read *to* her by poor Dot. That was the one she'd burned. "They do like their hyperbole, the broadsheets."

"You know, an MP shapes the future of the country, as you put it. My family of course, like yours, has a parliamentary seat and we have for centuries."

"In a country where things are done the way they've always been, over and over, and where people can't always choose their representation, because someone has inherited it."

"Right!" Giles said brightly, with satisfaction. As though she'd stated something delightful.

Anything else she said after that might have sounded seditious. She could not recall ever having seditious thoughts before.

"And he's . . ." She dropped her eyes briefly. "Oh, I am a bit abashed to say it."

"You can tell me anything," he said. "Haven't we usually confided in each other?"

Did he truly believe this? Perhaps they had, after a fashion.

"I think he's so *very* handsome." She lowered her voice. "Very."

Giles looked like he'd swallowed a fly. "He looks like the offspring of a tree and a cliff."

"Exactly," Lillias said dreamily.

It was admittedly gratifying to see that Giles had lost his grip on gallantry.

"Did you see Lady Flaxmont reach for her smelling salts when he walked through? He has made quite an impression."

"Perhaps she was frightened by his coat."

"Giles, that is very unkind. And his eyes are an unusual shade of blue. Quite extraordinary, really." It was odd to say this out loud to someone who wasn't Hugh, when it was something she'd thought from the moment she'd seen him.

"No doubt because he is the result of quite an unusual mix of ancestors. Many of them completely unknown."

This was also probably true. And clearly an argument in favor of having an unusual mix of ancestors. It was also meant to be insulting, but it was time to get to the crux of the matter.

"Giles . . . is aught amiss?"

Her heart began to pound when he was quiet.

"I cannot truthfully say," he said carefully, finally, "that while I would indeed suffer if you were unhappy, and your contentment has always been of concern to me, I would not grieve a little any circumstance that altered the consistent joy we have taken in each other's company."

Her heart twinged. It was such a lovely, lovely speech, and very convoluted and oblique and English in that it might contain an enormous amount of emotion and one would never know it.

"I shouldn't like you to ever grieve, Gilly. Or suffer." Even now, his apparent suffering was causing her heart to ache. He had a tender heart. Even if—how had Hugh put it?—he wouldn't have minded seeing Hugh dead.

"Lillias . . . I thought . . . I never thought . . ." Giles drew in a breath.

Then think, Giles.

Hope surged painfully. Perhaps Hugh was right. All Giles had needed all along was a little incentive. A reason to *try* in a life that had contained so very little need to try, when his life thus far had essentially amounted to a groaning buffet at a party. How much more of a prize she would seem then, if she was won away from a worthy competitor? Giles had won the Sussex Marksmanship Trophy one year, and he'd been chuffed about that. He liked competing.

She said very, very carefully, "I will admit to feeling a similar sentiment when you spoke to me of Lady Harriette two months ago."

He frowned, puzzled. "I was certain I'd made

mention of her well before that. Surely you know
of the Dervall family."

"Of course I know of them. But no, you hadn't
mentioned it. Giles . . . I would have *remembered if
you had.*"

Perhaps it was her tone.

But his expression changed subtly.

She could almost see the moment when he was
awakened to both ramifications and possibilities.

He was silent. Thoughtful.

"I do hope you and Mr. Cassidy are able to join
us at Heatherfield for a picnic."

"As he mentioned, Mr. Cassidy must away to
Portsmouth on a bit of business very early in the
morning the day after tomorrow. But I'm certain
he would enjoy a picnic in Richmond, and my parents would be delighted to join us, too, I'm sure.
Shall we arrive in the morning?"

"By eleven o'clock. We'll have a memorable day,
like so many other days we've shared."

She smiled. "I'm certain it will be."

Chapter Eighteen

❧❧❧

"Well, that went much better than I expected, Lillias!"

The countess had loosened her stays and was sprawling happily on one of the little settees in their sitting room in The Grand Palace on the Thames suite. "It was clever to wait for everyone to be more than a little drunk before we arrived, I think. They may or may not remember you announced an engagement at all, and may not have time to be shocked later."

Lillias stifled a smile. Her mother wasn't an imbiber of much beyond tea, usually, but when a social occasion featured a punch bowl she saw it as her duty to enter into the spirit of the festivities. Her cheeks were flushed and her hair was listing a little.

And she wasn't going to remind her that the Marquess of Landover had already informed half the *ton*.

Her mother noticed the smile and smiled back at her. "I do rather miss my lady's maid." Her mother gave her hair a push up out of her eyes. "A bit of a challenge to get all the pins out when one has had a cup or two of ratafia."

"Or three or four," Lillias said mischievously.

"Oh, why count?" her mother said breezily. The word "count" evolved into a wide yawn.

"But it seems Mr. Cassidy made a smashing impression on your father's friends. He knows so very many specific things." She lifted a hand languidly.

Now Lillias was curious.

That Hugh did know specific things was inarguable—how a finger drawn along the inside of her arm could make her nipples go hard as little beads, for instance. But she was certain he wasn't sharing that knowledge in company that included her father.

But she couldn't be in that room where they discussed all of those things. What did they talk about? How did they see him?

"What sorts of specific things did they talk about?"

"Oh, you know, money, buildings, investments, horses, guns, I believe the word 'balustrades' was used but I can't be certain and I don't know why, I stopped listening because you know how your father can go on."

"Mmm." Lillias did know. She rather wished she'd been in on the conversation. It sounded interesting.

"Gilly invited all of us to a picnic at Heatherfield tomorrow, Mama. Very impromptu. You and Papa are invited, too."

"Oh, that would be a nice little drive! Your father would like that." Her mother's voice trailed drowsily. Her eyes were closed now.

Lillias absently took up one of the pillows lovingly knitted by one of those ladies at The Grand

Palace on the Thames. And it felt like that, suddenly: like comfort and love and safety in its dense, plump little form. It was the entirety of the intent they'd had when they'd made it. She wrapped her arms around it, experimentally.

She toppled onto her side, clutching it.

The bliss, the *bliss* of being motionless.

She'd been caught and tossed by a merciless updraft of emotion for weeks. The vertiginous anticipation of seeing Giles followed by the near knee-buckling relief of discovering the long-dreaded Harriette nowhere near combined by the disembodying sensation of introducing a large and startlingly handsome American fiancé of no particular pedigree to a stunned *ton*—all of it was nearly bruising in its intensity. Then the smiling and smiling, deftly fielding the glancing blows to her pride, the oblique, insinuating little questions, and oh, yes, the envy. No one at that ball was going to up and marry a handsome behemoth from the wilds of America. They no doubt thought she'd lost her mind. Or her virginity.

But more than one woman would be lying awake tonight wondering what it would be like if Mr. Hugh Cassidy was lying next to them instead of Lord such and such. And well . . . there was a little satisfaction in the notion.

She breathed in.

Exhaled.

And for a time that's all she did, in time to her mother's soft snores, listening to the low fire pop and spit, sifting through images of the evening as though viewing it through a prism. And oddly kept returning to one impression again and again, only a few seconds in duration but somehow more distinct than others, like a tiny diamond among pebbles.

She reached behind to loosen her laces. Her fingers lingering at the fine hairs along her nape, reliving the feel of Hugh's fingers trailing along the bare skin of her back, as soft, secret, elemental as the night air, the two of them and their pleasure not separate from the trees, the sky, the stars, the hum of insects, the call of a nightbird.

Exactly like an animal.

How would she ever have known fingertips feathered across her neck could lead to a riot of sensation through her entire body if she hadn't smoked a cheroot in the Annex?

But the thrum of Hugh's restraint was in his touch; it transferred to her that spiky thrill of ferocious desire tightly leashed. *More*, he'd said. There's more. She was luckier than she deserved to be—of a certainty another man might not have been so restrained. And perhaps therein had lain part of the thrill, too. So easy to forget when one was in the throes of it.

It was a mercy it would never happen again.

Would Giles touch her the same way, given an opportunity?

She had never imagined him touching her that way, perhaps because before Hugh she'd had no idea of the possibilities. And yet she was daring once again to imagine herself married to Giles. And that was easy to do, because she'd imagined it for so long before.

Hearts are an encumbrance, Hugh had said. And yet apparently the flimsy traitorous things stirred and revived like dead flowers when watered with just a little hope. Hugh's plan offered that. And after her waltz with Gilly, it suddenly didn't seem at all outlandish.

If she and Hugh could both get what they wanted, this secret, fraught, wicked interlude would come to an end, and perhaps the ending would herald a blissful return of clarity, certainty, peace. "Forgetting" would no longer be so necessary. There would be no more need to distract herself from misery or to dull pain. She would be *herself* again.

She was certain she knew the kinds of things Hugh wanted to forget, though she suspected he'd deny it. He kept himself at the slightest bit of a remove from everyone, so slight that you wouldn't even notice it unless you, too, tried to keep the world from brushing up against wounds. It was a way to create a little pocket of peace for yourself.

Amelia. The name conjured one of those paintings of saints, eyes aimed beatifically toward heaven, halo pulsing around their hairlines. Perhaps this was unfair. After all, Amelia had bolted without a word to anyone. But Lillias knew too well that men often reserved reverence—and she'd indeed heard that telltale carefulness in the way he'd said her name—for women they didn't truly know.

And yet. Did it matter? When Lillias sat now with the idea of Amelia, this woman he'd pursued across an ocean, two surprising emotions sifted to the surface: envy and gratitude. Envy that she'd been the reason Hugh Cassidy wanted to stay alive in a battlefield hospital.

Nearly ferocious gratitude that he'd had one.

To be so needed. To be the source of someone's strength. That, suddenly, seemed the point of life.

She lifted her head abruptly when she heard a gentle tap at the door.

Lillias sighed. She found within her the fortitude to get off the settee to go and peer through the peephole.

She reared back when an enormous pale blue eye filled her view, so clear she half expected a meadowlark to go winging across it.

She opened the door to Dot, who was holding a tray upon which rested a little scone and a pot of jam.

Lillias stared at it, puzzled.

Dot curtsied and whispered, rather loudly, "I know you didn't ring for it, Miss, I mean, Lady, Lillias. But Mr. Cassidy said you hadn't eaten much and so he thought you might enjoy this scone. He hopes . . ." Dot cast her eyes upward, as though to try to access the ceiling of her brain ". . . he hopes you appreciate this great sacrifice, as he was going to eat it for breakfast."

Dot didn't say, ". . . and then he smiled at me and what choice did I have after that but do anything he wanted?" But it was absolutely what happened.

Lillias smiled. "Thank you, Dot."

Dot dropped a curtsy and Lillias closed the door, then ferried her plate to the settee and placed it on the little table, admiring it, quietly amazed.

Hugh's hand cupped lightly beneath her elbow. The odd, humble moment her attention had returned to again and again tonight. Somehow those few seconds transferred to her knees the strength to remain upright at the sight of Giles.

But how had he known?

He knew so many specific things.

Lillias looked across the scone at her mother and was beset by a swift wave of ferocious love and terror and gratitude. She could not imagine doing without any of her family members. Not even St. John.

It's the only thing that makes life bearable. And it's the only thing that makes life unbearable.

She thought she could concur.

She was suddenly just as grateful that she could play a part in his forgetting as she was desperately hopeful that the two of them would get what they each wanted.

And Hugh could go home again.

Lillias reached for one of those lovingly knitted coverlets and draped it over her mother. And then she settled back down on the settee across from her and devoured the scone.

It *was* heavenly. It *was* the food of angels.

She felt better than she had in weeks.

Replete, she caught up the other coverlet and dragged it over her, and lay back down. A few moments later she was lost in a blissfully dreamless heap across from her mother.

The earl tiptoed past them on his way in. He paused to plant kisses on both of their foreheads before he went off to sleep.

Chapter Nineteen

ↄ◌◌Გ

"A PICNIC! CAN I come along?"

Delacorte thought the day at Richmond sounded diverting. He and Hugh had encountered each other very early over breakfast, where they were the first at the table, and which they had enjoyed with the speed and wordless devotion Helga's cooking deserved. Now in the foyer beneath the chandelier, Delacorte was on his way out the door with his case to visit apothecaries. Hugh awaited Lillias and her parents and the arrival of the Vaughn carriage that would carry them all to Richmond.

"I wish you *could* come along," Hugh said, and he meant it. He could think of almost no greater pleasure than watching Delacorte suggest an impotency cure to the Earl of Bankham. "I'm afraid one has to be invited by the host."

"I don't know why anyone would want to be an aristocrat," Delacorte mused.

"I can't think of a reason, either," Hugh said.

"How was the ball?"

"Tolerable," Hugh said, summing up one of the most stunning, complicated evenings of his life in one word. "Lillias and I may have arrived at a plan to free ourselves honorably and gracefully from our hasty engagement."

Delacorte looked at him quizzically, furry brows drawn together.

Hugh stared back.

"Well, that would be a relief, wouldn't it?" Delacorte finally said, lightly.

And then Lillias appeared in the foyer in a striped muslin day dress and a straw bonnet featuring a green ribbon tied beneath her ears, and Hugh forgot how to speak.

"Good day! Enjoy your picnic!" Delacorte said, making haste for the door.

Neither of them heard him.

Hugh found his voice.

"Good morning. Seems a fine day for a picnic." He said this only a little ironically.

"Indeed," she said. Suddenly seeming a bit shy.

He lowered his voice. "Was your waltz with Giles illuminating?"

She cleared her throat. "I feel it's accurate to say he is quite shaken by our engagement and is awakened to . . . possibilities."

"Poor Giles, to be so shaken," Hugh said, after a moment. "The first time is always the hardest."

They were studying each other as though it was yet another new light, like the night on the roof or by firelight or in the full light of the garden. This one was a bit like the aftermath of a storm. A good deal had taken place the night before. The air had not yet cleared enough to see how the landscape had changed. But it was of a certainty changed.

"I look forward to shaking him even more," Hugh said almost lightly.

And then the Earl and Countess of Vaughn ap-

peared, as did their carriage, and they were off to
Richmond.

GILES AND HIS father and mother, the Earl and
Countess of Bankham, were waiting for them in
front of the house in a circular courtyard. They
were arrayed about a fountain involving what
appeared to be a tangle of frolicking cupids, all
spitting water.

Hugh stood back and gazed up at the mythical
Heatherfield.

Marbled, gilded, balconied, studded with row
upon row of windows glinting like diamonds in
the cooperatively brilliant sun, unhampered by
clouds today. Against the blue sky it resembled
nothing so much as a stone crown sitting on top of
the hill. It was built to last forever, intimidate, and
overwhelm. It succeeded on every count.

He hated it.

He'd been *prepared* to out of principle, and he
was rather glad to find that he truly did, out of a
sense of personal aesthetics.

And as it turned out, he hated the inside, too.

The harmonious, uniform proportion of the
rooms called to mind, incongruously, a livery
stable. The ceilings were quite high, boxed and
painted. The rooms were cavernous and full of
fussy things, objects chosen in order to induce awe
or envy in other people with lots of money—or in
people with hardly any—and to keep a regiment of
servants employed in dusting, polishing, sweeping, and laundering. In this Hugh supposed they
at least served a purpose. Miles of curtains poured

from the tops of enormous windows; satin-backed spindly-legged chairs faced each other before marble fireplaces in which one could have roasted a bull on a spit. All the shiny surfaces reflected the other shiny surfaces, as though the house was in love with itself and couldn't stop winking and preening. Voices and footsteps echoed and lent the place the ambiance of a dungeon. Although of a certainty it smelled better.

This is what people usually meant when they used the word "grandeur." He recognized and appreciated the quality of the craftsmanship; he surreptitiously touched the carved banister, imagining the brotherhood of craftsmen who had come together to build it, the pride and care they'd taken.

But that didn't make it feel like a home.

Hugh pondered again the charm of The Grand Palace on the Thames—everything lovingly chosen, refurbished, and arranged in such a way that one felt embraced from the moment one walked through the door. Nothing quite matched and yet for that reason everything did, and that seemed to include all of the people who lived there. And while Hugh did indeed aspire to a certain luxury, and had very specific notions of what that meant, for the rest of his life, when he walked into a room, The Grand Palace on the Thames would forever be the standard he held it to.

The Earl and Countess of Vaughn had gone up the long marble staircase to freshen up after their journey, leaving Hugh, Lillias, and Giles with the Earl and Countess of Bankham at the foot of the stairs, awaiting, they were told, footmen with a picnic hamper.

The Earl and Countess of Bankham had not met Hugh at the ball. They inspected him, and while it was clear he was a surprise and a curiosity and maybe even a bit of an affront, given he was neither English nor titled, it was also clear they struggled to find him truly wanting. Lady Bankham's eyes lingered on his face, traveled to his shoulders, then back to his face, purely for the pleasure of that journey.

The earl's eyes were large and brown like his son's; his jowls were a thing of majesty, like the ruff on an Elizabethan. His wife was petite and dark-eyed; her son owed his symmetrical features to her.

Lillias was standing a little apart from all of them, her expression pensive, as her eyes flitted from one object to another in that grand room.

She looked as though she belonged here. But in a way that troubled him. Softly illuminated by sunlight easing in through partially opened curtains, she might have been a beautiful statue, another ornament meant to contribute to the air of wealth, her personality subsumed by the house.

The thought made Hugh restless again.

And Giles, for his part, was clearly more at ease, relaxed, scrupulously groomed, quite glowingly handsome. It was clear to Hugh that he thought Heatherfield spoke for itself, and that it answered any question of perceived superiority.

They would just see about that.

"A pleasure to meet you, Mr. Cassidy," the Earl of Bankham said to him after introductions and bows. "Congratulations on the extraordinary good fortune of your engagement. Lillias is almost like a daughter to us."

He noticed that no one was congratulating Lillias on her extraordinary good fortune. This mordantly amused him.

"Thank you, Lord Bankham. I can hardly believe it myself. One of the advantages of recognizing extraordinary good fortune is the opportunity to be grateful for the rest of my life."

The Earl stood back and eyed him with pleased surprise. "Well said, young man."

"We understand you've been a soldier," Lady Bankham said, as though she'd been handed a pamphlet about Hugh to review just this morning. "Are you now in . . . trade?" She added this on a delicate hush.

"I've long been interested in politics, Lady Bankham. My intent was to run for mayor when I returned to New York, but . . ." He managed to produce a fond smile for Lillias. "Destiny had other plans for me. My interest and investments thus far are in transportation. Canals, lochs, railroads, ships. The swiftest ways to distribute goods and carry people to new destinations, of which there are an infinite number in the United States of America alone."

Lillias's expression was interesting. She was watching him, and appeared to be suppressing some sort of emotion he couldn't quite decipher. He wondered if she was imagining him in the context of this kind of house, and failing.

"In America, it seems a man can be elected to office just like that, Mother." Giles snapped his fingers.

"Just like that?" Her eyes widened as she studied Hugh. "Doesn't your family need a parliamen-

tary seat? I know nothing of American politics,"
his mother admitted.

"American politics will never be a thing you'll
need to trouble yourself over, dear," her husband
assured her, with a little arm pat.

"Well, in truth one must earn the votes of his
constituents by offering intelligent ideas for solving problems or making improvements. I typically
rather relish opportunities to improve the daily
lives of others. Just as I hope to continue to improve
the life of Lillias for the rest of our days."

It was possible he was overdoing the devotion a
little, but it had the desired effect of making Giles
shift restively from one leg to the other and everyone else eye him admiringly.

"In America, any sort of person can rise in the
world in unfettered leaps and bounds, it seems."
The Earl of Bankham said this quietly to his wife,
by way of explaining Hugh. "It's rather thrilling."

"Oh my. Unfettered. How startling." Lady
Bankham's fan did what her eyelashes wished to
do, which was flutter at Hugh.

Hugh offered her a smile, as if including her in
a joke between just the two of them.

She blushed like a girl.

Giles's square jaw was set like granite. Hugh
expected it was a matter of moments before a little
muscle began ticking in his jaw.

"Speaking of leaping, Giles leaped a drainage ditch on his new hunter the other day," Lady
Bankham offered. "Prettiest thing you ever did
see, soaring through the air like that."

Hugh gave Giles a bright smile, as if any efforts
Giles might make toward being manly ought to be

affirmed. "Well, if the drainage ditch is going to be in the way of things, it's a very good thing you knew how to jump it, I suppose," he encouraged him.

Giles's mouth made a valiant attempt at a curve, and only achieved a grimace.

Lillias so far had been merely observing. He wondered if it was uncomfortable to watch Giles gently flayed with strategic condescension.

"Lillias rides very well, too," said the countess. "I imagine it would be a useful skill when it comes to fleeing Indians, Mr. Cassidy."

"They don't shoot at you if you don't shoot at them," Lillias said, sounding a little bored. "And there are many different kinds of tribes. One doesn't just call them *Indians*. The Lenape Indians are part of the Algonquin tribe, for instance."

Hugh turned slowly to look at her in amazement.

Lillias lifted and let fall one shoulder, with a secret little smile.

Lady Bankham swiftly gripped her husband's arm, alarmed at this very specific thing Lillias seemed to know.

"I imagine you're quite the horseman, Cassidy," Giles said pleasantly. "One would need to be in order to outrun wolves and bears and the local tribes who might mistake you for a deer. And then, of course, one must be prepared to ride for hours to get to anywhere civilized."

"I *am* quite the horseman," Giles agreed. "And civilization is a matter of perception, though we've every comfort a human could desire within an easy walk or ride. But we're going to live here in England."

"Gilly won the Sussex Marksmanship Trophy one year," Lillias said. "He shoots very well."

"Oh, is that a great incentive to shoot well, then? A trophy?" Hugh pretended to be puzzled.

Giles paused. "I don't suppose you have a Manton's or anything of the sort in New York." Giles was all tender pity. "Where one could truly hone one's skill."

"If I didn't hit my target I wouldn't eat. Or I or someone I love might die. I always hit my target."

"Oh, *my*," Lady Bankham breathed.

Her husband eyed her balefully.

Giles studied Hugh. "Shall we do a little target shooting? We'll have a pair of Baker's brought out."

Hugh had loaded and shot Baker's more times than he preferred.

"*Must* we shoot things today?" the countess wondered, with a sigh.

"*I'd* rather like to shoot something," Lillias said suddenly.

"Have you ever done that, dear?" the countess wanted to know. "It isn't quite the done thing, but . . ." She stopped herself from adding, ". . . neither are American fiancés."

"I haven't," Lillias said firmly. "And I should like to."

The countess looked as though she intended to say something else. Then she paused and changed her conversational tack. "Well. We're so looking forward to spending the day with you and your Mr. Cassidy, Lillias, whether or not any shooting takes place. We'd so hoped Lady Harriette—she's the Marquess of Dervall's daughter—would have safely arrived by now but we've had a message this morning—they've been detained a week or more. I do believe it was stained with a little tear. I was quite moved." She placed a hand over her heart. "She's a dear thing—so petite and pretty and docile, you know, and hasn't yet surprised anyone."

Lillias knew this little criticism for what it was. She leaned forward and patted the countess's arm. "There's still time," she said, with great, feigned sympathy.

Finally Lillias's parents appeared at the top of the marble staircase and made their way down, and moments later two blue-liveried, bewigged footmen appeared with a hamper. Giles had a word with another footman about getting the groundskeeper to ready the rifle targets.

And then they all set out.

They'd passed the giant fountain featuring spitting cupids, heading out into an orderly avenue of sorts outlined by low green shrubs and tidily trimmed flowers that reminded Hugh of nothing so much as a labyrinth one could never escape. If they should inadvertently arrive at a minotaur, he was certain it would be the small tasteful English variety that spoke in cutting words.

Giles had flanked Lillias at once. Hugh took up her other side.

The earls and countesses fell back a little and let the younger people stroll ahead.

"Lilly knows nearly every inch of this house as well as I do, no doubt," Giles began. "Do you remember sliding across the foyer in your stocking feet? How your governess scolded you. You told her that day you were going to live here so what did it matter what you did?"

Lillias laughed. "She was a bit of a harridan, Mrs. Cuthbert. One just wanted to *bait* her."

"You were forever asking her questions she couldn't quite answer and she was infuriated by her inadequacy."

"I imagine inadequacy *would* be infuriating," Hugh said with abstracted sympathy, to Giles. He made it sound as though this was something Delacorte might have a pill to address.

Giles's determined confidence stuttered a little. But he ventured on. "And Lilly, do you remember the day you slid down the banister—"

She gave a shout of laughter. "—and you were at the foot of the stairs with a jam tart . . ." Lillias interjected.

". . . and when you flew off your face went right into it!"

They laughed together, delightedly.

For Hugh, it was the oddest sensation to feel elevated by her joy and yet oppressed by the source of it.

"I love to hear stories of when Lillias was a child," Hugh said. "How thoughtful of you to share them, Giles."

He said it because it was clear Giles was going to do his best to exclude him.

"How shocked everyone in the *ton* would be if they knew you were like that once, Lillias," Giles said. "You're such a fine lady now."

Her smile faded. "I suppose so."

Once again, Hugh knew that odd sensation of a belt tightened about his ribs on her behalf.

"The color you wore last night was about the

color of the stain left behind. A pale rose. Your dress was quite ruined. We cut it up into rags and St. John wrapped it around his shin and pretended to be a bloodstained, wounded pirate." Giles laughed.

Lillias didn't. She was at once abruptly silent.

She didn't look at him.

But Hugh knew she was thinking about that scar on his torso, and gunshot wounds, and the loss of his family members. And how he'd been alone in a hospital and imagined Amelia Woodley in order to have something to live for.

She looked up into his face, swiftly. Then away to Giles, who had never done anything so unseemly as kill or nearly be killed.

"It doesn't pay to just *wound* a pirate," Hugh said finally. "If you don't kill one outright, you're as good as dead. A bit the way you would an attacking puma. It's best to aim *right* for the heart. Or maybe throat."

This resulted in uniformly dumbstruck silence. Not one person knew how to respond to this unprecedented bit of information.

But it did put Giles in the untenable position of needing to ask Hugh how he knew how to kill pirates, which was both a gauche thing to mention and an inarguably, hopelessly manly thing to do.

"Mr. Cassidy knows a lot of very specific things," Lillias said. Her tone was indecipherable. She glanced at Giles worriedly, which Hugh found both touching and a trifle infuriating.

Giles refrained from taking up the topic and elected to brood a little.

"Everywhere I look there's a memory," Lillias said, absently. "That tree . . . the one with the knots on it that look like an old man's face?"

"We were there the day our new hound puppy Poppin jumped up and put muddy paws all over your dress?"

"A bear once nearly killed Hugh and his hound," Lillias said idly.

"The hound survived," Hugh said comfortably.

Giles, perhaps understandably, went completely silent.

"Things are often trying to kill you, Mr. Cassidy. I do wonder why," he said, finally.

This made Hugh smile slowly.

"My dear Mr. Cassidy, you must be relieved to be on English shores now and far away from so many terrible dangers." This came from behind them. Lady Bankham had promoted him to her "dear," which he supposed was flattering.

"Well, the primary danger to Americans in recent years has been the English," Hugh said, but with a mischievous sidelong glance at Lillias.

It was a statement that could be taken a number of ways, and was calculated to make all of the aristocrats both charmed and uneasy, and it succeeded.

They emerged from the hedge maze onto a vast swath of green surrounded by a low stone wall.

The groundskeeper, a patient-looking man with a mop of wiry gray hair and a face grooved in interesting lines, was waiting for them.

"Ah, look, the targets are set up for shooting." Giles sounded relieved. He was confident in his prowess.

"We'll just be over here covering our ears, dear," said the Countess of Bankham, speaking on behalf of all of the parents. "Do hurry, as the cheese will sweat if we don't eat it soon."

The groundskeeper had brought out a pair of fine Baker rifles, along with powder and cartridges. Gleaming on the low stone wall were two apples. He'd come equipped with a few others, should there be a call for it.

Hugh inspected the rifle he'd been handed.

It was inhale/exhale, to Hugh. Loading and shooting. Instinct. His hands were a deft, deadly blur of cartridge and powder. A half second of lining the apple up in his sights.

Then aiming.

And he fired.

The apple exploded.

He turned.

Giles went still. He was still ramming his powder.

"WELL DONE, MR. CASSIDY," enthused a temporarily deafened Earl of Vaughn.

"The cheese is about to sweat, Giles," Hugh said calmly.

And while Giles raised the rifle to his shoulder, Hugh reloaded his.

"FIRE!" the groundskeeper bellowed.

Giles did just that, adeptly turning the apple into smaller chunks of apple.

"We'll call it a tie," Hugh said generously.

Giles was silent. His mouth was a thin line. "Shall we have our picnic now?" he said, finally.

"I thought perhaps Lillias would like a go," Hugh said.

"I would like to have a go," she said firmly.

"Lillias, do you really think you ought to . . ." This was her mother, fretfully.

"I thought you were jesting, Lillias," Giles said.

"No," Lillias said into the silence. "I was serious. I'd like to shoot."

This was greeted by a nonplussed quiet.

Hugh glanced up at the groundskeeper, who understood it as a signal. He gamely jogged out to the wall and placed another apple, then jogged back.

Hugh was matter-of-factly showing Lillias how to hold the rifle.

"How do you aim?"

"Hold it up to your shoulder like so."

Hugh stood behind her to steady her arms on the rifle. She was slim but remarkably sturdy; he could feel her stubborn strength of will vibrating through her straight spine. Pride and contrariness probably had a bit to do with it, too.

"Once I have the target in my sights," he said, close to her ear, "I think of what I love most in the world. What will happen if I miss? Will they be harmed? Will they go hungry? Will I see them again?" He paused at length. "Because I've learned that once you know what truly matters in life, and once you know who and what you truly love, then you know who you are . . . and your aim will always be true."

She met his eyes across the rifle. Her own flickered with something he couldn't quite read. So intent was her gaze, so suddenly narrowed, for that instant, he felt as though she was frisking his soul. Or her own.

He stood back. "And *that's* when I pull the trig-

ger," he said softly. "In case any of that was helpful, I'll be right behind you. But brace yourself. It
has a kick."

He gestured to the group behind them and their
hands went up over ears.

She took a moment. He would have given a fortune to know what she was thinking as she got the
apple in her sights.

"Fire," he said quietly.

She pulled the trigger.

She staggered back into him and the apple exploded. He gently righted her.

They all stood back in silent awe.

"Well," she said. Sounding both satisfied and
abstracted.

For a long moment they simply looked at each
other.

"I never had any doubts," he said evenly.

She turned abruptly away from him. She lowered the rifle, staring at the place where the apple
had shattered. Pensive.

The groundskeeper walked over to take it from
her hands.

And then came an odd silence.

"When *I* shoot, Lillias," Giles said deliberately,
"I think about how blessed I am that I and my
family are wealthy enough to never go hungry
even if I never shoot a thing. About how fortunate we are to never know a danger other than
the odd storm or two. That we have a full staff of
servants to cook for us in our enormous comfortable house with grounds large enough for game
to roam . . . and yet I can still shoot for the simple
pleasure of it."

He offered her a little smile.

She gave him one of her own, out of habit. It vanished swiftly, however.

"When the stakes are low, everything is a game," Hugh said politely to Giles.

Chapter Twenty

༄ৎ৩৩৩৩

*T*HE MOOD of the day officially changed after that.

A hum of tension seemed to underlie every polite word uttered.

"May we *please* eat now?" the Earl of Vaughn wanted to know.

The footmen smoothed a blanket over the grass beneath the branches of a huge old oak, and began laying out plates and glasses, cheeses and fruits both fresh and preserved, various tarts and cakes and sliced cold meats, bottles of water and wine, and everyone settled in to feast. Conversation was pleasant and desultory and kept to the safer topics, the ones not likely to upset digestion. This meant dogs and horses, usually, and the weather.

Lillias hadn't said a word since she'd blown the apple to smithereens.

Nor had she met Hugh's eyes. She seemed, once again, filled with thoughts.

"It's been such a joy sharing Heatherfield Park with Lillias and her family over the years. Does the . . . Cassidy . . . family have an ancestral seat, Mr. Cassidy?"

Giles asked this. Hugh almost said, "Have you any more obvious questions? Because I can't think of one." He was tempted to point to the nether re-

gions of his pants and say, "All of my ancestors
had one, same as yours."

He supposed this was the sort of posturing
Lillias hoped for from him.

He took a sip of some of the ale brought out.

"Not as such. I helped my father build a cabin
from the ground up. We chose and felled the timbers. It was our first real home. My brother was
born there." Thusly Hugh provided his autobiog-
raphy in clipped syllables.

He didn't mention that his father didn't know
his own father. He was *sorely* tempted, but he
didn't want to subject Lillias to gasps.

"A . . . cabin?" Giles repeated. As if he wasn't certain one ought to say that word in polite company.
He turned a worried expression toward Lillias.

Lillias gave him a taut, distracted smile.

"A dear little house, Giles," his mother called
from behind them. "Made of sticks. A bit like a
bird's nest, isn't that so, Mr. Cassidy?"

"No," Hugh said.

He saw the startled expressions and drew in a
breath. Clearly that had emerged a little abruptly.
"Perhaps it's best to think of it as a cabin on a ship.
Simple, snug, immeasurably sturdy. One feels safe
in it when one sails across the ocean. And since I
built it and my father was there with me, I would
trust the safety and comfort of anyone I loved to it.

"My mother used to shoot dinner from the
porch," Hugh added.

"Oh. Oh dear," Lady Bankham muttered.

"A few years later, we built a home with plas-
tered walls and a roof because a woman deserves
a proper home. Four rooms and a door and win-

dows, stairs up to the attic room, flowers on the mantel, rugs loomed by my mother . . . it's still standing, too. Withstood battering storms and heat. That's where my sister was born. I'd hold it right up to Heatherfield in terms of endurance."

Judging from the faintly scandalized expressions of the Earl and Lady Bankham, this comparison was sacrilege.

"You're . . . you're not going to bring Lillias to live there?" Lady Bankham breathed. She surreptitiously touched Lady Vaughn's hand in support.

"Of course not. The house I want to build for Lillias will be . . ." He stopped. "Lillias and I will be living in England, of course. I would never want her to live in anything other than the style to which she's long been accustomed." He said this to soothe the worried, staring parents.

"They'll have the Devonshire house for a start," the earl said to the Bankhams, who nodded, of course, of course, the Devonshire house.

"Oh yes, charming place."

"And I'll have Heatherfield, eventually, of course," Giles said, with an arm sweep to indicate the ground and much deprecation, entirely insincere. "You might find it interesting to know that the marble was imported from—"

"Tell me about the house," Lillias said.

Her eyes were fixed on Hugh's face avidly.

"I beg your pardon?" he said.

"The house," she repeated evenly. "The one you want to build for me in the Hudson River Valley. Tell me about the house."

Instantly it was as though the two of them were entirely alone.

A blue butterfly took a moment to orbit them in floppy circles.

Giles cleared his throat. "But if the two of you are going to live in England . . ."

She didn't reply. She actually raised a hand slightly.

Hugh ignored him.

And her eyes compelled him.

He took a breath and released it. And suddenly he knew how to begin.

"Have you ever seen a beautiful woman wearing a diamond and think . . . while the stone is lovely, it's superfluous? Nothing could improve upon her beauty?"

He addressed everyone.

But he didn't take his eyes from Lillias's face.

Not one of the men present had ever had such a thought but they all wanted to be thought of as someone who had, so they nodded sagely. Which pleased two wives.

"I mention that because . . . that was my inspiration. I should also say—because this is relevant, too—that it's a little odd for me to hear you call her Lilly, Giles—if I may call you Giles—though of course it arises from long association, and it's a pleasure to know that others hold Lillias in affection." He smiled here. He'd chosen that mild little word—"affection"—deliberately. "But 'Lillias' sounded to me from the first like the name of a goddess. It suited her utterly. And that's what inspired the house."

The objective of his campaign had diverged from their original plan. It had, in fact, been heading in this direction from the moment he'd met her, and he was only now realizing it.

And he was a ruthless campaigner.

Inspiration unspooled, as if this was a story he'd told for lifetimes. As surely as it was a myth. "First I ought to tell all of you—Lillias knows—that the trees in America are like the spires of the grandest English churches. In the morning, the tops of them are often wreathed in mist, like they're all wearing halos, and the rising sun turns the cloud and mist into nacre and opal. The sunsets . . . colors you've never imagined hang up in the sky like bunting and feathers and the satin of ladies' dresses at a ball. Flame and purple and rose and gold, they change every moment and the shadows change, too. The smell is . . ." He took a long breath, trying to fit words to the things he felt. "Green and brown, ancient and dying, new and budding. And when you lay your feet down on the forest floor, a bit of that perfume rises up with every step. A place like that . . . it shows you who you are. I can't imagine Olympus holds a candle to it."

His audience was absolutely riveted.

But the only person who mattered was the one wearing the bonnet with the green ribbon, which fluttered loosely beneath her chin. She was rapt. Her eyes glittered with something close to fury in its intensity. Her features were taut.

The only sounds were birds trilling and the tiny leaves on the tidy shrubbery shivering in a breeze. He looked briefly away, across the smooth acres of green. The image came to him as clearly as a myth told for hundreds of years.

"Everywhere you look on my land, at every time of day . . . it's like living among a treasure chest full of jewels. And so I knew the house for her should both belong to the land and be a setting in which a woman like her can shine in all her true beauty. And it should look like something you'd stumble across if you should find yourself on Mt. Olympus. And in the Grecian style . . . a bit like a temple. Glowing in the sun, gold in the morning and bronze as the sun begins to fall. Clean-lined, majestic, elegant, serene. Ionic columns. A pediment, with a window, perhaps stained glass, that would catch the light. We'd welcome our guests onto a porch as generous as open arms. Over a sort of infinity of blue sky, mountains and trees and lakes like sapphires . . . we'd look out to . . . eternity."

Lord and Lady Vaughn exchanged glances.

No one said a word.

"Inside the house we'd have the finest materials . . . nothing shiny or spindly—I'm not petite, and the children—we'd want them to feel free to run around. Solid, elegant, comfortable, and lush. The rooms are filled with light and we've more wood than marble because good wood will give back light like gold does. It would be made to last forever. But mainly for us, and for two boys and two girls and cats and dogs."

He paused.

Lillias swallowed. Her jaw was set. Oddly, she looked very nearly furious. Or in the throes of some other fierce emotion.

He knew he was tormenting her. But he had an objective.

"Well, the sort of banisters one could slide down, of course. Lillias might want to get from one floor to another quickly." He smiled at that.

A little hush fell.

LILLIAS REMAINED ABSOLUTELY motionless. She didn't say a word. She was irrationally afraid that if she blinked, or breathed, the image Hugh had just conjured would disappear.

Two boys and two girls. It was what she'd always wanted, too.

She turned toward the group on the picnic blanket. The people she'd known her entire life suddenly seemed slightly unreal. A trifle distorted, as if she were viewing them through a window. She looked back toward Heatherfield; she could have sworn she saw a creamy white house fronted with pillars with a pediment window that caught the light. A terrible longing pierced her dead center. Fleeting, frightening, painfully beautiful.

All the things Hugh loved. All the things he could not have if he stayed here with her.

"It's so very American to want to build something entirely new," Giles said politely. "I suppose it's a country founded by those who've run away from tradition."

Hugh went rigid.

And the way he turned toward Giles slowly made Lillias's hands go cold with trepidation.

"No American has ever run *away* from anything. We've been fighting for our way of life since the country was born."

"You didn't quite win that last war, did you?"

Giles furrowed his brow as if his memory indeed required refreshing. When of course knowing about that war was unavoidable for any English person who read.

What the devil was *wrong* with him? Hugh could probably break him in half if he wanted to. And yet wasn't this the sort of thing she'd thought she'd wanted—this outright competition?

"Giles," she said softly. An admonishment. A gentle plea.

He didn't seem to hear her.

"Well, the British gave up," Hugh said easily.

Well. That certainly caused everyone to suck their breath in.

"Hugh," she said, very quietly.

But she might as well have been a ghost for how heard she was.

"A bit hard to keep two wars going for the British, of course," Hugh continued reasonably. "And arguably, I would describe the cessation of impressments of American sailors and the signing of a treaty as winning. But I'm certain they would have fared better if you'd had a commission, Giles. The commanders no doubt would have benefited from your military prowess. You could have shown them your Sussex Marksmanship Trophy."

The silence was more surprised than outraged. In fact, Giles's parents weren't even certain they'd heard correctly. Who on earth would have the temerity to say such a thing to a Bankham?

Lillias was suddenly a wishbone, violently pulled from opposite directions. She couldn't quite get a good breath.

"They probably would have, Giles, dear," his

mother said stoutly. "How lovely it is that you'll never have to fight a day in your life."

"Yes, how lovely, Giles, that you won't have to fight. For anything. Or anyone," Hugh agreed pleasantly.

There was really no way to charitably interpret this sentence.

Suddenly it was as if Hugh was the wolf set free among them and they'd only just noticed.

Nobody said a word, but the impulse to move back a few inches was almost comically palpable.

She realized now that Hugh's patience had been little by little abrading all afternoon. His quiet, confident contempt for their way of life, the things they loved, that *she* loved—was scarcely veiled now. Hugh had declared war. Whatever grip he'd had on patience and civility was lost, and what was worse, she couldn't blame him. And she knew that when he decided to fight, he went all in.

And yet. She'd begun to shake with something like anger. How dare he make all of these people seem frivolous in her eyes? Seem somehow less real than he was?

Everything seemed less real than he was.

"Mr. Cassidy lost his father and his brother in that war," Lillias's father said quietly.

Hugh still refused to meet Lillias's eyes.

It seemed almost a breach of etiquette to bring up their deaths on a sunny day on the flawlessly manicured lawn unfurling like a great carpet toward the huge home. But what was war if not death? Britain had paid its own terrible price in Europe.

No matter. It was as though Hugh hadn't heard. He still had Giles in his sights.

"A country only officially born in 1776, a country about as old as Lillias's father, has twice beaten back a nation with about nine centuries of conquering experience. Twice. I'll bet you your ancestral seat against mine, Bankham, that England won't make a third attempt. No empire remains an empire forever. Just ask the Romans."

Giles was white about the mouth now. The right scathing rejoinder was clearly eluding him, but then, one couldn't practice scathing rejoinders at Mantons. He was so naturally amiable. So usually gentle. He might know how to shoot brilliantly, but he didn't quite know what it was to fight.

And there was no denying the truth of everything Hugh had just said.

But she also realized that no one else could see it because they were layered in privilege as shiny and slick as silver. Everything reflected. Everything slid right off.

"We love our country every bit as much as you love yours, Mr. Cassidy," the Earl of Bankham said quietly. It sounded a bit like a gentle warning. And now all eyes were on him.

Lillias wanted to tell them to leave Hugh alone; he'd had enough pain. She wanted to tell him he didn't need to fight with anyone anymore; the war was over.

But she also knew he would always fight for what he cared about.

A strange pressure welled, filling her chest, her head. Her heart felt twined with thorny vines. She could not quite grasp an end of them to unravel it and get at the purest truth. Her own truth.

"Clearly," Hugh said gently. "There would indeed be no America without Britain. Remarkable, extraordinary Britain. I'm honored to call it home from now on. And there would of course be no Lillias without it, and that, as far as I'm concerned, is its finest accomplishment."

Lillias found herself propelled to her feet. She stood, rather blindly for a moment.

And then she turned and began walking. And walking. Toward the oak forest. She distantly heard her name. It was like so much wind in the trees.

And once in the trees, the walk became a trot, and then she was running like her life depended on it.

SHE KNEW HEATHERFIELD; she knew all the trees, the knots in their trunks, the patterns of light that fell between them; they whipped by out of the corners of her eyes, and they might as well have been a ballroom full of people standing. It was all a blur now, all of her life, her past. All the same. She furiously ran as though if she just got far enough she'd come upon the Lillias she once was. The one who'd been so certain of what she wanted and how her life would be.

"Lillias."

Hugh was fast. He was already upon her.

She stopped abruptly and turned.

They stared at each other.

The wind ruffled his hair and tossed his coat out behind him.

"How dare you?" she said finally. Coldly. She was breathing hard.

"Care to elaborate?" he said calmly.

"You're *barely* disguising your scorn for people I care about. And what gives you the right to scorn what I want? After all, it's *exactly* what you want."

He barked an astonished laugh. "I want to be married to Lord Milquetoast and live in an echoing mausoleum and do the same things, day after day, year after year, and let my family's ancient money feed me like a fatted lamb. *That's* what you've gleaned from our association so far?"

"You want everything to stay the *same*. For all your talk of building things and newness, you want things to be exactly as you've always had them. You want the same woman you've always imagined you wanted in the same place you've always lived, and the only reason you think differently is because almost everyone is *gone*. You've no history to uphold. No family to please. So spare. Me. Your. Scorn."

Her voice broke on the last word.

Because his face went whiter and whiter and she felt like a murderer.

She never loathed herself so much. She'd never known she could fight so filthily, could reach for someone's most vulnerable places and insert her sword. It was possible she'd never understood anyone else well enough to do that.

She wanted to apologize but only for inflicting pain. She wasn't going to apologize for telling her truth. Because she was right.

"It matters to me, Hugh. They matter to me." She said it desperately. Her voice cracked.

As though she was trying to convince herself.

And still it seemed he couldn't speak.

"Well. I suppose it's a good thing our plan is working a treat, don't you? Can't you sense Lord Bankham's first ever insurrection on the horizon, future Lady Bankham?"

He said it without rancor, but with much irony.

Why did it feel like a slap?

She drew in a breath. "Well. And then you can go," she said quietly.

"You left out 'to the devil.'"

"While that is quite true, I never used to have those kinds of thoughts before I met you."

He hesitated.

"I imagine you didn't feel a lot of things before you met me."

The words weren't snide or accusatory. He said them evenly. They were, perhaps, almost a question.

Her eyes began to burn. Furious tears tightened her throat, and she was damned if she'd let him see them.

She turned around swiftly, prepared to run back the way she'd come. In all likelihood she could have done it with her eyes closed. Weaving through the trees that were so familiar. Treading the paths worn over centuries.

But as it turned out this was overoptimistic because she still managed to trip on a little branch that had recently fallen.

She saw the ground rushing up to meet her.

She never got there.

She gasped when she was yanked back swiftly and tucked into the hard shelter of his body.

Hugh's arms were around her waist.

He turned her around, his hands holding her fast, reviewing her for damage.

She went still.

"Well? Are you going to kick me, like you kicked Gilly when you fell into the pond?"

"Bastard." She said it quietly.

"You didn't learn that word from me *or* from The Grand Palace on the Thames."

"If you'd just let go and give me a little room to do it, I'll kick you much harder than I ever kicked Gilly."

They stared fiercely at each other. He was a fearsome man—he could crush her if he chose. Perhaps he already had. In the way that petals release their truest scent when crushed. Like the forest floor exhales its layers when trod upon.

Don't let go.

The heretical thought lodged in her mind.

And that was just it: she somehow knew that no matter what, he would catch her. He would not let her get away with anything. He would make her say what she thought and he would be equal to hearing anything she said. He would know what she needed. He would know how she felt.

They remained rooted just like that, his hands resting at her waist. Lightly. Warm. She could feel the strength of him, like a tree or a ship or a little lath and plaster house that stood up to battering storms.

Never, never did he hurt her, except by the very fact of his existence, which could not be helped. He had cracked her open in ways she had not expected and did not welcome, and all the things she truly was were emerging. If she were honest, she knew the cracks had begun before he'd even arrived.

The wind soughed through the trees above them, and fallen leaves danced in a mad little circle, then lay still.

"Do you want me to let you go?" He said it quietly.

Why did he always leave the choice to her?

His features were taut. All that emotion he refused to show her, all that emotion he'd long schooled himself to hide because he was so strong and *manly*, all safely dammed up behind his beautiful features. But she could still see in his eyes how he saw her—the humor and longing, the sympathy, the vulnerability. The desire.

Suddenly it seemed wildly unfair that he should be so protected when she felt so laid bare. All she could think was that his eyes were surely the color of the ocean between England and America, and she had never seen anything so beautiful and so dangerously full of promise. She was as dizzy as if she were looking down and guessing the depths of the sea.

She closed her eyes.

She didn't pull away.

And he didn't release her.

Somewhere a bird called to another bird. Two plaintive trills exchanged. Then silence.

They were still away from the crowd.

She was aware, suddenly, that her cheek was moving softly as though against the sea. Lifting and falling. Somehow she'd eased up against him, as easily and unconsciously as a ship knows its part. She leaned against his chest. Slowly she uncurled her fingers from their clench, until they lay

flat against him. She felt the soft heat of his hand
right at the small of her back, hovering, then coming to rest there, where it seemed to belong.

Why should safety feel so infinitely perilous?
Why did she suddenly want to weep from a grief
she could not define, when the moment felt like a
hosanna?

"Lillias . . ." Her name like a whispered "Amen"
at the end of a secret prayer. It had a break in it.
"Do you want me to let you go?"

She heard the hint of a plea. The crack in all of
those words.

But there was no mercy for either of them.

She dragged her hands down and down until
she found the gap between his waist and trou-
ser and slid her hand inside his shirt. The jump
of muscles beneath her bare palm, his hot skin
smoothed taut over his stomach. It was brazen and
a hunger ignited so swiftly she was shaking.

She exhaled in pure surrender. She turned her
face up for his kiss.

He cupped her face in his hand, and she turned
it gently as his lips found her ear, her throat, her
lips.

At any time the group could come upon them.

He pivoted her up against the tree. And if there
was something desperate and maybe sordid in the
speed of what happened next, and in the deliber-
ate hiding, the terrible, terrible risk, she didn't care
and so be it. It would be the last time. That was the
danger and the dark, exquisite miracle of it. This
would be the last time. They both knew that.

Shockingly, with a deftness that didn't bear
thinking about, he lowered her bodice to free her

breasts and filled his hands with them. "Oh, dear God . . ." he sighed. "Lillias . . ."

He dragged his thumbs hard over her nipples, teasing and chafing, and her low animal moan shocked her; the pleasure was a revelation. How did anyone withstand it? She drew up hot jagged breaths.

He furled up her dress and lifted her up, slipped his hands beneath her arse, and pulled her against his groin, his cock hard behind the fall of his trousers, and moved against her.

"Hugh . . ." It was a plea. An exhale. She hardly dared hope he'd heard.

"Beg me . . ." His voice was a staccato rasp. He ground his hips against her again.

"*More* . . . quickly . . . Hugh . . . I want . . ."

And that was the trouble. *More* was the crux of everything. He'd known that from the beginning.

Somehow with one hand he'd unbuttoned his trousers, which suggested it was far from the first time he'd done that. His cock sprang free. It was long and thick and looked pulsingly alive, an impressive shock. It perhaps ought to have shocked her even more than it did. It was a measure of the madness of lust that all she wanted was to feel it between her legs. At once.

Her wish was fulfilled.

He furled up her dress and held it in one fist and he slid his cock against her cleft. A sob of pleasure caught in her throat.

He held her hips and moved against her again, and she rose up to meet him.

"Oh God . . ." His breath was hoarse against her neck.

Together they rocked in a swift, hard, desperate rhythm. It was a race toward something glorious. Then her head fell helplessly back and she was writhing as something extraordinary and inexorable came upon her from everywhere at once.

He slipped his fingers into her soft, slick heat and stroked hard and swiftly and she came apart. He pressed her head against his chest and held her fast, because he knew she'd been launched. Knew she wanted to scream in primal joy and triumph.

It was perhaps the closest to flight she'd ever come. She felt her consciousness sifting down, down, down, in glittering fragments.

She held on to him as his body shook hard with his own release.

He held her as their breathing settled.

But there was no time to savor. Dazed and flushed, he fished out his handkerchief and dabbed at her thigh to clean where he'd spilled. And then gently stood her upright, straightened her bodice, helped her smooth her skirts.

The world still spun, forever changed, and yet not changed enough.

He studied her, then with a faint, rueful smile produced a knife from somewhere in his boot, and she used the clean blade of it as a mirror to adjust the pins in her hair.

She would warrant anything Gilly would never pull a big knife from his boot to use as a mirror.

But she could imagine him sitting with her father at White's for years to come. She could imagine picnics on drowsy summer days. She had, in fact, imagined precisely that, for years now.

And then . . .

Suddenly, alarmingly, she could now imagine nothing beyond that.

It was as if those were the only things she could fit in the confines of a picnic hamper.

She looked back at Hugh. He'd put a good ten feet of distance between them, as though she were a fire burning, shooting off too many sparks. With alacrity, he was putting himself back together, smoothing hands over his hair, tucking his shirt in again. She could see his shoulders still moving as he caught his breath.

That was humbling, the somewhat ridiculous aftermath of passion, she supposed. Everything blown into disarrayed bliss must be reassembled again.

The sounds of voices were just audible now.

Fate had shown mercy this time, and she would not be caught with her breasts out. Blessings ought to be counted.

They had a few seconds still. Alone.

"I'll speak with Giles tonight," Hugh said quietly. "And if all goes well, I'll be gone before dawn."

She knew what he meant.

Still dazed, her body still singing whatever note it was he'd struck from her, she gazed back at him. The sun behind him picked out all the red in his hair, gave him a fiery halo. If this is what Persephone saw before Hades took her under, she must have willingly gone.

She knew definitively it was she who had to let him go.

She heard herself say softly: "Very well."

He hesitated. Nodded once, shortly.

Then turned and strode off deeper into the little wood.

She watched him go.

Slowly, slowly she turned toward the cheerful voices of the people she'd known all her life.

Chapter Twenty-One

⌒⌒◉⌒⌒

SHE HAD the sense that she had been talked about.

Their expressions—rather gentle, worried, a trifle indulgent, charged with some sort of secret understanding—gave her a hint of what her own expression might be. Her hair and skirts might have been restored to order, but internally she was nothing but a pulsating thundercloud. That flush in her cheeks could well be taken for temper.

"Mr. Cassidy thought he saw a . . . a hedgehog . . . and wanted to have a look." She explained Hugh's absence this way. It was met with bemused silence.

"Americans," the earl said sympathetically, finally.

"I told him I'd like to go back with you. He said we oughtn't to wait for him."

If things were not going at all well with Mr. Cassidy, they were all on her side. That much was clear. She saw no judgment, no glee. Perhaps there was a little hope. Her engagement was all of two days old, after all. And they were her friends, people who loved her, and she felt the softness of their care as they all moved back toward the house.

She knew a little mordant amusement imagining how the disappearance of Hugh Cassidy would brighten the worlds of a group of benignly spoiled aristocrats.

Just the thought of Hugh made her being contract with a pang like a lightning strike. Swift in brilliance and thrill.

And how much darker than before it left everything when it was done.

How odd to feel soothed as her family surrounded her like a cradle and Hugh echoed in her body. If she raised her hands to her face now, she could smell him on her hands.

She did that just now. It went to her head like a drug. She nearly stumbled.

Giles fell in beside her, and that was comforting, too.

The rest of their party fell back just a little.

Subtle!

Despite herself, there was no denying it was comfortable and familiar, and just those two things began to soothe her roiled emotions, if only just a little. Her feet on the grass, the sun above, even the birds singing were probably the descendants of the same birds who had sung at Heatherfield for generations.

"Lilly . . . Lillias . . . it has been such a pleasure seeing you here again," he said.

"It's always a pleasure to spend time with you, Giles."

"One could even imagine a lifetime of beautiful days just like this. Don't you think?"

She managed to smile up at him.

He smiled back at her.

At least she could make someone smile. There was some relief to be had in that.

He was her dear friend and she loved him, she did. She truly did.

She struggled not to turn her head to look behind her.

And soon the house loomed into view again, as it had hundreds of times before.

"DID YOU ENJOY investigating the hedgehog, Mr. Cassidy?" Lady Bankham asked solicitously.

Hugh slowly raised his head cautiously.

Perhaps this was a euphemism or a code of some kind?

Everyone was looking at him with pleasant expectation.

Lillias was studying her plate.

"Yes," he decided to say. "Thank you for asking. We don't have hedgehogs in New York."

"There's such a long list of things that are here and not there," Lady Bankham said.

"I suppose that's true," Hugh said, thinking of the list of controversial words Lady Vaughn had suggested compiling in the drawing room at The Grand Palace on the Thames. He did not say, "And the reverse is also true," because that would make for a very long dinner indeed and it simply didn't matter anymore. He'd caused enough consternation in the span of one picnic.

Because he could do what he needed to do no matter how battered he'd been, and do it with conviction, Hugh managed to keep aloft for nearly an hour a very uncontroversial conversation about carriages. Men were simple, as he'd said, and it worked a treat, as he'd known it would. All the men engaged in what was apparently a satisfying time reminiscing about their first barouches and their component parts—silver trim and lamps and the like—and about learning to drive a team, horses they had known, races. The ladies interjected now and again to assist with blanks needing filling ("Do you recall the name of that groom who . . . ?" and so forth).

Lillias spoke only once, to the footman trying to refill her glass. She said, "No, thank you."

She managed to appear interested in the conversation, propping her chin on her linked hands, eyes bright. It must have been something of a Herculean feat, but she was a veteran of ballrooms and soirees where almost nothing real was said.

When a lull set in, and stomachs were patted and napkins plucked from the collars of shirts and the footmen had ferried away the empty dishes, Hugh said, "I wondered if I can interest Giles in a game of billiards?"

Lillias stared at him then.

He met her gaze full on, because only a fool would miss an opportunity to gaze at her in candlelight.

As usual, it was like taking a dart to the solar plexus. If his soul was a target, the very essence of her hit that red center every time. He'd once resented it, and now he knew it for the magic it was. For the loss it would be.

But there was no hope for his soul if he played any part in her unhappiness. And there was redemption in playing a part in giving her the life she wanted.

GILES POURED BRANDY for the two of them.

Balls were racked. Cues chosen.

And then Hugh leisurely reached out and closed the door.

Giles froze in chalking his cue and eyed the closed door for a moment, somewhat warily.

He continued.

They shot two rounds before Hugh spoke.

"Bankham . . . I'd like to ask for your opinion about something."

"Definitely the barouche," Giles said absently, lining up a shot.

"It's about women."

He all but felt the man go rigidly still.

After all, Hugh was large and he was holding a long stick and they were alone in the billiard room.

"A confounding topic to be sure," Giles said lightly.

Hugh nodded. He eyed the table for his next shot.

"What would you do . . ." he leaned forward and took aim ". . . if you were concerned that the affections of the woman to whom you were engaged were . . . more strongly engaged elsewhere?"

The ball clattered across the table.

The silence was long.

The two of them stood at either end of the table as though this was a duel, and not a game.

"Interesting philosophical question, Cassidy. I should think it would be an uncomfortable realization, indeed." Giles didn't look at him.

Giles leaned forward and eyed the table for his shot. He drew the cue back, measuring, measuring again. "Out of curiosity, what do your sort do if another bloke intervenes in an engagement? Is it duels with pistols? Or do you simply snap them in half over your knee like a bundle of twigs?"

"We tie them up, coat them in honey, and leave them in the forest for the bears and ants to have their way with. They're not worth wasting good bullets on."

Giles missed his shot badly.

He stood upright again.

The assessing stare returned. Giles was wary now. His face hard. He had centuries of breeding behind him. Innate confidence bequeathed by money and the power of his family name. And he could lay claim to his own strength of character.

"But I don't think there's any honor in holding a woman to a promise if there was a certainty she could have the life of which she's long dreamed," Hugh continued. "And if there's a certainty she'd be cared for, protected and cherished by someone she cares for, only a brute wouldn't step aside."

Hugh knew that honor was more a thing of theory for Giles, who hadn't fought for his homeland, hadn't made choices about who and what to shoot. That he wasn't yet thirty and most of his life choices were already made for him, though he didn't realize it and it would never occur to him to view it that way. But he *was* a decent sort. He was intelligent. He was everything Lillias had said he was. And in Hugh's mind, while this was something of an indictment, it still brought him some small measure of cold comfort.

Hugh took his shot. The ball milled madly around the pocket, then sank very prettily in.

Time itself seemed to hold its breath as the two of them looked across at each other.

Giles was transfixed. At first. The evolution of his expression was subtle, but not unworthy of him: triumph, relief, sympathy, all had their flickering turn.

"I'm not a brute," Hugh said quietly.

The following quiet was elegiac. Something had ended.

Neither of them pretended to be playing billiards anymore.

"Well, then," Giles said quietly but very distinctly, as though he were issuing a statement before a magistrate. "As a man of honor, I can say with full certainty that it's safe for you to step aside."

SHE WASN'T TO know that after he wrote the first letter, he'd pulled another sheet of foolscap toward him and stared at it, and then turned to stare out the window. He saw in its reflection her face as he'd first seen her in the twilit dark of the Annex, a startling, arrogant, maddening, vulnerable jewel wreathed in smoke. She wasn't to know that she'd stopped his breath then and any number of times since, which meant the next breath he took after that was like the first one he'd ever drawn. So it was like he was being born anew every time he looked at her.

And she wasn't to know, though she might have guessed, that he'd followed Amelia to England in part because he had indeed wanted things to return to the way they were, when in truth his life would and could never be the same.

And she wasn't to know how he suffered torments over trying to choose words to capture something that was both one emotion and every emotion: fury and jealousy, a lust that awed him with its tenderness, shamed him with its savagery, and tested the limits of his considerable restraint; the terrible regret that his mother would never know her, and that Hugh would never know if she got a dog and a cat of her own. And the gratitude— for the surfeit of pleasure he took in touching her skin, for the revelation that he'd not been fully alive for a very long time. And he knew this for certain because now everything in him and on him hurt as though he was waking in that hospital in Williamsville again, or being cast into a new world, naked. But perhaps that was as it should be. And perhaps that had been the point. He hurt, and he was alive again, because of her.

And she didn't know that he'd watched, his hand trembling a little, the pendulum on the clock swing and swing and mark off the hours, and that as he did so he'd cursed, finally and for the first time, his inability to make words sing or ache. In the end, all he could do was write his truth.

So all she read was:

I wish you every happiness.
Yrs,
Hugh Cassidy

Lillias was motionless. She stared at the letter in her hands, searching every word for meaning, while behind her the maids began moving about and packing her things.

And then she drew in a breath, and tucked the letter into her sketchbook, like the final page in a story. Every page of the sketchbook was filled now. She'd been awake all night doing just that.

And then she stared out the window.

She couldn't see nearly far enough.

Chapter Twenty-Two

⊰∘⊱

Bankham,
I have reason to believe Lillias's
affections have long been engaged
elsewhere, and her attachment to me
likely resulted only from an expectation
of disappointed hopes. I shall not stand
in the way of a more appropriate match,
and will release her from her promise
should the future she desires become
available to her. Her happiness is all
that matters to me.
H. Cassidy

GILES BROUGHT the letter to Lord Vaughn, with whom he'd requested a private meeting in the library at Heatherfield.

"I found it this morning tucked beneath my door. He left before dawn."

Lord Vaughn stared at the letter for a good long time, and thought: *Good Christ, why did I ever* have *daughters?*

"You are the . . . 'elsewhere'?" He said this with faint amazement and looked up at Giles from beneath beetled brows.

Giles looked radiantly bemused. "It would seem so," he said delicately, and with not a little pride. "I believe Mr. Cassidy detected as such. And I believe this is his way of telling me that he will not shoot me should I wish to step in."

The earl lowered the letter. His frown remained fixed.

"I seem to recall hearing something of an arrangement with your distant cousin. Harriette," he said.

Giles cleared his throat. The earl's frown was having the intended effect, which was to make him uncomfortable just for the sake of it. He said carefully, "It is not a fait accompli, you see. My parents might perhaps be disappointed that we will not be upholding the tradition of an alliance with the Dervalls, but I cannot think they will ever object to my match to Lillias, who is not only the daughter of an earl but possessed of such a sterling character. I in fact think, once they learn of the depth of our mutual esteem, they would rejoice."

The earl listened to this speech with a good deal of rue, considering the girl in question possessed a character comprised of many and varied splendors. He loved her, but she was human.

"Esteem," the earl repeated. Finally. Musingly.

Giles, for a moment, wasn't certain what to do with this.

"Yes, sir. I thought it wisest to speak to you before I spoke to Lillias, as I should hate to cause her consternation if you did not approve of a match. And I do already think of you as almost a father."

Lord Vaughn stared across at the young man he'd known since birth. He was a fine lad, good-hearted, intelligent, level-headed. He knew nearly everything about him, thanks to their family's long connection. Certainly the town was plagued with far worse, young bloods who drank and whored and raced their highflyers at foolish speeds. St. John at this point could go either way, really, but the earl controlled the purse strings and St. John was tethered to those. He would simply need to take on faith that he and his wife had instilled proper values in their children and hope for the best while taking a firm hand. One didn't get to be a parent without understanding that much of life is out of one's control.

Once again he frowned down upon the letter left by Mr. Hugh Cassidy, who had departed for Portsmouth before dawn on a hired mount. This was not a surprise, as he'd said he'd be doing as such. It could not be said that he was stealing away like a thief in the night. And his stunning little letter indicated that he would also not, for instance, be calling anyone out or otherwise making a fuss should his engagement come to an end.

The still, gray, stunned face of his daughter over breakfast, during which she'd merely looked at her plate of eggs as though she'd never seen such thing before, was a bit jarring, however.

This letter rather explained a lot.

Was it true? Had she been secretly pining for her childhood friend all of this time?

He looked up again. Giles withstood another few potent seconds of his unblinking scrutiny without squirming.

And Lord Vaughn did appreciate the scene in

which he was now participating—the handsome, respectable, young titled man in the beautifully tailored clothing humbly begging an audience with his prospective bride's father. It was how he'd dreamed it would always be. It was infinitely preferable to standing in a small crowd when a curtain was whipped aside to reveal his daughter in the throes of what looked like an expert clinch with a man she'd met only a fortnight earlier.

And yet.

Why the *bloody hell* hadn't this young idiot sitting in front of him spoken before now?

It was a terrible pity it was too early to drink.

"Why the bloody hell didn't you speak before now?" the earl said out loud.

Giles blinked.

"I . . . I could not be certain that the depth of her regard was equal to mine. Everyone admires Lillias and she is in turn kind to everyone."

The earl turned his head toward the clock, mainly in order to think without the younger man's hopeful gaze upon him. He could have told Giles that no one is certain of anything *ever* by the time they were the earl's age. But he was tired, and it was very clear to him that his daughter ought to get married.

It was just that he knew how Mr. Cassidy looked at Lillias when he thought no one was watching. That mixture of wonderment and fury mixed with something like tender amusement and . . . awe. He suspected it was precisely the way Cassidy looked at the Hudson River Valley.

And he recalled how he had leaped to shield her

when that fateful curtain opened. Had touched her elbow in the ballroom. Helped her into carriages. A father notices these things.

And he'd of course done the absolutely right thing by Lillias, at the cost of his own dreams.

The earl looked down. He kept returning to the last sentence of Mr. Cassidy's letter.

He rubbed his forehead, where he was certain another wrinkle was forming at this very moment.

He did not look forward to explaining any of this to his wife.

He sighed gustily and handed the letter back to Giles.

"You know I hold you in the utmost esteem, Giles," he said slowly, only a little ironically, "and I think of you almost as a son. It would be a fine thing to have you as a member of our family and I see no objection to this match. No settlement funds have been transferred to Mr. Cassidy as of yet. As entanglements go, it is one easily enough undone."

If this was not precisely the warm and whole-hearted endorsement Giles had hoped to hear— he'd envisioned the earl exaggeratedly mopping his brow at the notion of ridding himself of the diffi-cult American—it was understandably English and understated. *My mother used to shoot dinner from the porch.* Good heavens. Giles would shudder every time he remembered those words in Mr. Cassidy's voice.

"*But . . .*" the earl said. ". . . I have two stipu-lations. The first one is that I leave the decision entirely in Lillias's hands."

Giles nodded. He anticipated no difficulty there. Lillias had been all brooding silence last night and all listless silence this morning. She was *not* a person of passions and moods, typically. So this meant she was done with Mr. Cassidy, of a certainty, and required only rescuing from her predicament. What a pleasure it would be to rescue her.

He didn't share with the earl the remarkable conversation he'd had with Cassidy the previous evening. That was between the two men, and he was certain Cassidy would like it to remain that way.

The grace of Cassidy's gesture wasn't something Giles would soon forget.

"And the second is . . . I request that you wait to speak to her until after we return to London and have moved out of our fine accommodations at The Grand Palace on the Thames and back into our townhouse. She's had an eventful week and I do think she will be in a more receptive frame of mind. We will depart this morning from Heatherfield and you may set a date to speak to her in London a week hence. Are we understood, young Bankham?"

Giles thought about Lillias as a girl, riding her horse at breakneck speed, shooting a target dead center just yesterday, sliding down a banister, wading into a creek. For all her delicate beauty, she'd never struck him as fragile. Perhaps she was now. He felt even fonder of her at the notion.

"Thank you, sir," Giles said. "Understood."

"I'LL MISS IT," Claire said wistfully.

Lillias stared numbly out the carriage window at the little gated park with its valiant sturdy greenery, the shining white building, The Grand Palace on the Thames's sign with its ghostly "rogue" still visible, the modest gargoyles. The rooftop where she'd sat and looked out over a part of London she would otherwise have never seen, with a man she would otherwise have never met let alone kissed, beneath stars, mist, and a half-moon.

She would not likely see any of them ever again. This strange, mad interlude in her life was over. Things would now go back to the way they were, and that's the way they would remain, forever.

Of course, nothing had explicitly been said. That wasn't the English way.

But Giles had said to her gently, after breakfast, "I'd like to call upon your father, Lillias, on Friday at five o'clock on St. James Square. I hope this is happy news to you."

Lillias had stared at him.

So Hugh had indeed spoken to Giles. And had apparently reassured Giles that he did not intend to run him through if she should wish to end the engagement.

She wondered what on earth had actually been said.

"It's always a pleasure to see you," she said. Truthfully.

By this time next year she would be married to Giles. Lady Bankham. One day mistress of Heatherfield.

It was everything she'd dreamed of. She supposed she even had Hugh to thank for it. It had been a remarkable detour in her life, and one day, perhaps, she would look back upon it and understand why it needed to happen.

Their driver snapped the ribbons and the Vaughn carriage lurched forward, out of the little courtyard, away from The Grand Palace on the Thames, forever.

By the time they'd gotten to the little bridge near the Barking Road, they found themselves stopped by what appeared to be bedlam. A clot of carriages and a crowd of milling men on horseback and on foot, shouting and gesturing wildly at each other, lamps held aloft.

There was a polite knock on the carriage door.

Her father slid it open. "What the devil is—oh, good evening, Mr. Delacorte," he said.

Mr. Delacorte's usually cheery face was grim and in shadow. He touched his hat. "Saw the seal on your carriage, Lord Vaughn." He was breathing as though he'd run quite a distance.

"What's all the hubbub about?"

"Well, it seems the *Tropica* was destroyed as it sailed toward Portsmouth, some hours out to sea—lightning hit her mast, went up in flame. The *Justice* found a few survivors floating on detritus at sea and they took a detour into the East India docks to bring them to shore and we're making room and trying to find accommodations for the men they've acquired. It's been a bit mad."

Lillias went still. "The *T-t-tropica*?" Her stomach iced.

"Oh, that is a too bad thing," her father said. "Poor souls."

She could scarcely breathe. But she managed to get the question out. "Mr. Delacorte . . . did they find . . ."

He knew she meant Uncle Liam.

Delacorte shook his head slowly.

Nausea struck, swift and dark. She nearly doubled over with pain.

She felt as though she were being pulled into a whirlpool. "Does he know?"

"He knows." His face was grim. "He's not in Portsmouth. He's back at the inn. In his room." He paused. "His room on the third floor," he added, rather superfluously and meaningfully. "I must away."

He closed the carriage door and was gone.

Her father shot the bolt and thumped his walking stick on the roof.

And they lurched hard forward again, but still, progress was halting. Measured in inches.

A roaring sound started up in Lillias's ears.

It was the sound of her own breathing. In her head was something between a sob and a scream, the sound a heart makes when it is near to breaking.

The carriage inched a few feet more forward.

"Papa, what time is it?" She heard her own voice as though it was coming from outside the carriage, from a great distance away.

"A quarter to eleven o'clock, child."

Her lungs were sawing now. In, out. In, out.

And then she shoved open the door of the carriage and leaped out.

Her father roared. "Lillias—Lillias! Christ! What the devil is she . . ."

She ran.

The wind yanked her bonnet from her head and it flogged her back, and her pelisse sailed out behind her. She dodged and wove and feinted through the crowds of men and carriages and horses, ignoring shouts of indignation, leers, oaths.

The wind stung her eyes into tears, blurring everything like her ruined sketchbook as she raced past. Her lungs sawed.

And when she finally reached the front door of The Grand Palace on the Thames, she seized the knocker and slammed it five times against the door. Praying.

"Oh, Lady Lillias," Dot said cheerfully through the peep hatch. "It's five minutes to eleven o'clock. You almost missed curfew. Have you forgotten something?"

"Dot. You must open the door *now.*"

"Oh, do you need a bourdaloue?" Dot whispered, with a sympathetic nose wrinkle.

"YES," Lillias said, thinking swiftly. "Will you go and fetch one for me? RUN!"

"I'll make haste!" Dot yanked open the door and vanished in the direction of the kitchen, losing a shoe on the way. Lillias slammed the door, bolted it, and hurtled up the three flights, stumbling only once.

The house was already slumbering for the night; the candles had all been doused.

She knocked on the door, gently.

He might not open it for her.

He might not open it at all.

Well, then, she would pound.

She heard the bolt slide, and the door opened. He was in trousers, a shirt open at the throat. Still in his boots.

Hugh froze. And then his face flared into fleeting brilliance. There and gone. His features carefully schooled to stillness.

Behind him, the lamp was lit and the fire was healthy and high.

"I heard," she said softly. "Mr. Delacorte told me."

His head went back a little, then came down in a nod. He stepped aside and she followed him into his room.

He closed the door and slid the bolt shut.

He sank down on the edge of the bed as if all of that movement was the last he was capable of.

She hovered in the doorway. Quiet. Inwardly frantic to bear for him the kind of pain that could not be assuaged.

"It's kind of you to come," he said finally, formally.

She couldn't quite breathe properly. "Of course."

"Giles?" he said suddenly. "Is he . . . ?"

She swallowed. "He intends to call on me tomorrow at five o'clock."

He studied her face, then nodded once. His features remained immobile.

He was, in fact, alarmingly still. The force that animated him, burned from him, seemed all but doused. He leaned forward, hands folded in his lap.

Her gut went cold.

She worked the knotted ribbon from beneath her chin and freed herself from her bonnet, tossing it on the chair. Then she shook off her pelisse and draped it over it.

She sat down, very gingerly, next to him. The bed had a surprising amount of bounce. They never stinted on the truly important things at The Grand Palace on the Thames.

The crackle of the fire was the only sound in the room.

Together they sat in silence for a time.

"The reason stories like *Robinson Crusoe* exist . . ." Hugh began finally, as though continuing a thought. His voice was frayed. He cleared his throat. ". . . is because people want to read a story about survivors. Survivors of things that smash our lives apart. There's something so satisfying in it, I think. And if anyone can survive . . ." He paused. The fire, his breathing, were the only sounds for a time. "Well, perhaps Uncle Liam will turn up one day with a pet . . . a pet parrot."

He tried a wry smile.

But he looked stunned.

And that's when she knew her heart had only ever been buffeted a bit before. She hadn't understood definitively that it belonged to him until his grief broke it open. His grief was hers.

He looked up at her. "But . . ." He gave a short, shamed laugh. *"Why?"*

The word was hoarse. He was embarrassed to ask a question that was so cliché. That had no answers.

She slid her arms around his waist and linked her hands. And then she held him tight and fast, so that in this moment of his shipwreck, she was the plank he could cling to. She was how he'd find his way to shore. She'd willingly be the island where he rose again, lived again, triumphed. She leaned her head against his shoulder.

He closed his eyes and exhaled at length. As though he'd been waiting for her and for this. As though her presence was a blessed relief.

And he turned and buried his face in her neck and wrapped his arms around her and held on.

She savored with a quiet, awestruck joy the miraculous rise and fall of each of his long, shuddering breaths. Because there was really no reason he ought to be here at all. He could have died a hundred times before. That was the dumb luck and the glory of life. She felt helpless to do anything but hold him, but therein lay the greatest, sweetest power and gift she'd ever known: he needed her.

He didn't weep, but she did, a little. Her tears swelled and spilled, softly. Since his heart was her heart, she could do the crying for him.

She turned her head to kiss his temple. Her hands unlinked and glided over his back, where other hard days and heartbreaks were etched in scars on his skin. She stroked his hair, gently.

He turned his head and laid his lips below her ear. He drew them along the clean line of her jaw. She took his face in her hands and brought her lips to his and he groaned softly at the sheer privilege and relief to be kissing her again.

Slow, slow. They'd never before had the luxury of leisure, and he drew her into a spinning world with kisses that were a revelation: languid and searching, sorrowful and tender, wholly inebriating, destroyers of boundaries. She was floating or spinning, divorced from gravity, clinging to him and taking and taking, their breaths staccato and rough now. The skillful glide of his lips, the carnal dive of his tongue, the meeting and parting to meet again, the hunger building and building until she was trembling and the world seemed to be falling, but when her head sank into the pillow she realized Hugh had lowered her there in his arms.

She was now flat on the bed and she knew what was about to happen and it shouldn't. But she wanted it to.

His lips, his breath, and his tongue applied in thrilling combinations and sequences continued their campaign of pleasure over her ear, along her arched throat, down into the shadow between her breasts, everywhere a river of sensation. Her own dress became a caress when, to her surprise, he peeled the shoulders easily down. The hands that had been playing at the nape of her neck had deftly undone the laces.

She slid her hands under his shirt, up over the furred, hard planes of his chest, and felt like a conqueror when his muscles jumped and he hissed in a breath of pleasure.

He reached behind him and through some magical contortion managed to drag it up and off over his head. The glorious world that was his torso lay before her.

He ducked his head and took her nipple into his mouth and sucked gently.

"Hugh . . ." His name was a stunned gasp. Pleasure arced through her.

She arched as he did it again, and he shifted his hips to unbutton his trousers before he filled his hands with the silky weight of her other breast, teasing, stroking, until she was rippling from the new and merciless pleasure.

He covered her mouth again and his hands were between the two of them. He dragged his own trousers down and there was his cock, hot and hard, pressing against her.

He gripped a handful of her dress and furled it swiftly up. She helped.

And suddenly she was bare to the waist and he was over her, and his hand slipped between her thighs. Her thighs fell wider when he slipped his hand along where she was aching and wet.

"*Hugh . . . I want . . .*" It was a whispered sob.

He guided his cock into her.

Her eyes flared wide, then shuddered closed, her breath gusting from parted lips.

She opened her eyes again to find him watching her as if he beheld a miracle.

How strange, how glorious, to feel him moving in her. The slow glide as her body welcomed and gripped him; locked together, side by side, their bodies began a cadence he guided, and then with which she colluded, arching up to take him deeper, urging him with the speed of her own hips, as they chased the ultimate pleasure. His eyes had gone nearly black and they burned into her and then he closed them as the cords of his neck went taut and his head went back hard against the building rush of need. He vanished when she closed her eyes to isolate herself with sensation. His hand on her hip; her hands against his chest; her head tucked into the hollow of his neck; there was no sound now, no world save the swift, desperate, rhythmic collision of their bodies and roar of their breathing. It was coming upon her again, that Roman candle release, gathering from the very edges of her being to a point of hot light. She distantly heard her own voice, *please, Hugh, oh God*, in harsh sobbing breaths.

And then bliss all but tore her from her body. She pressed her face into his chest as a triumphant scream, raw and nearly silent, tore from her, and she clung to him as her body was wracked with wave after wave of pleasure. From somewhere in the stratosphere she heard her own name as a groan as he went still, and then his body bucked, at the mercy of his own release.

Stunned, sated, amazed, they held on to each other as consciousness sifted back into their limp bodies.

She opened her eyes to a pair of blue ones staring down at her, as if memorizing her.

"Are you all right?" he murmured.

"Never better."

He smiled, and he could feel her smiling against his chest.

Their clothing was a shambles; her dress was mostly around her waist, his trousers trapped his legs. Together they helped each other out of the last scraps of decorum and it all ended up on the floor. He reached for her and she reached for him and utterly naked they held each other and savored the miracle of breathing together, of the feeling of bare skin all the way down.

The outrageous beauty of her. The wild gift of her passion. The cataclysmic pleasure. The generosity of giving her whole self to him when he was facing yet another unthinkable loss. Hugh could not think of a thing he'd done to deserve this moment, but perhaps, like fairness, deservedness was not a useful concept by which to live one's life. Perhaps the animals had indeed gotten it right. When such gifts were provided, the only sin was failing to be grateful. And the only safety was not thinking beyond this moment, her flesh hot against his, her trusting, sated, vulnerable body in his arms.

Her new life would begin—or continue, he supposed—tomorrow evening, with a proposal from an aristocrat. He wouldn't dwell upon the notion of some other man lying next to her any more than he'd love to dwell upon slowly bleeding to death from a bullet wound. There was comfort in knowing that he'd in the most unlikely fashion made sure she was getting the life she'd long wanted. And he would go back to America. He had a plan, after all.

But for this moment she was his. Only his. And no one knew how to appreciate a moment better than he did. It was all there was of life: moments of grace between the upheavals and changes.

Her hands had begun to softly, slowly move over him. Her fingertips traveled the deep gullies between his muscles, finding the raised scars, dragging her nails along him. Memorizing his textures. Her palms savored the texture of the coarse hair over his chest, the leather of his nipples. To the incomparable comfort and bliss of being so touched, he submitted, drowsily inebriated by the pleasure of it . . . then the gathering tension as desire was inevitably stoked and they were both reaching for each other and for more again.

He stirred and turned and her lips found his and it was his turn to savor. To revel in her discovery of all that his lips and hands could do, feeling her body ripple beneath him, or her eyes go dazed with wonder, then closed as she withstood the pleasure. And to glut his eyes and hands on the splendors of her body. He slid his lips down her throat, to her breasts, and gave each one a thorough appreciation, stroking the satiny weight of them, drawing his tongue around, then closing his lips over her nipples. He followed the silky divide between her ribs with soft fingers and his lips and breath, over her belly, and when he reached the triangle of auburn curls, he dipped his head to taste her and her gasp of shocked pleasure inspired him to do it again, and again, until her thighs had fallen open to abet this feasting. She moved with him, her hands curling into the counterpane, her coppery head thrashing back against his pillow, murmuring his name, turning it into a plea.

Nothing had ever been more erotic. The saw and cadence of breathing, her sighs and pleas, the curl and flex of her fingers in the counterpane, told him she was about to come apart, and he guided his cock into her and she did, her body bowing, her head thrashed to bury her scream in his pillow. She was still pulsing around him as he moved in leisurely, deep strokes, an attempt to postpone that moment of his own release, to build it to a mad crescendo. She turned her head again to meet his eyes. They reveled in each other's enthralled, lust-hazed expressions. He savored that view of her rippling body, the lift of her sweat-sheened breasts and throat as she once again arched helplessly, another release building. And then his own had its talons in him. He unleashed his restraint and he plunged again and again, hips drumming, until he was nearly blind with need. And then all at once he was fragments, shattered by the ecstasy he'd been chasing.

SIDE BY SIDE, they dozed. Lillias slipped in and out of dreams, naked in her sleep for the first time, apart from the warm arms around her.

She stirred and came fully awake when she realized his heat was gone.

Alert now, she sat up, clutching the counterpane to her.

His clothes were missing from the heap on the floor. Her heart gave a jolt.

And then she saw him, murmuring to someone through a crack in the door.

There was no clock, but the quality of the light through the blinds told her it was just before dawn.

He closed the door and turned and saw her and was still. As if he were memorizing her.

He sat down on the bed next to her.

The kiss was tender and lingering; his hand at her back, a slow caress. But then he closed his eyes and rested his forehead against hers. Turned his cheek to press against hers. His breath shuddered.

"I will never forget this, Lillias," he said. His voice was raw.

The breath stilled in her lungs.

She had a premonition about what he would say next.

"And . . . I am sorry. I ought to have . . . perhaps I shouldn't have . . ."

"What? What are you sorry for?" she whispered.

Her heart was jabbing at her rib cage now.

He closed his eyes and took a deep breath. He swallowed. "I am so grateful for the comfort. I perhaps ought not to have taken it when we don't love each other. But it was extraordinary and I will be forever grateful for . . . the beautiful gift of this night."

He looked into her eyes then.

She was falling and falling and falling without moving. Except there was no one there to catch her or to hold her close. Her limbs went cold. Her gut was cold. Her heart stopped beating.

And still somehow she was able to remain upright.

And somehow, words emerged from her mouth.

"Do not apologize. It was my decision, too. I wanted it. I came here of my own accord. And I enjoyed it thoroughly." Her words were raw and clipped.

She would claim it.

She would not allow him to take it from her.

But now she was staring at him, as if he were a stranger.

His complexion was gray-white in the wan light of dawn. Perhaps it was strain, or weariness, or grief. His hand was visibly trembling as he ran it over his jaw. She stared, mesmerized by the glints of copper whiskers along his chin, this profoundly intimate thing she had never seen because she had never awakened in bed with a man.

"Thank you," was all he said. He sounded broken. He was clearly in terrible pain. But what had she expected?

She could not accurately say whether any of his suffering had anything to do with her. Perhaps it was moot. Her own was blinding. Her own was crippling.

"For the forgetting?" Her shock sent the words out almost blithely.

His breath was audible.

"For the comfort," he said firmly. "And for the pleasure of your beautiful body."

The effort to say these words clearly cost him.

What was happening? She didn't know why these polite, honest, very true words were like a sword stuck right through her.

His voice was a graveled hush.

He said very carefully, "I have asked Dot to hail a hack. She thinks it's for me. It will be waiting outside. Your parents will be ill with worry if you aren't home straightaway. And we must have you out of here safely before everyone is awake."

She was already furiously moving, faster than she'd ever moved, yanking on her clothing, clawing her fingers through her hair to straighten it and twist it up into its pins, jamming her feet into shoes.

She seized her pelisse and thrust her arms in.

Could she blame him?

Grief could be a madness.

Same as love.

Same as love.

There was indeed no one to blame. She at least could truly say that. She'd wanted him. God, how she'd wanted him. He knew it. She'd taken and partaken. It had been glorious.

And now she supposed they were truly done.

Because Giles would arrive at their family townhouse at five o'clock and she would need to be there.

"Lillias."

But he said nothing more and she'd lost the ability to speak and it didn't seem to be anything more than a word, anyhow. A sort of "amen."

She turned and, with as much dignity as she could muster, made her way quickly down the stairs.

Chapter Twenty-Three

✎◦❀◦✎

"*A* PACKAGE HAS come for you, Mr. Cassidy. It was brought by a messenger."

Hugh had come down the stairs not more than an hour after Lillias left, though he wasn't certain why. He was vaguely aware that he was a little hungry. It could be Armageddon—and of a certainty, the morning after saying goodbye to Lillias felt like it—and he was fairly certain his appetite wouldn't leave him.

He was met in the foyer by Dot. The only maid who'd forgiven him for becoming engaged, and who had let Lillias into The Grand Palace on the Thames last night and likely knew precisely where she had gone and what they'd gotten up to, held the package out to him, eyeing him with a combination of pity and reproach, which was only what he deserved.

It was wrapped in brown paper and tied with a string. There was no indication who it might be from.

He took it from her.

Just as Delilah briskly strode across the foyer.

She glanced at Hugh and then her head whipped back for another longer look and she stopped abruptly.

They regarded each other.

He dully.

Her with alarm.

"Dot, bring Mr. Cassidy another pot of strong coffee and an extra scone, please. At once."

"I must look desperate, indeed." He was surprised to hear his voice emerging raw and tattered.

Everyone knew, and likely about everything. Not just about his uncle. About Lillias being in his room all night.

And they'd know soon enough about the end of his engagement.

His face must have reflected all of it.

He supposed the reception room was for grieving, because Delilah took him by the arm and steered him into it and urged him gently down until he sat on the pink settee where the king had once allegedly sat. The sun was pouring a gentle light through the parted curtains.

It was usually empty during the day—Delacorte, Hardy, and Bolt were all down at the docks. Mrs. Pariseau, thoroughly enjoying her widowhood, was usually out gallivanting with one of her many friends.

He pulled the knife from his boot and cut the string on the package. Delilah, married to a former blockade captain who never went anywhere without a gun, didn't even blink.

He parted the paper on the package and lifted out . . .

. . . a sketchbook.

He frowned.

And then his breath hitched. On the cover, in an elegant, tidy hand, was written:

Property of Lady Lillias Vaughn

But why had it been sent to *him*? And who had sent it?

Delilah peered down and saw the cover.

She said, delicately, "Mr. Cassidy . . . will you be all right if I leave you here?"

He nodded absently, scarcely hearing her.

Breath held, he turned to the first page, as if he'd been given the key to a treasure chest.

In pastels and watercolors and charcoal he found drawings that were accomplished and bursting with vivid character, and clearly quickly done.

A girl in a night rail, sailing over a darkened London, her hair like a dark cloud, her smile slight and dreamy, and below, a man in a billowing shirt who had hold of the string wrapped loosely around her wrist.

On the next page a man descended a ladder, strong sinewy arms reaching up to grip the rungs, his bare-to-the-waist torso illuminated in sunlight. A girl watched him, her face peeping around the corner of a doorway.

On another page was a woman standing on the porch of a cabin, aiming a rifle. His mother.

And then on the page following, in front of the same imagined cabin, a woman arranging tiny scraps of cloth on a rail, while a little humming-bird hovered nearby, eager to make her choice from among them.

His hands were shaking now as he turned pages.

And then there it was.

He huffed out a shocked breath. All the little

hairs on his arms and the back of his neck stood erect.

The Hudson River Valley. There was a sunset, spread out just as he'd described, with trees like great spired cathedrals, the hills undulating in overlapping purple and slate, on to forever.

On the next page: there it was at sunrise, the sky mother of pearl, the sun just kissing the tops of the hills.

Overlooking this view was a man on a brown horse, very tiny in comparison to all of the splendor.

And next to him was a tiny hound.

She'd given him a hound.

Tears were now burning behind his eyelids.

His heart was beating with anticipation as he turned the next page.

He did, and stopped breathing.

Oh God. The house.

Serene as a temple, the white bathed in amber afternoon sun. There were the pillars, the pediment, the carved pilasters, the balustrade. The windows above were arrayed toward the sun, and each one glinted. A path paved in stone led up to a wide generous porch, as welcoming as open arms.

On the balcony a man and woman stood. Their faces were indistinct, but their arms were about each other. And was that . . . there was a dog and a cat. No, two cats! One had stripes, and was waltzing along the balustrade rail, tail curved like a question mark. The other was gray and white, sleeping in a crescent on a chair.

He closed his eyes, and murmured, "Oh, my God."

She must have done this at Heatherfield. While

he was awake agonizing over five words that would be the last he'd write to her until the dawn broke.

He turned to the last page.

He covered his eyes with his hand, then brought it down again.

He saw himself. His face, not yet thirty years old. The deep hollows and strong bones. He looked tired, and handsome, and she'd captured the faint lines about his eyes and the little scar at the corner of his mouth. And his eyes as she must have seen them. Burning with longing, with hope, with humor.

How had she seen that? By what sorcery had she captured him so perfectly?

She'd seen him so fully.

As fully as he'd seen her.

And she must have drawn him from memory, little by little.

But the biggest surprise awaiting him were the two sheets of foolscap tucked into the back of the sketchbook.

One was the five-word letter he'd left for her. The word "happiness" was smudged, as if a tear had fallen on it.

That smudge seared his heart. He couldn't breathe.

The other letter was addressed to him.

> *Mr. Cassidy,*
> *Lillias inadvertently left this sketchbook behind at Heatherfield—one of the maids found it beside the bed. I thought you should see it.*
> *Giles, Lord Bankham*

Hugh exhaled roughly, stunned.

He covered his face with his hands. Then dragged them down and closed his eyes and threw his head back.

He sat for a moment. He took two long, deep, somewhat unsteady breaths, as something soft and golden filtered through the fissures in his being made by grief and exhaustion, knitting them, healing them. It was a peace unlike any he'd known before.

He closed his eyes to be alone, for the first time, with the certainty that he loved and was loved.

Was it enough?

Was it selfish to do what his heart now compelled him to do?

Perhaps.

He just knew that he had to do it anyway.

SECONDS LATER IT seemed—but the warmth and direction of the sun told him it was more like an hour—he jerked awake.

He apparently hadn't opened his eyes after he closed them. He'd dozed. He stirred, and stretched, and then turned his body.

And then froze.

Sitting on the opposite settee, staring at him, was a woman with flaxen hair spiraling from her ribbons.

Holy Mother of God.

"Amelia?" he whispered.

IT HAD BEEN just before dawn when their family's townhouse came into view, and the street was quiet and empty. Her parents would have been awake all night, and, as Hugh said, were likely worried sick. She was trying to decide whether attempting to go in through the servants' entrance or the front door was more advisable. There was really no way to avoid facing them.

She'd spent her time in the hack rearranging her hair as best she could without a mirror. That, and sobbing.

And then she saw a man slinking toward the servants' entrance of the townhouse, keeping to the shadows. He was carrying a hat and overcoat and walking stick. She thumped the roof of the hack hard, and it stopped.

There was no mistaking who it was.

She leaped out of the hack. "St. John!" she half hissed, half whispered.

St. John froze almost comically midstep. Then whirled.

And stared, agog, at the apparition that was his sister emerging from a hack just before dawn. Slightly disheveled, definitely probably still rosy in the cheeks and lips, eyes probably a little swollen. She'd done her weeping in the hack and that was the last place, she told herself, she'd do it. Although she wouldn't hold herself to that.

He clearly wasn't drunk, or if he was, not very. St. John's face reflected a dozen emotions and suspicions, but no doubt he'd come to some of the right conclusions. He wasn't a fool.

"Listen," she whispered, slowly, and said carefully, "I leaped out of our carriage when we were stopped on the bridge, because I suddenly needed to use the bourdaloue, so I ran back to The Grand

Palace on the Thames, where I encountered you, because you'd stopped in to say goodbye to Mr. Delacorte and arrange for more chess lessons. We waited until morning and then took a hack home together, because it was safer to travel in the morning and the roads were clearer."

St. John's face was quite the kaleidoscope for a fleeting moment. Alarm, concern, hilarity, curiosity scudded by as she watched. It concluded on sympathy.

That was the one that hurt.

He looked as though he wanted to say a lot of things.

Instead, he just reached out and straightened her bonnet.

"Got it," he said gently.

He looped his arm through hers, and they went up the front stairs together.

"How did you know I went to say goodbye to Mr. Delacorte?" he whispered just as he was about to turn the key.

She almost laughed.

"Good morning, Hugh." Amelia Woodley offered a little smile.

He stared at her. He was aware that he was frowning, but couldn't quite help it.

"What the . . . for God's sake . . . am I . . . dead? Are you?"

Perhaps he wasn't fully awake. He pivoted his head. Everything looked very much the same, but then it didn't seem unreasonable for heaven to look a bit like The Grand Palace on the Thames.

"Well, by now everyone knows I'm not precisely an angel, so this isn't heaven. You're alive. For a moment I wasn't certain, however." Her wobbly smile showed she was uncertain about the joke, too. "The maid called Dot made me tiptoe in. She said you needed your rest."

He hadn't even heard the knock on the door.

He stared at her, amazed. Waiting to feel . . . something. Perhaps he'd felt too many things in the past several days, or the pitch of his emotions had been such that any smaller emotions simply didn't register.

His manners drove him to his feet. "Amelia . . . I'm glad to see you. Are you sound?"

"Please don't get up, Hugh. I'm sound. And you? Are you well?"

At that, he slowly sat again.

And finally a distinct feeling penetrated his shock: the absurd banality of this exchange made him angry.

His gaze became one of rank disbelief.

She nervously looked away and tucked a spiral of her hair behind her ear.

He said nothing.

"The Clays told me you were looking for me. Hugh, I want to go home. And I don't know how to get there. I had only enough money to pay for this lark, you see." Her voice trembled.

He stared at her.

"Lark," he repeated carefully. After a pause.

She knotted her hands in her lap and then studied them. He inspected her swiftly. Her blue dress was rumpled. She did indeed look a trifle hard done by.

"Six weeks' passage across the ocean, Amelia. Months in England. Not a word to anyone since. Your father is worried unto death. He would have given you the moon, had you asked."

His words emerged clipped and scalding.

He, who had lost so many, was nearly dizzy with disbelief she would put anyone she allegedly loved through such torment for a . . . lark.

"But he never would have let me go without him, and when would that have ever happened? Kathryn Clay said I was pretty enough and rich enough to catch an English lord who lived near her and he never would have consented to me going for that reason."

He gave a short laugh.

"Well? Were you? Pretty enough?" he said sardonically.

Through his disbelief wound a thread of utterly mordant humor. Apparently Amelia Woodley had harbored ambitions beyond Hugh Cassidy. Here was someone else who'd learned that life was equal parts dreams and disillusionment. He couldn't fault her for dreaming, really.

She flinched. But didn't reply.

"And did you?"

After a moment, she shook her head, shamefaced. Mutely. She returned her gaze to her clasped hands.

"Did one catch you?"

"Hugh!" She gasped. She'd taken his meaning, all right.

He wasn't sorry. He was too tired to be sorry or polite. "You've no right to any indignation, Amelia. If we're to find a way to get you home, I shall need to know if you're with child, and if that's the reason you've finally surfaced. We'll need to make accommodations accordingly."

She was wide-eyed and scarlet now. This was not the deferential Hugh Cassidy she recalled. "No, Hugh. I'm not. I just want to go home. I want to go home. And I am . . . so *sorry* for everything."

Sorry! Hugh was reminded once again of the inadequacies of the English language.

Amelia began to weep then, prettily but copiously. She was a fool, and she was exhausted. And he *was* immensely relieved she was alive and unharmed. Despite it all, his heart squeezed. He sighed, found a handkerchief in his pocket and handed it over, and while she buried her face in it, he sat for a moment in reflection.

The corn silk hair that spiraled around her jaw, the sweet round face and dark brows . . . she was indeed lovely. But he understood fully now that just as she'd never really known him, he'd never really known her. How could he? He hadn't fully known himself, until Lillias turned him inside out.

But he was grateful to Amelia for being a grace note in his life when he'd sorely needed one. She'd been hope, when he'd had none, and nothing else to cling to. And for being the reason he was in England, where he had learned what it really meant to be in love.

By that definition, he supposed Amelia Woodley really was an angel.

"We'll see about finding accommodation for you here and a chaperone for your crossing when we're able to buy passage for you on a ship. Your father has provided me with enough funds to make sure you get safely home," he said gently.

Relief animated her at once. And then uncertainty flickered.

"But you . . . won't you be going home to America now, too?"

"Yes." He stood up. "But not with you."

HE HAD A quick private word with Mrs. Hardy and Mrs. Durand, explaining in as few words as possible who Amelia was and why she was here, something he'd long kept private for Amelia's sake. Stalwart women that they were, they didn't even blink. They assured him they would find accommodations for her at the top of the stairs, give her some small bit of distracting work to do, and not let her out of their sight.

Mrs. Durand in particular had some experience with the foolish decisions young girls are inclined to make about men.

She *could* tell Amelia that her life wasn't over. That life was full of second and third and thousandth chances, that gambles and choices in fact happened every minute. That luck and faith were all most people had in the end, and that one day, after a number of twists and turns, she might end up happily running a boarding house by the docks with the most unlikely best friend, married to the last person on earth she'd ever thought she'd marry.

But she didn't tell her any of that. Not yet. They fed her a scone and gave her potatoes to slice so that she could be surrounded by the soothing, feminine camaraderie of the kitchen.

While Hugh shaved, got into his coat, grabbed his hat.

And operating on faith, he went out to take the biggest gamble of his life.

Chapter Twenty-Four

❧◈❧

WHETHER THE haggard parents waiting up for Lillias believed them or not proved moot. Lillias let St. John do the talking. He repeated the story she'd given him with admirable accuracy. They maintained an impenetrably united front for two people in their respective conditions (one deflowered, sated, and distraught but hiding it well, one a little drunk and displeased to be out the five pounds that he'd lost at a gaming table, and hiding it well).

Her parents did what appeared to be a limb count, performed sweeping glances to determine if anything on them was bleeding or torn, and they were allowed to go straight to their bedrooms.

"Remember Giles will be here tomorrow at five o'clock, Lillias," her father said. Probably thinking that madness like leaping out of carriages would end once she was good and married.

"It's not something I would *ever* forget," she said.

St. John paused to stare at her on the landing, eyebrows up around his hairline.

"Good night, St. John," she said.

"Good luck, Lillias," he said, wryly.

They went to their separate rooms.

THERE WAS A clock on the mantel in the sitting room down below, and from her room she could hear it softly bonging out the hours, the half hours, the quarter hours. Because she didn't sleep. Or if she did, it was in scraps of time, minute as the silk a ruby-throated hummingbird might weave into her nest. Her thoughts were just as fragmented. She ached everywhere in ways she'd never ached before. She was sore between her legs. Her very soul was bruised. Like Persephone, she'd been yanked from the heights to the depths.

And she knew that no matter what he'd said, if Hugh were to climb into bed with her now, she would turn to him for more.

More. That's what Giles had said. She was always a little "more."

It occurred to her that he saw it as something to solve. Perhaps something to *rectify*.

Hugh saw it as something to give her. To show her. To watch her become.

Once you see one, you'll never forget it, he'd said, when he told her she looked like a Hudson River Valley sunrise. *They steal your breath.*

We don't love each other.

He didn't say things he didn't mean.

The clock bonged six in the morning.

Perhaps he was right about this. Perhaps this lust was so potent and consuming and messy and dangerous that one was tempted to call it something more noble in order to justify indulging again and again. Perhaps it was how addicts felt about opium, and everyone knew opium was a bad idea in the long run.

Once you know what truly matters in life, and once

you know who and what you truly love . . . your aim will always be true.

Why would he lie to her?

Nothing is like us.

Perhaps this would all fade like a fever, once he was gone again.

Perhaps he already knew that's exactly what would happen. Which is how he was able to let her go.

Nothing is like us.

It was too soon to imagine herself underneath Giles's naked body. She would need to be, as that's how the heirs would get made. It wasn't as though the thought was distasteful. It was that she simply couldn't form a picture of it, as if her mind kept it behind a closed door. Which is where sex ought to have been kept before she was married, if she were truly a lady. But then, she'd always been a little *more*.

She exhaled roughly, sat up, pressed her palms against her eyes, then looked about her familiar room that soon enough she'd move from and into, presumably, one day, Heatherfield. The rose and cream and green carpet and the curtains in spring green. Her wardrobe and writing desk and the portrait she'd drawn of her mother and father in pastels, the first work she'd thought good enough to frame.

How could she ever do without any of these people?

She closed her eyes.

Tentatively, reluctantly, she raised her arms before her, then curved them into a wide circle. Inside them she could conjure the heat and shape of

Hugh; she could feel the rise and fall of his back. The powerful, precious feeling of knowing his breathing had steadied because he'd turned to her, and she'd held him. And with it, an ache of loss that almost gutted her.

How set free she'd felt, naked in his arms.

And just like that, he'd sent her away.

She slammed her fist down on the bed in grief and frustration, and it nearly bounced back and hit her chin. If that wasn't a metaphor for her entire life at the moment, she didn't know what was.

She sank back down against her pillows.

But at five o'clock she would be set free from ambiguity. And eventually, this anguish would end, because it must. She would get on with things, as Hugh had needed to do so many times after disasters befell him. That was simply the nature of life.

But she would marry Giles. There was no reason not to do it. She would have a fine life. It had been her dream, after all. How many people could say that their precise dreams had come true, even if this particular dream had expired?

And her new life—which would be more or less like her old life—would begin.

THE DAY BOTH crawled and raced.

She didn't emerge from her room until noon, and she took one look at herself and realized she would need at least a few more hours to look like she hadn't been thoroughly ravished the night before. She called for a bath. Her body stung in surprising places, yet not so surprising given how thoroughly those places had been used last night. Honestly, if she could bottle the smell of him she would.

And if she'd had a choice, she never would have bathed again, so she could smell like him forever.

But she washed herself in French milled soap. She could not meet Giles redolent of sex with another man. And perhaps she could consider this a ritual washing away of the past, because as of the moment she'd left him, Hugh was of necessity officially the past.

And then she chose a dress—the pink muslin day dress, with the spray of daisies at the waist and hem. It usually lightened her mood, that dress, and she knew she looked fresh and lovely in it. Pink slippers. With the help of her lady's maid, her hair was braided and coiled, and two curls were allowed to trace her jaw.

Giles would be brought through to her father's study upstairs when he arrived. And then, she supposed, he would seek her out. She refused to hide in her room.

Smelling like lavender, a feast for the eyes, she went downstairs to the little sitting room at half past four to wait by the fire, and tried not to feel a thing.

She held herself very still, until the heat of the fire made her close her eyes.

She might have dozed just a little, because they opened again only reluctantly, and only after the clock chimed the quarter hour.

She stirred and stretched and then went still.

Standing before her was Hugh Cassidy.

Her hand flew to her throat. Her heart had immediately flown there.

For about three heartbeats, they regarded each other.

And then:

"I love you," he said.

"*Oh.*" Her breath rushed out of her.

Not a bludgeon. A catapult. She was instantly soaring like a gyrfalcon.

"I didn't want to leave you in suspense as to the purpose of my visit." He sounded so serious. He wasn't smiling. "May I sit beside you? Those three words about took all my strength."

She nodded slowly.

She was trembling.

But she'd spent all of her strength on that one word. *Oh.* She didn't need to speak ever again. It seemed unnecessary, anyway. He was here, and he loved her. What more would she ever need?

Gingerly, he lowered himself to the settee next to her.

"Lillias." He took a breath. And then another. "Sweetheart . . ."

He turned to her.

He blurred as the cool, cleansing tears filled her eyes. She knocked them away so she could drink him in. He blurred again.

"Letting you leave this morning was the hardest thing I've ever done." His voice was hoarse. "I just . . . didn't want you to go into your new life with regrets or heartaches. I could not have lived with myself if you left thinking you may have broken my heart. And I . . . I could not be sure that you loved me. I thought . . ." He cleared his throat.

"It would be the height of selfishness. I thought it would just . . . I thought it would just prolong your misery."

He paused to draw in a long shuddering breath.

Gently, she reached out, and laid her hand on his.

He looked up at her slowly then. And his face lit like the dawn.

She was awed at this extraordinary power she'd learned she possessed. She could bring comfort and strength to this man by just being herself. Just by loving him. He threaded his fingers through hers.

"I thought love was meant to be an easy, peaceful thing, Lillias. But it's like life itself. It's maddening. And beautiful. And changeable and funny and passionate. It's . . . like a Hudson River Valley sunset. Underneath all that fire and glory the sky is ever constant. It's like you. For me, it *is* you. Do I make sense?"

She nodded. Her heart was pounding so her ears were ringing. Joyously as church bells.

"I realized . . . that I, in my way, have actually been courting you from the moment I laid eyes on you. And I thought . . . we get few enough opportunities in our lives to love or be loved at all. And no matter what, she ought to know she has my love, wherever life takes her. And so here I am."

She didn't mean to make him wait. But it was a moment before the words could emerge, because they had to travel from the depths of her heart, and her heart felt as vast and deep as the sea now.

"I love you, too." Her voice was trembling.

Her words had made him softly brilliant. He looked like he contained the very sun. "So I gathered."

She gave a little laugh and a sniff.

She reached for him as he reached for her. He pulled her into his lap, which was just as sturdy and comfortable as she'd always dreamed. Her tears were cool against his temple. And they just held on to each other. Lulled and enchanted by the very fact of each other, by the gentle sway of each other's breathing. Like ships finally at harbor. Dumbstruck by their luck. Awestruck that they were loved by each other.

"You will marry me?" she murmured.

"Sweetheart, I will marry you."

"I want to live in New York with you."

"I know."

"I don't want to lose my family . . . I don't want to hurt them . . ." She swiped her tears. "I love them so. But . . ."

"You never will lose them. And we'll have a family of our own."

". . . but I want to love and be loved. Fiercely. Forever."

"I know exactly how to do that."

There was no doubt in her mind.

"I want to see and do and feel new things and create a new life in a new place. I want two boys and two girls. I want you. I need *you*."

"I'm yours. Forever," he murmured. He kissed her nearly senseless.

Against her lips he paused to whisper, "You are sure? You're not scared?"

"So scared. And so sure."

"We are going to have a wonderful life, Lillias. And we are going to soar so high."

"Oh, I *know*," she said.

THEY WERE LUXURIATING in slow, slow kisses, made possible by the fact that they now had all the time in the world to indulge in such things, so they didn't hear the approaching footsteps. First on marble, then muffled by Axminster.

Which is how the Earl of Vaughn discovered not young Bankham waiting for him, but his daughter in Hugh Cassidy's lap.

The earl threw an arm up over his eyes.

"Arrgh! Dear God . . . what on . . . *again*?"

They didn't fly apart from each other. They did stop kissing. They looked at him, expressions glazed with wonderment and happiness.

"No, no, don't get up on my account," the earl said acerbically.

But Lillias gracefully and unapologetically slid from Cassidy's lap, gave her skirts a shake. And then Hugh stood.

Cassidy looked like he hadn't slept in two nights, which was more or less true.

"Papa . . . I'm going to marry Hugh," she said calmly.

The earl had no words.

Hugh reached for her hand, and gently, inexorably as a vow, they laced their fingers together.

They were already a united front. They might have been married for years. He knew what he was witnessing.

And while this was almost precisely what he'd thought would happen when he'd told young Giles to wait a few days to speak to her, the earl also sensed what Lillias was about to say next. He felt every muscle in his body bracing for it.

"And I am going to live in New York with him," she said gently.

She wasn't asking permission.

He'd never before been in the presence of such radiant, peaceful happiness, such certainty, and the earl was surprised at the *relief* he felt. This was rightness. They were the embodiment of the quiet after a storm. Two more besotted people never lived, he thought. Unless it was, once upon a time, he and his own wife.

He heaved an enormous sigh. "Well," he said, quietly, somewhat gruffly.

Cassidy remained quiet. No arguing, no attempt at persuasion, no superfluous words, no triumph. He waited, hovering like a sheltering tree. Because he knew how the earl felt, and how Lillias felt. This was their moment.

But there was no mistaking it. Their decision was mutual and unequivocal. Lillias was now his. And Hugh, as he'd said the other night, would protect what was his.

Life sundered. And life joined.

The countess quietly entered the room, and he sensed her there, as he had so many times before, and he slipped his arm around her. Her eyes didn't even widen when she saw Hugh. She and her husband had talked about this probability the night before.

"Lillias, daughter . . . we know your heart," her father said. "We may not know all of its intricacies, but we have more of a sense of you than you know. I was waiting for you to know your heart, too. And . . . I . . . we . . . think you have made the right decision. Mr. Cassidy is a fine man. We are very glad indeed for you."

"Thank you, sir," Hugh said.

"And . . ." her mother added, through tears. "We think you *should* go to America. You've our blessing. We will miss you desperately. But we will come to visit."

Lillias's smile then would be a gift they would remember for the rest of their lives.

"And of course you'll have all your settlement money," the earl said. "Get rich. Change the world. And build her that house, Cassidy."

GILES HAD NEVER set out for London at all that day.

He remained in the familiar, soothing surrounds of Heatherfield, nurturing a rather bittersweet heartache and singed pride.

Once Giles had seen the contents of her sketchbook, he had known the conclusion was foregone. He loved Lillias. But he didn't love her the way Cassidy loved her, and she didn't love him the way she loved Cassidy. He had sense enough not to want to compete with that for the rest of his life—or to deprive Lillias of her true love for the sake of their mutual sentimental attachment to a past they were both understandably reluctant, maybe even afraid, to release.

But things could never go on being the same, even if he'd married her. *He* was the same as he'd always been; Lillias was not. But Giles found relief in knowing she would now be who she was meant to be.

She was indeed more.

He was not. And this was fine with him. He didn't want more. He didn't want challenge. He was uniquely happy in that he wanted exactly what he already had. He would pick up the thread in the family continuum, and be part of the weave of history.

And besides . . . Harriette might actually turn out to be quite a nice girl.

Epilogue

❧❧❧

One year later . . .

THE MAYOR of Wolfdale and his bride made love like pagans all over their beautiful property.

On a blanket beneath towering trees on sultry summer nights.

On the shores of the lake after swimming naked, like otters.

In meadows, observed by squirrels and deer.

By the warmth of a leaping fire in winter, after they'd skipped flat stones across an icy pond to make them sing.

And then came the perfect clear night when she'd stretched her nude body out on green grass beneath a black sky full of stars and a fat half-moon, and he'd pretended to be Hades discovering her. The ensuing ravishing left them all but floating up among the heavens.

And as a result of that moonlit midnight magic, the lovemaking today—near a sheltered overlook, beyond them the mountains rippling outward in greens and blues, below them the sapphire wink of a lake, and behind them the pearly glow of the house—was slow and tender. They would be parents in seven months.

And their happiness gave everything a radiance.

Lillias had brought with her tiny scraps of silk and wool from clothes once worn by her mother and father and brother and sister.

The day she told Hugh about the baby was the day she laid them out on the balustrade rail for the hummingbirds who would soon be mothers, in solidarity and with blessings. Every nest was a miracle of strength and fragility. Even her own.

They'd at once dispatched one letter to Baltimore to Hugh's sister, Maeve, who would come to stay with them when the baby arrived, and two letters across the ocean: one to Lillias's family, and one to Mr. Delacorte. Lillias and Hugh had decided to ask him to be the baby's godfather.

Lillias thought nothing could be more appropriate. Still, she was somewhat resigned to a certain inevitability. "His—"

"—or her," Hugh said. They were talking about the baby.

"—first word is going to be 'bollocks,' isn't it?"

Hugh laughed.

Hugh had learned from Lillias that it was Mr. Delacorte who waylaid the Vaughn carriage and sent her running back to The Grand Palace on the Thames.

"I *saw* how you looked at that girl," Delacorte told him at the wedding celebration held in the new Annex ballroom, the first event apart from Hugh's proposal to take place in the room. "The same way Hardy looks at Brownie, or Bolt looks at Goldie. I thought I'd see if I could prevent the two of you from being fools by breaking up your engagement, terrifying as she is."

By the time they'd boarded the ship for America, Delacorte and Lillias very nearly liked each other.

Both letters took about six weeks to travel across the Atlantic. When Delacorte received his he let out such a whoop in the middle of The Grand Palace on the Thames that it traveled the thousands of miles across the ocean and soughed in the trees outside of the Hudson River Valley.

At least this was the story he and Hugh and Lillias told Hugh's children for the rest of their lives.

The Earl and Countess of Vaughn were ecstatic about their first grandchild—many happy tears were shed—and while St. John was pleased enough at the idea of being an uncle, when his parents started intimating that it was high time for him to get leg-shackled and produce grandchildren, he was tempted to board the next ship to China. As it was, all of the Vaughns would be descending upon New York when the baby came. Claire missed her sister very much, and was beginning to wonder if there were any more handsome Americans roaming about in New York, a conjecture she was wise enough not to share with her parents.

Back at The Grand Palace on the Thames, Delacorte mourned the absence of Hugh—as dear as Captain Hardy and Lord Bolt were to him, Hugh was his bosom chum—but was consoled somewhat by the unlikely friendship of Lord St. John Vaughn, who often came around for chess lessons in the evenings and was soundly beaten every time.

From among her many friends, Mrs. Pariseau

had located the perfect chaperone for Miss Amelia Woodley's trip back to New York: a cheerful, shrewd, no-nonsense, worldly widow who was returning to America and would find keeping a young lady out of trouble child's play.

The search for a footman seemed about to bear fruit right as Lillias and Hugh sailed to America. And just when there was a wistful lull and absences they began to truly feel at The Grand Palace on the Thames—with the Vaughns and Hugh Cassidy departing—Delilah and Angelique received a letter from a gentleman interested in a private (*very* private), quiet (*very* quiet) suite in which to write his memoirs. He was the kind of formidable war hero—a legend, really—who awed even Captain Hardy . . . and . . . they weren't certain how they would break the news to Delacorte . . .

. . . he was also a duke.

LILLIAS AND HUGH were so in love.

With each other, and with the land, and with Hugh's new role as mayor and her new role as mayor's wife. All the ladies of Wolfdale were kind and helpful and quite in awe of her, which was practically Lillias's favorite combination of things for people to be. She looked and sounded like the daughter of an earl, but she was so enthralled by the beauty of the Hudson River Valley and so eager to learn everything about it that everyone was quite enchanted. They loved experiencing it anew through her eyes—the dramatic and brutal winters, the melting summers, the fiery autumns, the heartbreakingly beautiful springs. She'd brought with her gifts of pattern books and bolts of silks and velvet to share with them. The ladies of Wolf-dale were now among the most stylish of New York State.

At the foot of the bed at night slept two cats, one gray and one ginger, both soft and fat. And in a basket by the fireplace slept a seven-month-old bloodhound called Happy, named for what he was all the time.

Hugh's own awestruck happiness renewed it-self, found new levels and heights, every time he shared something new with Lillias. Every time they learned something new about each other. From every skirmish (and there were skirmishes) and every reconciliation.

They stood and peacefully rearranged their clothes, helped smooth each other's hair, rolled up their blanket, and stood and set out back to the house.

She'd gotten accustomed to a husband who kept a knife in a boot and a pistol in his coat. His rifle, locked, was slung over his shoulder. She found it rather thrilling, actually. Especially since she could shoot nearly as well as he could now.

They strolled back, hand in hand, when Lillias said, "We've a visitor. Somebody is standing on the porch."

This wasn't surprising, really. They frequently received visitors and had come to love entertaining. In a cozy parlor reminiscent of the one Hugh loved at The Grand Palace on the Thames—although, as both Hugh and Lillias had envisioned it, a tri-fle more plush with velvets and wools, furnished with fine locally made tables and sturdy chairs and cabinets and Lillias's framed watercolors on the walls—conversation ranged freely over politics and investment and crops and animals and art and music and how Hugh was establishing an American outpost of the Triton Group. A visitor merely meant they would ask their cook to set another place. Lillias was hungry *all* the time now.

"What's on his shoulder?" Lillias shaded her eyes to peer. "Is he . . . is he wearing a uniform? It looks a bit like . . . could it be epaulets?"

Hugh squinted. They could see that the man— and it was a man—was wearing a long dark coat and tall boots and a beaver hat. Like any gentleman of the day.

But against the backdrop of the cream-colored house, something a bit odd, brilliantly red and green, was visible on the man's shoulder.

"Hugh?" Lillias turned to him.

Because he'd stopped abruptly.

His face was a stunned blank.

"Lillias," he said slowly. "That's a parrot."

A thrill suddenly traced her spine.

Because even from this distance, something about the man's posture . . . his height . . . his way of *being* . . . seemed deeply familiar.

And then she realized: the man reminded her of her husband.

Hugh's face illuminated to a painful brilliance.

Her heart lurched with hope.

And then he reached for her hand. He gripped it tightly. They didn't run. But the closer they got, the longer and swifter their strides became. They slowed as they climbed the porch, as if they were suddenly entering a dream.

His blue eyes were vivid in a face brown and creased from wind and elements, gorgeous with wear and experience, rugged as the mountains. A tiny gold loop glinted in his ear. A handsome parrot tipped its head and regarded them peacefully from his right shoulder.

"Hugh, my boy, you won't believe what I'm about to tell you," said Liam Cassidy.

His eyes were wet.

Hugh hurled himself into his uncle's arms, and they were a blur. Lillias brushed the back of her hand across her eyes.

"This is my wife, Lillias." Hugh's voice was gravelly. He stepped back to let Liam and Lillias have a look at each other.

"*Enchanté*," said the parrot, with great sincerity.

"Thank you," Lillias replied politely.

Uncle Liam's eyebrows went up and so did the corner of his mouth in a wicked grin. "Hugh, my boy, I think your story might be even better than mine."

And then they all went inside.

Don't miss the next book
in Julie Anne Long's bestselling
Palace of Rogues series,

AFTER DARK WITH THE DUKE

On Sale November 2021